Saints On Fire

A Spiritual Warfare Novel

The Fire Series (Book 3)

Eric M. Hill

Published by SunHill Publishers
P.O. Box 17730
Atlanta, Georgia 30316
ericmhillauthor@yahoo.com
www.ericmhill.com
www.twitter.com/EricMHillATL
www.facebook.com/ericmhillauthor

This book is a work of fiction. Names, characters, places, incidents, and plot are pure imagination. Any resemblance to any person, living or dead, events, or locales is incidental.

Cover design by Cora Graphics

Chapter 1

He was a spirit of pride.

He slithered on the floor among the girls, sliding over their feet, enjoying the good feeling of bad flesh, unrepentant flesh emboldened by hearts set on fire of hell. The long snake circled the bare calf of one of the teen-age girls and made its way up her bare thigh.

"Do it! Do it! Do it! Do it! Do it! Do it!"

Four girls in bikinis. Four guys in swim shorts. Jumping up and down in unison encouraging a girl who needed no encouragement. She tightened her beautiful blue eyes and raised her hands and bounced her head and torso with the chants of the group who had immodestly named themselves *In.*

If you weren't *In*, you were out. You were lame. There were two simple ground rules for being *In.*

You had to be rich.

You had to be beautiful.

The bouncing girl was both of these.

The snake slid on and around the bodies of each of the young people before coming back to the bouncing girl, the host of the pool party. She had planned this party immediately after it had been planned by a ruler spirit named Slavery.

Pride encircled the girl's legs, then her torso, finally her neck. He wrapped loosely one last time around her delicate neck and opened his mouth, baring four surprisingly white fangs. The snake's eyes widened. His wide mouth froze open.

A mercy angel had stepped out of nowhere. The snake looked at the angel's large head and obnoxiously large mouth. This type of pride demon was not a fighting spirit. So why had a mercy angel crashed their party? And on what grounds could he crash it? No one here had prayer cover. And the girl—

"You will not kill her." The angel spoke to Pride and to the other demons in the room. He looked inquisitively at the small, jelly fish-looking demon who was draped over the girl's head and face. It called itself Ugly.

Pride knew this angelic intrusion wasn't right. The other demons knew it wasn't right.

The mercy angel looked at each demon. Rejection, Self-Hatred, and Look-At-Me were in the crowd. There were snarls and mutterings, but no challenges. Tangling with the mercy of God almost always ended badly for demons, so their ugly silence wasn't a surprise to the mercy angel. Mission accomplished. He disappeared.

The snake closed his mouth and waited for his stomach to settle. *Where do those big head mercy angels come from?* Finally, he gathered enough courage to follow his craving. He opened wide and sank his fangs into the girl's delicious neck.

"Yeah!" screamed the girl, with balled fists and her eyes closed, facing the high living room ceiling.

"Yeah!" screamed eight other teenagers filled with either booze or pills or a dangerous combination of both.

The girl sat on a sofa.

"She's really going to do it," said one of the girls.

"What? Did you think she wouldn't?" whispered one of the guys to the girl. "She's one crazy—" The guy's mouth stopped when he saw the needle.

The new silence in the room was odd.

Holly looked up. She had the second filthiest mouth in the room. Caitlyn was the proud number one. Holly saw Caitlyn waiting for her to break her one day vow of not cursing. "Look at you," she smiled at her best friend, Caitlyn, "*female dogs*. I would never say *itches*."

That won her a mischievous grin. "Oh, now you are one naughty nun," teased Caitlyn.

One of the guys, Jared, sat on a chair and pulled out something small wrapped in foil. Inside the foil was a tiny balloon. Everyone but Holly watched in frightened awe disguised as bravado as he prepared the heroin.

She wasn't afraid. She had told everyone here that she would prove heroin addicts were weak-minded people looking for something or someone to blame for them being losers. People were hooked on drugs for two reasons. One, they were idiots. And, two, they wanted to be hooked on drugs.

Specifically, she was going to prove her point by taking heroin in what was supposed to be its most addictive form. She'd take it once in front of witnesses and never again, showing that only weak people and fools were hooked on drugs.

Jared skillfully inserted the needle into a vein in her arm. There was hardly a prick. He pressed the top of the hypodermic needle and smiled. Holly had never given him any play, but she was on his turf now. Play would come soon enough.

No one saw Slavery approach. He was simply there. The dark mass of evil didn't smile like Jared. He couldn't smile. But he did exhale deeply when Jared pressed the enslaving poison into his new property. He watched the chemical travel through Holly's bloodstream. It reached her brain in seven seconds and found the molecules on cells called opioid receptors and locked a thick chain around her mind and soul.

Holly looked around the room with a beautiful smile of confidence. She didn't feel the drug yet. All eyes were on her. This is what she needed. She wasn't ugly. She wasn't rejected. She did belong. "Mr. Heroin," she started derisively, "you can kiss my pretty white....ugh." Her head dropped.

A warm sensation slowly moved across Holly's chest. Suddenly, there was an explosion of delight that blew away one reality and rushed her into another. Every part of her being filled with an ecstasy beyond description. A hurricane of pleasure carried her into places never before imagined. She had no control over her mouth or any part of her body. So she couldn't respond to the body, mind, and soul orgasm with a scream from her mouth. Instead, she nodded once, clumsily.

Slavery looked at the beautiful, rich, white girl in her bikini, and at her fake friends gawking at her. "You stupid—" He called her the name she wanted to call the others earlier. "We'll see who kisses what." He glanced at Jared and smiled.

Slavery looked menacingly at the subordinate demons and left this stupid dirt in the hands of Jared and her fake friends.

***

Annus was one of many demons who had been recently reassigned to Atlanta to help fight the revival. He would never have volunteered for such a dangerous assignment. But now that he was here, he was going to do two things. First, he was going to make this work for his career. And, second, he was going to have some fun.

His eyes lit up when he spotted a lady on a stretcher against the wall. And she wasn't in the back of the church; she was in the front. What kind of a crazy church brought paralyzed people to church?

Annus twirled his arms wildly and wiggled his long torso. He had to loosen up. He pushed his head from one side to the other. He approached the paralyzed lady with a wicked grin.

***

Sharon greeted Ms. Dixon. She was the paralyzed lady's mother. "Thank you for bringing Rosa." She bent down and kissed Rosa on the forehead. She rubbed her face. "How are you, Rosa?"

Rosa was technically a quadriplegic. She had no use of her legs, next to no use of her arms, and her fingers and thumbs didn't work at all. She had been accidently shot in the spine at a club on Moreland Avenue in East Atlanta two years ago. She didn't have children. She had never been married. And now it was all but certain, she would live in a wheelchair the rest of her life and die alone, with no one but her mother in her life.

"Hi, Sharon," Rosa smiled.

Sharon was grateful for the smile, but she saw the pain lurking in the shadows.

"Is Andrew here?" Rosa asked.

"What? I'm not good enough?" Sharon knew that her little brother had a special place in Rosa's heart. And why not? He was the one who had led her to the Lord while she and her mom had been out shopping at the *Farmer's Market*. Sharon patted her on the hand. "I know. I know. He's here. I'll tell him you're here. But first, Rosa, I want to say something."

Rosa looked up from the makeshift bed that the church had so compassionately provided for her. She could sit in her chair, but her condition made it really uncomfortable. They had insisted on going the extra mile for her. Sharon's eyes were lovely. Filled with true love and concern. She'd listen to anything this girl had to say.

"I don't know what you're going through. But I know the devil. I know that Satan is telling you it's over. That your life is worthless. He's telling you all the things you will never have. He's telling you that you're a burden to your mom."

Both Rosa and her mom's eyes filled suddenly with water.

"He may even have told you that suicide is the answer."

"I knew it!" said a suicide spirit who had been trailing Rosa since the accident, trying to find an open door. "I knew she'd open her big mouth. Why does she talk soooooooo much? Oh, I hate her. I hate her. I hate her."

Suicide wasn't the only spirit who had targeted Rosa. There were many spirits following her like buzzards waiting for an opportunity to rip away their victim's flesh. Hopelessness, Despair, Anger, Self-Hatred, Depression, they all were there, as were others.

Surprisingly, Unforgiveness, who ordinarily would have been securely buried deep in her soul and strategically positioned to let the others in, was on the outside, too. For one of the first things Andrew had done in his presentation of the gospel to Rosa was to explain that forgiveness from God could only be received if she were willing to forgive others. She surprised Andrew and his father by immediately forgiving the man who shot her.

One of the spirits looked with sleepy eyes at the ranting suicide spirit. "What an original thought. *I hate Sharon.*" The unimpressed demon looked into the crowd of evil spirits. "He hates Sharon. What demon doesn't hate Sharon?"

Sharon lived up to the expectations of the crowd of demons. "But suicide is not the answer," she said to Rosa. "Anger and bitterness is not the answer. And your life is not over. Andrew introduced you to your God and Creator. He has a plan for your life, and that wheelchair over there won't stop it.

"I'm so proud of you coming here on a Saturday morning. Most people wouldn't mess up their Saturday to come out and pray. But you did, and that says something about you, Rosa. You're not a quitter. And as tempting as it is, and I'm sure as tempting as it's going to be in the future, you're not going to spend the rest of your life obsessing over what could've been. You're going to fulfill your call."

Rosa looked into Sharon's face with the intensity of a person whose eyes had been glued wide open. Others had told her similar things, but their words weren't like Sharon's. Sharon's words had power. They had life. It was as though she were telling her something that God had told her face to face. "How?" she asked. "How do I fulfill my call? And what is it?"

Rosa's mother put her hand to her own face and let her tears course over her hand. She had never seen her daughter so hopeful after the accident until they had met these people. She waited for the young woman's response with as much eagerness as her daughter waited. For the mom had fought overwhelming feelings of insignificance and self-rejection all her life. Maybe she would hear something that could help her, too.

Sharon held Rosa's limp hand. A hand that was numb. A hand dead to sensation.

But Rosa's heart felt what her hand could not. *This girl didn't know her, and yet she loved her. A cripple.*

"What's your call, Rosa? It's to love and obey God. Make Him smile. Make Him your everything."

Mother and daughter pondered Sharon's short statement.

"Give, and it shall be given unto you. If you give God your very life, if you make Him everything, if you search for Him like rubies and gold, your heart will find peace. Rosa, don't wait for the perfect moment. Don't wait for the pain to leave. Serve Him in your pain. People who don't give life don't receive life."

Sharon looked at her, knowing how difficult it was to understand what she was saying, and wondering whether Rosa had caught any of it with her heart.

The mother caught it all. She buried both hands in her face and released fifty-four years of rejection. Her shoulders bounced up and down as she cried.

Sharon hugged her around her shoulders with one hand and placed her other hand lightly on the lady's forehead. "Lord, I ask You to touch Ms. Dixon. I ask You to take away the pain and heaviness and disappointments of life. I ask You to remove every lie of the enemy, the effects of every harsh word, every cruel act, every tormenting memory. Have mercy on this precious woman, Lord, for whom You died."

"I've had it!" said one of the demons. "This is all I can stand. I know where this is headed. I am *not* going to be here when she starts calling down the power of God."

He took off, saying nothing else, and not looking back.

Almost immediately the other demons scattered.

All but one.

His name was Annus.

***

The demons stood and watched the spiritual flames rage over the church building in hapless futility. Every few moments a fireball shot from the building and into the air like a guided missile.

Missiles. *Guided missiles.*

That's exactly what these fireballs were. They were explosive fireballs of prayer launched by sons and daughters of Adam who had no more value (at least in the eyes of the demons) than spit on the bottom of a shoe.

It was disgusting, but what could they do? They couldn't physically *make* these wretched children of God stop their contemptible prayers. That kind of direct interference was rarely allowed—even angels were limited in their direct interactions with people. Sure, if someone was dumb enough to open the door to witchcraft, they could suppress them more than others. But even then...

The evil spirit recounted his eviction from his Gadarene victim long ago—it was recorded in what the angels called the blessed book. He and a horde of vicious spirits had invaded a man. Not all at once. The invasion actually had begun when the man was but a child. One night his father had done an exceptionally good job at entertaining his five-year-old son with a scary bed-time story.

To the father, it had been a harmless tale told by a father who adored his children. Children loved stories. But to little David, son of John, it had been a torturous adventure filled with evil monsters.

When David had cried so hysterically that it abruptly ended the bed-time story, his father thought it was a combination of his scary story and a little boy's vivid imagination. It was both. But what the father didn't know was there was a third reason his son screamed uncontrollably in terror that evening.

Little David's mind had been too tender and impressionable to discern between fiction and reality. It was a story to his father, but it was real to him. When the loving father reached the scariest moment in the story, the part where the demon grabbed the little boy, a demon of fear grabbed little David. David literally saw the evil beast. That's why he screamed so terribly all night.

The sound of the prayer missile taking off, and its mammoth size, suspended the demon's recollections of his ancient activities in Gadara.

That thing is huge, he thought. *My darkness, I'd hate to be on the receiving end of that thing.* His thin, dark, rubbery lips rolled like a sea's wave. He shook his head. *They must have touched and agreed on something.* Eyelids with too much skin hung half-way over his dark eyes. Dark eyes that followed the big fireball until it disappeared in the eastern horizon. Oh, well, it wasn't him. His mind drifted back to little David.

Little David never recovered from that night's scary story. The spirit of fear that entered him that evening eventually opened the door to other spirits. Those spirits opened the door to other spirits. And on and on it went until that fateful day Jesus confronted them by the seashore.

This eviction had happened so long ago, and yet the bitterness of its taste was still in his mouth. He spit a wad of something hideous from a mouth that harbored breath that came from hell's outhouse.

They had been so comfortable! They had driven David mad. He was living in a graveyard, naked, compelled by hallucinations of his mind, and tormented by compulsions of demons who expressed their evil desires upon his flesh.

They had him!

They had him!

Then who comes waltzing from the boat, the boat from nowhere? Jesus. The Son of God Himself. Yet even though they had been startled by His appearance, they had not been overly concerned with being cast out. After all, their victim was crazy, and there were so many of them, and they had been there thirty years.

But out of nowhere. Before they knew what was happening. Crazy as their victim was, the putrid son of Adam somehow saw through the darkness of their thirty-year-old stronghold and caught enough of a glimpse of God's light to get hope.

David rushed toward Jesus and began to worship Him. Of course, they immediately shut that foolishness down. They took control of the man's mind and put up a ferocious fight, but they had known all along their cause was lost.

Now as the evil spirit shared his thoughts with the burning church and his bitter eviction, he mused that the thing that made this defeat even more deplorable was that the enemy had recorded it in that wretched book. Three times. *Three times!* In Matthew, Mark, *and* Luke. Did that sound like a God of love? A God of humility? Gloating about their humiliation and recording it for all the world to see? *Yeah, right! He's no better than us.*

The evil spirit bunched up his nose. Something stank, like burning flesh.

"What are we going to do, Contemptus?"

Startled, Contemptus turned, looking over his right shoulder. Had it been an angel, he'd be in three or four pieces before he had even known what hit him. He had to get a grip. He couldn't let his mind wander like this.

He looked at the scorched demon. He was a raw mess from top to bottom. No need to ask what had happened. He knew what had happened. That church is what happened. Or more accurately, the prayer meeting in that church is what happened.

"What are we going to do?" repeated Contemptus. He didn't mean to speak contemptuously, but it was his nature. Only with extreme effort could he speak any other way.

"Yes," the raw demon answered. "Ever since Sharon escaped from the sex guy—"

"She didn't *escape*. The heifer didn't escape. God killed *the sex guy,* as you call him. After God finished with the place, there was nothing left to escape from. She simply got in a car and rode away with the sex guy's wife and daughter."

The demon's raw face was still able to show his surprise.

Contemptus blew out a short, disdaining breath without opening his mouth. "You didn't know, did you?"

The demon didn't answer. This was not the story he had been told.

"Just because we're demons doesn't mean we have to be stupid," said Contemptus. "Lying to others is one thing. That's proper. Lying to yourself..." He looked dismissively at the demon's exposed flesh. "It can get you," he paused, "burned."

Contemptus outranked the injured demon, so Annus dared not answer the way he wanted. He tried to ignore the pain that seared through his badly burned body. His words passed through gritted teeth. "What are we going to do about the church's new militant position on prayer?"

"What can any demon do about a praying church?" Contemptus's words were filled with anger. "There's a few things we can do, Anus."

"Annus. It's Annus," the demon corrected.

Contemptus frowned as he looked critically at the demon's wounds. "If you say so." He continued. "One, we can hope they get bored or sidetracked."

"And if they don't?"

Did this idiot just ask me what I think he asked me? "Anus...Annus, *if they don't?* Have you looked in a mirror lately? That's what happens if they don't. Two, we can try to distract them ourselves. Distractions usually work. So I suspect that's what we'll be ordered to do." Contemptus looked thoughtfully into the flame and at periodic eruptions of fireballs. "Do you know what concerns me even more than this prayer—"he pointed at the sky—"and even more than those fireballs?"

The aching, scorched raw demon looked at his superior with a purposefully blank face. *No, high and mighty. What is more important than a fireball of prayer?*

"It's what they do after they pray. They are taking their prayers to the streets. They're following that blue mist of conviction all over the city."

Contemptus didn't say it. He wouldn't. But this was crazy David in the graveyard all over again. These saints were on fire, and they were carrying God's light into their darkest strongholds.

"Look!" screeched Annus, pointing at the church's front door.

The blue mist of the Holy Spirit came out of the sanctuary. It hovered over the ground about twelve inches like a thick fog and moved purposefully in different directions. The scene resembled a great body of water overflowing and finding new paths, creating streams and rivers of life.

The demons, however, saw the movements of the mist not as streams and rivers of life flowing into the cities and suburbs. This scene was more like menacing tentacles going forth into previously forbidden places to strangle the life out of their strongholds.

The church's front door opened. Contemptus shook his head in fleeting denial, wanting desperately to not believe what he was seeing. The demons were far away enough from the church to not draw attention to themselves. Nonetheless, Annus found himself shakily stepping backward. He was already burnt raw in several places. He couldn't take another fireball.

What had gripped the demons' attention could be described as a sharp, two-edged sword. One side of the blade was the blue mist of conviction of sin that hovered over the ground and now snaked its way in several directions away from the church. The other side of the blade were the Christians—accompanied by angels!—who were leaving the church building and getting in their cars and unknowingly following the mist.

"That is trouble," Contemptus said to the new demon. "Have you ever seen this before, Anus?"

Annus stared at the procession, not answering.

"Aaaaaanus, have you ever seen such a thing? Do you have this kind of thing in San Francisco?"

"Huh. Oh. No. Never."

"Do you know what you're witnessing?" asked Contemptus.

"Uhh, not really."

"Figures. Why would they send a San Francisco demon to a revival hot zone? Can you answer me this?" He looked at him dismissively. "No, of course not. We're sent lambs to help us fight lions."

"I didn't want to come."

Contemptus slowly shook his snarled face. "Yeah. I guess it's not your fault." He turned his eyes back to the mess. "That, An—"

"An-nus," the spirit interrupted. "The a is soft."

Contemptus looked at the inexperienced demon in ugly silence for several seconds. "Soft a. Of course, it is. Annus, that trash you see in the parking lot is following the Lord's mist into battle. We have better success with Christians who go out with good intentions, but no prayer covering. Fighting them is sometimes like fighting a courageous, but blind and deaf army." His lips pulled back into a wide smile that revealed discolored teeth that appeared to be in battle against one another. "They don't *see* us. They don't *hear* us. Until it's too late."

"Why sometimes and not every time?"

The smile raced from Contemptus's face. A frown replaced it. "I knew you would ask that?" He eyed one of the streams of mist as it led out of the parking lot and down a street, while three cars followed it. He smacked his lips and turned back to Annus. "It's *sometimes* because the enemy is arbitrary. He's unpredictable. He's a liar. You never know what he's going to do. Sometimes he stands by and watches us devour his dupes. And sometimes just when we're about to pounce on them, out of nowhere an angel or a..." he surveyed again the burnt demon's wounds, "...a fireball or a lightning bolt fries us on the spot."

Annus saw it in the more experienced demon's face. His superior thought he was an idiot.

"Most demons not of my kind don't know how to take me, Annus."

Spare me, thought Annus.

"I don't *always* mean ill when I speak."

He outranks me. Why doesn't he just flap his jaws and get it out?

"What happened to you?" Contemptus blurted. "You've been here, what...?"

"One day."

"One day and you're a marshmallow on a stick. What in the name of darkness happened to you?"

Annus knew he'd get this question a lot until he recovered from his humiliating wounds. Most of his hair would never grow back. The fire had seared much of his body. But, hopefully, his large patches of red would one day have skin again. "There's a cripple lying on a cot. I go to her. The other demons scramble when Sharon—"

"Oh, my god!" spat Contemptus. "Sharon. *That* pain in the darkness. You tangled with Sharon? She's a friend of God," he said, as though Annus should have known. He shook his head at the ignorant demon. "Finish your story."

"No, it wasn't Sharon. Sharon left the cripple. It was just me, her, and her mother."

"Rosa and Diane," said Contemptus.

"Yes, Rosa's the cripple."

Contemptus knew he shouldn't judge Annus too harshly for his ignorance. But this didn't stop him from looking at him as though he were a pile of dog poop. "There's a *cripple* lying on a cot. I went to *the cripple*. Rosa's *the cripple.* I know exactly what happened. You saw a *cripple* and thought you'd kick her around like a can on the street. Do you want to last more than a few days here, Annus? Maybe lengthen your life span to at least a week? Darkness knows there's not much of you left to save."

"That would be my preference." Annus wasn't entirely successful at masking his anger.

"The next time you see a son or daughter of God in a wheelchair or on a cot or even lying down hooked up to a machine that's breathing for them—"Contemptus bent forward and got uncomfortably close to Annus's face. He smelled Contemptus's breath. *Horrible! Absolutely horrible!*—"forget what they look like and judge them for who they are. They are sons and daughters of the Most High."

Contemptus saw it in the dumb demon's eyes. "That's for us, not them! We tell them they're crap. And if we can get them to believe it," he paused, "if we can get them to judge their worth by how they look or feel, or by what someone says about them, we got 'em! But if you want to live, don't start believing your own lie. You understand?"

Finally, Annus seemed to understand.

"Yes," said Contemptus with a smile.

"The cripple burnt my darkness to a crisp."

The smile faded angrily from Contemptus's face.

"But she's more than a cripple. She's a daughter of God. Even if God's children don't know who they are, *I* can't ever forget."

Contemptus's smile returned. Maybe this soft *a,* San Francisco misfit could become a real demon after all. "Not if you want to live.

Come on. We've got to join the others. Mist or no mist, if the enemy wants a fight, he's going to get it."

Chapter 2

The blue mist that Diane, Rosa, and Sharon unwittingly followed was six feet wide. It had already reached its preliminary destination at Cumberland Mall. This was two specific side-by-side parking spaces close to *The Cheesecake Factory* restaurant.

Actually, they were the spaces closest to the street just across the driveway. As usual, the Saturday crowd had converged on the mall with a vengeance. The only open spaces were far away across the parking lot on the opposite side of the street. Even the spaces for the disabled were taken.

The mist enlarged itself into a wide circle over the parking spaces and marked the ground by deepening its color before proceeding to the doors that led inside the busy mall. This marking gave the appearance of a flow chart made of blue smoke.

An angel with a sword in one hand and a dagger in the other descended hard within the blue circle. These empty parking spots were reserved.

***

Diane drove the big van around the mall's crowded parking lot in frustrated circles. Were they at Cumberland Mall or a rock concert? She looked left and right, contemplating which way to go. She shook her head.

Oh, well, we can park across the street. It's not that far, she thought. She decided to turn left and put on her turn signal.

"You probably should go to the right and circle back around," an angel said to Rosa.

"Mom, try the right," said Rosa.

"The right?" she said, looking in that direction at the long line of cars, all apparently looking for parking spaces. She changed her signal. "Alright."

"To the right, it is," Sharon joined in. "Reminds me of Andrew. 'When in doubt, go to the right. You go right, you can't go wrong.'"

Rosa gave Sharon a questioning look.

"What does that mean?" asked Diane.

Sharon laughed at her brother in his absence. "*Exaaactly.* It means he should seriously not consider comedy as a career."

"Oh," said Diane.

Sharon smiled at Rosa. "Don't worry. He's still wonderful."

"Sharon?" Rosa was afraid to ask.

Sharon was smiling. It was a beautiful day, and the day's beauty found its way onto Sharon's face. "What?"

Rosa's face didn't carry the day's beauty. Her expression was caught somewhere between hopeful and troubled.

"Rosa?" said Sharon.

"Wednesday night—those people who testified. The lady with the frozen arm."

"Janice," said Sharon.

"You know her?" asked Rosa.

"Yeah. She's been coming to the church for uhhh, six...seven months now."

"So her arm. You'd know..." Rosa wanted to know for certain, but she'd heard the question in her mind and it sounded one hundred percent inappropriate and accusing. She smiled. "Forget it."

"No, Rosa. What is it?" asked Sharon.

Rosa didn't answer.

"Ohhh, Janice's arm," said Sharon with a wide mouth. "Was she really healed?"

Rosa smiled tentatively.

"We were talking about it," said Diane, waiting behind the snail-paced moving line of cars. "We've never heard of anything like that before." Diane had to qualify this statement. "Well, I mean you've got those guys on TV who claim to heal people. Maybe some people are being healed in their ministries, but I just can't get past..." She let the thought drop. The last thing she wanted to do was offend someone who had been so kind to her daughter.

"The money?" asked Sharon.

Neither Diane nor Rosa answered.

"The constant begging for money," Sharon said with resignation.

"Sharon, it's not just the begging. It must cost a lot to do what they're doing. Somebody's gotta pay for it."

"It's all of the other stuff that goes with it?" asked Sharon.

"Yes, I guess that's what it is," said Diane. "The outlandish promises they make to raise money."

Sharon heard a brokenness in the lady's voice that pointed to something deeper than a passing concern over televangelists. "Ms. Dixon, did you send them some money?"

She sniffled. "Yes."

"I hope you don't mind me asking." Sharon glanced back at Rosa. "A lot?"

"More than I could afford."

Sharon didn't have to ask why. She knew why. She rested her elbow on the edge next to the window and looked sadly out her window.

"I'm sorry, Momma," said Rosa.

"You have nothing to be sorry about, Rosa. You didn't shoot yourself. I'd give everything I have if it meant you could live a normal life."

Sharon turned her head more away from Ms. Dixon. She was trying to hide the tears that poured from her tender heart.

"She told me she was going to send the money," said Rosa. "I should've told her to not do it, but I was scared. I don't want to be like this the rest of my life."

"Sharon, do you think people really get healed through those people?" asked Diane.

Sharon quickly wiped her eyes. "I have a friend, Jonathan, who explained it to me this way. Do you remember Samson in the Bible?"

"The strong guy with the long hair?" said Rosa.

Sharon laughed and shared a smile with Diane. "That's the guy. He was a prophet. He was chosen by God to deliver his people from an occupying army. But Samson had a problem with women."

"Sex?" asked Diane.

"Yes," said Sharon. "Jonathan jokes that Samson was the only prophet in the Bible who had more girlfriends than prophecies." Sharon looked back at Rosa. "Samson was anointed of God. He had supernatural strength. When the Spirit of God came upon him, he'd do things that were humanly impossible. One time he fought and killed a lion with his bare hands. One time he had a fight with a thousand Phil—a thousand guys, and killed them with the jawbone of a donkey."

"He killed a thousand guys with just a bone?" asked Rosa.

"Yeah. God helped him." Sharon's voice dipped. "Then one night he had sex with a prostitute. His enemies were waiting to jump him. At midnight he tore the city's gates down and carried them off somewhere." Sharon could tell the women didn't understand what she was saying. "Ancient cities often had walls around the city to protect them from attack. Samson somehow singlehandedly tore down the city's gates and carried them away. The gates must have weighed thousands of pounds."

"This was *after* he had sex with the prostitute?" asked Diane.

"Yeah," said Rosa, "how can you go to bed with a prostitute and still work miracles? Didn't you say he was a prophet?"

Sharon's heart lifted. She knew their questions were prompted by heaven. "He was. That's the part that confuses people. God is good and faithful and compassionate even when we aren't. When you look at guys like Samson, it's easy to think either that God's not using them or that God approves of their behavior. I used to think like that, too, but Jonathan shared his own experiences with me. And he showed me in the Scriptures that God is greater than the weaknesses of men."

Diane finally reached the end of the row and made a right.

"Turn back down this row, Mom," said Rosa.

"Rosa, there's cars lined up waiting for spaces. There's nothing there."

"Try it, Mom. Something told me we should go down this aisle. The preacher said we walk by faith, not by sight. Right, Sharon?" Rosa smiled.

"Right!" Sharon agreed.

"No fair ganging up on me." Diane let out a breath and nudged forward, waiting impatiently for an opportunity to get off the main street and to turn down the row. "So you think God is really with these preachers? What about the guy who wears the red suit all the time?"

"The one that got caught with the male prostitute," said Rosa.

Red suit? Male prostitute? Ugh! "I've never heard of that one," said an embarrassed Sharon.

"That one's a real mess," said Diane.

"God couldn't use that one, could He?" asked Rosa.

"I know how it sounds, but God is God. He's not limited to only using good people. And He's not limited to only using perfect people. If He were, He wouldn't be God. And since there aren't any perfect people, He wouldn't have anyone to use."

This didn't make a whole lot of sense to either woman. "How can God use a homosexual preacher?" asked Diane.

"Wait a minute," said Sharon. "I want to make sure we're on the same page. I am *not* saying God approves or overlooks *any* kind of sin. And it doesn't make a difference whether we're talking about a preacher or the person who sits on the last pew. What I am saying is that God owns everything and everybody. He can get His will done through someone even if they don't serve Him. Can I give you some examples, Ms. Dixon?"

"Sharon, please call me Diane." She laughed. "If for no other reason than my vanity."

Sharon laughed, too. "Okay. Let's go back to Samson. He had a serious problem with lust, but God still used him. There was Judas Iscariot, one of the original twelve apostles. He was a thief, but God still used him to cast out demons, work miracles, and heal people. Oh, and one time Moses worked a miracle in a way he wasn't supposed to and God still did it for him."

"How?" asked Rosa.

"How, Moses?"

"Yeah. If God is the one who gave Moses the power to work the miracle, how could he do it wrong?"

Sharon looked back at Rosa. Rosa's body was trapped in a shell of flesh that was broken beyond human repair. She couldn't comb her own hair. She couldn't brush her teeth. She couldn't bathe herself. She couldn't do anything from the neck down. And yet...

Sharon smiled broadly as she looked beyond Rosa's paralyzed body and into her spirit. It was nothing supernatural, not a fruit of her growing prophetic gifts. It was the questions. When Peter had answered Jesus's question of "Who do men say that I am?" with "You are the Christ, the Son of the living God," Jesus had said to Peter, "Blessed are you, Simon Barjona. For flesh and blood has not revealed this unto you, but My Father who is in heaven." That's what was happening here. The Father was communicating with Rosa—and Diane.

Sharon reached back and held Rosa's hand. "I love you, precious Rosa." The tears that rolled down Rosa's face humbled Sharon. She squeezed her hand again. "God told Moses to speak to a rock so water could come from the rock. Did you see the original Ten Commandments movie? The old one?"

"No," said Rosa.

"Well, this is when they were wandering in the wilderness. There were hundreds of thousands of people who needed water. Instead of speaking to the rock, Moses hit the rock with a stick."

"So they didn't get the water?" asked Rosa.

"No. They *did* get the water. That's the point."

"But Moses didn't obey God. How'd they get it?"

"God made water come from the rock even though Moses did his own thing," said Sharon.

"I don't understand, Sharon," said Rosa. "Why would God make water come from a rock from someone who disobeyed Him?"

Sharon knew this was it. This is where God had been leading the conversation. "Rosa...Diane, God made water come from the rock because the people needed water. He gave them water *in spite of Moses,* not *because of Moses.*" Sharon turned around in her seat, saying nothing as she looked at the cars in front of them. Jonathan had said sometimes preachers talked too much. Sometimes it was best to deliver your message and be quiet.

Almost at the same time, both ladies asked, "So then how do you know who's really serving God?"

"Fruit. A tree is known by its fruit, not by its miracles. We're not supposed to follow someone just because they have miracles. We're to follow them only as they follow Christ. So if their lives don't line up with the Bible...."

"Hmp. That's interesting," said Rosa.

"Yes. It is." Sharon looked out the window and turned back to Rosa. "But sooner or later we reap what we sow. It's easy to think people get away with stuff. Even Moses had to pay for what he did."

"What happened to him?" asked Rosa.

"God didn't let him into the Promised Land. After all that walking around in the wilderness. Forty years with those people and one act of disobedience cost him. Same with Samson. God kept using him even though he was sinning. I guess Samson interpreted this as God not caring about his sin. One day he went out to fight his enemies and he thought God was still with him and He wasn't. He got his eyes put out, and his enemies put him in prison."

Rosa smiled. "I see. God is patient."

Rosa had reduced everything Sharon had said into three words. This brought a smile to Sharon's face. "You said it, Rosa. God is patient."

Diane watched car after car ahead of her pass by the empty parking space. "Yes!" she said, when the car directly in front of her passed it up.

Rosa smiled. "See, Mom. We walk by faith."

Sharon looked into the back at Rosa, smiling.

They got out of the car. Diane gripped the wheelchair, and a lady approaching the beat down car parked next to the van, said, "Rose? That you?"

Rosa looked at the three women. She didn't know one of them, but if she was with Shanice and Jasmin at the mall, she was most likely a thief. But there was something about the girl that was unlike the two women she used to party with. Something deeper than the contrast in her striking beauty and the attractiveness the other two had tried unsuccessfully to create with exaggerated make-up and fake hair that appeared to have been made with plastic. There was something about the girl that screamed *I don't belong here!*

"Girl, they said you got shot." This was Shanice. She was about a hundred pounds overweight, which helped her career of shopping without money. It was amazing how much merchandise she could stuff into her large outfits. "They shoot you bad?"

Jasmin was maybe twenty pounds lighter. "We been meanin' to come see you. You still on English Avenue?"

Diane held her tongue. Her daughter had gotten shot two years ago.

"Yeah. Still there," said Rosa, without bitterness. She had never expected to be visited by either woman.

"Uh huh," said Jasmin, looking back toward the building, scanning to see if there was going to be any drama. "Okay, girl."

"Nice seeing both of you," said Rosa. "

The two big women glanced toward the mall doors and moved purposefully toward the safety of the car. The third girl smiled at everyone and started to join her cousins. Rosa pushed her words. "What's your name?"

The girl turned with a pleasant smile. "Kim."

"Kim, we came to the mall to talk to people about Jesus."

"You're Christians?" she asked, as though they were water in the desert.

"Come on, Kim. Let's get outta here," said Shanice.

"Hey, will you keep me in your prayers?" asked Kim.

A surprised Rosa smiled. "Yes. Yes, I will."

"Anything in particular?" asked Sharon, as the girl approached the car.

She hurried back playfully to Sharon and Rosa. "Ask the Lord to watch over me. I had a problem with a boyfriend and had to leave Baltimore. I'm staying with my cousins for a while in *Mayhem*." She rolled her eyes in an exaggerated way. "It—is—dangerous—in—Mayhem." She turned to join her cousins. For some reason, she stopped. “Hey, you mind if I call you some time? Maybe I can visit your church.”

Rosa’s eyes widened with excitement. “Yes.” She gave her the number.

Kim hurried back to the car and hopped in.

Rosa, Sharon, and Diane watched the car drive away. Diane wasn’t as giddy about the chance meeting as they were.

“Did you see her face when she asked if we were Christians?” asked Sharon, beaming.

“Wouldn’t it be something if God set this meeting up?” said Rosa.

“I think he did,” said Sharon. Her smile faded. “If He did—and I think He did—she must really need someone to pray for her. She said it’s dangerous where she lives. Rosa, it looks like God has given you a job.”

A warmth defied Rosa’s disability and moved across her entire numb body. She *felt* it. Her eyes widened. Just as quickly as her deadened body felt the warmth, it was gone. Another wave of warmth went through her. This time it went through her spirit. She smiled.

Almighty God had communicated to her. To her. *A cripple.*

Rosa heard Sharon, but she answered God. “I’m going to pray for her. I’m going to pray for Kim day and night.”

***

Slavery stood two blocks away with an entourage of demons who followed him everywhere. Addiction and Hopelessness were at his left and right. Pride was a step behind. This was not his preference. He would have loved to have been up front. And this was exactly why he was a step behind. Slavery had no toleration for egomaniac demons. Well, there was *one.*

The demons could have flown to their destination. Or rather, Slavery’s destination. But they walked instead. They always stopped flying and walked when they got within two or three blocks of *Mayhem Courts.* Of course, the official name wasn’t *Mayhem.* It actually was *Mahem.* Named after some dead son of Adam. But those who had been cursed to live in one of the two thousand units of Atlanta's last public housing project rightfully called the place *Mayhem.*

For so it was.

Slavery always chose to walk the last couple of blocks to *Mayhem* because he wanted to look at it in all its oppressive glory as he approached. This was the last of his Atlanta Housing Authority projects, and he was going to enjoy every moment of it while it lasted. Not that he was planning on losing *Mayhem Courts* any time soon. But history had sadly proven that his precious prisons weren't guaranteed to be around forever.

And it wasn't the Christians. They were the least of his troubles when it came to his prisons. For the most part, they left him alone. They were too scared to bring their wretched gospel to his dangerous property, and they were too unconcerned or busy to pray any difficulties his way. Well, that last statement wasn't entirely true.

Fortunately, most Christians were ignorant of the *true* power of prayer. They rarely understood how God used prayer to rule the world and to limit or destroy works of darkness. And they didn't have a holy clue of the secondary effects of prayer. *But what good was ignorance if the enemy still insisted on using these dirt people!*

That's how he had lost his hellish housing projects. People made from dirt, and seeing through a glass darkly, had prayed for revival in Atlanta. Did they know such prayers would shut him down? Did they know that that hideous Spirit of God would take their contemptible pleadings and use them like a wrecking ball to demolish strongholds of poverty, pain, and misery that had brought Slavery pleasure for decades? No!

And yet....

In 1994, a hole-in-the-wall church of fanatics cried out to God for revival. Slavery remembered the night as though it were last night. The prayers had been added to a bowl that had held Atlanta revival prayers for twenty-four years. When the angel poured the prayers into the bowl, it tipped to the right and emptied all the contents back onto the city of Atlanta.

Specifically, the prayers landed on City Hall, the Atlanta Housing Authority, and forty-three public housing projects. Mysteriously, the forty-fourth, *Mahem (AKA Mayhem) Courts*, was missed.

Slavery knew what had happened with the prayers because of the dog of heaven's insatiable ego. Truly, the powerful demon didn't know who talked about himself more, Satan or God. *I am that I am. I'm the bright and morning star. I'm the lily of the valley. I'm the first and the last. Come unto me. Look unto me. Eat my body. Drink my blood.* It was all so nauseating. Satan in one ear, God in the other. Both so full of themselves.

On that fateful day in 1994, the Great Ego pulled back the curtains of heaven. Suddenly, the kingdom of darkness saw the solemn prayer ceremony taking place in the far distance of a different dimension.

"The priests of the earth have declared life in Atlanta. So shall it be."

That was it. That's all the angel said. Barely a mouthful of words. The next thing Satan and his kingdom saw was a bowl tipping over and blue liquid scattering all over Slavery's beloved housing projects. Some landed on the U.S. Department of Housing and Urban Development, and some even on the White House. *Something big was going on.*

Two years later Slavery watched *Techwood Homes* get demolished. A few years after that, Slavery watched *Perry Homes* give way to the wrecking ball—literally. Some said that the great demon actually cried. One by one the Spirit of God tore down the rest of Slavery's concentrations of evil. And when his beloved *Bankhead Courts* were destroyed, he cried uncontrollably.

But as devastated as it was to lose nearly all of the Atlanta public housing projects, he still had *Mayhem.* And he still had hundreds of thousands of people in his grips. Some didn't look like slaves—he thought of his proud, self-deceived, affluent suburban slaves—but they were his, nonetheless. Better dressed and better educated than his ghetto slaves, but in some ways worse off. At least his projects slaves knew they needed help. His suburban slaves were too stupid to see their real need. *They'd find out their true need a moment after death. Ha, ha, ha...a moment too late.*

Slavery and his crew walked the last block to *Mayhem.* He surveyed the several rundown high-rise buildings that comprised part of his west Atlanta kingdom. The group stopped in the middle of the large, dead lawn that separated the parking lots on the left, right, and center. That's where the buildings were, too.

Slavery looked to his left. He walked to the little playground and swiped his hand across a wooden bench and put his fingers in his mouth and sucked. The blood from last week's murder had long been gone. But Slavery could still taste the memory. It was good.

Oddly, Slavery would have stopped the murder if he could. Dead people made horrible slaves. His nature craved slavery, not death. But he was a demon, was he not? The enemy loved his dirt people. So although Slavery would no longer be satisfied by Jerome's slavery, God would never have the satisfaction of knowing that dead, wannabe thug as son. Slavery had lost a slave. God had lost a potential son. God's lost was infinitely more. That made Slavery's lost bearable.

Now, to check on his property.

Slavery turned back toward his crew and froze in disbelief and horror. The other demons saw his fear. They whipped out their weapons and spun around to fight the angels who until now hadn't bothered their *Mayhem* property.

One of the demons was so unnerved by what he saw, he dropped his dagger. He quickly scooped it up and involuntarily stepped backward.

"What is *that* thing doing here?" screamed Slavery.

That thing was a blue mist that hugged the ground and moved in a straight line toward them. The demons scurried out of the way and watched in horror as it passed them and went into the center building.

Slavery was dumbfounded. First, that the visible presence of the Holy Spirit had invaded *Mayhem.* Second, that he didn't know what to do. Should he just stand by and watch as this thing tried to rob him? No, he couldn't do that. He rose in the air above it and followed its path. He needed to know who this thing was after. His crew followed.

The mist went through the front door and up several flights of a smelly, darkened staircase. It went inside the door that led down a long, dark hall. The demons watched the mist take an abrupt turn into *G6*.

Slavery could've gone inside, but he decided against it. "Who lives here?" he barked.

Hopelessness rattled off several names. "And Shanice and Jasmin," he finished.

"And that new dirt. Kim," said Despair. "The one who acts funny."

Slavery rubbed his chin. "Yeah, she does act funny, doesn't she?" He thought it over for a few seconds and went inside. He watched Shanice and Jasmin try to talk her into smoking some marijuana. For a moment it appeared that she would do it. Then that mist went all over her.

"No. I told y'all I don't want any." Kim stood up and went into a back room, leaving the women by themselves.

Slavery's eyes blazed at her. God was trying to take his property. "No way are you going to take what's mine. She serves me or she dies." He shook his fist at the ceiling and shouted, "You hear me, Mr. I Am Wonderful? She serves me or she dies!"

Chapter 3

"So how do you feel?" Jonathan asked, with a slight grin.

Edwin put his hand on his belly. "Hungry."

"Oh, come on. This is only the third day," teased Jonathan. "Anyone can go without food for three days. We only have until dinner. Jesus fasted forty days."

"Breaking news, Jonathan. I'm not Jesus."

"You're not? Hmp. I never would've known."

"You do this a lot, don't you?" asked Edwin.

Jonathan put his hand on his belly and jiggled. "Not by choice. As you can see, I like to eat. Although it's not as big as it used to be. Liz has been helping me."

"The things you do—the miracles and visions and all the other stuff, you think God uses you like this because of your fasting?"

"Edwin Styles, that is a good question. You can do a lot of stuff without fasting, but sooner or later you're going to run into a situation that doesn't respond to your prayers or commands. You can pray to God and shout at the devil until you fall out from exhaustion. Nothing happens. Nothing. You turn down the plate and get alone with God and you tap into His power."

Edwin rolled his fingers thoughtfully on his desk.

"You remember in Matthew 17 and Mark 9? The guy with the son who had a demon?" asked Jonathan.

"Uh huh. It's not like you don't mention the poor guy every other time you speak somewhere."

"Nine apostles, Edwin, standing around one demonized boy, trying to cast it out. Demon doesn't go anywhere. Jesus comes on the scene and asks what's up. The man tells Him that he brought his boy to his disciples and they couldn't help him. You remember what Jesus said?"

"Yeah, bring him to Me."

Jonathan's eyes gleamed. He bounced his index finger at Edwin. "He did *not* say, 'Nothing happened? Oh, must not be God's will to heal him.' That's what we would've done. Something's hard, we pray for something and nothing happens, must not be God's will. Jesus didn't think like that. He said, 'Bring him to Me.'"

"But, Jonathan, that's Jesus. Of course, He'd say that. He's the Son of God." Edwin had obviously said exactly what Jonathan wanted him to say. "You set me up, didn't you?"

Jonathan grinned. "If you can't count on your friends to manipulate you, who can you count on? Edwin, Jesus didn't say, 'Of course, you couldn't cast him out boys. You're not the Son of God.' He said the exact opposite. He rebuked His disciples for not healing the boy, and later when they privately asked why they couldn't cast the demon out of the boy..."

"Their unbelief," said Edwin.

"And?" asked Jonathan.

"And what?"

"And how did He tell them they could get rid of the unbelief?"

Edwin made a humming sound. He pulled his head back and tilted it upward in thought. "Prayer and fasting."

"Most people think of getting rid of the mountain by prayer and fasting. That's true. This kind of mountain doesn't go away except by prayer and fasting. But I like to take it a step farther. I like to think of it as getting rid of the unbelief through prayer and fasting. If you get rid of unbelief, you're left with faith. Faith moves the mountain."

This brought up another question in Edwin's mind. "But they had faith, didn't they? I mean, they were commanding the demon... I guess they didn't have faith. Jesus said they didn't."

"It's easy to mistake commotion for faith," said Jonathan. "You got nine apostles commanding a demon to come out of one little boy. You'd think at least one of those rascals had faith. Jesus said they didn't. What they had was experience. What they had was momentum. They figured this demon was like the others they had faced." Jonathan smirked. "He wasn't. Sometimes momentum can get you bitten in the butt."

"I think I see what you're getting at," said Edwin. "It looks like they were on a hot streak when they ran across this little boy. They tried everything they had tried before and when it didn't work, they lost faith."

"Yep. That's it. And this could've been prevented had they gotten rid of the unbelief *before* they faced this demon." Jonathan saw the question coming. "I know. Let me put it this way. Jesus said prayer and fasting was the answer to unbelief. He lived in prayer and fasting, so He didn't have a problem with this. The apostles couldn't pass up a *Popeyes* without getting a three-piece combo. So they did have a problem."

"Just that simple? Pray and fast and you can move every mountain?"

The light in Jonathan's expression dimmed. His eyes suddenly seemed distant and saddened by Edwin's question. "There's very little about life that's simple. Faith doesn't automatically come just because you fast and pray. The Pharisees fasted and prayed and they killed Jesus. The object of prayer and fasting is to humble yourself before God, to intensify your search of Him, to hear His voice. If you don't hear His voice, chances are your story will have a bad ending. Jesus lived off of hearing His Father's voice. That's why He had no problem with faith."

The men said nothing to one another for a few minutes. The conversation had been rich and they both sensed the Holy Spirit's presence. Some of Edwin's thoughts had brought water to his eyes.

"God is willing to give us all things. We're seated with Christ in the heavens, but we choose to live in the basement, don't we?" said Edwin.

"Yep." Jonathan smiled at his friend. "But not today. Today we're out of the basement. You're ready to go see Octavius?"

Edwin tilted his head, still finding what he was about to do hard to believe. "If making a pastoral visit to the man who kidnapped me and my family and beat my daughter is coming out of the basement, then I guess I'm out of the basement."

Jonathan smiled. "What better way to put this prayer and fasting to use than to go to one of the most dangerous neighborhoods in the nation to preach Christ?"

Edwin gave Jonathan a sick look. "I can always count on you for a word of encouragement."

"Always," said Jonathan. "To live is Christ, to die is gain."

"Ugh," said Edwin.

***

Edwin's eyes skipped and bounced nervously onto and off of one thing then another. They were only a few miles from downtown Atlanta, but it felt like he was in another country. Atlanta was such a beautiful city. Ever since the Olympics, it had gone on a renovation rampage. He thought of Centennial Park, the Georgia Aquarium, the new World of Coca-Cola building, and a large mixed income community that had replaced a neighborhood of rundown homes, abandoned buildings, and a dangerous public housing project.

He thought of how private investors and the city had taken a defunct steel mill and had turned it into Atlantic Station, a thriving residential, business, and retail district. The transformation had been truly amazing.

But west Atlanta was not Atlantic Station. Edwin looked down to his right.

"Doors locked," said an amused Jonathan without looking at Edwin.

Edwin shook his head and resumed to looking out the windows in every direction. How could an area like this exist not even five miles from downtown? Every so often there was a small home that showed its residents hadn't totally given up. But for the most part it was block after block of raggedy houses and buildings in disrepair.

Really, *raggedy* and *disrepair* were compliments to some of the structures that challenged Edwin. He looked at one house and told himself that there was no way someone actually lived in it. He hoped he was right. The door of the house opened and a guy stumbled his way to the top stair and sat down. Edwin watched him put a liquor bottle to his lips and drink as though he was trying to quench a burning thirst.

"Rotgut."

"What?" said Edwin, turning to Jonathan.

"*Mad Dog*. Rotgut."

They sat at the light watching the man, Edwin keenly aware of how long it was taking for the light to get to green. *Was it even working?*

Jonathan shot out a short prayer for the drunken man. "MD 20/20. But true aficionados of horrible wines call it *Mad Dog.* It used to be sold in twenty ounces. Was twenty percent alcohol, too. That's where the 20/20 comes from." Jonathan shook his head. "Now it's only thirteen percent alcohol."

"Sorry for your loss," said Edwin.

"Don't tell me. You never had Mad Dog?"

"Don't hold it against me," said Edwin.

"I'm not, Edwin. Nobody's perfect."

Mercifully, the light changed. The car didn't move. Edwin turned to Jonathan. He was staring at the drunk. He put the car in park, pushed the parking brake, and pushed the button for the hazard lights. He opened the door.

"Where you going?" asked Edwin.

Jonathan stepped out. "I'll be right back. Gotta say a little prayer for my Mad Dog frat brother here."

"You can't just leave the car in the middle of the street." Edwin looked all around him. Thank goodness no cars were coming.

"Sure you can," said Jonathan.

Edwin watched in amazement. Nothing spectacular happened. It was just as he had said. Jonathan sat next to the man and talked to him for a minute or so. He then took him by the hand and prayed for him. The man lowered his head as Jonathan prayed. Edwin watched with a gaping wide open mouth as the drunk took a long gulp from the bottle as Jonathan prayed for him.

"Incredible," said Edwin to himself.

Jonathan hopped back into the car and drove off. "That, my boy, is something you will never have the joy of experiencing. Spending quality time with a frat brother. And do you know why, Edwin? Don't be offended. But it's because you were a terrible sinner."

"Glad I could disappoint you."

"Well, it's too late to join the Mad Dog brotherhood now." He turned to Edwin, "Some things you have to give up when you come to Christ," he said with mock seriousness. "But it's not too late for you to make some interesting friends."

Edwin looked out the windows. He looked at a liquor store to his right. There must've been fifteen men hanging around the parking lot of the small store. Most of them looked as though alcohol had beaten them senseless. Dirty and tattered clothes. Puffy faces. Dull, reddened eyes. Zombie-like walks.

But the thing that tore at Edwin's heart was the sense that he was looking at a tragic puppet show. The men were the puppets. The puppet master was the alcohol that had robbed these men of whatever dreams and dignity they may have had at one time.

"I've never seen such a concentration of liquor stores before in my life," said Edwin.

"Hopelessness and addiction are big business in the ghetto, Edwin."

Jonathan turned a corner and drove slowly. The scene stiffened Edwin's back and pushed him forward. He glanced downward at the door again.

"Door's locked, but that won't help any, Edwin. The glass isn't bulletproof. Remind me to fix that if we make it out of here."

Edwin was too nervous to laugh at any of Jonathan's *I'm-a-living-martyr. Nothing-bothers-me* jokes.

The street was narrow. It was lined with run down houses. About a third were clearly abandoned. *So many abandoned homes on one street.* Several people ran behind homes or scurried into houses when they saw the approaching car. Those that remained were a rough-looking bunch who sat on porches and steps. Everyone stared warily at them like they were the enemy.

Edwin looked on the other side of the street at a house that had been burned nearly to the ground. It had a look about it that said it had been in that condition for a while. *Why hadn't the city knocked it down? Didn't they know what that would do to property values?*

Jonathan stopped the car in front of a sad structure of a house. Three black men sat on the porch. They looked every part of every negative stereotype. This could easily have been a movie set. But it wasn't. It was real life. He turned the ignition off.

Edwin didn't know where his heart had gone, but he was certain it was no longer on the left side of his chest.

"Edwin, do you know where we are?"

"Beverly Hills?"

"No, that's two miles east of here. We're in *The Bluff.*"

"Of course. That's where we said we were going, right?"

"Right," said Jonathan. "Would you like to know what's going on around us right now?"

"Would you like to talk about this at *The Marietta Diner?*"

"Nice try. No," said Jonathan. "Two unfamiliar faces just drove down a street that is famous for its drug dealing, especially heroin. Two blocks away a spotter gave a signal to another spotter who called someone on this street. They think we're cops. That's why no one has rushed the car trying to sell us drugs."

"They think we're cops?" This sounded awful to Edwin.

"Smile. That's a good thing. We're not in danger until they find out we're *not* cops."

"And tell me again why I'm here?" said Edwin.

"Compliments of your wonderful daughter. She led Octavius to the Lord. Octavius lives here. She wanted to come, but you had a fit when she asked to go with me to visit him. You shut her down by offering to come."

Edwin felt nauseous. "Oh. Yeah. I volunteered."

Jonathan looked at his friend with admiration. "Yes, you did. And, Edwin, you didn't do this just for Sharon. You did it because you're an awesome man of God who wants to know what it's like to follow the Holy Spirit no matter where He leads. No matter what the cost."

Edwin looked at the dash. His fears faded as he thought on Jonathan's words. He was absolutely right. In the past year he had experienced God in ways he could only describe as thrilling, almost unbelievable. Still, he couldn't get past the unrelenting pull toward something greater. Whatever that *something* was, it was just beyond the fence of fear, safety, and comfort.

"You ready?" said Edwin.

"What's the hurry? We're cops. We can sit here all day."

"Ha, ha," said Edwin, grabbing his big Bible.

They opened their doors and got out of the car. Edwin looked at the three men and started up the stairs first. Jonathan smiled inside.

Two of the guys sat across the stairs, blocking their path. The third guy leaned on the bannister. Only one of his hands could be seen. "What y'all want?" said one of the guys on the stairs.

Edwin looked at the guy's long braided hair. "We're looking for Octavius." Edwin wondered if his voice cracked.

"Octavius? Only somebody wantin' *Octavius* is po-po," said the man.

Edwin looked at the man. *Po-po? What's a po-po?* he wondered.

"We're not po-po. That's Reverend Edwin Styles. I'm Jonathan."

"Congratulations. What y'all want with Prince?"

"He's a friend of my daughter," said Edwin.

"Yo' daughter?" said the man. "How old's yo' daughter?"

Edwin hesitated. What did that have to do with anything? "Seventeen."

The man leaning on the bannister spoke. "Prince is friends with yo' seventeen-year-old daughter?"

"Yeah," said Edwin.

"You ain't got no problem with that?" he asked.

"No."

"You got a picture?" he asked.

Edwin hesitated again. "Yeah."

The guy looked at Edwin as though the picture should've already been in his hand.

Edwin looked at all three of the men, then pulled out his wallet.

"You don't have to take it out of the wallet. I'll give it back." The man smiled. "I promise."

Edwin ignored him and pulled the picture out and handed it to him.

"I don't mean no disrespect, Rev, but yo' wife must be slammin'. Look at that booty. You don't mind no little black babies running around the crib?"

What picture did you give him? thought Jonathan. *Aww, Edwin, you gave him the full body shot*. Jonathan held back his laughter.

"Any child that my daughter has will be my grandchild."

"Man, stop playing with yo' self and let us see the picture," said the guy on the bannister to the dude who had the picture.

They passed around the picture, making statements that gritted Edwin's teeth under his façade.

The guy with the long hair handed it back to Edwin. "I think I wanna serve the Lord."

"Now, do you guys mind if we go up to see Octavius?" asked Edwin.

"Yeah, go on up." The guy with the long hair looked at the guy on the bannister and communicated something to him with his eyes.

The men moved out of the way. Edwin and Jonathan walked up the steps and stood at the door.

"Go on in," said one of the men.

Edwin and Jonathan stepped inside. Immediately the three men rushed behind them and shut the door. A man came out of a back room with a black gun in his hand. The gun was pointed at the floor and not at them, which was a good thing. The bad thing was the man was very convincing at looking like a killer in a bad mood.

"Believe it or not, I got a concealed weapons permit. But I don't need a permit to have a gun in the house. Now I haven't yet pointed this gun at you. I promise you, though, if I point it, I'm going to use it. You got a warrant?"

"Warrant? We're not cops?" said Edwin.

The man with the gun jabbed his finger in the air. "Now *that's* what this is all about. We been jacked by cops who think they can come in here and take what they want because they have a badge."

"We're not cops," said Jonathan. "Go ahead and search us."

"Let me call my wife," said Edwin. "I'll put it on speaker. You can listen. She'd know if I were a cop. Right?"

The three men who had been on the porch looked at the guy with the gun.

Edwin continued. "Or my daughter. I can call my daughter."

"Let's just make it easy," said Jonathan. "Octavius obviously isn't here. Why don't you call him? Or better yet, use my phone to pull up Edwin's church. You'll see his lovely face."

The men searched Edwin and Jonathan and checked the church website. They had Edwin call Barbara and Sharon and listened as he spoke to them. They did the same with Jonathan.

The four men sat down. Mike, the one with the gun, lit up a joint. He took a long hit. "Man, y'all crazy as hell coming in here like this. Bible study?" He threw the words out of his mouth. "Whoever heard of somebody from the burbs coming down here for a Bible study?" He took another long hit and held out the joint to Edwin.

Jonathan put out his hand as though he wanted it, looking at Edwin. "Paul said that he became all things to all men that he might by all means save some."

Edwin's eyes widened in shock. His open mouth joined his eyes.

Jonathan looked at the man with the joint and the other men. They all cracked up laughing.

"Hilarious," said Edwin. "Is anyone here going to tell us where we can find—?"

"Your son in law?" joked one of the men.

Edwin just looked at the guy.

"I'm sorry, Rev," the man said laughing. "Prince at Mayhem."

"Mayhem Courts?" asked Jonathan.

"How you know about Mayhem? I know you ain't gone try and have a Bible study up in Mayhem. Not if you wanna live."

Jonathan looked at the man with the long hair. "Hadn't thought about. What do you think, Edwin? Bible study in Mayhem?"

"Can we just go see Octavius?" said Edwin.

"Rev done had enough of y'all crazy niggas." This was the guy who had been leaning on the bannister.

They started walking toward the door.

"You gentlemen mind if we pray for you before we leave?" asked Jonathan.

Edwin wasn't shocked that Jonathan would ask four drug pushing thugs if he could pray for them. But he was shocked at their response. The only word he could use to describe it was *enthusiastic*. Four criminals enthusiastic about someone praying for them. Who would've thought?

He figured he'd step out in faith. "Let's hold hands," he said, holding out his hands.

Jonathan put his hand to his mouth and covered a grin.

The men frowned.

"Man, I ain't holdin' no nigga's hand. You must be crazy," said one.

The one standing next to him said, "Naw, man, we ain't holdin' hands. You gotta come better than that, bro."

Edwin looked at Jonathan.

Jonathan stepped backwards with his palms facing Edwin. "I like you, Edwin, but I'm not holding your hand either." He laughed at Edwin's scowl. "Gentlemen, we don't need to hold hands. We'll save that for the ladies. God can touch you without us holding hands."

Without any prompting, all four men stood at an angle with their arms hanging before them and one hand crossed over the other. Their heads were bowed, but their eyes were open, looking at Edwin and Jonathan.

Edwin tried again. "Do we have any prayer requests?"

"Yeah," said one. "I want you to pray for me and Jantell."

Edwin smiled ever so slightly, encouraged. "Anything in particular?" asked Edwin.

"Yeah, I want you to pray that she give up them drawls."

"Man, be for real," said another. "Dude's trying to pray for you."

"Nigga, I am for real." The man jutted out his neck with every other word to emphasize his point. "That girl ate her food. Then, Dawg, she ate six of my wings. Man, it was a ten-piece. So I got fo' wings left. She ate half my rice. Took her to the crib. She drank two brews. Then she gone talk about she got to go babysit for her sister. She should've told me that before her big behind ate up all my food."

"See, that's what got you," said the thug, looking at his friend with a nasty smile. "That big behind."

"Yeah, Dawg, I had plans." He rubbed his hands together like a fly. "Had salt...pepper...catsup...hot sauce—"

Another of the men chimed in. "I was with you, bro, up to the catsup. But that girl don't need no hot sauce. She already hot." He looked at another of the men. "Am I right, Dawg?"

"Don't need no hot sauce," the man agreed, shaking his head.

"Q, you know how that girl eat. How you think she got all that booty? She played you, man."

"That's alright. That's alright," he answered. "I ain't throwing away my hot sauce. Rev gone pray for me, and I'm gone make her pay! Gone get back my wangs. My rice. My brews. With interest. Watch and see." He looked at Edwin, ready for him to pray and ask God to help him get Jantell's drawls.

Everyone was laughing except Edwin and Q. But Q was smiling.

Jonathan stepped in when he and the others stopped laughing. "My friend doesn't have a lot of experience with these types of prayer requests, but I do." He lifted his hands. "Lord, I thank you for leading us here to meet these men. I thank you for preserving their lives. I ask that you open their eyes to the truth of who You are." Jonathan opened his eyes. "Gentlemen, it was no accident that we came here today. God knew that Octavius wasn't here. He wanted us to meet you. You know why He wanted us to meet you? He wanted us to tell you that Almighty God wants what's His."

"Wants what's His?" This was the guy with the gun. He sounded offended.

"Yes. He wants what's His." Jonathan looked intently into the man's eyes. "*You* are His." He looked at each one, saying the same thing. "You've been very kind in inviting us into your home, and in not shooting us. Believe me when I say this: we're very grateful. But can I ask one thing before we go? Jesus Christ is Almighty God. He died to wash away your sins. But He rose from the dead. He's alive.

He's here in this room with us, and He wants to show you His mighty power. Can I have your permission to ask Him to show Himself to you?"

Edwin's face turned slowly to Jonathan. Praying for four thugs—one holding a gun!—was one thing. Standing in their house and telling them that Jesus was going to show Himself to them was something totally different. *Jonathan, oh, Jonathan.*

"Shoot, man," said one.

"Whatever," said another.

"Got no problem with it," said another.

The one with the gun was the last to answer. "What you mean He's in the room? You saying He's gone do somethin' *now*?"

Edwin's eyes were fixed on Jonathan.

"Well, that's the idea. That's what I'm hoping."

"Hoping? You said He's in the room, right? If He's in the room, He need to step up. Step up or shut up."

"Now I can go with that," said Jonathan. He closed his eyes. He wasn't as confident as he appeared. God didn't work in his circus. He couldn't make Him jump through hoops on demand. *Lord, have mercy on these men. Please show Yourself to them. If there is anything in my life that is offensive to Your precious Holy Spirit, please forgive me. Don't let my sins stand in the way of You revealing Yourself to these men.*

He reminded Himself of Matthew 28:20. *"I am with you always, even to the end of the age."* He reminded himself of Mark 16:20. *"And they went out and preached everywhere, the Lord working with them, confirming the word with signs following."* He reminded himself of John 14:13, 14. *"And whatever you ask in My name, that I will do, that the Father may be glorified in the Son. If you ask anything in My name, I will do it."*

"You gone pray today?" snapped the man with the gun.

Jonathan looked beyond the man's intimidating appearance and loved him. He smiled slightly. "Yes," he said softly. He lifted his hands above his head and looked beyond the low ceiling. By faith, he saw himself standing before the throne of grace. "Lord, I have told these gentlemen that Jesus Christ is Almighty God. I have told them that Your Son died for their sins. I have told them that You raised Him from the dead. I have told them that they belong to You, and You want them to come home. I have told them that Jesus Christ is in this room with us. Now, Lord, show these men that we are Your servants and that our message is true."

Edwin didn't move an inch. Surely, only seconds had passed, but it felt much longer. Beads of sweat climbed from under his hair and rolled embarrassingly down his face. He'd only draw attention to his nervousness if he tried to wipe it away, so he stood there, motionless, hoping no one looked at his face.

"Just wait for a few moments," said Jonathan.

The man with the gun appeared to be running out of patience. His face was turning into a frown.

"Man!" said one of the men. "Whew! I'm burnin' up." He put his hand on the back of his neck. "My neck burnin' up." He bounced and rolled his shoulders as though he could dislodge the heat.

"Satan, let these men go!" said Jonathan.

The man who wanted Edwin to pray Jantell out of her drawls rubbed his stomach. He felt dizzy. "What the...? Man, I feel sick. I'm gonna throw up."

"Throw up?" said the man with the gun. "You better get yo' black a— to the bathroom."

The man stooped over, holding his stomach as he walked slowly to the bathroom. "Aawww man. Aawww man. My stomach."

The man with the gun watched him as he went. He looked at the other guy furiously rubbing his neck and claiming to be burning up. He said the heat was going down his back. The man with the gun looked at Jonathan.

"Could be coincidence. Could be God. What do you think?" said Jonathan.

"Dawg, look at my neck." The man asked the other guy without the gun.

The man looked at the back of the guy's neck as though something might jump out and grab him. His eyes widened. "Antoine, that nasty crap is gone. I ain't lying, man. It's gone!"

The burning man whipped around and looked at him like he was crazy. He pulled his shirt up over his head and turned around. "What you see, man?"

The man's head involuntarily went back in shock. "Dawg!" He put his hand to his mouth and bent to the side. "Dawg!"

"What, man? My back on fire! What you see?"

"Nothin', man."

"Nothin! I'm burning up. You see *somethin',* I know!"

"Naw, Dawg. I'm serious, man. I mean nothin'. All that nasty stuff is gone, man." He looked over at the man with the gun. "Tell that nigga that stuff is gone."

The stuff he was talking about was a severe condition of erythrodermic psoriasis. An incurable skin disease that caused the skin on his neck and large areas of his back to break out in a huge, inflamed rash that peeled and burned intensely. There were short periods when the rash lessened in its severity, but it was never entirely gone. This latest flare-up had been exceptionally bad.

The man with the gun walked slowly toward the burning man. He looked like he was looking through the man's back. He turned to Jonathan. "G building, man. Number thirteen. That's where Prince at."

"Step up or shut up is what you said, right?" said Jonathan.

"G13," said the man.

"That's it? The Lord heals your friend and all you can say is G13?"

The man looked at Jonathan. Edwin looked at the man. He had a strange expression. It was like he was on the verge of either crying or shooting Jonathan.

"Thank you," Edwin said to the man. "Let's go, Jonathan."

Jonathan looked at the man. "We're going to G13. But remember. God wants what's His."

Chapter 4

The blue mist of the Holy Spirit coursed down the narrow streets of *The Bluff,* passing its many dilapidated homes and their residents. A peculiar thing happened as it turned right on Turner Street.

Aisha was fourteen and already beat down and tired from life. Somehow a seed had been planted in her heart that she could be a doctor. No one knew where she got the crazy thought. She didn't even know. Certainly, no one she knew would've encouraged her to be anything other than a whore like her mother. She sure was pretty enough. Even prettier than her thirty-year-old mother used to be. Before the drugs and butt whippings from so-called boyfriends quieted her good looks.

Donte knew Aisha was fine. That's where the baby came from. She looked both ways before pushing the cheap stroller out into the street. She didn't know she was pushing her screaming baby into the path of heavenly traffic. The blue mist of the presence of God, and the armed angels with serious expressions, were hidden in another dimension. The only thing on her mind was this screaming baby.

Aisha thought the child was just being bad. She'd screamed, "Shut up!" to the child every several feet and threatened to whip him if he didn't. Although the exact language she used would've been more appropriately used in a rowdy bar. The child didn't shut up because he had an ear infection. The only way he knew to tell his young mother that he was in terrible pain was to scream.

She grunted in frustration. "You make me wanna slap you!"

Those were her words, not her heart. She loved Ray-Ray. But what was she going to do? She was fourteen years old with a baby. Her momma was a crack hoe. Her daddy was in and out of jail. This was one of those *in* times, and his worthless butt was going to be there a long time this time.

Aisha shook her head. She wanted to cry. Tears wouldn't fix anything, though. They wouldn't take her back in time to the moment before she had finally given in to Donte saying, "I love you, baby. We gone make it together." Tears wouldn't take her back in time and cause her to be born in a good family. It didn't have to be a rich one or even middle class. Normal would be good enough.

Not ghetto normal. Just regular normal. The kind of normal where she'd have two parents, or maybe just one. Just as long as that one wasn't a hoe or a drunk. Just be somebody who would say, "Aisha, did you do your homework?"

Aisha and her baby were in the middle of the street. The baby screamed what seemed to his mother as his loudest scream ever. Before she could explode in angry cussing, something happened.

One of the warrior angels who walked in the mist felt the mother's pain. He had worked and fought in many ghettos of the world. He knew from experience that poverty and hopelessness often covered beauty with their ugliness. He saw the seed of potential in her heart. The young daughter of Adam wanted to be a doctor.

He was an angel, but he wasn't the Almighty. So he didn't know if the unlikely seed within her would miraculously bloom, or whether it would go the way of so many others in the ghetto and be ruthlessly dug out of her heart by harsh circumstances. She wasn't his assignment. So he had little to offer her. But perhaps in this quick passing moment, he could do just a little. The angel touched the baby's ear. The sickness and pain left.

God opened Ray-Ray's six-month-old eyes. He bounced in his stroller and smiled at the angel who was looking back at him and smiling as he marched away with the other warriors.

***

Jonathan waited for the girl with the stroller to cross the street and made a right on Turner. He and Edwin looked several blocks ahead at the imposing buildings that awaited them. Jonathan's lips pressed hard against another. He exhaled. What was waiting for them in those buildings?

The closer they got to the hi-rise public housing projects, Edwin wondered had he reached the deepest level of fear possible for a human, or was there a fear greater than what was trying to strangle him to death.

"Edwin, you alright?"

Edwin didn't lie. "Uh uh."

"Me either." Jonathan abruptly pulled over into a convenience store parking lot.

Edwin kept looking directly ahead of him.

"Edwin."

"Uh huh."

"Remember we went to the game and we were going to go half on the parking and you didn't have any change and I took care of it and you promised to pay me back?"

"Uh huh."

"I want my money. I want my five dollars."

Edwin turned. "Jonathan, do you see where we're parked?"

"Yep."

"Did you see those buildings waiting on us?"

"Yep. I did. I most certainly did."

"Jonathan, I know high on your *To-Do* list is to be martyred. You've been beaten and tortured and—"

"Strangled," Jonathan interjected. "Got choked real good in—"

"Strangled in who knows where and who cares where?"

"Oh, now that hurts."

What I'm getting at, Jonathan, is my wife is a *fabulous* cook, and I happen to know she has planned a *fabulous* meal this evening. I'd love to enjoy that meal."

"So would I."

"But that *To Do* list of yours, Jonathan. That list is not going to let us enjoy that meal, is it? We may not make it out of there. The name of this place is *Mayhem Courts. Mayhem!* Do you know what Mayhem means?"

"You want me to look it up on my cell phone?"

"No, I just happen to have it right here on mine. Here's a short one, but it's descriptive enough: actions that hurt people and destroy things: a scene or situation that involves a lot of violence. Actions that hurt people. Lots of violence. Somehow that and a wonderful meal this evening sounds contradictory."

"Right."

"And you're worried about five dollars."

"Exactly, Edwin. I'm doing this for your own good."

Edwin looked at him and nodded that he was ready for the punchline.

"Okay, here's my rationale. You owe me five bucks. The good Lord and I have given you plenty of opportunities to give me my money. You on the other hand have deliberately—"

Edwin gave him a hard look.

Jonathan raised his hands. "Or *ignorantly* passed up these opportunities. Now out of your own mouth, you admit that I may get to mark martyrdom off my list today." Jonathan scooted a little closer to Edwin. "Edwin, if that happens and you haven't given me my money, I fear for your soul."

Edwin chuckled and shook his head. "It's true," said Edwin, reaching into his back pocket for his wallet.

"Do not be deceived. Neither fornicators, nor idolaters, nor adulterers, nor homosexuals, nor sodomites, nor thieves...thieves, Edwin, will inherit the kingdom of heaven." Jonathan smiled and rubbed his hands together before Edwin pushed the money into his hand. "What's true, Edwin?"

"Jonathan, when the thought first came to my mind that you were crazy, I thought it was God. Later when that thought resurfaced, I told myself it was the devil. Now...."

"Now what do you think, Edwin?"

"Now I don't know whether it was God or the devil. I only know that whoever said it was telling the truth."

"This is turning into an abusive relationship, Edwin."

The men sat silently for several seconds.

"Why'd you really stop?" asked Edwin.

"Besides the five bucks?"

"Besides the five bucks."

"You know, Edwin, I don't really have a death wish. It only looks like I do. I really have a life wish. I know that to die is gain. The moment I die, I go to be with the One Who died for me. I go to a place where everyone loves righteousness, where everyone loves the Lord. So I have no fear of death.

"You're a good man, Edwin. You have a good ministry. You have a wonderful family. Everyone is called to do what God called them to do. I'm me. You're you. It's not fair for me to take you out of your world and to thrust you into mine." Jonathan's face was serious. "I face death constantly. But that's my call and my choice. I won't romanticize this. We're going into a stronghold of violence and drugs and rebellion. We could die in *Mayhem* today. You don't have to go."

Edwin searched his heart. "Braised chicken," he said.

"What?"

"Braised chicken thighs with carrots and potatoes. That's what I'll be missing if you get me killed today."

"Aaahh, they're probably having something better in heaven anyway. Probably not chicken. Maybe some kind of fancy manna," said Jonathan.

"I guess if we lead someone to the Lord, we owe it to them to disciple them," said Edwin.

"I've always thought so," said Jonathan. "Good choice." He put the car in reverse.

"Wait a minute. How'd I do back there at the house," asked Edwin.

Jonathan smiled. "Aaaaaahh, at the house."

"Yeah. How'd I do?"

Jonathan started laughing.

"That bad, huh?"

"No," he said, holding his belly. "You did—"he laughed some more—"did you really think I was going to smoke that weed?"

Edwin pulled back, waving his head, then shaking it. "Look, I didn't know what you were going to do. We're in a dope house with criminals. One's got a gun. They offer you dope. I didn't know you could say no."

"Edwin, no matter what the circumstance, you can always say no. You just have to be willing to pay the price for saying no." Edwin saw seriousness in Jonathan's eyes as he said that. "Besides, I'm a holy man of God. I haven't smoked weed in weeks."

"You're not going to get me on that one."

"You're on to me," said Jonathan.

"What about the guy and his girlfriend?"

"Ah, yes. Jantell and her drawls."

"That didn't bother you? A guy asking us to pray for...."

"You can say it, Edwin. God knows what drawls are."

"He was talking about her panties," said Edwin.

"Panties. Drawls. Same thing."

Edwin shook his head. "I just—he—the irony of it. He asked a minister to pray that God would help him get Jantell's panties off."

"He said drawls."

"He wants to have sex with her."

"That's probably why he wants the drawls off, Edwin. Did you and Barbara adopt your children?"

"Jonathan, I just can't get over someone asking a preacher to pray for him so he can have sex with his girlfriend. And that didn't bother you one bit. You were laughing."

"It was funny."

Edwin needed more than "it was funny." His expression said so.

"Edwin, I don't mean it was funny in an absolute sense. You and I both know that only a person who is totally ignorant of God would ask something so foolish. If the young man dies in this condition, he's going to hell. That's not funny. That's why we're risking our lives. Because there's nothing funny about someone living in rebellion and dying in his sins.

"What was funny, Edwin, was the moment. I'm used to this stuff. You're not. You're sheltered. You're only used to clean ministry with clean people. You're easily shocked. If you could've seen your face." He laughed briefly.

Edwin knew that Jonathan wasn't in the least way trying to criticize him, but he was chastened, nonetheless. He sensed that the chastening was the Holy Spirit revealing his heart to him. "That's why you're so successful winning so many kinds of people to the Lord. Nothing shocks you. You don't let their lifestyles or mannerisms keep you from ministering to them."

Jonathan looked at him keenly, recognizing God at work. "Edwin, we're the salt of the earth. Salt must come into direct contact with whatever it's trying to season. We can't be so afraid of or be offended at the world that we stay away from them. A lot of things you just have to learn to ignore or laugh at if you're going to reach people."

"Can I ask the obvious?"

"What about their sin?" asked Jonathan.

"Yeah. What about their sin? We can't compromise what we believe in the name of reaching people."

"Good point, Edwin. Let me put it this way. Have you ever noticed how little space is given in the epistles to denouncing the society they lived in? There was abortion back then. Even worse, infanticide. Have a kid. Don't want it. Lay it out in the woods somewhere. Let it die. There was homosexuality. Slavery. You name it, they had it, and more of it. I'm not saying if you live in a country with a government that lets Christians get involved, we shouldn't say something.

"But here's where I detour a bit from some. I've noticed that for every ten preachers who speak publicly against homosexuality or abortion only one of those ten will speak against racism, worldliness, fornication, gluttony, greed, self-worship, contempt for the poor—you get the point.

"Paul told us in 1 Corinthians 5 that we should be more concerned with judging the sins of the church instead of judging the sins of the world. I think if we spent half the time judging ourselves that we spend judging the world, we'd have enough integrity and spiritual power to command respect from the world. Instead, the world sees a bunch of chronic complainers and finger-pointers preaching about a dead guy they don't imitate.

"Edwin, how long are you going to let me babble like this? You know I won't stop if you don't stop me."

"How do you know that's not the plan? To let you talk until it's too late to go to *Mayhem?*"

"It's never too late for mayhem, Edwin. Never too late." He got back on the road.

Only two blocks left before they would enter *Mayhem Courts.*

"How did you know the Lord would manifest Himself to those guys at the house?" asked Edwin.

"I didn't."

"That's comforting."

"That's another long discussion, Reverend Edwin Styles. Don't have time to talk about it right now. I'm working on my *To Do* list."

Edwin smiled. "Ha, ha. Brilliant comedian moonlighting as a preacher."

Several people suspiciously watched the car approach. It wasn't recognized. Neither were the two men in it. One of them was white.

Edwin was careful to not give eye contact. It was awkward trying to not look like a cop. But how could a white man in *Mayhem Courts* not look like a cop? "Jonathan, I was reading Matthew 28. The part where Jesus said, I am with you always."

"Yeah?"

"I know it's in the Bible. So spare me the sermon. You said you didn't know whether or not God was going to manifest Himself to those guys at the house."

"I knew He would manifest Himself. I just didn't know how or when. I asked Him. So I knew He'd do it."

"And how do you interpret Jesus's promise to be with us always?" asked Edwin. "Specifically, right now."

"Well, Edwin, you've picked an odd time for one of my faith-building messages. Jesus was with Paul when he worked miracles, and He was with him when he was stoned by the Jews. He was with him in Acts 16 when Paul cast the spirit of divination out of the little slave girl, and He was with him when he and Silas were beaten and thrown into prison for casting that demon out. He was with the apostle James in Acts 5 when an angel freed him from prison, and He was with him in Acts 12 when he got his head chopped off in prison. Whether we live or die, He is with us. Would you like more faith-filled examples?"

"Lovely," said Edwin. "There goes a good supper."

They parked and got out of the car.

***

Several rough-looking black men were at the entrance of the building, maybe six or seven. They were huddled, discussing something and looking intermittently at Edwin and Jonathan as they approached. The men weren't at all enthused about two cop-looking strangers in *Mayhem.*

"We're here to see Oct—Prince," said Edwin.

"Why you telling us?" It wasn't a question. It was a demand. The man who made this demand had long hair like the guy who wanted Edwin to pray about Jantell's drawls. He wore a tight-fitting t-shirt. It wasn't tight because the shirt was too small. It was tight because the man's muscles were too large for the shirt.

"Somebody here look like his secretary?" The man who said this had red eyes. He looked like he hadn't slept in days.

"I doubt seriously that any of you gentlemen are anybody's secretary." Jonathan looked at the muscled man. "Especially you. Anybody hittin' iron like that...." Jonathan looked at them all. "The reason we told you we're here to see Prince is because this is your place. We're visitors. No one here knows us. We didn't want to be disrespectful."

Edwin thought this was a fine speech. He searched the men's faces to see whether they thought it was a fine speech. It appeared to lessen the level of hostility—a little.

"Whachu wont?" one of the men asked.

Edwin hesitated.

"With Prince, nigga. You said you wanna see Prince. You wonna see 'em or don't cha?"

Edwin was over forty years old. He had been born a white man. As far as he knew, he was still a white man. He had gone the entirety of his life being recognized as a white man. And yet for the second time in one month, he had been called "nigga." By a black man, no less.

"Yes, we want to see Prince. He's a friend of my daughter."

"Prince is friends with your daughter?" said one of the men.

"Yes. We had the pleasure of meeting him when he tried to carjack us. Well, actually, he did carjack us."

The men's expressions turned tense. The one man who was sitting on the step stood up. He looked as though he had something in mind.

"It's not like that." Edwin waved. "Prince and I, we're cool. Like I said, he's a friend of my daughter."

Edwin saw that one of the men, a young man with a red scarf wrapped around his head, was studying his face. The man stepped forward, holding up his pants with one hand and bouncing his finger at Edwin with the other. "You da one me and Prince jacked at Kroger's." He started bouncing around, holding his hand to his mouth and laughing. "Ah, ha, ha, ha, aaahhhhh, ha, ha, ha. Dawg, his daughter liked to kill that nigga. He couldn't even talk when he got back to the crib."

The guy was unable to stop laughing. His laughing and bouncing around loosened up the men.

"Man, go on up. Tell Prince he bet not smoke up all my weed, either." This was the man with the red eyes.

"I'll make sure to tell him that," said Jonathan.

Edwin and Jonathan went inside the building. As soon as they got to the second floor, Jonathan touched Edwin's arm and stopped. He was smiling. "Prince and I, we're *cool?* You and Prince are *cool,* Edwin?"

"How'd I do?"

"That was..." he shook his head with a turned up lip, "...good. It was good."

"What? What I do wrong?"

"Nothing. It was good. Now, it would have been awesome had you said, "Me and Prince, we cool."

"I am *not* talking like that," said Edwin.

Jonathan slapped him on the shoulder. "Good. Me either. Unless my life depends on it. Let's go."

They continued up the darkened stairs.

"Jonathan, that's the second time someone black has called me the N-word."

"What? *Nike*?

"No, not *Nike*. You know what word."

"How many times has someone white called you that word?"

"What?" said Edwin, incredulously.

"You said that's the second time someone black has called you the N word."

"You know what I mean."

"Edwin, remember what I said about some things you laugh at and some things you ignore? Here's a wonderful opportunity to do either. If I were you, I'd laugh. If I can laugh at a white gentleman in South Carolina calling me an uppity nigger, or an old white woman in Louisiana referring to me as boy, you can laugh at a black man in *Mayhem* calling you nigga."

Edwin stopped climbing stairs. He had a shocked look on his face. "Someone called you that?"

"Edwin, we're fighting for people's souls. We can't let petty things like this get us off track. I don't care what the devil calls me. I'm going into the strongest of his strongholds, and I'm going to set God's people free. I can't do that if I've got thin skin. You gotta love people. Even the ones who treat you bad. Just like Jesus. Come on. I've got to tell Octavius to not smoke all that guy's weed."

Edwin shook his head as they climbed the stairs. "What's he doing smoking marijuana? I thought he got saved. Sharon led him to the Lord."

"That's why we're here," said Jonathan.

They climbed the last stair and opened the door to the long hallway. There were light sockets in the long ceiling, but only a couple of sockets had working bulbs. Some bulbs were missing.

That, coupled with the dark floors, made for a dark hallway. However, there was a little light coming from the small door window at the opposite end of the hall. But it was so little as to not be any use.

What the hallway lacked in light it made up for in noise. If it wasn't the strong bass on someone's music pounding on the doors, it was someone yelling or laughing or a baby crying or a television with loud as its only option.

"Edwin, wait," said Jonathan as he stood by a door.

"What? This isn't G13."

"I know. It's Tupac. *Dear Mama.*"

"Who?"

"You don't know him, Edwin. He was a rapper. Was murdered in '96. Drive-by. I know some of his people. He wrote this song for his mother."

"Is there anyone you don't know?"

Jonathan was saddened again. That was one he couldn't save. Maybe they could save Octavius.

They stopped at G13.

"What's that smell?" asked Edwin.

"Ohhh, boy," said Jonathan. He knew. He knocked on the door.

The door opened. A strong rush of marijuana slapped Jonathan and Edwin. Their eyes widened involuntarily. A woman who was maybe close to thirty stood before them with a beer in her hand. She was dark-skinned, attractive, and surprisingly not shy about opening the door wearing only a long shirt that Edwin felt wasn't long enough. She looked at the men and bobbled her head as if to say, *And who the h— do you want?*

"Who dat is?" said a little five-year-old in the background.

"I told you, Mark, stop talking like that. You sound so ignorant. *Who dat is?* It's who is it? Ugh." This was Michelle. His nine-year-old sister who loved to read. The lady standing at the door was her mother. She carried a long robe to her mother. "Here, Momma."

"Oh, so now you the momma?" she said to her daughter. But she took the robe and put it on with a smirk.

"I'm Reverend Styles, and this is Jonathan. We're from Glory Tabernacle. We're here to see Octavius."

She laughed. "Church people here to see Prince. Maybe y'all can make him stop drinking my beer."

"We'll give it our best shot," said Jonathan.

"Prince," she yelled over her shoulder. "Y'all come on in."

They stepped inside.

Another little bare-chested boy around three-years-old came out of a back room. He had on a heavy disposable diaper that had come unfastened on one end. He sucked his thumb and with his free hand, he held up his diaper. He looked at Edwin and ran to him screaming, "Daddy! Daddy! Daddy!" He let go of his diaper and it fell to the floor. He hugged Edwin's leg tightly. His little legs danced up and down in excitement like a jack hammer.

"That ain't yo daddy, little nigga. Let go of that man." The momma cussed to make sure the little boy understood his mistake of hugging a white man's leg and calling him daddy.

Jonathan looked at Edwin with a sly grin.

"Jonathan, just...don't."

Out of the back room came Octavius. A fat joint was in one hand. His lungs were tight with a long puff. He wore no shirt. His chest and abs were well defined. That kind of definition didn't just happen. Edwin lifted weights himself and appreciated what kind of effort this guy was putting in at the gym.

Octavius opened his eyes wide with surprise. He went to Edwin and exhaled the marijuana smoke directly into his face. He cussed. "Oh, man, I'm sorry. Didn't mean to shotgun you raw like that, Cuz. I thought y'all was just talkin' when you said you was coming for Bible study. How y'all know I was here?"

"God knows where you are, Octavius," said Jonathan.

"Okay, let me get rid of this first." Octavius began to raise the joint to his mouth.

Jonathan said, "Uhh, this will probably work better if you don't do that. And your friend downstairs, the one with the dragon eyes, he said don't smoke all his weed."

Octavius smiled widely. "Oh, yeah. Yeah." He bobbed his head. "Yeah." He handed it to the woman, who was shaking her head in disbelief at Prince.

Edwin recalled how this man had kidnapped him and his family and had pistol whipped his daughter in front of him. Now he was in the heart of the ghetto, in this man's living room—full of marijuana smoke—about to have Bible study with a guy who was high on drugs.

"This is going to be an interesting Bible study," said Edwin out loud to God.

Octavius bobbed his head and smiled, showing off a gold tooth. "Yeah. Yeah. We gone get some Jesus up in here."

***

Some Jesus was already *up in here*.

The blue mist was thick in the living room. Four demons, what was left of them, were scattered in the small house. Outside in the dark hall, the bodies of demons were stacked three and four deep. The calm of that floor's interior was exact opposite of the ferocious hand-to-hand fighting going on outside.

This unprecedented affront by the kingdom of light on their property had caused Slavery and Annihilation to talk of a temporary truce. One thing that was unspoken, but clearly understood among them was that there must be a severe penalty for this intrusion. The residents of *Mayhem Courts* would pay dearly.

Chapter 5

Slavery and a handpicked task force of demons neared the posh neighborhood. He looked contemptuously at the homes as he landed a block away. He and his posse would walk the rest of the way to their target's luxury home. There was a lot on his mind. He could use a few extra moments to contemplate the day's developments.

Despite the fact that business was booming in slavery, there was much to be concerned about. The day had started off bad and had gotten worse. To help him steady his nerves, he had chosen a safe home as the first on his suburban route. He didn't need any more surprises. He'd had enough for the day.

A quick, but thorough inspection of the property revealed no prayer. Not even prayer residue. *Good. That stuff was horrible. What didn't blow you up, asphyxiated you. How many demons had ruined their lungs getting even a scant whiff of that stuff?*

The scouting demon motioned them forward.

The approaching troop of evil spirits were formidable in appearance. Their large number for one young girl with no prayer cover seemed overkill. More than one of the demons felt their large number was more a response to the humiliation of *Mayhem Courts* than a real tactical advantage against this unprotected girl.

Slavery had brought with him a contingent of fighting spirits. Prayer support or none, you never knew with the enemy. *He and His criminal mercy!* He also had several spirits who carried clubs. They would join the Rejection and Abandonment spirits who were already pounding her.

Slavery and his demons stood on the large, deep green, professionally maintained lawn. He looked to his right and smirked. That was his next visit. Nearly five thousand square feet of heated space. Luxury cars in four garages. Degrees from prestigious universities hanging on the walls. One highly esteemed psychiatrist. One shake-the-planet investment banker. Three adorable college-bound children.

One pervert. One drunk. One hooked on prescription drugs. One hooked on pornography. Another on the way to being hooked. Four and a half out of five ain't bad.

"Heh, heh, heh," he laughed. "Things aren't always what they seem."

The demons followed Slavery into the target's home. To his left and right were spirits of addiction. Behind them were addiction specialists. Gluttony. Pornography. Alcohol. Tobacco. Several others, and a host of spirits who seemed out of place. One never knew when an opportunity might present itself. One had to be ready.

Ahhh, yes, and then there was Heroin.

He wasn't *the* star of the show, but he could've been had this spot not been reserved for Slavery. Many spirits mimicked human speech patterns and slang, mannerisms, and surprisingly even clothing. This was a by-product of their extreme envy of the sons and daughters of Adam.

The Lord had arbitrarily and unjustly created these beings in His own image from the dirt—*the dirt!*—to share His very throne. Imitating their usurpers—and, of course, living through them—was the closest thing they could do to claim what was rightfully theirs. Heroin took this to a whole new level.

He was already a fascinating personality with irresistible charm. His presence was magnetic. So there was no need for him to dress and act so outlandishly. Nonetheless....

He appeared as a hybrid demon-man. He wore soft blue pants with a matching shirt. And, of course, blue shoes and a blue scarf. This was odd enough, but he added a long, blue sequin cape that had fluffy white ruffles at the ends of the sleeves, and a blue hat with a feather in it. He was obviously a demon and not a man. Yet one couldn't tell by what he portrayed. It was all so ridiculous, even to demons.

But he *was* Heroin. So between derisive whispers and muffled laughter, they tried to focus on his legendary powers to enslave and not on how far he was taking this imitation thing. But this was hard to do when a demon of such prowess and fame chose to walk in the back of the troop so no one would step on his flowing cape.

Slavery stood in the kitchen, only a few yards from the target. "Here's our precious white dirt."

"*Hoooolly.*" Heroin cocked his head to the side. "Holly, baby."

All eyes looked to the back of the posse.

Heroin lifted his hands halfway and fluttered his fingers backward. "Time to talk to Daddy, baby. Let's go upstairs."

The demons parted to the left and right, creating a path for the flamboyant demon and his flowing cape.

Slavery was a dignitary. A general. As such, he had worked with and commanded all sorts of demons. This was an exceptional challenge. For the effects of losing the Great Rebellion had been devastating not only for the obvious reason of one day being cast into the lake of fire to suffer God's wrath forever. It was devastating because of how it had affected their appearance, intelligence, desires, abilities, and for some, their sanity.

Some demons, like Heroin, were a mixture of brilliant and eccentric. Others were in any language chosen to describe them...*crazy*. Perhaps functionally crazy, but crazy still.

Slavery looked at Heroin with the patience of a championship winning coach who knew how to get the most out of a team—no matter how odd one of his star players.

Heroin turned to Holly's mom. "Mom, Holly's going to eat in her room. Is that okay with you?"

"Mom, I'm going to eat in my room. Okay? I've got some studying to do. No rest for surgeons in the making," said Holly.

Mom and Dad shared a smile of accomplishment.

"Sure," answered Mom.

"MCAT's in trouble," said Dad, going back to his *Wall Street Journal.*

Holly took her plate and a bottle of water and headed for the staircase. Heroin put his hand across the back of her neck and onto her shoulder, his long, skinny fingers dangling. The demons started after him.

"Wait," said Slavery. "Give him space." He answered the demons questioning looks by looking at Heroin's dragging cape.

"Sheesh," said a demon, shaking his head. "This is ridiculous."

"Rejection and Abandonment, give him a few minutes and then get up there," said Slavery.

Heroin looked at Holly with a grin. "Pride will make you do some dumb things, won't it? But it never really was about pride, was it? Whatever. A girl who wants to be a surgeon should have a better appreciation of chemicals." Heroin shook his head. Deep lines formed in his face as he pushed his lips down in mock disapproval. "Drugs are bad news. But not heroin, baby. Heroin's good for you."

Holly sat her food and water down on the bed. She walked slowly to her walk-in closet, moved some stuff around, and sat against the wall in the dark. She couldn't believe it. *This can't be happening to me!* She held out her arm and looked at where the needle had entered. Her arm dropped limp against her side.

This...simply...can...not...be happening to me!

Holly bowed her face and shook her head in her hands. *No! No! No!* A half gasp pushed from her throat, but got caught in her mouth between her twenty-thousand dollar teeth. Compliments of a daddy, who like everyone else, thought Holly had a beautiful smile, but who loved his little girl so much that he didn't put up much of a fuss if it meant helping her low self-esteem.

He and his wife had stood united in their denial of Holly's request at age fifteen for a boob job. So far they had successfully resisted two years of her regular requests for something that time had proven totally unnecessary. But she had prevailed upon them for lip implants.

Holly trembled. This was different. This wasn't low self-esteem. This wasn't just in her mind. Well, it *was* in her mind. But what made this different was *something* was in her mind.

Not just a thought. *A thing.*

Something had been driving her ever since she came out of that....

Holly shook her head in denial at the word *high.* She had been high many times. Marijuana. Booze. Even OC a few times. But whatever that was she felt when she took the heroin was insane. What it had done to her. Where it had taken her. There was no imagination, no movie, no dream. Nothing could ever describe the kind of paradise that had filled every atom of her being.

But paradise was gone.

In its place were two things. One, a craving for paradise. And, two, the near certainty that paradise was forever lost. It was the latter that was more cruel than the former.

The *near certainty.*

Given the options of two horrible possibilities, it would be better to crave something she knew she could never have, than to crave something that cruelly tormented her with the thought that if she stretched her fingers just a little more—*just a little more, Holly!*—she'd grasp a reality that would forever exist only as a memory.

She'd only taken heroin one time. Why did the thought of it fill her mind with such ferocity? Like a hungry tiger clawing wildly for food? Somehow she knew that her body was not yet enslaved. It was a battle in her mind.

Enslaved.

Was she really even thinking like this after only one time? This was ridiculous. Slave? She wasn't some inner city dope fiend. Some ghetto junkie. She had taken one shot. One shot. That's all. Just to prove to everybody how lame it was to blame heroin for their problems. *Anybody can stop if they want to,* she had said. *Just stop.*

She trembled in the corner. That's what she had told her friends. Only stupid people became junkies, and only weak people stayed junkies. She wasn't a junkie. So why was she even thinking like this?

She unconsciously mumbled the thought that was carried into her mind like a feather riding the wind. "It's impossible to leave paradise." She followed this with her own thought. "This isn't paradise. It's hell."

Matter of perspective, thought Heroin.

For the next few minutes, Holly gave herself a pep talk. And during that time, Heroin held out his arm and stroked with the other as though he were playing the violin.

"I'm smart. I'm strong," said Holly.

Heroin stopped his mime. "Now, Holly, I was with you until you said smart and strong. If you were smart, you wouldn't be in this situation. Smart people don't listen to Pride. And so far as being strong, that's irrelevant. Not a one of you dirt people is as strong as I am." He shook his finger at her in a scold. "But I've never run into one, not one, Holly, who didn't believe he was stronger than me. Every single one of you—including *you,*" he punctuated in a falsetto pitch. "Get up here!" he yelled for the others.

Rejection and Abandonment came running. They watched Heroin hug her until he disappeared inside. He yanked his cape in behind him. Both demons carried two clubs. They knew what to do with them. They'd join the others who had been there since the day she had been given up for adoption.

The beating began.

***

An army of demons was to the left.

An opposing army of demons were to the right.

His voice carried a cold draft. "I don't like this one bit," said Annihilation.

"That makes two of us," said Slavery.

Annihilation peered at Slavery warily. None of their previous truces had ended well. Why should this one be any different? "We have irreconcilable differences."

"You want to kill them all," snapped Slavery.

"Yes." Annihilation's answer was without shame. "I want every single one of them dead. I hate this black dirt."

"Why the obsession with black dirt? Go somewhere and annihilate white dirt. Dirt is dirt, is it not?" Slavery didn't know why he was wasting his time with this animalistic killer.

Annihilation's wide, dark face was hard with contempt for his competitor. "Must I say it, Slavery? Africa. It's where the enemy began this humiliation! He and his Garden of Eden."

"Dirt is dirt! You idiot!"

Slavery's insult stirred both armies.

Slavery lifted his hand. "Stand down!" he shouted without taking his eyes off Annihilation.

Annihilation's intent upon Slavery was evident in his eyes. "Your next insult of me will not make it fully out of your foolish mouth."

Slavery was unimpressed with the threat. "Perhaps. Perhaps not. This would be what, our fifth or sixth fight? Both sides lose a bunch of demons. You and I cut and stab one another and return to have this same conversation again."

"Perhaps this time I make sure there will be no next time?"

"Calm yourself, Annihilation. We're competitors, not true enemies. The enemies are those who would take *Mayhem* from both of us."

"I am hungry," said Annihilation. "I have to kill black dirt. No one is as committed to feeding my fire as this black dirt. Their rage. Their unforgiveness. Their self-righteousness. Their lawlessness. Their self-hatred. It's dependable, Slavery. This ungodliness makes them kill one another. I have no one like this black dirt who delights in killing black dirt with such passion. I used to have the KKK, but that was so long ago," he stated sadly.

For a moment, Slavery tried to see things from Annihilation's eyes. He was right. There was no dirt like black dirt that could be depended upon to so routinely kill itself. "What about Mexico? The Mexicans have been butchering one another. Or Syria or Iraq. Now that would—"

"I'm stuck here," he interrupted. "I've tried to get a transfer to more bloody places. I'm stuck. They won't let me go anywhere. They said if I want more blood, I need to shed more blood. They told me to stop trying to steal another demon's blood."

"Since when is stealing bad?" asked Slavery.

"Exactly. Anyway, I've got to get my own blood, and the only dirt I can count on to give it to me is black dirt."

"We have irreconcilable differences," said Slavery.

"Brilliant assessment," said Annihilation.

Slavery had known this all alone. He was being selfish in contending with Annihilation over *Mayhem.* But as commendable as selfishness was, it really didn't make any sense to hold on to this old policy of fighting for scraps. They weren't fighting for scraps. *Mayhem Courts* had nearly eight thousand residents. Besides, if anyone was fighting for scraps, it was Annihilation. He did get a lot of blood from violent crime. But he had been living off of only one or two murders a month. That had to be tough on him.

He on the other hand had an ever increasing supply of slaves from alcohol, tobacco, pornography, drugs, hopelessness, fear. Oh, he could go on forever if he so desired.

"But our common threat is greater than our differences," said Slavery.

"What do you propose this time, Slavery?"

"I may surprise you, my friend."

Friend? What is this trickster up to now? thought Annihilation.

"I propose more than a truce. I propose peace. Let's stop fighting. You do what you want. I do what I want. There's enough dirt to go around."

"No more fighting among ourselves? What's your angle, Slavery? You always have an angle."

Slavery hadn't seen it until that moment. He cussed. He spit on the ground and cussed again. He pointed behind Annihilation's army. "That is my angle!"

A man engulfed in a light he didn't see emerged from the G building.

"I know that is *not* Octavius," Annihilation said disbelievingly.

"Oh, yes, that is Octavius," spat Slavery.

"Look!" Annihilation pointed to Turner Street.

A car with a suspicious glow drove up and parked. A young lady engulfed in a light got out of the car and walked across the parking lot. She was with two big women.

"And who's that?" asked Annihilation angrily.

"That's the new dirt. Kim. Look at that blue mist. Someone's praying for her. Do we want that kind of wickedness on our property?" said Slavery. "Trace that mist back to its source," he ordered a demon. "Find out who's praying for that girl."

"Today's battle at G building was just the beginning. The enemy's planning something big." Slavery looked at his new ally.

"Slavery, we need to stop this."

"How?"

"We need fear," said Annihilation.

"Spirits of fear? They'd need something—"

"No. Not spirits of fear. We need a heavy blanket of fear. We need *Mayhem* to live up to its name. We need to put the fear of darkness into anyone the enemy might tempt to invade our property with the gospel. We need crime. Vicious, violent crime. Blood," he said with spit dropping from the corner of his mouth. "We need blood. We need murders. We need everyone to know that *Mayhem* is off limits."

Slavery looked at Annihilation with new respect. Why had he waited so long to team up with him? "I do have some soft targets."

Annihilation smirked. "I always knew you did."

***

The demon's displeasure at having been selected for such a dangerous mission was evident on his bony face. He saw the amusement on the faces of a few demons who were standing close to him when Slavery chose him.

"Good luck," said one of them without an ounce of sincerity.

The frowning demon gave him the finger as he walked away and told him to do something to himself. He heard demons laughing at him as he left.

The mission was as simple as it was dangerous. Follow the mist. Find out who was praying for Kim. Tell Slavery.

Dangerous part. Try not to lose weight by being sliced and diced by an angel's blade.

He would've loved to have hovered high in the sky and simply look down at the mist from a safe distance. But things hadn't been simple since the Great Rebellion. Their warfare with the kingdom of light and the sons and daughters of God was like the human's guerilla warfare. Guerilla warfare with a million *Rules of Engagement.*

So many rules! So *maaaany* rules! And if it wasn't a rule for this or a rule for that, it was the ridiculously complicated environment in which they had to fight. Sometimes they could fly. Sometimes they couldn't. Sometimes they could see through physical objects. Sometimes they couldn't. Sometimes they could spot angels ten miles away, so to speak. Sometimes angels stalked them right under their noses, hidden in prayer. Or worse, hidden by the arbitrary and unjust sovereignty of God. He made and broke His own rules whenever it served His purposes!

The demon's thoughts and murmurings stopped. He followed the blue mist with his eyes to a house. He looked around warily. No threats. Correction. None that could be seen, he reminded himself.

The demon entered the home through the kitchen wall. Diane was washing dishes. His cheeks and lips rolled in displeasure at her. He left the kitchen in search of the mist. He saw it in the hallway, coming out of a room with a closed door. He tried to look into the room without entering. He couldn't. He cursed and stepped through the door.

What he saw was both unbelievable and despicable. A woman in a wheelchair sat with a Bible on her lap. It was opened and she was praying. The demon tilted his head. *This woman is crippled.* In a flash, he understood the severity of her physical condition. This is when his faced turned hateful.

Cripple, why are you praying for someone other than herself? Where's your bitterness? Why aren't you consumed with self-pity? No unforgiveness! How can this be? The demon let out a long, hot breath of disgust. *What is this world coming to? A cripple who should be focused on her own problems...focused instead on trying to free this Kim dirt from our prison. What would happen if more people tore themselves away from focusing on themselves?*

He shook himself. "Just the thought of this—whew! I've got to tell Slavery—"

"What you have seen."

The demon felt his weapons being snatched from his waist. He spun around and was immediately hit in the forehead by the angel's large fist. The demon stumbled backward and fell on his back.

The angel rolled him over onto his stomach. He wrapped him in a chain, locked it behind him, and put a shackle around the demon's neck. He snatched him to his feet. He had to hold him up until his senses unscrambled.

Eventually, the demon's eyes groggily opened. Then fear chased away the grogginess.

"What...what...?" he stammered, more from fear than the after-effects of his caved-in forehead. There was much to fear. The angel's size. His hard stare. But most of all, there was something about the angel's glow that told him he had been captured by an angel of the Lord's presence. *How had he crossed paths with such a high-ranking angel?*

The angel roughly grabbed the demon's neck with both hands and shot into the sky. The demon's confusion nearly matched his fear. The angel wasn't taking him to hell. Where was he taking him?

The angel stopped.

The demon looked around and saw nothing but blackness. Although they had gone up, the spirit now realized just how disoriented he was. They weren't up or down. They weren't in or out. They just *were.*

Suddenly, the demon was in a massive room and surrounded by too many angels to count. The demon's shocked head swung and jerked in every direction. Where was he? Why was he here? What were these angels going to do to him?

The angel who had captured him put his large hand around the demon's neck. "It is written, 'The manifold wisdom of God might be made known by the church to the principalities and powers in the heavenly places.' You have been chosen by the Most High to take a message to your master. You will tell him everything you see. If you fail to obey, another of your kind will perform this task." The angel looked at him coldly. "But I will return for you."

No bravado. No posturing. Just a weak, "I understand," he answered.

The angel pushed the demon by his neck, directing him to a spot. In a moment, the demon's dark mind was blown. Disorientation fell on him again. Was he as close to the unbelievable as it seemed? But how could he be this close and at the same time be so far away. It was like not knowing whether his hand was a few feet away or a billion miles away.

He shook his head in amazement. This couldn't be true! There was no way he was witnessing this! He saw the throne of God! The Almighty, and the Christ on His right hand! Why was he being allowed to see this?

Then he saw something that was infinitely more amazing than seeing God and Jesus seated side by side. An innumerable host of angels stood before the throne. As though it had been rehearsed a million times, the crowd parted perfectly for someone wearing a flowing white robe.

The demon's head stretched forward against the shackle. The angel felt the tug of the chain, but didn't look at the demon. He knew that this dark spirit was shocked and overwhelmed.

The person in the robe walked through the path of the perfectly formed lines on both sides as though he had been there before and belonged there. Suddenly, the demon's eyes could see the event more clearly. The person in the robe.

"My darkness," he exclaimed. "It's her. It's the cripple."

"She's not crippled here," said the angel who held the demon's chain. "She's a priest of the Most High God."

"She has access to the Most High? The very throne room of God?"

The angel looked at the wretched creature. He was an eternal enemy of righteousness. A rabid spiritual dog capable of nothing but destruction. Under other circumstances, he would not hesitate to separate his head from his body.

The demon seemed to pick up on these thoughts and lowered his eyes.

"More," answered the serious angel.

The demon wanted to scream, *"More? What is more than the throne room of God?"* But he thought better of it. In a moment, even he in his depraved condition understood what the angel meant by *more.*

Rosa walked to the bottom of the thrones. She looked into the faces of the Father and the Son.

"She's praying." The words came involuntarily out of the demon's mouth. This was an astounding event. Dirt was standing before the very throne of God. Blessing Him. Worshipping Him. Making petitions. Even making declarations. Declarations! She spoke boldly to the Most High! *Why, they'd burn me at the stake if I tried that,* he thought.

"You did try that. And for your offense, you'll be burned soon enough."

The demon whipped his neck and looked into the angel's eyes. "You know my thoughts?"

"There is no creature hidden from His sight, but all things are naked and open to the eyes of Him to whom you must give account."

The demon looked into the angel's eyes until he thought another moment of eye-to-eye contact would get him destroyed. He swallowed hard and turned back to Rosa.

"I told you Rosa has access to more than the throne room of God. Now you will see the unlimited graciousness of God, and the culmination of His eternal plan."

The angel's words were too much. The demon shook his head at the implication. He was about to see *more? Something greater than he had already seen?*

Then it happened.

Both the Father and the Son motioned for Rosa to sit with Jesus on His throne. The demon's foul mouth opened wide in shock as Rosa walked up the stairs and sat with Jesus. Dirt was seated with Christ!

"Rosa is not dirt, demon. She is a daughter of the Most High God, and sister of the Lord's Christ. Have you never read that the saints of the Most High are raised up together with Christ, and are made to sit together with Him in the heavenly places? Have you never read, 'To him who overcomes I will grant to sit with Me on My throne, as I also overcame and sat down with My Father on His throne'?" The angel's contempt for the demon peeked from behind his official non-expression. "Of course not. Your kind does not value the words of our Lord."

The demon had no time to digest the angel's words. In a moment, he was being dragged faster than lightning back to earth.

"Tell everything, or I will come for you."

That was the last thing he heard before the angel hurled him toward the streets.

***

Slavery and Annihilation felt good about their plans. Their respective armies felt good about their masters' plans. The enemy had come in like a tsunami and had made a mess of things. But things were going to get back to normal. And in a hurry. They were going to show the Lord that He couldn't push them around.

Slavery and Annihilation and their armies jumped when they saw the object hit the ground hard and bounce several times toward them. Thousands of demons crouched with outdrawn swords, daggers, and other weapons.

Finally, the bouncing object rolled to a stop.

"Go see what it is," Slavery ordered a demon.

The demon went warily to the object. He looked at it and laughed. "The last time I saw you, you were giving me the finger. What happened? You tried that with an angel?"

"Just go get Slavery! I have a message for him."

The amused demon went back to Slavery and whispered to him.

Slavery went alone to the chained demon. He got on one knee and listened to the new intelligence. The demon's message fascinated and infuriated him. "Did you tell the other demon what you have told me?" he whispered.

"No. No. Of course not. He'd run his big mouth and scare the darkness out of everyone."

Slavery crinkled his lips and nodded his head. "Well, maybe that's a bit of an embellishment. But I'm glad you understand my position."

"Sir?"

Slavery stood up and whacked off his head. A head without a body couldn't wag its tongue.

Annihilation watched without emotion. Discipline was necessary to maintain order. "What was that about?" he asked Slavery when he returned.

"He disgraced us all. Annihilation, you'll have your blood tonight."

Chapter 6

Holly sat against a tree alone. It was a beautiful April day, but she didn't see its beauty. Her legs were up to her chest and her arms folded protectively around them. She watched students in the distance, sure that every whisper was about her and that every eyeball was upon her. She wondered why she had even gotten out of her car. She had skipped her first two classes.

It was only Tuesday. Only the third day from when she had shot up. And yet it seemed so long ago. How could three days last so long? How could they be so unbearable? So excruciatingly dark and dismal?

Holly looked across the grass of the interior of the track field. She saw the spring colors that girls were wearing. But somewhere between the bright colors and Holly's brain, the colors turned black. She knew they were bright. *But they were black to her.* Everything was black. The sun's rays were black. The sky's blue was black. The birds chirping were mourning. Everything was dark and getting darker.

She still told herself that she wasn't a junkie. She'd even gone on the Internet and read everything she could about heroin. None of it was good. Except that there seemed to be a consensus that one shot of heroin wouldn't get someone hooked. She grasped this thought as though her life depended on it.

Another thing that gave her slight hope was that she hadn't suffered any physical withdrawal symptoms. No sickness whatsoever. But this was almost meaningless. *For her mind was filled with thoughts of heroin from the moment she awakened to the moment she went to bed.*

Went to bed, not went to sleep. For Holly, going to bed no longer meant going to sleep, because she didn't go to sleep, at least not for a long time. It took at least two or three hours of obsessing about heroin before she'd fall asleep. Then she'd dream about it until she awakened in the morning feeling like someone driving a car had a chain around her neck forcing her to run wherever he drove.

She could resist, refuse to run. But then she'd simply hit the ground and be mercilessly dragged until the ground had torn her flesh from her body. She'd actually had this very dream. Saturday. Sunday. And Monday.

A creature wearing a blue suit, a blue hat, and a long, sparkly blue robe drove her around town. Every so often he'd look back out his window and smile at her and say, "Come on, Holly, baby. That's my girl. Run. Run. Run. If you stop, you die."

Holly was dead tired. She'd slept maybe eight hours in three days. She dropped her head on her knees and closed her eyes.

"Holly. Holly."

Holly was running...running...running.

Come on, Holly, baby. That's my girl.

"Holly," the guy shook her shoulder.

Run. Run. Run. If you stop, you die.

"Holly!" the guy said louder.

Holly grunted and looked up. It was Jared.

He looked down at her smiling. There was something wrong with his smile. "You alright? What are you doing out here?"

Holly put on her game face. "Jared, hey, what's up?"

His smile seemed to carry a secret he was loving. "You're what's up. Sitting out here by yourself."

"Yeah, it's been hectic, you know." She pulled out her phone and looked at it. She cursed. "I've got to get to biology class." She went to get up and Jared pushed her shoulder down. His hand touching her body was repulsive, even if it was just her shoulder. She looked at that awful smile of his. A smile other girls thought was beautiful, but which she thought was horrible for one unfixable problem. It was on his face, and his face belonged to a narcissistic creep who used girls as his doormat.

"How you been since Saturday? Some people are beginning to think you're avoiding your friends."

She gave her best impression of who she used to be. Or at least who she used to pretend to be. "If I were trying to avoid my *friends*, my *friends* wouldn't have to wonder about it. I have a way of making myself clear. You of all people should know that."

In the past, she had responded to his confident overtures by using every word and expression she could think of to crush his huge ego and to make it clear that he was out of his league.

She glared at him. This was more out of habit than for anything he had done here. Of course, there was that awful, obnoxious smile.

Jared slowly clapped his hands.

"What?" she asked, annoyed.

Jared's smile disappeared. "You're a fake, Holly."

"What?" she said, her face twisted in anger.

"Everything about you is fake." He looked her up and down.

Holly could've thrown up when he did this.

"I know why you've been avoiding us," he said.

She looked at him and shook her head. "You're pathetic." She walked past him.

"I've seen it before, Ms. High and Mighty. The great Holly Burton is a heroin addict. A junkie!" he spat.

This stopped her instantly. Anger filled her chest. *This self-aggrandizing, miserable retard!* She spun and marched back to him. Less than a foot separated them. She had emasculated him before. She'd do it again. Whatever he had left of his manhood, he was about to lose it.

"You worthless—" she began.

He lifted his finger and put it to her lips as though they were actors in a movie. "You're a junkie, Holly."

His words paralyzed her mouth. The anger that she had tried to hide behind drained out of her feet. She stood there mute, feeling naked before a guy whom she despised. She momentarily tried to force a brave face. That brave face that she had shown the world whenever the truth of her fragility was close to being discovered. *It wouldn't come.* All she could muster was a sick expression, like she was about to pass out.

Run. Run. Run. If you stop, you die.

"Stay with me now, Holly," said Jared.

Turn around. Walk away. Leave this creep standing here to play with himself. Just leave, Holly! she ordered herself. Her legs wouldn't move.

"They say the truth hurts. It's probably a new sensation for you." He smiled even more wickedly than before. "I know you have to get to class." He stepped up close. Only inches separated them. "So I'm going to make this short and sweet. Most people can take heroin straight like you did one time and not look at it again. At least that's what I've heard. I wouldn't know from experience. I'm not stupid enough to put that poison into my body. But there's a small percentage of folks, like you, Holly, who pop that vein and that's it." He snapped his finger.

His finger snapping sounded like thunder in Holly's ears.

"Holly."

She stared at his chest in a daze.

"Look at me, Holly," he said with an edge. She looked up. It felt like rape looking into his eyes. "That's good. Now, no one knows about your addiction but me."

"I'm not addicted," she heard herself say, surprised and relieved that she could finally speak.

"Course not, Holly. You're strong. I remember now. You took that crap to show the world how strong you are. Holly, baby, listen to me. Nobody's stronger than heroin. Not even you." He looked intently into her eyes. "It's driving you crazy, isn't it? All you can think about, right? I know exactly how it works, Holly. Ask me how."

She didn't answer.

"Ask me how, Holly."

She knew exactly what this creep was doing. He was trying to control her. She wouldn't give him the satisfaction of—

"Ask me," he demanded.

She submitted. "How?" She didn't know why she gave in, and hated herself for doing so.

"My older brother was a junkie. I say was because he's dead. But his legacy to me before he OD'd was to pass on this valuable information that I'm sharing with you."

Holly felt her anger returning. She was relieved. "What do you want?"

"Holly, don't flatter yourself. I've had you once and—"

"What do you mean, you've had me? You've never...."

"Go on. Finish what you were saying."

Holly couldn't believe it. She had thought something happened to her when she was high on heroin. The thought of this dog raping her made her sick. Then mercifully, she remembered there were seven other people there. "You're lying. My friends wouldn't let you touch me."

"We are both going to be late for class, but this is so worth it. Holly, two things. First, you don't have any friends. Well, let me not lie to a junkie. I'm not heartless. Caitlyn is your friend. That brings me to number two. Caitlyn had to go."

Holly shook her head in a disbelief that she was desperately trying to hold onto. "But they wouldn't let you...."

"Holly. Holly. *They* wouldn't let me? *They* were with me. You'd be surprised at how many people don't like you."

This was preposterous. It was the imagination of this demented monster. Everything he was saying was a lie. This was simply Jared being Jared. It was why she had always hated him. Now she hated him even more.

Jared shook his head with a confident smile. He pulled out his phone. He pulled up a video and showed it to her. "No," he playfully smacked her hand aside. "Look, but don't touch."

The videos—there was more than one—seemed to never end. When they did, Holly was weak-kneed and gutted.

Jared put his hand under the mute girl's arm and walked with her toward the building. "Holly, if it helps any, I was as shocked then as you are now. You knew me from the beginning. I told you I wanted you and that I was going to have you. But the others. Man, your girls flipped on you on a heartbeat. And the guys, well, you know guys."

"How could you?" Holly said, as she walked robotically arm in arm with someone she hated.

"How couldn't I? How couldn't I?" he corrected. "There you were. In your bikini. Totally gone. It was easy. Holly, the next time you're going to be wide awake. And I'm going to use my phone to video you begging me for it."

"I'm never going to bed with you, Jared." Holly had been gutted. She'd been compromised, humiliated, betrayed, and raped. She didn't know how she was going to recover, how she was going to make it, but she would never go that low.

He gave her an *Oh, really?* look. "You mean not *again*." He whispered in her ear, "Junkies don't make the rules." He squeezed her neck affectionately and left her standing numb by the door of her building.

***

Holly was physically standing, but she had been mentally and psychologically knocked out. A suicide spirit that had been watching from a distance came in for a landing. He stopped, then moved in a little closer. He'd seen enough. He took off in the opposite direction as fast as he could go.

The big mercy angel that stood next to Holly watched the suicide spirit retreat. The angel had destroyed two other suicide demons whose compulsive nature had gotten the best of them that day. They had gotten threateningly close.

He held her up as she walked haltingly down the hall. In her stupor, she wondered why she was going to class and not running for the refuge of her car. She entered her AP biology class and took her seat next to a girl wearing a cast on her arm.

***

Dr. Dawkins placed both elbows on his wooden lectern and looked condescendingly at Sharon. "You disagree."

"What?" Sharon snatched a glance around her. He was talking to her. "Oh, I didn't mean—"

He furrowed his brows and lifted his hand gently and waved his palm toward her. "Noooooo. Noooooo. Noooooo. No need to back down. This is an AP biology class. Intelligent questions are encouraged here."

"I don't have a question," said Sharon.

"But you do disagree with evolution."

"You mean that we came from monkeys?"

"That's a bit simplistic, but for the sake of time, yes."

Sharon laughed lightly. "Of course, I disagree."

"Why, may I ask?"

"Of course, Dr. Dawkins. I encourage intelligent questions." She smiled at him.

He knew enough about Sharon to know she wasn't trying to embarrass him. She was just having some harmless fun. He smiled at her. "We're waiting, Ms. Styles."

"Dr. Dawkins, what is your degree in?"

"Which one?" He smiled.

"Your doctorate." She returned his smile. "You're not going to say, which one, are you?"

"No. I only have one doctorate. Straight biology."

"And I haven't yet finished your AP biology class."

"Your point, Ms. Styles?"

"My point is that you've forgotten more about biology and science than I'll ever learn."

"So," the teacher clapped his hands once, "you're turning tail and scurrying off into the woods."

Sharon smiled and looked at her teacher. He wasn't a bad guy. He was as kind as he was cynical, but he could be surprisingly dogmatic. He had known she was a Christian, but this was the first time he had called her out like this. She wondered what was really going on.

Lord, are You up to something here? If so, please help me. Give me Your words and power. I ask You to move by your Holy Spirit.

"You're praying, aren't you?" he asked.

"That's not fair, Dr. Dawkins. Mind reading is unscientific. But full disclosure. I was praying, and you're in for it."

"Oh, goodie, goodie," he said, without meanness.

"And in response to your comment about me turning tail and scurrying off, no. I'm just smart enough to know that I don't know enough about biology and science to debate you. Plus, I know that you dogmatically accept the obvious fallacy that nature created itself. Another thing," Sharon said, maintaining her smile, "I suspect that were I to get the best of you," she clapped one time, "you'd turn tail and scurry off into the woods of circular reasoning."

Dr. Dawkins and several students laughed. "Well, Ms. Styles, I have to admit to two things. One, you have a fascinating imagination. And, two, you're smart enough to not pick a fight you can't possibly win."

"Ouch!" said a student.

"Don't be so mean, Dr. Dawkins," said another.

Dr. Dawkins raised his hands in mock humility and shook his head. "I didn't want this fight. But when peasants rush the castle, no good can become of it."

"Peasant, huh?"

"No offense meant, Ms. Styles."

"None taken, King Dawkins."

He smiled. "Well, enough of that."

"This is a science class, right?" asked Sharon.

Dr. Dawkins grimaced. "Oh, you again?"

"Yes, one of your lowly peasants."

"Yes, this is a science class," he answered.

"Let's conduct an experiment."

"What kind of an experiment, Ms. Styles?"

"The kind that will demonstrate why I think evolution is silly, and why I find it impossible to believe it." When he hesitated, she added, "You're not scared, are you?"

"Oh, Dr. Dawkins, you can't let her front you like that," said a male student.

"Yeah, Dr. Dawkins, make her kiss your diploma," said one of Sharon's girlfriends, not wanting the skirmish to end.

"Make her kiss me, Dr. Dawkins."

Sharon turned and looked at the guy who said this. "Don't make me go back there, Brent."

"Just kidding, Sharon," he said laughing. Then under his breath, he said, "*Please* come back here." But it was loud enough for her to hear it.

She shook her head without looking back. "Well, Dr. Dawkins?"

"What do you need? How long will the experiment take? What will you prove?" asked Dr. Dawkins.

"I need a bunch of volunteers. It will only take a few minutes. I'll prove that God is real."

Dr. Dawkins' eyes lit up. He clapped his hands once. "That—God—is—real? What is it with peasants and castles?"

The talk of proving God's existence in a few minutes pierced Holly's stupor of pain. She raised her head and rested it on one elbow, looking at this strange girl.

"Deal, Dr. Dawkins?" asked Sharon.

"Sharon, the king is in a good mood. Anyone who promises to prove the existence of God, uhhh, I'll give you an extra two minutes. Now you have five." Dr. Dawkins smiled around the room.

"Can I stand up in the front, Dr. Dawkins?"

He motioned her up. "By all means."

She went up front.

Oh, precious Holy Spirit, please, please, please help me! This is a once in a lifetime opportunity. So many souls, Lord. "Okay, it's a simple experiment. Everyone knows I'm a Christian. So...anyway, what I'm going to do is ask God to manifest Himself to my volunteers."

"Intriguing," said Dr. Dawkins, as he rested on his lectern with one elbow propped up as he rubbed the hair on his chin. "How do you propose God will show Himself?" Then he tossed in for effect, "Or should we take it by faith that He's here?"

"Real funny, Dr. Dawkins." A thought came to mind. "Tell you what," she said, as she went and got a piece of paper and started writing, "I'll write down some of the signs here, and you read the signs to the class after the experiment."

Dr. Dawkins smiled and reached for the paper. "Like taking candy from a baby."

Sharon pulled the paper back with exaggeration and folded it. "Or pouring tar over the castle walls onto the poor peasants?"

Dr. Dawkins' eyes twinkled.

She handed the folded paper to him. "Put the list in your inside jacket pocket."

He did it.

"After the experiment, you'll read the list out loud and we'll see if any of these things happened. This way I won't compromise the behavior of my volunteers. Satisfactory?"

"Ms. Styles, I'm a merciful man. There's still time for you to skidaddle into the woods."

"And I'm a merciful woman. There's still time for you to confess that God is smarter than you."

He stretched forth his neck with a frowned face. "Not on your life, peasant."

She stretched forth her neck with a frowned face. "Then we have a deal?"

"Deal," he said.

The class clapped, roared, and stamped their feet.

"Now who wants—?"

Every hand shot up.

Holly looked around at all the hands raised in the air. She noticed that her hand was also raised.

"Okay, everybody. Thanks. This won't take long. Here's my premise. If Jesus Christ answers my prayers here in front of all of you, then He obviously is real. If He is real, then the Bible's testimony of Him is true. If what the Bible says about Jesus Christ is true, then what it says about creation is true. We're good?"

"We're good," someone answered.

Sharon looked around. No one seemed to object, so she went on.

Holly studied everything about this girl's appearance. She was beautiful, but Holly knew from experience that beauty didn't necessarily make you confident. How could she stand up there in front of everyone and claim that God was going to answer her prayers in front of them? Was she crazy?

She didn't look or act crazy. A thought pushed itself on stage. *But then I don't look like a junkie, either.* She grimaced inwardly and refocused on Sharon. *She's sweet. Genuinely sweet.* Another possibility other than insanity came to mind. What if she was so confident because she really did know God this way?

"Okay, let's start...*now!* Come, Holy Spirit. Show my friends that I have spoken the truth about the Lord Jesus Christ."

Holly and the others followed Sharon's instructions.

Close your eyes.

Lift your palms upward.

Say, God if You are real, and if Jesus Christ is real, I ask you to show Yourself to me now.

Wait.

Listen for His voice.

Be aware of His touch.

Dr. Dawkins had been truly enjoying himself up to this moment. He looked at Sharon. She was standing before his Advanced Placement biology class with her eyes closed and hands lifted to the heavens, like Joan of Arc, waiting for something that would never happen. But she wasn't Joan of Arc, and nothing was going to happen. Except she would be humiliated. *I should have never let it get this far,* he thought. He looked at his watch. *I'll give her a couple of extra minutes when her time is up.*

***

Adaam-Mir looked at Sharon, then at his mentor, Myla. He had learned a lot since being selected to train for frontline work. But it seemed every new thing he learned birthed a hundred new questions.

"Did the Spirit tell her to do this?" he asked.

"No."

"Then why did she do it?"

"For the Lord's honor," said Myla.

Adaam-Mir wasn't as reluctant now to ask questions that in his earlier training he would have thought to be inappropriate. "Is this not presumption? To claim to speak for the Lord when He has not spoken?"

"That would be presumption, my brother. But the Lord has spoken."

Adaam-Mir searched for the answer with his eyes.

"In His word," said Myla.

"But where in His word does it talk about...*a classroom experiment?"*

"Adaam-Mir, you ask good questions."

Adaam-Mir smiled.

"Do you recall when Paul went to Cyprus and was explaining the faith to the proconsul, Sergius Paulus?" asked Myla.

"Yes!" The passionate angel gestured with a balled fist. "The false prophet, Bar-Jesus, tried unsuccessfully to turn him from the faith."

"Unsuccessfully. Why unsuccessfully?"

"Because the blessed apostle Paul called blindness upon him. This showed the proconsul the truth of our blessed Lord."

"Where in the blessed book does it talk about calling blindness down upon those who oppose the preaching of the faith?" asked Myla.

"It doesn't, my brother. But he was filled with the Spirit when he did it."

Myla looked at his protégé, waiting for him to understand the revelation of his own words.

The angel lowered his head. He turned it to one side, then the other, as one thought produced another.

"You see, Adaam-Mir, the children of the Most High *walk* in the Spirit. They *live* in the Spirit. Sharon's experiment didn't start in heaven. It started in her heart. A heart submitted to the Spirit."

"But is that not the same thing as saying, the Spirit told her to do the experiment?" asked Adaam-Mir.

"No, it is not. That misunderstanding is why so little is done in the power of God. The sons and daughters of God are waiting for

God to act, so they can act. Our blessed Lord is waiting for them to act, so He can act.

"Adaam-Mir, the blessed words of our Lord: 'And whatever you ask in My name, that I will do, that the Father may be glorified in the Son. If you ask anything in My name, I will do it.'"

Adaam-Mir's eyes brightened. "I think I see! 'If you abide in Me, and My words abide in you, you will ask what you desire, and it shall be done for you. By this My Father is glorified, that you bear much fruit; so you will be My disciples.'

"Sharon didn't hear the Spirit tell her specifically to have the experiment—like Paul. She's not operating out of revelation. She's operating out of her relationship."

"Exactly," said Myla. "The same way we often do things we know will please our Lord even though He hasn't commanded us to do them. You can do things because you hear His voice. That is good. You can do things because you know His heart. That is better. The first acts as a servant. The other as a son or daughter."

Adaam-Mir looked at Sharon admiringly. "This daughter of God is remarkable. She is asking what she desires—*what she desires.* Just as it is written in the blessed book. And her desires are honored by God because they are kingdom desires. She's doing this experiment to get fruit for the kingdom."

Boom!

Both angels looked up into the heavens.

"What is that?" asked Adaam-Mir.

"The Lord has opened our eyes, my brother. It is a great honor," said Myla.

A thunderous voice spoke. It seemed to come not only from the heavens, but from every direction, even from beneath them. The ground trembled until the last word was spoken. "The eyes of the Lord run to and fro throughout the whole earth to show Himself strong in the behalf of those whose hearts are perfect before Him."

Out of a huge whirlwind of fire came seven chariots driven by beasts with eyes in the front and back and on the both sides. The chariots went in different directions at amazing speeds. In a moment, they moved too quickly to see anything but seven blurs coming from and going into different directions."

"Adaam-Mir, this is the presence of the Lord searching for faith in all the earth."

Suddenly, a stream of fire came across the sky from the east. It moved directly overhead and turned toward them.

Adaam-Mir felt like his heart was going to explode for joy. He looked at his mentor. "This fire, it is for Sharon?"

Myla spread his arms and closed his eyes. "Yes," he said, as the fire fell upon the classroom.

***

Holly felt sweat pouring from her forehead. She opened her eyes and looked at her right arm, especially the place where the needle had entered. She touched it. It was burning up. She looked around the room, trying to make sense of what she saw.

A few students were sniffling and trying to mask tears. One of them started sobbing loud enough to draw attention to herself. The girl wore a cast on her arm.

Dr. Dawkins' head moved with the agility of a bird. He would no longer look at one student before he snatched his head in another direction.

"Casey, is the Lord doing something?" Sharon said to the girl wearing the cast.

A girl went to Casey's side and put her arm around her neck and shoulder. "It's okay, Casey. It's okay." The girl looked up from Casey at Dr. Dawkins and mouthed, *I don't know what's wrong with her.*

The girl was crying hard, but apparently not in distress. There was clearly a smile on her crying face. "My *aaaaaarm,*" she cried.

Someone said, "She had a terrible accident."

"I broke my arm," the girl cried. "The bone was sticking out."

Dr. Dawkins hurried to the girl. "Casey, do we need to get you to the nurse? Do you have painkillers?"

The girl looked at Dr. Dawkins through her tears. "I'm not in pain."

He shook his head. "Well, what's wrong? Why are you crying?"

The girl burst out in tears.

Dr. Dawkins looked at Sharon.

"Casey, what's going on?" Sharon asked.

With difficulty, Casey was able to stop crying. Her voice trembled as she spoke. "My arm, it—got hot. It got really hot. Then I felt something happening to my arm. Inside of it. Like it was being fixed."

Sharon told herself to not shout. "Casey, do you feel any pain?"

"No."

"Casey," Sharon turned and looked into Dr. Dawkins' eyes, "I think the Lord Jesus Christ, the Savior of the world, has healed your arm. You wanna test it and see?"

The girl's gushings started again. "I *know* He healed me."

"Okay, let's just be careful and test it. Maybe you could—"

Casey lifted her cast and slammed it against the desk.

Everyone screamed in horror.

Dr. Dawkins doubled over in a near fetal position.

Sharon clutched her chest. She gulped some much needed air. "Casey. Oh. Hmm. Okay."

Casey starting taking off the cast as though she was on a mission.

"Casey," Dr. Dawkins began. *Don't do that*, is what he started to say, but he was as curious as everyone else to see her arm.

The cast came off and Casey popped to her feet. She walked around the classroom crying and waving her arm over her head. "Sharon, He did it. He really did it. I didn't think He would do something like that for me."

When the commotion finally died down, Sharon asked her shaken teacher to read the list of signs to the class.

With trembling hands and scrambled thoughts, he pulled the paper out of his pocket and unfolded it. It read:

Crying
Shaking
Speaking in tongues
Falling out
Feeling heat

Hearing God's voice or getting a strong thought

Seeing a vision

Healings

Something obviously strange, out of the ordinary, or supernatural

Dr. Dawkins didn't get to cover any of his content, but the class did have a lively discussion about God, the Bible, and miracles. When class ended, Holly caught up with Sharon.

"Can I talk to you?" she asked.

Chapter 7

Sharon sat in Holly's Mercedes with her after school. The girl had asked a lot of questions after biology class—she didn't have time then to answer them all, so here they sat. Although Holly had come across as hard and self-assured, there was something beneath her shell that sounded like a veiled cry for help. So Sharon knew the small talk was about to end.

"You know Casey?" Holly asked.

"Yeah, I guess. I've eaten lunch with her a couple of times."

"Her arm—that was—I don't know how to take that? Everyone says it's real."

"You sit right next to her, Holly. You saw what happened with your own two eyes. Take it as you saw it."

Holly said nothing for a couple of minutes. Neither did Sharon. She used the silence to pray.

"I've never thought of God like that."

"Like what?

"Like...like real. Close. We don't talk about God in our house. Mom used to take me to church when I was little." She paused in thought. "But when her mother died, the last time we went to church was her funeral."

"It's hard to lose a loved one." Sharon thought of Christopher. "Your mother—and I'm sure you losing a grandmother, it's not easy."

"She's not my mother." Holly was as shocked by her words as Sharon was surprised. She looked at Sharon as though she had just spilled punch all over her prom dress. "I didn't mean to—I don't know why I said that."

Sharon looked tenderly at Holly. She appeared humiliated and terrified that she had blurted this out. "Does anyone else know? I mean here at school?"

"Oh, my God, no. No. No one knows." She begged Sharon with her eyes.

Sharon reached for Holly's hand. Holly slowly moved it closer to Sharon. She took Holly's hand and squeezed reassuringly. "I'm honored that you'd share your heart with me. Whatever you say to me will never leave this car. I'll never betray you."

I'm hooked on heroin. I'm a junkie. I was raped while my friends watched. Oh, and I don't have any friends. My adoptive parents love me, but I'm the loneliest person in the world. I'm seventeen and my life is over. Holly felt like her throat was closing. She pushed a swallow that felt like it didn't go down.

"Are you okay?" asked Sharon.

I'll never betray you. Those words sank into her heart like water finding its way to the deprived roots of a thirsty flower. "I asked around. Everyone says you're like some kind of school priest." Holly's heart hurt, but she managed a broken laugh. "Maybe that's why I told you about—" A single tear punctuated her thought.

Sharon smiled. "Really? That's what students are saying?"

"Not just students."

Sharon's eyes started watering. "Hmp, that's..." she took a deep breath and let it out, "well, that's why I'm here."

"What do you mean that's why you're here?"

"Holly, you saw what the Lord did in there today. That's why I'm here. It's why I'm alive, to show the love and power of my Father."

"You're talking about God."

"Yes, I'm talking about God."

"You call Him *Father.* I mean, like a real father," said Holly.

Sharon felt a joyous warmth in her belly and chest. She smiled at the peace and satisfaction that was enveloping her. "Holly, God is my Father. I am His daughter and servant. He loves me and I love

Him. He'd do anything for me, and I'd do anything for Him. And, yes, I'm one of his priests. Every child of God is a priest."

Holly was in an emotional tornado, spinning violently from one extreme to another. One moment, she saw nothing but a dizzying array of reasons to not live. The next, she was standing sure-footed and calm in the midst of the violent winds, imagining she were a daughter of God like Sharon.

"Do you have a lot of friends?" Holly asked.

"Yes. I have a lot of friends." Sharon looked intently at this hurting girl, seeking to know her beyond her beautiful but guarded and hard shell. "But more importantly, I *am* a friend to many people." She smiled. "What about you, Holly? You have many friends?"

No, I'm all alone. There's no one, but me. "Yeah, I have lots of friends." Her words sounded hollow.

"That's good, Holly. Good friends add so much to our lives."

The mercy angel that had guarded Holly by the tree and had helped her to class saw Sharon feeling Holly's heart. He nodded his head in satisfaction. There had never been a doubt that this fearsome warrior of the Most High would care for this wayward soul. But he had to wait for her to commit to carrying her before he could join their hearts.

Question?"

"Yeah?" said Holly.

"Got room for one more?"

"Friend? You? Really? Yeah. Yeah, that would be cool." Holly noticed the joy in her own answer and wasn't ashamed of herself for appearing eager. This kind of honesty was different, but it felt good.

The mercy angel had to speed the relationship up. The kind of danger Holly was in couldn't wait.

Sharon's wide smile disappeared. She suddenly looked troubled.

Alarm gripped Holly. Sharon must've come to her senses. This was definitely the shortest friendship she'd ever had. "What's wrong?" she asked.

Sharon stared at the floor mat. Her face filled with anguish. She put her hands to her face and bent over. She cried into her hands. "Oh, Lord, Lord, Lord. You want me to do this?" Her head rocked as the tears poured from her eyes."

Holly didn't know what to do. She was afraid to say anything. She didn't know how, but somehow she had already lost Sharon as a friend. It had been stupid anyway to think that someone like Sharon could be her friend. And even more stupid to think that God would have someone like her. She closed her eyes and trembled, waiting for Sharon to say it.

In a few minutes, Sharon lifted her head. She wiped her eyes and face. "I have to tell you something."

Holly tried again unsuccessfully to push down a swallow. She braced herself. She tried to summon anger. Anger would keep her from crying. It was bad enough to cry over a guy. She was *not* going to cry over a girl.

"What I'm going to tell you, I haven't told anyone. Not even my parents. Holly, a little over a year ago something terrible happened to me." She thought back and felt the pain. This surprised her. She had cried out to her Father about this many times, until she felt it had been adequately dealt with.

"I had a best friend, Toni, who did something horrible to me. We went out on a double-date. I didn't know the guy she set me up with." Sharon wondered why God wanted her to tell something so personal to a stranger. *What if Holly tells someone? Lord, I'll just have to trust You.* "Well, he drugged me. It was part of the plan. Part of my *best* friend's plan to set me up to be raped. Holly, I was a virgin. I was being faithful to the Lord with my body. I was saving myself for marriage. Something was taken from me that I can never recover."

Holly's mouth parted in astonishment. This girl who could get God to come into their classroom and touch people was sharing secrets with her that she'd only—Holly's astonishment increased, as did her heart rate—*that she'd only tell her closest friend. She hadn't told anyone about this.*

The heavy weight of Sharon's sad words dropped on her. *Something was taken from me that I can never recover.* Holly found herself crying for this strange angel who had surprisingly offered to be her friend. A friend who knew God, and a friend whom she knew would never betray or abandon her.

The tears on Holly's face rolled over a smile that hadn't made itself from her heart yet. It didn't make any sense to her, but somehow caring for someone else's problems had taken the edge off her own.

"I don't know why, but the Lord wanted me to tell you my story," said Sharon.

Holly looked at her with an open mouth. She slowly turned and gazed out the windshield. It was bright. The sunlight was bright. The sky was blue. All of her car's windows were up, but she heard birds singing. She turned to Sharon and with both hands squeezed her arm. "Please, Sharon," she said through tears, "tell me how I can make God my Father. I want to know Him like you do."

***

Heroin stood at a safe distance observing the thorn and the big angel with his property. He licked his finger and thumb and traced the front of his blue brim. "Too late to jump ship now, baby. You jump, you're just going to land on my island. Nobody but you and me on *Paradise Island*. Sharon's not going home with you. Sooner or later you, gotta stand on your own two feet. I'll see you at the house, baby."

***

Upon the last word of Adaam-Mir's song of worship, he fell to the ground overcome with emotion for Holly's salvation. He was sure his friend and mentor Myla had seen this many times. But he had only been on the frontlines a short while. It was still an awe-inspiring event to him.

A soul saved from eternal damnation....

After several minutes of lying on his belly in reverence, Adaam-Mir opened his eyes and got to his knees. He looked at Myla who was standing and exhibiting little of the joy angels usually had when a soul was saved.

Adaam-Mir studied his mentor's face as he stood up. "What is wrong, Myla? Why do you not rejoice over Holly's salvation? She is safe now. Sharon is her friend, and the mercy angel is with her."

"No, my brother, she is not safe."

Adaam-Mir's face turned somber. "Is her conversion not real? Is the soil of her heart not good soil?"

"Her conversion is real, Adaam-Mir, but she was born in the furnace of addiction."

"But God can keep her!" said Adaam-Mir.

Myla understood his friend. He had little experience with human nature or spiritual warfare. So he was prone to looking at the human experience in a clinical way. The blessed book promised victory, *and there would be victory!* His friend had not yet learned to reconcile the positive promises and victories of the blessed book with the negative realities and failures recorded in that same blessed book.

"It is never a question of God's ability to keep anyone, Adaam-Mir. Do we question the Most High's ability to keep any of his blessed martyrs?"

The weight of this thought quieted the angel's energy.

Myla saw that the thought had hit home. "And yet they die. There's not always an easy answer to fit every situation. Remember Job's friends? It's dangerous to trust in formulas to interpret every mystery. Sometimes they're right. Sometimes they're wrong. Often all they produce is simplistic reasoning, self-righteousness, legalism, heartbreak, and unbelief."

"Where does that leave Holly? She gave her life to the Lord. She *belongs* to the Lord," the angel emphasized.

"Yes, she did, Adaam-Mir. She belongs to the Lord. Just as the lion cub belongs to its mother."

Lion cub? What is this? thought Adaam-Mir.

"Adaam-Mir, a mature lion is safe. A lion cub is not. Holly is a lion, but she's a cub. There are jackals and hyenas that will take advantage of her present vulnerability. Heroin is her jackal. He has her by the throat. There aren't many cubs who escape the jackals of heroin."

"He has her by the throat? How can he have a child of God by the throat? This doesn't make sense, Myla."

"Adaam-Mir, every chain isn't immediately broken when a son or daughter of Adam repents of sin. Yes, their sins are washed away and they are declared righteous before the Almighty. But forgiveness of sins doesn't mean every bondage and habit is immediately broken."

Adaam-Mir knew that Myla would not be mistaken. Yet he shook his head at this statement. "But the salvation of God is complete. It lacks *nothing*, my brother."

Myla moved closer to his friend. "It lacks nothing," he agreed. "But there is a time appointed for the full effects of sin to be removed. Until then, the sons and daughters of God must use their authority to rid themselves of any bondage of the devil and of the flesh that didn't immediately leave when they submitted to the Lord. That is the message of much of the blessed book. Especially of the part they call the New Testament."

"But what about the alcoholics and other drug addicts who were miraculously delivered at Glory Tabernacle? Brother, and the blessed book specifically named alcoholics when Paul said in Corinthians, 'Such were some of you.' Such *were* some of you. Were these alcoholics not totally delivered from our enemy?"

"Adaam-Mir, it is a difficult truth to comprehend. Some truths seem to contradict others. This makes them difficult to understand." Myla patted his friend on the shoulder. "There is total deliverance available from every bondage, every addiction. But the craving of the addiction usually doesn't immediately leave. Those whom Paul spoke of in Corinthians were in fact free. This freedom may have happened immediately." He looked at Adaam-Mir seriously. "Or it may have come after an intense spiritual, mental, and physical battle."

Adaam-Mir slowly shook his head. "Myla, I know what you say is true." He shook his head more emphatically. "I just don't understand why every salvation doesn't produce immediate victory in every area of life."

"Adaam-Mir, the sons and daughters of Adam are spirit, soul, and body. You remember what Paul told the Thessalonians: 'May your whole spirit, soul, and body be preserved blameless.' The spirit is made alive and reunited with the Creator at the moment of true repentance. But the soul and body must be put under subjection by the new creation. It must be put under subjection because it is in rebellion.

"This is what is meant by the many Scriptures that say things like, 'Be not conformed to this world, but be transformed by the renewing of your mind,' or 'put to death the deeds of the flesh.'

"Holly has genuinely come to the Lord, but the craving is still in her mind. It is a driving, tormenting, irresistible craving. You see the heroin spirit over there stalking her."

Adaam-Mir looked contemptuously at the demon dressed as a human. "But she can say no."

"Yes, Adaam-Mir, she can say no. But you must understand the intensity of the warfare. It is not a regular temptation. It is an all-consuming fire that refuses to be put out. It requires extreme trust in God, faithful support from the church, and a high tolerance of pain."

"Tolerance of pain? You said the battle is in her mind," said Adaam-Mir.

"There is such a thing as mental pain. It is as real as physical pain and often more tormenting." Myla looked tenderly at Holly in the car. She was laughing, enjoying the freedom he knew would be challenged the moment her new friend was gone. "She is blessed that the craving hasn't reached her body yet. I hope we can keep this from happening."

Adaam-Mir gripped his mentor's large bicep. "The craving gets inside of the addict's body? Is it a demon?"

"Demons are attracted to addictions. Any time you have an addiction, no matter how harmless it appears, you're probably dealing with a demon at some level. Even if they don't directly cause the addiction—and they usually don't—they can make it worse."

"What happens if the craving gets into the body?" Adaam-Mir asked, fearful of the answer.

Myla's expression carried the pain of what he was about to explain. His friend had seen people who had been miraculously delivered from drug addictions. But he had not yet witnessed the horror of watching a heroin addicted son or daughter of Adam go through the torturous battle of trying to break free of its chains.

Adaam-Mir listened in saddened awe, deeply moved by what his mentor shared. Actually, his eyes revealed he was shocked. "The drugs change their bodies? They put things in their bodies that literally change the design of the Creator?"

"I know how unbelievable this sounds, my brother, but yes. It becomes nearly impossible for them to stop taking the drugs because their bodies become dependent on the drug to live without pain."

"This—is—too—much!" yelled Adaam-Mir, but not at Myla. He flailed his arms. "They take a drug to make them feel better. The drug changes their body's chemical composition and makes them a slave to the drug. And now they have to take more poison into their body to satisfy the physical craving they created by taking the drug in the first place."

Myla watched his animated friend pace back and forth, shaking his head in denial of something they both knew could not be denied. Adaam-Mir stopped and rubbed one hand roughly through his hair. Both angels looked at the laughing girls in the expensive car.

"This girl. What will become of her?" asked Adaam-Mir, his tone revealing his fear that the craving may get into her body and make her battle harder than it already was.

Myla walked towards the girls. Adaam-Mir followed. They stood only a few feet from the girls.

"That depends on a lot of things, my brother. The Lord is sovereign. She could leave here and never have another craving for heroin."

"Or?" said Adaam-Mir.

"Or she could leave here and enter a level of warfare greater than anything she has already suffered."

"A greater battle?"

"Yes. When a person comes to Christ, the enemy knows he has but a short time. He moves quickly to discourage the new convert before she learns of her authority and of who she is in Christ. Each day the new saint is exposed to the word of God and prayer and the blessed Holy Spirit, she gets stronger. Satan has to destroy her before she gets too strong for him. That's why it often gets worse before it gets better."

"Then there is hope!" The angel's enthusiasm was back. "If she resists him until the worst is over, she can prevail."

Myla answered his friend's exuberant inexperience without taking his eyes off of Holly. "It is hard for us to imagine human hardship. But try, my friend. Imagine being buried alive in a coffin. Now add a couple of hungry rats. Holly is already in the coffin. If the enemy spreads his bondage from her mind to her body, those are the rats."

Myla looked at Adaam-Mir. "You and I and Sharon know Holly can be set free." Myla pointed his finger at his friend. "But we are not in the coffin. She is. Now what if Satan offers to immediately get her out of the coffin? All she has to do is take some more heroin."

"But that choice...it's not," Adaam-Mir vigorously shook his head, "it's not right. She will see no way out but the poison."

Myla grabbed both shoulders of his friend. "This is what the addict sees, and what the church fails to understand. Holly is in the coffin. You saw the heroin spirit. The rats are coming."

Chapter 8

Tears were in Sharon's eyes. She held both parent's hands. "Mom, Dad, thank you." She looked admiringly into Edwin's eyes. "Thank you for encouraging the church to use their homes to show the love of Christ through hospitality. This means so much to our Father."

Edwin grinned at his angel.

"Mom, God is proud of you."

She smiled also. Still questioning her and her husband's sanity for agreeing to invite Octavius for dinner. Holly was a lovely girl. But Octavius? Him smashing that gun into her daughter's head would never leave her memory. "It will be an interesting evening, I'm sure," she said, looking at Edwin.

Edwin saw it. He couldn't agree more.

"They're here," yelled Andrew.

"At the same time?" said Barbara.

"I'm sure they didn't ride together," Edwin joked.

Barbara looked out the window. Holly was halfway up the walkway. Octavius was parking his vehicle behind Holly's. "Edwin, he's driving a Mercedes."

Edwin looked out the window. "Hmp. So is Holly. You think she carjacked someone?"

She looked at him with a half-serious scold. "I don't have any experience with Holly, but I do with him."

"Dad and Jonathan say he's doing good, right Dad?" said Sharon.

"Yep. He is. Hasn't killed anyone since we started having Bible studies with him."

"Edwin, that's not funny," said Barbara, as she walked toward the kitchen.

Andrew stopped laughing. "Dad, you're asking for it."

"I agree with Mom," said Sharon. "You better be good." Sharon went for the door.

"Hey, I'm the one risking his life having Bible studies with him in *The Bluff*. I'm the good guy. It's okay for the good guy to crack a joke about his friend."

Sharon opened the door. The girls squealed and hugged one another, rocking from side to side. "I'm so glad you came," said Sharon. "We haven't seen each other *innnnnnn*—"

"Three...hours," said Holly, leaning forward with each word, as though this were a ridiculous amount of time to be apart. Holly handed her a small wrapped gift.

"What's this?"

"Don't open it now. Just hold on to it. You'll know when to open it. Okay?"

"Okay."

"Promise me, Sharon, you won't open until you you're supposed to."

"Weird, but I promise." Sharon put her arm under Holly's and walked with her to the restroom so they could wash their hands. "So, tell me, Dr. Burton, what *have* you been doing since I saw you last?"

What have you been doing?

What have you been doing?

What have you been doing?

Sharon's words peeled back the skin of her friend's smile. Holly felt the heat of harsh truth hitting her bared and humiliated soul. She quickly returned the smile to its proper place, but she found herself unable to lie to her friend.

"Secrets, huh?" Sharon smiled. "I better not hear about my friend and some guy from anyone other than you. Is that clear?"

Holly was glad she was walking by Sharon's side when she said this. She was sure her friend would see through her if they were face to face. Holly found a way to physically hold herself up under the weight of Sharon's words.

"Sharon. Holly," Barbara called, as she walked towards the girls. She stood by the bathroom door and hugged Holly. "So nice to see you again, Holly. Why don't you just move in? We have the room. I'm sure Sharon wouldn't mind. Right, Sharon?"

"Let's do it!" said Sharon with a smile that couldn't get any wider. "That way we could really be sisters."

Holly saw Sharon's enthusiasm. It wasn't mere playfulness. She'd do this in a heartbeat. Sharon was such a wonderful, giving person. *I wish I could, but then you'd come to hate me as much as I hate myself,* she thought.

Holly laughed to keep from crying. "*Okaaay,* you put it out there, Mrs. Styles. Don't be surprised...." she said, smiling at Sharon.

"Edwin, the door," said Barbara as she walked back to the kitchen.

Edwin and Andrew went to the front door. Edwin opened.

Octavius wore a black *Philadelphia 76ers* basketball cap with a battery powered flashing fiber optic emblem. The cap was turned partly to the side. His long locks of hair sat on the collar of his oversized shirt. He flashed a smile. "What up, Rev?"

Edwin surveyed his swollen lip and the bruises on his face. Andrew stared at the cap. "Hello, Octavius. Glad you could come." Edwin stretched out his hand. Octavius gripped his hand and pumped it once and turned his fingers to grip the inside of Edwin's. Edwin followed clumsily.

"Yeah, that's it, Rev."

Andrew shook Octavius hand like he had grown up down the street from him. Octavius smiled, then laughed. "Where you been hangin'?"

"I get around," joked Andrew.

"You betta keep yo' eyes on that one, Rev. He got secrets."

Edwin looked at Andrew. "I think that's a good idea. I will. Let's get to the dining room before I get in trouble. The warden doesn't like to serve cold food."

"Warden? Ugh. Let's not even joke about prison, Man." He said this grinning at Andrew.

They entered the large dining room. Edwin didn't like red dining rooms, but red it was.

"Octavius, the only person you don't know is Holly. She goes to school with Sharon," said Edwin.

Holly and Octavius looked at one another oddly.

Sharon popped up and hugged Octavius. "Prince, you came! Dad and Jonathan tell me good things about you."

He smiled. "Can't say nutin' else. Every thang good about me, Sharon." He saw the blood drain from Barbara's face. It had also drained from Edwin's face, but he didn't see that. "Naw. Naw. It ain't like that," he laughed toward Barbara. "I'm talkin' 'bout the new creation. What happened when we prayed."

"When we prayed?" Sharon's eyes were large with excitement.

"Naw, not the first time, when Rev. was gone lock me up," he said, grinning at Edwin. "That was the cat with the shallow soil. I received the word, but hell, what else could I do? Rev. was gone send my—oh, I'm sorry everybody. Still trying to get the devil off my tongue."

"It's okay, Prince. Everyone here has things they're working on. Back to the shallow soil," she said excitedly. "You're talking about the parable of the sower and the seed? Luke 8?"

"Naw, I don't like that one. Too weak."

Sharon looked at him questioningly.

"Yeah. Luke 8 don't bring it like Matthew 13. Mark 4—that's tight, too. But Matthew's big dog."

Sharon smiled and looked at her father and mother, then turned back to Octavius. "Matthew's big dog? You know all three places? I mean, not that you wouldn't. But, Prince, most people don't know all three places where that parable is. And anyway," she punched him lightly on the shoulder, "you've only been a Christian a little while."

Holly lifted one brow.

Prince smiled. "Yeah, well I been hittin' it hard. If you gone do it, do it. Right? Plus, I got a good memory. Don't even really have to try. It just sticks."

Andrew let out a breath. "I wish it worked that way for me. Ms. Hennigan is killing me."

"Why don't you two have a seat? We can finish the conversation after Edwin says the prayer," said Barbara.

Octavius smiled. "Wait," he said. "Smell me, Sharon."

She smiled and sniffed, shaking her head with a smile. "What?"

"Uh huh. Yeah. Get a little closer and do it."

Edwin's and Barbara's necks craned forward. Andrew looked at his parents and covered his mouth and put his elbow on the table. He tried to inconspicuously cover as much of his face as possible as he laughed.

Sharon got closer and sniffed. "I don't smell anything."

"That's right. Nut'n. Get a little closer and do it one mo' time."

Sharon smelled his chest area first. She shook her head. Then she got on her tip-toes and rested her hands on both shoulders and sniffed one side of his neck. Andrew looked at his parents and covered his face with both hands, but peeked out through his fingers. His belly bounced up and down as he silently laughed as he watched his parents' faces lose their color. Sharon went to the other side of his neck and took a long sniff with her eyes closed.

Andrew couldn't take it. He closed his eyes and buried his face in his hands and begged God to help him stop laughing.

Sharon bounced back to the floor from off her tip-toes. "I don't smell anything."

"No weed!" he declared in triumph, with a wide smile. He looked at Edwin. "Tell 'em, Rev. We be kickin' it at the crib, don't we?"

Andrew wiped tears from his eyes as he furiously fought to not burst out laughing.

"We, Octavius?" said Edwin.

"Now come on, Rev. You know I shotgunned you a hit the first time we had Bible study. At *Mayhem*."

"That was hardly by invitation," answered an embarrassed Edwin. He reminded himself what Jonathan said about not letting anything get him off track when he's trying to reach someone for Christ.

"Y'all, I'm just playin.' Rev's not lightin' up." He looked at Edwin. "*I'm not either*. I put that sh—"he changed the word he was going to use—"stuff down. I read where the word says to be sober. I can't serve God if my mind ain't all there."

Edwin finally was able to stop Sharon and Octavius from talking long enough to pray over the food.

"Prince, the parable. You were going to tell us when you really gave your heart to Christ." Sharon wasn't letting this go.

Holly looked intently at Octavius as he spoke.

"Yo' father know *The Bluff*, a little about *Mayhem*. Nothin' but death there. If it ain't already dead, it's dying. I was serious when I prayed with you after you went crazy on me when I tried to jack you."

Sharon smiled. "Not your average church girl, huh?"

"Ain't nut'n 'bout you average. You be killin' it, Sharon. Almost killed every d—"he dropped the word he was going to use—"body."

Barbara was horrifyingly fascinated by whatever this was that was going on around their table. This could've easily had been a *Woody Allen* film. One moment, her daughter was on her tip-toes holding the shoulders of the man who had cracked her in the head with a gun and was slowly sniffing all over him with closed eyes.

Really, Sharon! Must you always be so gullible? The whole world is not as innocent as you are!

The next, he was telling her in some kind of inner city lingo that she was hot. But the mere lunacy of the moment was too ridiculous to interject herself into the conversation. It would've been like trying to jump on a merry-go-round that was spinning at sixty miles an hour. She'd bypass the dizziness—for now.

"I was serious when I prayed with you, but when I got back to the crib, it was like, I'm glad that white man didn't send me to prison, but this ain't me. I can't do no Jesus in *The Bluff*. And I *damn* sure can't do no Jesus in *Mayhem*. Every nigga in *Mayhem* got a gun." Octavius grimaced. "I didn't mean to cuss, Sharon, but that's the real—"he changed the word—"deal. That's exactly what I said to the Lord."

Barbara saw that merry-go-round speed up. She chewed slowly on her green beans and dabbed at her mashed potatoes.

"That's what God wants from us, Prince. He wants honesty," said Sharon. "So it's really dangerous where you live, and you didn't know how you could serve God in such a dangerous environment? You didn't think God could take care of you."

"How many people you know that done got shot?" said Octavius.

"No one," said Sharon.

"Stabbed?"

"No one."

"Beat to death?"

"No one."

"I see that—"he changed the word—"stuff all the time. All the time, Sharon. You call the police when somethin' happens. We don't call 'em. You know why? Two reasons. One, we handle our own business. Somebody do something, handle it. Plain and simple. Two, we don't call 'em because that's like callin' in the KKK. Honestly, I'd rather face those crazy niggas in *Mayhem* than the police. At least you can fight a nigga back."

"Why do you call the police the KKK?" asked Andrew.

"Because where I live, the cops do whatever the he—" He stopped himself. "Let me say it this way. I ain't never met Officer Friendly, and I don't know anyone in my neighborhood who has."

"But if people don't break the law, they don't have to worry about the police," said Andrew.

Octavius finished chewing a mouthful of Barbara's tender pot roast. He drank some tea while bouncing his finger at Andrew. "That's your neighborhood, Andrew. Where I live, cops treat you like you the enemy just 'cause you live there. They beat yo' a—they beat you just 'cause you live there and just 'cause they can. They arrest you 'cause you fit the description. They shoot you 'cause they thought you had a gun."

"You said everybody in your neighborhood has a gun," said Andrew.

"Ain't no nigga crazy enough to go around shooting at the cops. We don't shoot cops. We shoot each other."

"Well, *that* makes sense," said Barbara. She couldn't help it. "You ever think that that one fact alone has anything to do with the cops assuming their lives are in danger whenever they stop one of you?"

Edwin scanned every face and ended with Barbara's. She had stopped eating. Her lips pressed hard against one another. One hand was on her lap. The other was on the table. She gripped her fork and bounced it in her hand, looking more like someone preparing for a fight instead of finishing her dinner.

"Well," began Edwin.

Sharon jumped in. "This is good dialogue. The only way to understand one another, and maybe change the way things are, is to have honest conversations. Mom has made a good point. Prince, why do people in your neighborhood hurt one another the way they do?"

Octavius rolled his lips and slid his tongue against the back of his top teeth. "Sharon, I grew up in *Mayhem.* Literally. Momma was hooked on heroin and doing whatever she needed to do to take care of us."

"Where was your father?" Sharon asked.

"Father? Anyway, one day some church ladies came to the crib. Moms was sick 'cause she was trying to get that," he heard the word before he said it and changed it, "stuff out of her."

"What happened?" Holly asked timidly.

Octavius looked at her for several seconds. "She kicked heroin in his—"he stopped—"God healed her."

Holly's eyes watered. She thought of Casey and her arm. With a hopeful expression, she asked, "God gave her a miracle?"

"I guess some of it was," he answered. "She had tried to kick it probably...oh, I done forgot how many times. It was a lot, that's all I know. But when these ladies laid hands on her and cast the devil out—"

"Cast the *devil* out?" said Holly.

"Look, that's what they said. Moms was on the floor. These ladies nearly drowned her with olive oil. They told the devil to come out of my momma. I still remember what one of those ladies said. 'You filthy spirit of heroin, I break yo' power of addiction. I bind you and cast you out of this woman. Leave her right now, and take yo' craving with you.'"

"What happened?" asked Holly. "Did the craving leave your mom?"

"Honestly, no. At least not right away. For a few weeks she seemed worse than she had ever been. I thought Moms was gone die on me. But something changed when those ladies prayed for her."

"What?" Holly asked, like someone coming from under water after holding her breath to the breaking point.

"Moms said—"Octavius shook his head with a smile—"I don't know how many times Moms gone give this same testimony. Every Sunday. Every Tuesday. That's prayer night. Every Wednesday. That's another church night. She gone give that same testimony." He laughed. "Anyway, she said when those ladies cast the devil out, she felt chains breaking off her soul. She said she could hear 'em, too. *Snap! Snap! Snap!* You gotta hear her tell it."

Tears trickled down Holly's face. "She felt chains snapping?"

"Yeah, but heroin ain't no pu—"he changed the word—"punk. He gone make you work for it now. Those ladies told Moms she was gone have to stand on the word. They said some people had to fight the good fight of faith until everybody in heaven and hell knew they meant business.

"I remember seeing Moms high as hell, sittin' there with a big Bible on her lap. One time I tried to move the Bible off her lap 'cause I thought it was gone fall. Her eyes popped open and she slapped the s—"he changed his word—"snot out of me. She said she was standing on the word."

Octavius shook his head, smiling. Then his eyes glazed and tears rolled down his dark cheeks and disappeared into his well-groomed facial hair. "I thought she was crazy as hell. Sittin' there high with a Bible in her hand talkin' 'bout standing on the word. Huh, I was the one crazy. Moms knew what she was doin'.

"Holly, sometimes you gotta fight for what God gives you. Like when God gave the Promised Land to His people. They had to cross the Jordan River and go over there and beat down the Canaanites before they could enjoy it. The devil's not just gone let you have all God want you to have just because. If you don't want it bad enough to fight fo' it, God's like, cool...whatever."

Sharon and Edwin looked at one another in amazement. Sharon was sure she saw her father's chest poke out to match the grin on his face. Barbara's and Andrew's expressions matched their surprise, too.

"Got to the point where we just left her alone," Octavius continued. He looked dreamily into the past. "Then it happened. Just happened. She was worshippin' God. Playin' some white music. Like some of that stuff y'all do at y'all church. She jumped up off her knees and started screamin'and—" He dropped the word he was going to say. "Said she heard God say, "Enough."

"Was it enough?" asked Holly.

"Must've been. She ain't done that—crap since that day." He smiled, then laughed. "Now she Prophetess Ebony Monroe of *Worldwide Apostolic Church of International Deliverance and Glory.* Moms said she asked God to help her get her family out of *Mayhem*. When I was sixteen we moved to *The Bluff.* From *Mayhem* to *The Bluff.* That was our promotion. Well, anything's better than *Mayhem.*

"But it was too late. You can't live in this kind of," he paused, "environment for that long and not be infected."

"Infected with what?" asked Sharon.

"Hopelessness. Rage."

"Why the rage?" asked Andrew.

"Because of the hopelessness," said Octavius. "God didn't create people to live without hope. It's not natural. You take away hope, what's left? Frustration. People gone find a way." He shook his head. "Then you got the *Vice Boys*. Those crazy niggas a make Mother Theresa start carryin' a gun. They like roaches. They everywhere. Dude named Sonny Christopher runs thangs. Sometimes he say he the Christ."

"The Christ!" said Sharon. "You mean like Jesus Christ?"

"That's ridiculous," said Barbara.

"I feel ya' on that, Mrs. Styles. Everybody know Jesus ain't fat," said Octavius.

Andrew laughed.

Octavious added. "Says half his last name is Christ."

Mrs. Styles? A barely noticeable, cautious smile formed on Barbara's face. "I know you've visited the church a few times. And my husband has been telling me that the Lord has done a wonderful work in your life. So now you're a changed man?"

"Not as changed as I'm gonna be," he said.

"And no more urges to assault young girls?" said Barbara.

Octavius sat back fully in his chair. He glanced at Holly as he answered Barbara. She lowered her head. "No more urges to assault young girls."

"That would be a radical change of heart. The last time we were this close to one another, you were holding a gun and threatening to kill us."

Sharon looked at her mom, wondering whether she should try to intervene. Barbara looked instinctively at her daughter. Sharon read the look loud and clear and lowered her head in prayer.

"That's your message, isn't it? The gospel? That God changes our heart?" Octavious's manner was surprisingly polite. "If Jesus can only help so-called good sinners, what good is He? If your gospel doesn't work in *The Bluff* or *Mayhem*, then I've misinterpreted the Bible. I read today that Jesus said, I did not come to call the righteous, but sinners to repentance."

Barbara looked at him in contemplation. Everyone was quiet, waiting on her response.

"Mrs. Styles, I don't blame you for having your doubts. You right. I kidnapped you. I robbed you. I threatened you. I hurt your daughter. And I'm going to tell you something. I was going to kill you. All of you."

Everyone but Octavius felt a chill of fear drape over them.

"But that's not me any more. God changed my heart."

"When?" asked Barbara, her eyes watering. It wasn't obvious whether she was moved by his story or so angry dry eyes were impossible. "When did God change you from being a robber and murderer?"

Barbara's words had an effect on Octavius. He blinked several times in thought, glancing at things on the table. He looked up with eyes that may have gotten moist. "It started when my momma got off heroin. We all knew it was God that saved Moms. Then Momma started praying for us and preaching at us. Some of that stuff she say just stick with me. All that stuff she say about God loving me and having a plan for my life.

"To tell the truth, I been trying to get that stuff out my head for years. But then when we jacked y'all, and crazy Sharon—oh, boy, that girl—took off like a bat out of hell, everything just started falling in on me. I knew I was going to prison for the rest of my life. But y'all forgave me."

His eyes were watery. The evidence was a solitary tear rolling down his face. "Then everything Moms said about God was right in my face. Sharon telling me I was a prince of God. Then when your husband and Jonathan came to *The Bluff* and *Mayhem* to see me—"he shook his head—"I knew in my heart that what my momma said was true. God was after me.

"They didn't act like they were better than me. They didn't condemn me. They didn't act funny. Well, maybe Rev. when my little nephew grabbed his leg and called him Daddy and peed on his pants."

Sharon looked at her father. "I wonder why this is the first we're hearing of this?"

"Just let Octavius talk, honey," he said.

Andrew covered his face again, shaking his head, laughing.

"I got a lot of sin in me. A lot of bad habits I'm trying to get rid of. Gave up smokin'. Gave up drinkin'. Cussing. Still tryin' to give that sh—" See what I mean? But I read Romans over and over. I know that eternal life is a gift from God. I know I got it through faith in what Jesus Christ did for me through His death and resurrection. I know righteousness is a gift."

Octavius looked at Holly. "But I didn't *really* know it was real in me until I saw some dudes nearly skipping and hopping into an abandoned house in my neighborhood. A white dude was parked outside with a big, stupid grin on his face. I went inside the house. They had this white girl in there."

Holly's eyes filled with terror. She shook her head at Octavius and silently mouthed, *"Please don't."* Everyone's eyes were riveted to him. So no one saw her silent begging.

"She was scared to death. We get a lot of girls in there. Drug hoes, mainly. But this girl didn't look like no hoe. I saw what they was doing to her, and my first thought was if she was working for Santa Claus, I was gone get my present, too. So I got in line."

"What do you mean she was working for Santa?" asked Andrew.

"Andrew, go to your room," said Barbara, as though the room would catch on fire if he delayed one moment.

"Octavius, does it get any worse than this?" asked Edwin.

"Naw, it's not raw like that."

"Okay. Let him stay, Barbara."

"They made that girl look back at us."

Holly was trapped at the table. She didn't want to hear this, but she couldn't run away either. No one saw the tears that rolled one after the other down her face. Nor did they see her heaving chest.

"When she did, I heard God say, "She is my daughter, and you are My son. What are you doing? Help her."

Holly gasped.

"You heard God?" asked Sharon.

"What did He sound like?" asked Andrew.

"I didn't know what to do. When I heard his voice, it was like I came out of a trance. Then I got confused. Her down there, she didn't look like no daughter of God. Then there I was standing in line to take advantage of some girl who looked like she had fallen into quicksand."

"What did you do?" asked Barbara, fully engrossed in the story. "Please tell me you helped this poor girl."

"That's how I got these decorations on my face." They studied the busted lip and the bruises. He pulled up his pant leg. "Got shot here." He pointed to his calf.

"*Whaaaaaat?"* said a fascinated Andrew. "You got shot?"

"Wasn't no real gun," said Octavius.

"It was a BB gun?" asked Andrew.

"Naw. A double-duece."

Andrew frowned in thought. "A 22!"

"Yeah." He looked at Edwin. "I told you, you gotta keep an eye on this playa." Octavius grabbed the front of his shirt. "He shot me in the back, too." He pushed back the chair.

Barbara put her hand up in a *Halt!* position. "We believe you, Octavius."

"Why'd somebody beat you up and shoot you?" asked Andrew.

"Because some dudes don't like it when you tell 'em the girl they slammin' belongs to God and they gotta stop. They don't stop. You gotta make 'em stop."

"Whoooaaaa. How many were there?" asked Andrew.

Octavius glanced quickly at Holly and turned from her. "It's not important. More than one."

Everyone sat in silent awe.

Holly was clearly moved to the depths of her soul by Octavius's story. She didn't try to hide the tears. She couldn't if she wanted to. They wouldn't stop. But everyone just figured she was as overwhelmed as they were.

"You said God called the girl His daughter," she said to Octavius.

"That's what He said," said Octavius.

"How can He call a girl who would let herself be used like that His daughter? How? How can He still love someone like that?"

"That's what I used to ask myself when I saw my momma high on heroin, clutching her Bible. I asked her one time how she could call herself a child of God and be hooked on heroin? I still remember exactly what she said, and she quoted it, too. She said, 'Everybody's hooked on somethin'. Then she said, 'I am confident of this very thing, that He who has begun a good work in me will perform it until the day of Jesus Christ. He will never leave me. He will never forsake me.' Holly, if God's only there when we're strong, what's the point?"

An hour passed.

"I was reading some stuff in the book of Acts about being filled with the Holy Spirit," said Octavius.

"Yes! Dad, let's talk about the Holy Spirit," said Sharon.

"Sharon, I'm going to go now," said Holly.

"No. No. Noooooo. You have to stay, Holly. You need the power of the Spirit in your life."

"No, I'm going to go, but if you have time tomorrow after school," she smiled, "we can have church in my car."

"Ooh, okay. I can wait until tomorrow." Sharon said this with a sad smile that was designed to show her friend that she really wanted her to stay.

Octavius looked at her with a message in his eyes as well as in his mouth. "You sure, Holly? I think this is something you *really* need. I know I do."

She walked over to him and took both his hands and squeezed them. "Thank you," she said, looking intently into his eyes. She pulled his hands up and closed her eyes and pressed their hands against her face. "Thank you so much." She reached up and hugged him. "I love you, Prince. I owe you my life, and I'll always be grateful for what you did."

No one knew what to quite make of that good-bye.

I love you, Prince? I owe you my life? Barbara wondered what kind of animal magnetism this man possessed that two young, suburban white girls felt so drawn to him. One sniffing his chest and neck like she was in a bakery. The other hugging him and telling him that she loved him and owed him her life—because of a story he told.

Whatever kind of genie is in your bottle, it's not coming out on my daughter, she thought.

***

Heroin sat on the passenger seat of Holly's car waiting impatiently for her. He perked up when he saw the front door open.

"Hurry up and get your butt down here. Paradise is waitin' on you, baby."

Chapter 9

Sharon looked at the door, smiling. She couldn't wait to talk to Holly about the previous night. Part of her was bouncing and turning flips because of what the Holy Ghost had done to Prince. *What a powerful baptism of the Spirit!* She wasn't ashamed to admit that she was a bit jealous, and she was going to hold God accountable for this.

I thought I was Your favorite, she thought.

Another part of her was sorry that Holly had left before the fire fell. There was nothing like the baptism of the Holy Spirit. She had spoken to Holly a few times about receiving the power of God in her life. She'd listen with such openness, and she'd appear so eager to receive. But then her expression would change and she'd disengage.

She never admitted it, but something was eating away at her soul. Something was sucking away her confidence in God's love for her. Whenever Sharon had mentioned going deeper in God, Holly would light up and smile. Then a dark, heavy blanket of guilt, shame, and unworthiness would drape over her.

Sharon shook that thought. Today was the day. Holly had promised that they'd have car church after school. She was sure the Holy Spirit had no problem with falling upon someone in a car.

One of the vice principals approached Dr. Dawkins and whispered something in his ear. Whatever it was, it wasn't good. He looked stunned, then sad. The vice-principal looked sympathetically at the class and left.

Dr. Dawkins took off his glasses and rubbed the brow of his nose and put them back on.

"Mrs. Rose has just given me some terrible news." He looked at Sharon. "Holly has had an accident."

Sharon's mouth dropped open. "What happened?"

"*Eyyeeee*..." he cleared his throat, "the details are unclear."

Sharon trembled. "Well, how is she?"

Dr. Dawkins' eyes dropped. He looked up. "She's dead."

The air left Sharon's lungs. She clutched her chest. Her lips opened and closed rapidly as her closed throat tried to suck in air that wouldn't come. Dizziness and weakness added to her lack of air. She strained against the gravity that pulled against her as she tried to rise. With a burst, she pushed herself up on her wobbly legs. Two steps and she was down and out.

***

Edwin hurried around to Sharon's side of the car. He opened the door. She was between wails. "Come on, Sharon. I'll help you in."

She looked up in a daze. Her head bobbed and circled, as though her muscles were too weak to carry it. "Dad-dy...Dad-dy...my friend—"

"Come on, let me help you. It's going to be okay." He reached in and held her under both arms. Her pained face came up.

"Daddy, my...soul hurts." She gripped her father's forearms. "My heart. I'm dying, Daddy. Please help me. I can't take this. I can't take it. God is killing me. My Father is killing me. Why is He doing this to me, Daddy? He knows I love Him. What have I done?" She stood up wobbly, holding on to her father with one hand. The other was at her throat. She panicked. "Daddy! I can't," she choked, "breathe."

Edwin snatched his daughter up in both arms. "Barbara!" he yelled. "Barbara, open the door!" It didn't open. He put her down and placed her against the garage door wall and pushed his shoulder into her chest to hold her up. "Hold on, baby," he said, as he opened the door. He swooped her up and hurried to a sofa.

"My God, what's wrong?" said Barbara. "What's wrong, Edwin?"

"Sharon, calm down," said Edwin. "Try to take a breath."

"What's wrong with her?" said Barbara.

"Baby, look at me. Can you breathe? Do you have any pain?" asked Edwin. "It's Holly," he said to Barbara and turned back to Sharon.

"Daddy, I'm in pain. I hurt all over. I'm dying. I can't do this. I don't want my heart any more," she cried. "It hurts too much. Toni's gone. Holly's gone."

"Edwin, what does she mean, Holly's gone? Did they have a fight?"

Edwin looked up from one knee. "Barbara, Holly's dead. The school called me. Said when they announced it in class, Sharon passed out."

Barbara's hands went to her face. She dropped to both knees in tears. "Ohhhh...ohhhh, Holly, noooo."

Sharon looked at her mother. "He took her from me, Mom. He took her from me. He gave her to me and took her away. First, Toni. Now Holly." Sharon dropped her head. She grimaced and shook as though she were trying to shake away confusion. One heavy breath followed the other, each deeper than the one before.

Edwin saw what was happening. "Calm down, Sharon."

Sharon's hands lifted before her face. Her fingers were curled and filled with tension. "I ca—I ca—I ca—I ca—I ca—"

Barbara pushed her way between Edwin and Sharon. "You can't what? You can't what, Sharon?"

"I ca—I ca—I ca—"

Barbara gripped her daughter's face. "Look at me, Sharon."

Sharon looked at her mother like she were a little child. Her mouth was moving, but now nothing was coming out.

"You are going to let this pain out. Do you hear me?" This wonderful child was practically dying from grief. Barbara felt her baby's pain. She cried as she said, "You—are going—to let this pain go. Scream, Sharon. Open your mouth and scream."

Sharon's mouth moved desperately. Nothing would come out.

"Let it out, Sharon." Barbara's tears got stronger. "I am not going to watch you die of a broken heart. I said *scream*."

Sharon's face filled with even more grief. Her silent mouth still moving.

Barbara's heart burst with her daughter's agony. She shook her daughter's head in her hands. "In the name of Jesus Christ, the Son of God, I—said—scream!"

"AAAAAAAAaaaaaaaaaaaaaaaaaaaaaaaaaaahhhhhhhhh hhhhhh!"

"More!" screamed Barbara.

"AAAAAAAAaaaaaaaaaaaaaaaaaaaaaaaaaaahhhhhhhhh hhhhhh!"

"Scream again!"

Sharon screamed over and over and over as her parents took turns holding their screaming, hurting daughter.

***

An overdose? Her friend was an addict and she didn't know it? What kind of friend had she been to Holly?

The next day Sharon didn't go to school. She had no intentions of getting out of bed.

Holly's gift.

She sat up and paused, then threw the covers off and got the gift and sat down. She looked at the wrapping and bow. The paper had golden angels on it. There was a little name card. It said *To my angel, Sharon.* She would've cried, but couldn't. Her bitter tears felt like they were in her belly, unable to make their way to her eyes, but not unable to make her feel sick. She had a trash can next to her bed just in case the bathroom was too far away.

Sharon rubbed her fingers and thumbs over the top and bottom of the gift before opening it. Now suddenly as she began opening it, she felt tears forming in her eyes. She blinked and water came down her cheeks.

She opened the box. It was a journal. A used journal. Holly's journal. A note was included. It read:

> *Sharon, if you are reading this, I am in trouble. I hope I am not dead. I don't want to die in this condition. Not after tasting the Father's love. But since you are reading this,*

> *I have probably not yet learned to trust in our Father's love enough. So it's very important to me that you know that even though the past month or so has been the worst time of my life, it has also been the most wonderfully fulfilling and love-filled time of my life. Despite this poison, I am finally whole. I'm sorry, Sharon. I hope you are not ashamed of me. I hope you don't hate me for my weakness. If what you have taught me about our Father is true, and I believe it is, I will see you again. If not here, then in heaven. My earthly and eternal sister, I am the thief on the cross. I have little to be proud of, but my trust is in Him who said, "Today shall you be with me in paradise." I will see you again.*

Sharon sat with her back against the large headboard and read the journal many times. Sometimes she cried. Sometimes she laughed. But there were entries that made her have to ask God to not hate the people who had hurt Holly.

Her friends.

Jared.

Why was it so easy for people to be cruel?

But not everyone was cruel. Prince wasn't cruel. Holly was the girl being taken advantage of by those guys in that house in *The Bluff.* Jared had blackmailed her and had brought her there to be humiliated. But Prince had put himself in danger to save her. He was a hero.

She hugged the soft leather journal to her chest and cried softly. Sublime thoughts of self-sacrifice and heroism faded as she thought of the tragedy of losing a friend who had become so important to her in such a short period of time. It was as though God had knit their hearts together.

Satan.

The Bluff.

Heroin.

They had all stolen her friend. Even worse, they had stolen God's daughter. She thought of the tragedy of Holly and the irony of Prince. How many more Holly's would *The Bluff* destroy? How many Prince's? How much longer would they allow Satan to sit as a king and terrorize the people of that community?

Her father and Jonathan were already having periodic Bible studies with Prince at his house in *The Bluff* or at his sister's house in *Mayhem.* It was time to do more. It was time to take the battle to the enemy.

***

Later in the day everyone gathered for a meeting at Sharon's request. Edwin, Barbara, Jonathan, and Elizabeth.

"No. No. Absolutely not," said Barbara.

Sharon looked at her father.

"I love you. I know you're hurting. But the answer to one tragedy is not to have another one. I have no intentions on losing a daughter to *The Bluff.*"

"Then what about *Mayhem?*" asked Sharon.

Edwin and Barbara looked at her as though she had just certified herself as crazy.

"What about *Mayhem?* I'm not losing you to *The Bluff* or *Mayhem* or anywhere in between. Now I am sorry about Holly. She seemed like a wonderful young lady, but I'm sure if she loved you the way you say she did, she'd be with us on this." Edwin looked at the disappointment on Sharon's face. "I'm sorry, Sharon. This is final."

Barbara looked relieved.

"Jonathan, what do—?" started Sharon.

Jonathan quickly jumped up. "I have to go to the bathroom."

"Oh, no you don't," said Edwin.

"We'll be right here when you get out," said Sharon.

"You will?" said Jonathan. He looked at his watch and tapped his head. "Oh, I forgot...about a meeting...."

No one was buying it.

He grimaced and wagged his head once. His eyes popped big and he lifted a finger. "What if I turned in my *Uncle* card?"

"That's the only way you get out of here without going on record," said Edwin.

Jonathan looked at his brokenhearted friend. "Never." He got what he wanted. A tiny smile.

"Well? Tell me why we should do nothing." Sharon spoke with sad resignation.

Jonathan adjusted the tie he wasn't wearing. He cleared his throat. His words were quick. "I agree with Sharon. Okay, Liz, let's go." He acted as though he was about to stand up.

"What?" yelled two shocked parents.

"Are you crazy?" said Barbara.

"Let me answer that, Barbara. Yes. He is insane," said Edwin. "We should call someone to have him picked up."

"Would you send Liz down there?" asked Barbara.

"She's been in far worse places," said Jonathan.

"Bravo." Edwin clapped twice. "Proud of you. What a guy. Send your wife down there. We'll be praying for you. No offense, Liz."

She shook her head with a smirk. She'd seen it all before.

Jonathan looked at Sharon and winked. "The dynamic duo. Are they always like this? I guess they can't be the dynamic duo. Edwin could be Batman, but Barbara—she can't be Robin. Catwoman! She *can* be Catwoman. Look at those claws."

No smile from Sharon.

No smile from Edwin.

Definitely no smile from Barbara.

"Okay, okay," said Jonathan. "I was *not* saying that you should let Sharon go down there."

Barbara exhaled. "Well, he's not crazy."

"Don't get your hopes up too high, honey. He's not through yet." Edwin looked at Jonathan. "Are you, *Uncle*?"

"Well, no, Edwin." He smiled. "How did you know? Gifts of the Spirit? A vision, maybe?"

"I know you, Jonathan."

Jonathan looked at everyone. "Sharon is right. We should do more than we're doing. Not because Holly overdosed on drugs presumably bought from *The Bluff. The Bluff* and *Mayhem* have been killing people forever. We should do more because God wants more done. And He wants it done through us."

"The whole world needs to be evangelized, Jonathan. Where'd the sudden certainty come from that God wants us full force in *The Bluff*?" If they were going to attack that kind of stronghold, they'd need more than a hunch to go on.

"Sharon, you have the answer," said Jonathan.

"I do?"

"Yes, you do. You're a prophetess, aren't you?" said Jonathan.

Sharon dropped her eyes. She had been with Holly nearly every day for at least thirty days straight, and she hadn't seen that she was on drugs. What kind of prophetess was that?

"Do you believe Elisha was a prophet of God?" he asked.

"Yes."

"Sometimes people romanticize being an Old Testament prophet. We think all they did was run around performing miracles and hearing God talk," he flicked his first two fingers in the air like a bird flying away, "in the most clear speech imaginable. Most likely British. Truth is only a few of 'em did miracles. And God didn't talk to 'em as much as we think He did.

"Sharon, some of those guys went months or years between messages. And we won't even mention the beatdowns they got. Let's not give God any ideas. Remember Elisha and the Shunammite woman?"

"The one whose son died and he raised him back to life."

"Yep, that's the one. Buried in all that miracle talk is something he said that you need to take to heart."

"What?"

"When the lady fell down and grabbed him by the ankles, his rogue prophet-in-training pushed the woman away. Elisha said,

'Leave her alone. She's distressed, and the Lord has hidden it from me, and has not told me.' Get used to it, Sharon. God's not going to tell you everything."

No one said anything as she thought on Jonathan's words.

"A good prophetess doesn't just get visions and hear God speak. She interprets signs."

Sharon looked up.

"She connects dots," said Jonathan.

Sharon turned her head to the side.

"Sharon," said Jonathan.

She looked at him.

"The sons of Issachar had understanding of the times. Remember? They used their understanding to connect the dots and tell Israel what they were supposed to do. Be the Lord's prophetess. Connect the dots."

"How? Where do I start?"

"Start with Michael Bogarty."

She looked at Jonathan, chilled by the mention of that name.

"Start with him and see God's hand."

"He kidnapped me. This brought me to where he was keeping the girls. I was able to see what he was doing." She thought some more.

"Didn't you say there were some girls there that said you were the answer to their prayers?"

Sharon smiled. "Yes. Eliana and Kimberly."

"You didn't exactly arrive first class, did you?" said Jonathan. "Hearing God speak is one level of revelation. *Seeing* God speak is another level. This kind of revelation is available for every child of God, but they're usually too earthly minded or busy too figure it out. God sent Joseph to Egypt to save his family from starving, but how'd he get there?"

"As a slave," said Sharon.

"That's right. *Slavery Airlines.* Now look at what has happened and *see* God talk."

She looked at him the way an athlete would look at her coach.

"Time to grow up," he said.

She focused and sorted her thoughts. "Dr. Dawkins called me out. I asked the Holy Spirit to come. He healed Casey. Holly was there. She came to me after class." Crying fell upon Sharon, and she quickly wiped her eyes. "I led her to the Lord. We became best friends." She smiled. "In some ways even better than me and Toni." The smile left. "She died."

"Now fill in the blanks the way a daughter of Issachar would. Look at everything the way a prophetess would," said Jonathan. "Don't see accidents and coincidences. See providence."

Lord, give me Your Spirit of wisdom and revelation. "Holly was hooked on heroin when she approached me. Jared got his drugs from *The Bluff.* Prince!" she screamed. "Oh, my God! Prince carjacked us. We led him to the Lord. He lives in *The Bluff.* You're doing Bible studies at his house. Jared took Holly to that horrible place so those guys could— Prince was there. He stopped it."

Sharon put her hands to her face and began to rock back and forth. The tears came freely. "We invited them both for dinner, not knowing what had happened at that house. We're connected to Holly. We're connected to Prince."

"What a coincidence? Right?" said Jonathan. "Joseph's brothers sold him into slavery, but God meant it for good. Satan inspired Prince to rob you, but God meant it for good."

"I see. I see." Sharon felt joy entering her heart. Her friend had gone to heaven prematurely, but God's plan was to use her death as part of His plan to take life to *The Bluff.* "God destroyed Anthony Righetti and the Family. He destroyed Michael Bogarty and his sex gang. He wants to destroy—" She stopped. "*The Bluff* and *Mayhem* is not one guy."

"It's a mindset, Sharon. A mindset of hopelessness, anger, addiction, immorality, violence, poverty—you name it, it's there."

"How do we go after something like that?" she asked.

Edwin cleared his throat. "In two stages. Frontline and back at the ranch. We set up something there—in the community. We can figure that out. Since Jonathan is so skilled at overthrowing governments—"he smiled cynically at Jonathan—"you are now the director of our new inner city outreach department." He looked at

Sharon with a hard father smile. “You are the coordinator of our new inner city outreach department.”

“I am?” Sharon hardly believed her ears.

“Yes, you are. And that position is located firmly and inflexibly in a Glory Tabernacle office. Electronic ankle bracelet provided at no cost to you.”

A frown formed on her face.

Edwin continued. “Of course, since you are the pastor’s daughter, you may work from home any time you like.”

Sharon looked at Jonathan.

“Great idea, Edwin” Jonathan quickly answered.

“Fantastic idea,” said Barbara just as quickly.

A slow smile came to Sharon’s face. “Thank you, Dad. Mom. Thank you, Jonathan.” She teared up. “I just couldn’t stand thinking that her death was in vain.”

“Maybe her death is a seed that will produce a crop we can’t even imagine,” said Barbara.

The angel took his hand off of Barbara’s shoulder.

Chapter 10

Earlier, Slavery had addressed his large army and had shown his extreme displeasure by separating several demons' heads from their bodies. Now, Annihilation was addressing his own. He was furious. Unlike Slavery, he didn't punctuate the end of his meeting by sending a handful of demons to the *Dark Prison.* Why wait?

Annihilation began his meeting by lining up ten bound demons in a row. He used his short dagger to cut out each of their hearts. He slammed each on the ground and stomped with his large boot until there was nothing but mangled demonic flesh and black goo.

He stood before his huge army. His large body had gotten larger with the increase of bloody violence and murders in *Mayhem.* "Soldiers without heart will have their hearts removed. Soldiers who do not see what is happening in Mayhem will have their eyes removed." He pointed to one of several demons who was assigned to watch the *G* building. "Him."

In a dark flash, four of Annihilation's elite soldiers were upon the demon. They stood before the angry ruler. One of the four demons side-kicked the back of the demon's leg. The terrified spirit fell to his knees. He instinctively dropped his head.

Annihilation grabbed the top of his head, his claws piercing a half-inch of flesh. He jerked it back. "What do you see happening in *Mayhem*? What do you see happening in *G* building?"

"Great general! Great general!" The spirit raced for a satisfactory response.

"Enough!" Annihilation shouted.

He dug his claws into the demon's eye sockets and yanked them out. He threw the eyes into the crowd of soldiers.

"Get this howling fool out of my sight. Don't kill him. Unbind him and drop him off into some dry place. Let him wander."

Two of the four spirits took away the blinded demon.

The ruler spirit looked menacingly at his army. "I hope I have your attention. Octavius has been reading the cursed book almost non-stop. The book of Acts, especially. He's been praying like he's some kind of apostle. He's been flapping those big lips everywhere he goes. Jesus this. Jesus that. Jesus. Jesus. Jesus. He's even praying for people. Next thing you know, he'll be asking people to forgive him for all of the glorious works of darkness he's done. I'm sick of it!" he screamed.

He bared his teeth in a prolonged way, as though he were posing for a picture. Then he exploded in fury. "He was baptized in the Holy Ghost! This criminal! This drug pusher! This thief! This fornicator. Baptized in the Holy Ghost! It wasn't enough that he got saved! No, he received power from on high! And for what?" His voice dropped, but the low tone masked none of his fury. "For ministry. To supernaturally spread the kingdom of God. To bring the kingdom of God here to *Mayhem*."

A murmur broke out in the vast army.

"Shut up! Whispering about this empowered black dirt won't stop him." The ruler paced back and forth with his hands folded behind him. "We need action. We need to shut him down before he becomes too big of a pain in the darkness to shut down."

Annihilation's eyes glared at his servants. If something worthy of praise doesn't happen soon to this threat, we will meet again to discuss *heart*. Is this understood?" he yelled.

"Yes, my lord!" the army bellowed.

"Now go get me that dirt!"

***

It had been a difficult day for Rosa. When she was shot, and woke up in a hospital bed paralyzed from the neck down, she had nearly gone crazy. *Her life was over.* But as the excruciatingly long days went by, she found that death would have been a gift. What could be worse than lying on her back all day, looking at the ceiling? Or sitting in a wheelchair and looking at a cup she could never again pick up? Or having her mother feed her like she was a baby?

Then the dreams. The terrifying dreams.

She began having a recurring dream about killing someone's lamb and being caught by the police. When it came time to stand before the judge, he offered her mercy. Instead of accepting the judge's mercy, she spit in his face. Then the terrifying part of the dream.

The judge was so angry that he sentenced her to death. She cursed the judge even as they strapped her in the electric chair. Curses were coming out of her mouth when the first jolt of energy started frying her flesh. But instead of the electrocution ending in death, it continued. On and on and on. The fire never stopped shooting through her body. She never lost consciousness. Her heart never stopped.

An everlasting execution.

Then came the day that freed her spirit from the wheelchair. Her mom had taken her to the *Farmer's Market.* They were there at the meat section looking at lamb. A young man approached them and asked if he could talk to them about God's lamb.

Rosa smiled, recalling how nervous Andrew had looked. He was so scared, and his words so jumbled, that he appeared on the verge of turning and walking away. He didn't know that she had been having dreams about a lamb.

When he asked if he could tell her about God's lamb, the dream exploded in her mind like fireworks against a dark night. And when he got to the part where he said her sins had crucified God's lamb, she was certain that her paralyzed body was trembling. She was already asking God for mercy in her mind when Andrew told her that the penalty for rejecting God's mercy was everlasting punishment.

Yes, she was paralyzed. Crippled. Her body confined to a chair. But she was not in that electric chair in her dream. And she never would be. Not only had she escaped God's judgment, her record had been wiped clean, and she had gained Him as her Father.

She looked around her room. The walls that used to move toward at her. The door that used to taunt her. The ceiling that used to lower to within an inch of her nose, threatening to crush her. No more.

The torturous thoughts that cruelly held the mirror of her inabilities before her eyes—no more.

The room that tried to suffocate her—no more.

But today had been a tough day. That mirror was back, and the walls and ceiling were closing in on her. Rosa knew why. She remained free only as long as she took authority over her thought life. And for her, this meant thinking from an eternal perspective. She had to see things as they really were, and not as they appeared to be. *She had to see herself as God saw her.* What did the Bible say about her? That's all that mattered.

"In Jesus' mighty name, Satan, get out of here!" she said. "This chair is temporary. I have a new body coming. But until that day comes, I'm going to love God and serve Him through my prayers. Now, out!"

"Did you say something?" said her mother in the next room.

"Yeah, she said something, lady," said a demon of self-pity, one of the three trembling spirits in Rosa's room that now felt like a big bull's eye was upon each of them.

"Don't go anywhere," Idolatry ordered the two self-pity demons. "If you go, I have to go. And I'm not ready to—"

Four angels stepped out of another dimension.

"Gotta go!" said Idolatry. He was gone before the self-pity spirits heard his whole statement.

They joined immediately. Why fight? They could always come back when she was more focused on herself.

***

The demon had grown fond of his heart and eyes. So he wasted no time racing to Annihilation to report the blue mist that had started at the cripple's house and was snaking its way through the neighborhood. If that thing came into *Mayhem*, he'd be covered.

***

The goal was not complicated. *Stop Octavius.*

Fifty demons followed him everywhere. Fifty demons went ahead of him in anticipation of where he might go. Three companies of one hundred were on standby for immediate reinforcement.

The fifty hovered around the tiny house. They couldn't get any closer than two hundred feet. The house was on fire. Every now and then a flame would shoot out beyond two hundred feet. The hovering spirits would screech in fear and fly away. But they were demons. So as soon as it looked safe to get closer, they'd do so. Until another flame erupted. And off they'd go in a screech.

This continued until the threat came onto the porch. He looked around with a determined look. "Yeah. Yeah. It's on, Satan."

"What do you think he meant by that?" asked a demon to any demon willing to answer.

An evil spirit shook his head at the stupid question. "That's where the term, dumb devil, comes from. Why don't you go ask him? I'm sure he'll tell you."

***

The fifty advance party demons descended upon the little house in *The Bluff.* They joined many who were already there. Some who came and left, traveled with the people who frequented the crack house. But some never left. They were attracted not by a person, but by the environment.

"That didn't last long," said a demon watching Octavius. He looked at another with a silly grin.

The grin wasn't returned. "You idiot. Why do you think he's carrying the cursed book? He's not here to do drugs. He's here to preach the everlasting gospel. He's here to rob us." The demon looked at his idiot comrade, shaking his head contemptuously. He flew to the other side of the demon horde.

The house was on Oliver Street. It was the middle of three small abandoned houses. The three hotly contested the title of being the most raggedy. But the middle house, the one that Octavius stood in front of contemplating what he was about to do, had a slight edge. This was odd, since this was the one most popular with addicts. But then that's where all the trash came from that was strewn around the house.

That's it. The junkies made the house more ugly. What was it about junkies and trash? thought Octavius, unaware that he was thinking so deeply about three raggedy houses he'd seen for several years.

"Junkies are trash," said a demon.

The thought stopped Octavius on the second of four cement steps that led to the elevated lawn of dirt and weeds. He thought about his mother. She wasn't trash. He thought about Holly. She wasn't trash. He thought about how things could have been different for him. He wasn't trash.

Octavius knew this was the Vice Boys' house. They'd hear about this sooner or later—probably sooner. Unless God did one of those miracles he read about, preaching in their house was definitely a suicide move. He tapped his Bible and looked into the bright sky. His thoughts went to Stephen. A dude he had read about in the book of Acts. *That cat saw Jesus standing at the right hand of God.*

Octavius left heaven and looked at hell. At least as close to hell as a person could get before actually going there. The door of the crack house was open. *The door to hell was always open, wasn't it?*

He walked across the wide, creaky, wooden porch. What those junkies had done to this porch. This wasn't trash. It was garbage. His face hardened. He turned from the trash and toward the door, aware that something had changed in him. He was looking at trash and garbage like he was some kind of ghetto philosopher.

Octavius stepped into the Vice Boys' house with his big Bible. The place was as trashed inside as it was outside. Spaced-out folks were laid out everywhere. Some lying on the floor. Others propped up against a wall. It wasn't *sitting* against a wall. That would imply consciousness. These people were *propped*.

His eyes fell upon a girl who used to be as fine as they come. She was smart, too. Had he not been so saddened by what he saw, he would've let go of an awkward chuckle. Samira Knox was her name. She was mixed with something. Nobody knew. But whatever it was, it added something exotic and unique to her flawless white skin and long pretty hair.

The unexpressed chuckle was because Samira was too good for the Prince. She wasn't arrogant about it. She had just told him nicely three years ago in that out of place white girl voice of hers that she was from Chicago and visiting her cousins for the summer—a white girl with cousins in The Bluff? How did that happen?

She was in the University of Chicago studying sociology and urban planning. She had come to *The Bluff* because she was going to use the experience to write her thesis when the time came.

Octavius looked at Samira. Her name was still pretty, but she wasn't. Somehow her long, pretty hair was still long and pretty. *How was that possible?* But it was like a beautiful frame around an ugly, marred painting.

Samira's face had been battered so much by men, especially the Vice Boys. For some reason, they hated her for the same reasons they turned her out. She was beautiful. She didn't look black. She was a college girl. She enunciated her words. She talked about helping people. She wanted to help black people. *They hated the fact that she wanted to help black people.* They said she thought she was better than them. Why else would a white person try to help a black person?

Then there were the sisters. They jumped on her all the time because as much as the brothers talked about her like a dog, they were on her like a rabbit. Blind envy compelled them to try to beat the beauty off of her. One time they even held her down and cut off her hair.

The Vice Boys didn't appreciate that one bit. Samira was still fine at that time. So cutting off her hair would cost them money. They beat those three girls like they were men. One of them almost died.

Octavius looked at Samira. *You came here to help us—to help me.*

This was his fault. He knew exactly how the Vice Boys operated. Kidnap the girl. Take her somewhere. Put chains on her. Force her to take drugs until she was good and hooked. Use her up until they were through with her. Throw her away as a worthless junkie.

He had heard that the Vice Boys were going to turn her out. He could've warned her. He didn't because she had hurt his pride by turning him down.

You could be somewhere up in Chicago doing yo' thang, helpin' people.

But she wasn't in Chicago helping people. She couldn't even help herself. He remembered how heartless he had been when he heard that the Vice Boys had her. He knew that soon she'd be so messed up that he could have her any time he wanted her. But he didn't want her like that. He wanted her straight. Mind all there. Looking in the nigga's eyes who she had turned down. So he went shopping and did what he had to do to get enough to rent her before they put her in treatment.

Octavius hadn't thought of Samira's expression when he had entered her room three years ago until this moment. She had been sitting on the floor in a corner, her arms wrapped around her knees. She wasn't wearing anything, but her panties and bra. She looked up terrified. Then her eyes widened with hope when she saw who it was.

"Prince," she gushed, with her mouth wide open. "Oh, my God. My God. My God." She jumped up and wrapped her arms around his waist.

He remembered how powerful he had felt when this beautiful, mixed, whatever she was, college girl held him. Her head resting on his chest. Her trembling body pressed hard against his. He remembered how aroused he became at her trembling.

Then he pulled her arms from around his waist and looked her coldly in her eyes.

"You're not here to help me, are you?"

Now he understood. *That* was it—the moment of death. Over time, *The Bluff* and *Mayhem* had made this girl ugly, but that was the moment Samira died. It was the moment he had destroyed everything good she believed. Nausea coated his belly and rose upward. The Bible suddenly became too heavy to hold. It pulled against his thick fingers and dropped to the dirty floor.

Samira looked up. "Prince," she said, with a smile that haunted him. "What are you doing here?" Her words were crisp, clear, in defiance of her surroundings.

Octavius watched as she prepared to shoot some heroin. He wanted to snatch it from her hand and shout, "What are you doing? You're supposed to be in college! You're supposed to be fixing this crap!"

But where did he get the nerve to think something so stupid? Something so hypocritical? He had destroyed this girl. He had created this junkie. Now he was standing over her acting like that dude who had shot Dee-Bop dead, and later joined the crowd on the street looking at the body, saying, "Awww, man, that's cold. What happened to Dee-Bop?"

Now here he was standing over Samira doing the same thing. Octavius turned and started to walk away.

"You're forgetting your Bible, Prince."

Octavius froze. Junkies had a one-track mind when it was time to get right. That wasn't Samira. *That was God.* He turned slowly and looked down. She was having a hard time finding a clean shot. He got on one knee.

"Samira, wait."

"I can't procrastinate on this issue, Prince. I'm sick."

"Please, Samira, just for a moment."

"I'm sick, Prince."

Prince's face imploded in guilty grief. "I know you are," he said with tears.

"What's wrong?" she asked. "Can I do anything to help you?"

Prince dropped the other knee and doubled over. "I did this. I did this to you. I could've helped you. I could've stopped this from happening." Prince lifted his face toward heaven, with eyes closed. "God, I did this to Samira." He screamed, "I did this to her!"

He was on his hands and knees on a filthy floor and didn't care. His muscled body bounced as he broke further. There was nothing good in him. He was an animal. A selfish animal who had hurt someone because she was too smart to get involved with a thug.

When his remorse gave him a moment, he looked at Samira. Her head was slumped in a heroin stupor. He knew he had no right, but he needed to. He touched her hair. It felt good. And he felt guilty for touching it.

God had saved her hair. He grimaced and cried through a closed mouth. He looked at her face. She wasn't ugly. She was beautiful. She was a beautiful person who had run into ugly people. Even now, there was something good in her that had miraculously survived all they had put her through. How could she bring herself to ask if she could help him?

He grabbed the Bible and sat next to her. He wrapped his arm around her and nestled her limp head onto his chest.

Octavius remembered his mother. He put the Bible on the lap of Samira's dirty pants. "I didn't help you when I was supposed to. I needed help myself. But if God gives me the power, Samira, I'm gonna help you now. My momma was a junkie. She used to get high and put the Bible on her lap. We thought she was crazy, but she was standin' on the word. That word snapped her chains."

Octavius burst into tears. "God...God...Father, I can't take back anything I did to Samira. I'm asking you—I'm begging You, please snap her chains."

He sat for an hour with the girl whose dreams he had stolen and whose life he had wrecked. He had had plenty of sex from plenty of women, but he had never had a single moment of genuine tenderness with any one of them. He turned his head and smelled Samira's dirty hair. It smelled like perfume to him. He kissed her hair and rested his forehead on her head.

Suddenly, he hopped up. He ran to the door and trotted to the corner of the street and looked both ways. He ran back into the house, lifted Samira in his arms, and ran out onto the porch and leapt onto the ground. In a few moments, he and Samira was in his SUV. She was laid across the back seat as he hurried away.

***

On the dirty floor of the Vice Boys' crack house was a big black Bible. A gold inscription on the cover said, *Prince of God.* Inside the cover was written, *To my friend, Prince.*

***

"Like watching a river of lava flow down a volcano," said Slavery. He spit in disgust, without taking his eyes off the blue mist that was moving across the large field.

One of Annihilation's cheeks turned up. "You see it coming, but what can you do?" He gave his own wad of black spit.

They watched the mist enter the building at one of the doors. They knew where it was going. It had come many times. It was coming for Kim. That was bad enough. But something that took this to the level of being insulting was how the mist went through the doors.

It wasn't limited to doors or windows or anything. It went wherever it wanted. Yet it made a practice of going out of its way to honor the decisions of the children of Adam—even their physical doors. The enemy was so committed to honoring their decisions that he did it even if it meant his precious dirt would be hurt.

And what was this charade really about? Because he had truly given this world to them? No. It was just another of his self-serving ploys to cover his incompetence. He had made a mess of their world. And now by supposedly honoring their decisions, their so-called free-will, he could blame them for their problems.

Slavery broke away from his musings. "Once the lava has *left* the volcano, there's nothing that can be done with it but to get out of its way."

Both ruler spirits turned to one another. A single raised eyebrow of Annihilation joined Slavery's grin.

"Shut down the volcano, yes. We have tried, but Rosa has resisted," said Annihilation, looking for an answer that would match Slavery's grin.

"She has resisted self-pity. A surprise, for sure. It's normally such a successful weapon at shutting down saints." Slavery's grin turned into a smile. "Maybe she'll listen if we're a bit more forceful."

Chapter 11

Prince drove around for hours. He didn't know where to go. He'd drive a million miles if it meant at the end of the journey, Samira could be fixed. His word choice stabbed him in the heart.

Fixed.

Hadn't he *fixed* her enough? His sad eyes looked in the rearview mirror, first for cops—he was taking a big risk—second, at Samira. He had stopped and put her seat belt on. But she had taken it off and was lying across the long seat on her side. Her golden hair buried most of her face. Her closed eye, lips, and nose were uncovered, though. She puckered. He turned away.

What am I doing? He shook his head.

Prince. Oh, God! My God! My God!

Then...

You're not here to help me, are you?

His tears blurred his vision. He looked at the large truck fast approaching opposite him. Only two double lines separated him from what he deserved. His heart should have been beating fast. His body should have been tense as his punishment got closer. Instead, he felt nothing but a sad calm rest over his guilty soul.

Guilty.

His face hardened at the thought of his last act proving that he belonged on the other side of those double lines. He didn't care about anyone but himself. He hurt people and felt nothing. He took what he wanted. And now his last act was to go to his grave never paying for his sins.

A thief to the end, he thought.

The truck was almost there. He narrowed his eyes. His SUV drifted to the left.

Boooaank! Boooaank!

Prince exhaled deeply, looking at the truck's grill that would soon be in his front seat.

"Prince," he heard Samira say softly, unaware of the danger.

Prince swerved hard to the right. He missed the truck only by inches. Somehow he had forgotten that Samira was in the backseat. Now his heart slammed furiously against his chest.

"Samira," he said, looking behind him, as though he had just snatched her from death. She was sound asleep.

His hands gripped the steering wheel hard. It wasn't enough that he had turned Samira into a zombie. Now his killer selfishness had shown itself again and had nearly killed her for real. He panted for air. Air he didn't deserve.

He glanced in the back seat. How could she call his name at just the right moment, then immediately go back to sleep? Was this a coincidence? Or had God saved their lives? He thought of his momma's prophecies that he would preach all over the world. Sharon had said the same dumb thing. They were both wrong.

It couldn't happen.

He drove a nice ride because he was good at selling drugs. He had a pocket full of money because he was good at taking what he wanted. He was alive because he was good at making other niggas dead.

Prince drove another hour before he pulled into a Super 8 motel parking lot. He looked back at Samira's sleeping face. He looked harder. Was she smiling? Must be the heroin. She sure had nothin' else to smile about.

He quickly weighed his options. He opened the glove compartment, got a pen and paper, and wrote a note. It read: *Samira, please don't leave*. He tucked it under her hand and went inside.

He came back and she was standing outside the vehicle, obviously trying to figure out what was going on. About fifty feet separated them. She began to walk away.

"Samira," he called.

Samira stopped. She looked warily at Prince. She was like a cat who had learned that behind the most tender wooing could be cruelty beyond description. Running was Samira's only defense.

Prince saw it in her face. If he took one more step, she'd run.

Please don't run, Samira. I need to talk to you. If you run, I'll die. He heard himself. Again, it was all about him. He had basically on the spur of the moment kidnapped this woman. Even now he didn't know why. He only knew that when he saw her in that dope house, he felt like a rope was dropped around his neck and he was yanked in the air. He was choking on guilt.

"Samira, please don't run."

Her eyes darted.

"I'm not going to hurt you."

"What do you want, Prince?"

He lifted both his hands, then dropped them. Emotions pushed inside his chest. "I just want to talk. We're in Chattanooga. I found you at the V-Boys' house on Oliver. I'm sorry, Samira. I just need to talk to you."

"You need to talk to me at a motel, Prince?"

"Samira, please. I been drivin' around with you fo' hours. If it was like that, I didn't need to come to no motel."

She looked suspiciously around the parking lot. *Was he trying to sell her to somebody?*

"Samira, there's nobody else but us. I got us a room...so we can talk. 227. Can we talk?"

"Go back toward the entrance, Prince. I'll talk to you there."

"Okay."

She met him in front of the automatic door.

"Samira, we can talk in the lobby if you want to."

The doors opened. A uniformed police officer approached them. "Everything okay here?"

"Yeah, everything cool," said Prince.

"Is that right, Ma'am? Everything cool?" the big officer said, not taking his eyes off of Prince.

She hesitated.

The officer took a step backward. His right hand rested on his holster. "Sir, step away."

"Samira," pled Prince.

"I'm not going to tell you again," said the officer.

Samira jumped between them. "Officer, we were just having an altercation about his choice of motel. I was sleeping and when I awakened, I found that my boyfriend had selected a *Super 8*. Is a *Holiday Inn* too much to ask?"

"Really?" he asked.

"Really," she said, smiling.

He looked at Prince. "Wait right here. Don't go *anywhere*. Ms., may I speak to you privately?"

She smiled widely. "Samira Knox. And of course you can, Officer Jacobs."

The officer looked over her shoulder at Prince. "Is everything okay? Are you safe?"

"Yes," she answered immediately. "I'm safe. It was just a silly argument." She looked at the officer as though he was being foolish.

"Are you here of your own free will? Does he have a gun?"

She appeared shocked. "A gun? No. Of course, I'm here of my own free will. Officer Jacobs, I appreciate your concern for my safety, but I assure you my safety is secure."

"Where are you and your boyfriend from?"

"Atlanta."

"Where are you going?"

She turned and looked at Prince.

"Please look at me, Ms. Knox."

She kept looking at Prince. She remembered now. The house. Him talking tenderly to her. Him on his knee crying. What would make a man like him cry?

"I hope Chicago," she said.

"You hope?" asked the officer. "You don't know?"

She smiled. "No. It's a surprise. Maybe you can get it out of him." She couldn't tell whether or not he believed her.

"Okay, Ms. Knox. Would you mind not looking toward your boyfriend while I speak to him?"

"Sure," she answered, energetically.

"I had a good talk with Ms. Knox," the officer said to Prince. "She said you two are going to Saint Louis."

Lord, please, I don't know why I have this woman. "Not if I can help it," he said.

"Where you going?"

Prince remembered that she was from Chicago. "Chicago."

"Chicago, huh?"

Prince didn't say anything. He was cool. Then he remembered what he had in his truck and almost had a bowel movement.

"People get nervous when they see folks arguing in the parking lot."

Yeah, don't you mean white folks get nervous when they see a black man talkin' with a white woman in the parking lot? What y'all got—a three-second rule in Tennessee? "I hear you."

"You two have a nice trip."

Prince watched the officer walk toward Samira. He waited for her in the lobby. He was relieved when she came in and sat at his table. He let out a long breath and held his head, with his elbow on the table. He was as surprised and confused about Samira going alone with this craziness as he was for doing it.

Samira looked across the table at him. He almost couldn't believe what he was seeing. Anyone with eyes could see that she had been through it, but now she didn't look half as bad as she did in the house. Actually, she looked kind of good. Like a Mercedes with mud on it.

"Prince, I don't know what I'm doing. I mean *here*. Why didn't I disclose to that officer that I am here without having the slightest notion as to why you have brought me here?" She leaned into the table and asked without emotion. "Why were you crying? What could make someone like you cry?"

Her question rolled around in his mind. Then, without mercy, it found his heart. "That," he answered softly. "Someone like me."

Samira's blue eyes narrowed with questions. "Go on."

Prince looked at the beautiful damaged goods sitting across the table. She had a million questions that only he could answer. He had kidnapped her and brought her here to talk, and now he couldn't put two words together.

"I've done a lot of things."

"A lot of *things*?" Something clicked and a look of disbelief came to her face. "Things."

Samira fought the fear that was clawing at her insides. She had been beaten and tortured so many times for doing nothing but what she was told or forced to do. He had never beaten her. But he had abused her. Sexually. That once. For hours. After that she only saw him in passing.

Now here he was calling her rape *things*. He didn't even have the decency or courage to call it what it was. Instead, he had reduced the most horrifying night of her life, and the beginning of her now horrifying life, under the generic category of *things*.

You raped me, you coldhearted monster! Call it rape! Her memories empowered her fear. She said nothing.

Prince felt his chest about to explode. "Samira, you mind if we go to the room I got? I got a lot of things to say, and—"

"You got some smack, Prince?"

He remembered her as she was before the Vice-Boys got her. *I'm going to use this experience to work on my thesis.* Now it was *You got some smack?* Tears came out of both of his eyes. He wiped them quickly. "Yeah, I got you."

She was puzzled at his tears. But tears or not, he was a criminal who made other killers tremble. She mustered all the courage she could. Her blue eyes looked into his. "I lost the ability to say no a long time ago, Prince. You know I'll do whatever you want."

Prince strained to keep from bursting into tears. He looked at a *Super 8* sign on the wall. He had over three grand with him, and he was about to put Samira up in a motel. What was wrong with him? Did everything he did have to show how bad he was?

"Samira, you mind if we go somewhere better than this? You mentioned *Holiday Inn*. Is that cool?"

She looked at him without saying anything. She stood up and walked toward the door.

He saw it in her eyes. She didn't have to say anything. Samira had been a slave for three years. What else was she going to say? Prince closed his eyes and tightened. The tears came anyway. He wiped them away and followed her to his vehicle.

***

Prince stood before the door of their new room. She was behind him with closed eyes. The fear that tore through her body was indescribable. She felt her organs trembling.

Oh, God, please help me to endure it, she prayed.

Prince turned. Samira's eyes were closed. She was crying silently. Everything in him wanted to reach up and wipe away her tears. But the thought of putting his hand on her seemed sick, like molesting a child. He had no right to touch her.

"Samira," he said, softly. He held the door open widely.

Her eyes parted. She looked into the room. It appeared empty, but they could be in the closet or bathroom. Her lips parted to let her rapid breaths escape. She had gotten used to using her body to get heroin. She had even gotten used to being humiliated. But she could never get used to the beatings.

Prince searched her wet face. He looked in the room and looked at her. "Oh," he said, feeling sick at having to say this, "there's no one else here. It's just you and me, Samira. You can come in. Remember...I let you pick the hotel...and the room?"

She looked at him. Her expression conflicted with facts and fear. She stepped inside, took a few timid steps forward, and stopped, never looking up from the floor. When she heard the door close, she collapsed to the floor on her knees.

Samira clasped her hands together near her panting mouth. "Oh, God, please. Oh, God, please. Oh, God, please. Oh, God, please."

Prince watched the crumpled woman before him. She was terrified. What had she been through? He knew what he had heard. But what had she *really* been through?

She looked up at him. Her hair partly covering her face. "Please don't beat me, Prince. Can we just do sex? Please?" she begged.

He looked down into her pleading eyes and realized painfully that he was looking *down* at her. He fell to his knees a few feet from her. "Samira...Samira..." He looked at her trembling lips and dropped his head. He looked up. "You don't have to—" his voice broke. He took several long breaths, trying to not cry. "We're not...oh, Samira." He looked back at the door latch. He stood up and went to it. "Samira, you know how this latch works?"

"Yes."

"If you put it on, no one can get in here, even with a key." He took both plastic cards from his pocket and tossed them on one of the beds. He got on one knee. "Samira, can I touch you?"

She started to undo her top button.

"No," he said, with his palm up. "No, Samira. Can...can I touch your hair?"

It wasn't the request to touch her *hair* that puzzled her. It was the *request.* She didn't have any rights that could be violated. So why had he asked? She looked at him without answering.

"Samira?" he asked softly.

She nodded.

Prince put forth his trembling hand. He lifted a handful and let it lay across his open palm. He stared at it. God was talking to him through her hair. He closed his eyes and lifted her hair and pressed it against his face. He breathed in slowly. Somehow God had saved her hair. He felt it in his heart. *Somehow God was going to save her life.*

Prince's strange behavior had stopped her tears. Why was he holding her filthy hair to his face? Why was he smelling it? Why was he crying into her hair? Silence and stillness was the only appropriate reaction.

Prince opened his eyes. "Thank you, Samira. I got what you need; so don't worry 'bout that. I'm going to sleep in my ride. I want you to put the latch on the door. Take a shower or a bath. Relax. Go to sleep in a real bed. No one's gone bother you. Nobody in the room, but you."

Samira didn't answer. She couldn't. There was no answer for this—only questions.

"I've given my life to the Lord, Samira, and I'm really sorry for the things I did." He went to the door and looked at her. "God's going to save you, Samira."

He heard the latch on the door as soon as it closed.

***

Prince returned a few hours later.

Samira looked through the peephole. She was glad he was back. He said he had heroin. He came in carrying several bags. She shut the door, locked it, and put the latch back on.

"What's all of this?"

He had bags from everywhere. There were bags in bags. *Gap. Old Navy. Macy's. Banana Republic. Bath and Body Works. Verizon. The Limited.* And others. He put them on the second bed.

"I'll be right back," he said.

She put the locks on the door and went to the bags. One by one she looked inside. The stuff inside was all for women, except for the phone. She dumped one of the bags on the bed. An assortment of body lotions, body creams, bubble baths, and soaps fell out. She dumped another bag. Out came five kinds of perfume. What was going on?

He heard a knock. She looked through the peephole and opened the door. In he walked with a *Chipotle* bag and a *Starbucks* cup.

"Prince, what is all of this? Who is this for?"

He stood before her with the expression of a man who knew he was trying to fix a shattered, priceless vase with glue. "It's what you had the time you let me take you to get something to eat."

"Why are you doing this, Prince?"

"I remembered your sizes. I remember you talkin' 'bout your sister, and how she'd sneak and wear your clothes. Even your shoes." He looked at her hair. "Good. You haven't washed your hair yet. There's some stuff—"

"Prince," said Samira, as loudly as her fear of him would allow, "please tell me what you're doing?"

He let out a pained breath and stretched out his hand at what she was wearing. "You don't belong in that, Samira."

She lifted both hands a little, looking down at her dirty, tattered clothes. "Prince," she pointed to the stuff on the bed, "that's not who I am. That's who I used to be." She looked down at herself. "This is who I am. Please don't be angry with me, but I'd like you to return your merchandise."

"Samira, these clothes are dirty. They have holes in them."

"Prince," she stressed timidly, "don't you see? *I* am dirty. Everything about me is dirty and ragged and worn. I've accepted who I am." She shook her head sadly, put her hand over her heart, and cried, "I don't have a soul." She stepped closer to him. "I—don't—have—a soul. I don't deserve what you've purchased."

"Samira, no. You're wrong. I don't deserve to give them to you, but you do deserve them." He thought about something he had read in the Bible. "Just think of it as a gift from God. Please, Samira."

The blank expression on her face didn't convey her sadness, but her eyes did. "A gift from God? I begged God to free me the night the Vice Boys kidnapped me. They joked and laughed about all the stuff they were going to do to me. They beat me and had taken off all of my clothes except my bra and panties.

"Just when they were making me take them off, too, they got a phone call. Somebody told them to leave me alone. They locked me in that room. Then a nice guy I had gone out to dinner with showed up in that filthy room. I was so happy. All I could do was say—"

"Oh, God."

"Yes, Prince. Oh, God. That's what I said. Over and over and over. And what gift did He give me that night? What gift did I get the next morning? All that day? All that night? The next three years? Now that I'm nothing...now that I'm dirty...now that no decent man would ever want to touch me, He uses *you* to purchase me clothes and dinner?"

A God that would stand by twiddling His thumbs, watching while she was repeatedly gang raped and tortured, and while she was brutalized and homeless for three years, seemed worse to her than the people who had hurt her. At least they were only people. People were capable of evil. But God? *The God of love?*

A world with people like Prince. And a God who used them for curb service. At this point Samira didn't care whether Prince beat her or not. If she were lucky, he'd kill her. She only hoped it wouldn't take too long. Maybe then she could get away from God and people like him and finally have true peace.

Her words stung. There was nothing he could say. It was all true. And this was just what he'd done to her. What about all the others?

"Samira, I'm glad you haven't taken your bath yet." He tried to smile. "Now you can use some of that bubble bath stuff. I'm goin' back to the car. You can take your time. I got the new phone activated. I put my number in there. Just call when you finished."

"Why'd you bring me here?"

He turned. He shook his head. "I don't know, Samira. I saw you in that dope house and—"

"You've seen me many times, Prince. You never even gave me eye contact. Do you know what that did to me? Do you even care? I only ask because of all of this," she said, sweeping her hand at the bags on the bed.

"Yeah. I care."

"You care?"

"Yeah. I do. I care."

"Three years later you care. Prince, why do you care three years later?"

He knew how hollow this would sound. "Can I sit down?"

"It's your room, Prince."

He sat in a chair. She sat in the middle of the bed with her legs folded.

"One night, 'bout a month and some change, I was out doing some dirt. Carjacked some people and it turned on me. This crazy girl, Sharon—well, she ain't really crazy—anyway this chick took off with us in the car. We were going like a hundred, hundred and ten. She made me throw my gun out the window. I did it. She stopped the car.

"We was on 400. So it wasn't like I could run somewhere. The girl, Sharon, talked her father—he a preacher—into not calling the cops. Sharon said God brought me to them so I could be saved, and so I wouldn't end up in prison."

"What does that have to do with us?"

He looked at Samira with remorseful eyes. "Everything. Those church people started coming to my house and having Bible study with me."

"They came to *The Bluff*?"

"Samira, they even came to my sister's crib in *Mayhem*. Then they invited me over for dinner."

Samira's face did her talking.

"I'm serious," said Prince. "The people who we jacked came to *Mayhem* for Bible study, and then invited me to their crib for dinner. I ain't lying. I know how it sound."

"Okay." She didn't know what to make of this story, but she waited for more.

"I mean these folks was saying some of the same stuff my momma been saying to me forever. About God and Jesus and stuff. But then when they started coming to the house—"

He found himself afraid to finish.

"Prince, is this your way of telling me you found God?"

"Yeah."

"And all your sins are forgiven?"

Prince stood. He couldn't look her in the eyes. Finally, he did. "Samira, the statute of limitations for rape in Georgia is seven years. I know God has forgiven me, but what I did was wrong."

"*What* did you do to me, Prince?"

He dropped his head and turned away.

"No!" This time she did yell.

It startled him.

"What did you do to me?"

He grimaced. "You know what I did to you, Samira."

"Sit *down*, Prince."

He didn't. He was caught up in surprise.

"If there is *any* thing decent in you, I'm asking you to please sit down. You brought me here. You said you wanted to talk. Now talk."

He sat down.

She pointed an index finger at him whose nail she hadn't cleaned since the first rape. "*What* did you do to me?"

He buried his hands in his face, then lifted his head. "I became your friend. I talked to you. I tried to make you think I was better than I was. You saw through it. But you were still nice to me. You let me take you out." Prince gazed into that moment. "Told me about your family. You shared your dreams with me." He wiped away a tear.

"I shared my dreams with you, Prince. Do you know why? I knew you were a criminal. I knew you did bad things. But I shared my dreams with you because I saw something in you. I saw something more than a criminal. I saw a handsome, smart guy who had potential to be good. I saw someone worth saving.

"I thought that by showing you kindness maybe a little ray of light would penetrate your darkness and you'd reach for more than *Mayhem.* I didn't reject you, Prince. I went as far as I could with you. I considered you my friend."

"I made a mistake, Samira. I'm sorry."

She turned away, gripping her head as though she couldn't bear any more. "You did *not* make a mistake, Prince." Samira's face flashed an energy and sureness he hadn't seen before. "Did you drive me away to another state to tell me you made a mistake? Prince, take me home. Or at least take me somewhere that I can catch a ride."

Prince dropped to his knees. He reached behind him and pulled out a gun. Samira froze. She watched him pull back the chamber. The hand with the gun dangled by his side. He stared at the floor.

"Samira, I knew they were coming after you."

Her mouth opened in stunned disbelief. She shook her head. *No, it couldn't be true.*

"I knew they were coming and I didn't say anything. Part of me panicked when I heard. I knew I had to get to you. Part of me—the part of me I hate—put out the word that I wanted the first taste."

Samira backed up deeper into the room. "First taste?"

He looked up. His eyes had a determined look. "You wouldn't go to bed with me, and I felt I had a right to it. So I waited for the call."

Samira's head was swimming. Three years of hell could've been prevented with one phone call from someone she considered a friend. Her dream of getting her doctorate degree was never going to happen. Her dream of helping others was never going to happen. Her dream of having a family of her own was never going to happen. She felt sick.

"See, Samira? The only one who can help me is God. The only one I can ask to forgive me is God. I betrayed you and I raped you. It's too much to ask you to forgive me. Ain't no nigga should get away with that."

He closed his eyes and let his heavy tears course unhindered down his face. He held the gun out, butt first.

Samira looked at the man who had destroyed her life. She held her belly with one hand to keep herself from throwing up. She took small steps toward the gun. She took it out of his hand and backed up.

Prince still had his eyes closed. He widened his arms and said, "What I did to you wasn't a mistake. I raped you. I ruined your life. What I did was evil. Samira, make sure that I'm dead. I don't want these niggas bringing me back. Just shoot 'til it's empty."

Samira gritted her teeth as she looked at him. In a moment, she saw a movie of a thousand horrible scenes, one after the other. The scenes muted Prince's prayers.

"Lord, I'm sorry for what I did to Samira. I deserve this. Lord, I'm sorry for what I did to Sharon and her family. Lord, I'm sorry for all the dope I sold. Lord, I'm sorry for the niggas I shot, and I'm sorry for the ones I killed. Lord, I'm sorry for the stuff I stole. Lord, I'm sorry for being evil."

He prayed until he ran out of things to say. He opened his eyes. Samira was staring at his chest with a glazed look, like she was in a trance. “Samira.”

She shook her head. “Hmp? What? Oh.” She looked at her rapist and tightened her jaws. She pulled her finger. It trembled, but didn’t touch the trigger. She shook the gun and pulled her finger as hard as she could. “Please, God,” she cried, “let me kill him.”

“You can do it, Samira. You’re just nervous. Take a deep breath. Then...pull.” Prince took a deep breath.

“It won’t work,” she cried desperately.

Prince dropped his arms. *Are you kidding me? I don’t believe this.* He took the gun from her and looked at it. He knew nothing was wrong with this gun. He slowly put it back in his holster. “Now what?” he muttered to himself. He wasn’t killing himself.

“I guess I’m not a killer,” said Samira.

It was strange how a few moments could make someone think straight. Prince was disappointed that she wasn’t a killer. *Now he was going to have to deal with some hard issues.* But he was glad that she hadn’t killed him. Had she killed him, he would’ve been the reason for her going to prison. *Was he ever going to stop messing up this girl’s life?*

“You have the smack?” asked Samira.

Prince’s heart sank. Death would’ve been better. At least for him. “Yeah, I got it.”

“I guess I may as well use some of the stuff you bought. I haven’t had a bubble bath in—” she muffled a cry. “It’s been a long time.”

“I’ll leave you the gear—got some new needles—and wait in the truck ‘til you call. Or I can sleep all night in the truck. Yeah, that’ll probably be better.”

“Prince, I don’t forgive you. I’ll never forgive you. But I think you’ve shown that I no longer have to be afraid of you.”

Prince smiled in his heart. She didn’t forgive him, but he didn’t think she hated him. That was worth the trip. It was worth risking his life. He looked at her long hair. Now he smiled. He knew why he was so fascinated with it.

Samson. Samson's power was in his hair. The enemy took him down by taking his hair. But God had mercy on him and caused his hair to grow again. When his hair grew back, Samson asked God to restore his strength. God answered his prayer and Samson took down everybody.

After all this girl had been through, there was no way her hair should've come out looking like this. Her hair was prophesying the faithfulness of God. For a fleeting moment, a crazy thought came to his mind. *No way! This girl may kill me for real.*

Samira went to the bed and started looking at the bath stuff. She picked up some shampoo. "Prince, earlier why did you give such attention to my hair?"

"Uhh, yo' hair?"

"Yes. You smelled it and put it to your face and closed your eyes. I thought that was your prelude to having sex with me. Then you stopped. What was that about? Was that a good guy, bad guy moment?" There was not the slightest hint of an invitation in her question.

"No, Samira, that was all good guy. Your hair is beautiful. When I saw you in the dope house, it stood out. It didn't belong there. It was like God was talking to me. About you. About me."

"God was talking to you through my hair?"

"Yeah. It was like I could feel God saying, Her hair is a sign. Her hair is beautiful and it doesn't belong here. She is beautiful and she doesn't belong here. I saved her hair, and I'm going to save her life. I think that's where I went crazy and drove off with you."

"You got all of that from looking at the filthy hair of a homeless, junkie prostitute?"

"It was the Holy Spirit talking to my heart. But, yeah, it started with your hair."

She looked at the shampoo container and read its claims. She smiled and cried. "Something happened when you handed me that gun. It's obvious that you've changed." She paused in thought. "I don't forgive you, but I no longer hate you." Then she whispered to herself, "I'm going to wash my hair."

Prince had gotten more from this surprise trip than he ever could have imagined. The only thing that disturbed him now was his missing Bible. He had left it in the Vice Boys' house. He wondered what would be waiting on him when he returned home.

***

"Is anyone fond of losing their heart or eyes? I didn't think so. Then tell Slavery and Annihilation nothing about what has happened here. And make sure no one says anything about that angel stopping Samira from killing Octavius. They won't care a thing about the prayer cover Sharon gave him. All they'll see is one angel having his way with a hundred demons."

Chapter 12

Prince's black Mercedes came to a slow roll. In most neighborhoods, close to midnight meant folks were sleeping. But this was *The Bluff*. Vampires didn't sleep at night. This is when the biting was done.

He stopped his car a hundred feet from the house, on the opposite side of the street by a bunch of trees. He glanced into the trees, seeing nothing, but knowing that seeing nothing didn't mean something wasn't there. Somebody taking a leak. A hoe tricking. Vice Boys checking on things. But if that's who was in the dark of the trees, they weren't just checking to be checking. They were looking for him.

He rolled toward the dope house at a couple of miles per hour. There was no one on the street when he had taken Samira. Of course, that didn't mean no one in another house saw him. Plus, one of those junkies may have been sober enough to see and recognize him.

He parked against traffic on the side where the middle house was. Everyone in the neighborhood knew his car—it wasn't like there were a lot of Mercedes' in his neighborhood—but he locked the door anyway. Two things you never did with junkies. Never trust them. Never underestimate them. Dope had a way of making niggas do stupid stuff.

Prince glanced back at his SUV.

Like try to steal a nigga's ride who everybody knew had shot niggas for less than that.

Two dudes were on the porch. One standing, one sitting. He recognized them both as junkies. When he was close enough for the men to see what he was doing, he reached behind him and took his gun from his back waist and put it in his front waist. He kept his hand on it as he got closer.

One of the junkies was old, not in chronological age, but in dope age. He had ten heroin years on him. That gave his forty-year-old mug a sixty-year look. A bad sixty. He lifted his hands and laughed. It sounded like his throat was full of something he needed to spit out. "Whatever it is, I didn't do it."

Prince ignored him as he walked past. But he didn't ignore the other much younger junkie. He stared coldly into this man's eyes until he had entered the house.

Prince surveyed the room. Same pathetic chaos as always. He looked at a couple of dudes on their knees working on some *burn. Burn* was what some stupid white people bought when they came to *The Bluff* to buy heroin and didn't know they were buying cornstarch from a junkie. Real dealers didn't do that because they wanted repeat business.

Another dude was sitting on a box with a little table in front of him. On the table was a small water bottle. He mixed some water with heroin in a metal bottle cap and heated it with a lighter. He had his dirty needle on the table, ready to fill it with the mixture so he could inject it into his body.

Prince knew the only thing that had kept him from ending up sitting on a box in this garbage can disguised as a house was seeing what heroin had done to his mother. Still, this was pathetic. Nobody should live like this.

They don't know Me as you do.

The thought put Prince on pause. He looked around slowly, suddenly feeling the darkness that was in this place. The darkness on each person. In each person. The smell of urine in buckets and bottles in the bathroom and bedrooms rushed into his nostrils and down his throat. He frowned as he tasted it. The smell of feces joined the taste of urine in his mouth.

I'm getting out of this hell hole.

He went to where he and Samira had been sitting. Lots of things strewn about on the floor. Old razor blades. Vials. Needles. Metal bottle caps. And the usual filth. But no Bible.

Who will help them out? asked the Voice.

I don't know, thought Prince, responding to the thought.

Who will deliver My junkies?

My junkies? Wait a minute. Was this God speaking to him? Jonathan had told him to listen for thoughts that sounded out of place. He had said that was one of the ways God spoke. Prince knew these junkies weren't *his* junkies. So this thought must've been God calling them *His* junkies.

But why would God say these junkies belonged to Him? They belonged to the devil. Didn't they? Another thought pushed its way into his mind. *The earth is the Lord's, and all its fullness, the world and those who dwell therein.*

The room was dark. But He who shines light in darkness had turned on a bright light in Prince's mind. *The junkies...the hoes...the gangstas. Everybody...everythang belong to God. The devil is a thief. Nigga just takin' thangs. That's why Jesus came. To take back what that nigga stole.*

Three days ago Prince had read Luke 14:12-14. "When you give a dinner or a supper, do not ask your rich friends, your brothers, your relatives, nor rich neighbors, lest they also invite you back, and you be repaid. But when you give a feast, invite the poor, the maimed, the lame, the blind. And you will be blessed, because they cannot repay you; for you shall be repaid at the resurrection of the just."

The word gripped Prince so much that he had come to this crack house to preach. Who was poorer than a junkie? At the time, he didn't know what good that was going to do. But as stupid as it was, he knew he couldn't receive forgiveness and eternal life and not tell somebody. Then he saw Samira.

After that crazy spell that had caused him to run off with her disappeared, he was left with a deep feeling in his soul that maybe there was something good in him. *He had rescued Holly, and now Samira.*

He shook off the thought that maybe he simply had a thing for pretty white girls. He thought about the trouble he could be in. Naw, that wasn't it. Wasn't nobody that fine. White, black, whatever. He was acting crazy because ever since he had given his life to Christ, something had come over him. Something messing with his mind. And it had gotten worse when he got baptized in the Holy Spirit. *Power shootin' all through me like that.*

He still was trying to wrap his head around that craziness. One thing was now clear, though. His one-day ministry in the crack houses was over.

Prince took slow steps toward the wall adjacent to where he and Samira had been sitting. *I helped Samira. I don't know whose gonna help the others,* he thought.

I will send you. You will help the others. Be strong and of a good courage. Do not be afraid, nor be dismayed, for the Lord your God is with you wherever you go.

The force of the thought stopped him. *What the—?*

The blow to the back of the head dropped him.

***

Prince slowly opened one eye. Eventually, the other eye caught up. His eyes looked at his lap, but his brain didn't interpret what it saw. A groggy thought that a junkie had cracked him upside the head fought through the confusion. He lifted his head. It felt like it had been split open.

Now his brain worked with his eyes. *Oh, —,* he cursed inside. Even in this situation, he found himself thinking, *God forgive me for cursing.* There it was again. That thing that was changing him. A slight, momentary smile followed the thought and good feeling that came with it. His predicament wouldn't allow anything but a momentary smile. He wasn't in the crack house. *He wished he were.*

Prince moved his arm to touch the throbbing. It didn't budge. He looked at his arm.

"Precautions," said the smiling man that sat directly across from him by a few feet.

Prince knew the man well enough to know it was a shark's smile. The two dudes who stood by his sides weren't smiling. They had their killer looks on. One of them, Russell, was legit. He had shot a few people—killed one. He was good with his hands, too. Not like the punk standing on the other side of the shark. AJ, lots of mouth. *Nigga probably never even shot a gun*, thought Prince.

He heard something and looked behind him. A couple of more dudes. *Figures,* he thought. "What's this?" he asked, looking at the ropes that wrapped his arms to his sides.

"Prince, my brotha, that's insurance. I want to keep things civil." The man lifted a hand that had rings on three fingers and studied the liquid in his glass. "I love Brandy. I love to drink it *neat*. No ice. No mixer."

"You got me tied up in this chair to tell me how you like yo' Brandy?" AJ looked at his boss like he was waiting for the word to teach Prince some manners. Prince wasn't impressed. *Probably wipes his fat butt for him.*

The shark smiled at Prince. He put the glass close to his chest and sniffed with his eyes closed. "You don't want your senses overwhelmed when you take your first taste." He brought the glass to his face. "Like making love. The difference in a two-minute man and one who takes his time to appreciate the beauty of the female body. The beauty of the female body. Reminds me of Samira."

Prince felt like he had just been dunked naked in iced water. *Somebody saw me. He knows!* Most of Prince's hardness left. There was only the thinnest veneer left. So thin that the poke of a finger would make a hole, exposing his fear.

The shark put the glass to his double chin and took a deep breath through his nose. He concentrated on the smell of dried fruit aromas in the Brandy. He then put the glass to his nose and smelled through his nose and mouth. He took a tiny sip of the Cognac.

"Anybody can *drink* Brandy," he said. "A camel can drink Brandy. But does the camel appreciate the process of making Brandy. Does it appreciate the quality of the Brandy? This is *Prunier. VSOP*. Very Superior Old Pale. Jean Prunier got this gig going in the 17th century. Only uses grapes from the Grande Champagne Cru.

"A Cru is one of the six Cognac production districts. Six districts, Prince. And guess which one is rated number one by the French government?" The shark's chubby cheeks bubbled up and he showed his teeth through a menaced smile again. "Secret's out—Grande Champagne district. *Prunier* is special because of where it's created." He wiggled his index finger again. "All of this talk makes me think of Samira again. Samira's a hoe. We know that." He looked at AJ for agreement.

"She a hoe," said AJ.

Prince's fear didn't keep his lip from turning up at AJ's *Yassuh, boss* behavior. Nigga was pathetic.

"Aaahh, but Samira's like this Brandy. She's a special hoe. You know why she's special, Prince? The Cru she's from. Special district. White. Cultured. Privileged. Educated. Idealistic. Well, not any more." He looked intently at Prince, without the smile. "I think she held onto that idealism until you showed up and rocked her world." The shark laughed. "Now, Cuz, *you* are no two-minute man." The man looked at his four bodyguards. "Had I known my cousin was going be that long with her, I would've charged him more than a thousand dollars."

The shark looked at Prince with a puzzled expression. That fiendish, teeth-filled smile was back. "Just how many ways can you drink Brandy, Prince?" He sat back in his chair. "Oh, well, that's none of my business. That's between you and her. You paid top dollar for it."

Prince could tell by the look on his fat cousin's face that the playing was over.

"Nothing against the sisters around here, but they're not Brandy, if you know what I mean. You apparently appreciate good Brandy as much as I." The shark's eyes were dark. "So imagine my surprise when I reached for *my* Brandy and she was gone." The shark looked at one of the men behind Prince. "Gimme this nigga's Bible," he snapped, his high culture act suddenly gone and replaced by the cold-blooded inner city criminal he was.

Prince closed his eyes. *Lord, You have to help me. This nigga's gone kill me if You don't stop 'em.*

"Open yo' eyes!" AJ yelled.

The man from the back of the room handed the big Bible to the shark. The shark tossed it onto Prince's lap. "I don't know where it is, but somewhere in that Bible is something about stealing." He looked coldly at Prince. "Thou shalt not steal. That's in there, isn't it?"

"Yeah, it's in there."

"It's in there?"

"Yeah, it's in there."

"Then where's my Brandy? Where's my special hoe?"

Prince didn't answer.

"Prince, we grew up together. We're cousins. I knew you when you were just Octavius. Now you're Prince. A prince who steals." The shark pulled out a gun and rested it on his leg. "How many niggas have been beat to death in this house? Hmp," he pressed for an answer.

"I don't know," said Prince.

"Three."

"What about Jerry?" said AJ.

"He died at the hospital. Okay, we'll count him. Four," said the shark. "How many niggas been shot in this house?"

"I don't know."

"Five." The shark looked at AJ. No corrections. "Five been shot. Right where you're sitting now." He stared at Prince for several moments, his fingers ominously tapping the gun. "Cousin, I genuinely don't know what I'm going to do with you. One part of me says you can't kill your own cousin. Another part of me says this is business. If your cousin crosses the line, you have to kill him. Otherwise, business will suffer."

He looked around at his bodyguards. "Otherwise, niggas start thinking lines were made for crossing. Too many lines get crossed, and my boss—whoever he is. I know he some cracker sittin' behind a desk somewhere—may start thinking I don't have a handle on things. We can't have that in *Mayhem*. Everybody agree?"

Everyone, but Prince nodded.

"Cousin, I've been more than fair with you. Everybody in *Mayhem* pays taxes. But *you* don't pay taxes. I gave *you* an exemption. *Gave* you an exemption. And why is that, Prince? Because of blood." He frowned his face. "I let you and your little posse do business," he shook his head and fluttered his hands, "wherever and whenever you wanted. And this is how you repay me? Nigga, this is how you repay me? You are driving around in a fifty thousand dollar SUV because of me!" he yelled.

"Let's smoke this nigga," said AJ.

The shark looked at AJ like he had lost his mind. "Nigga, you gone kill somebody in my family? In *my* family?" he said, pressing his finger against his own chest.

AJ looked to be straining to keep his pants dry.

"Watch your mouth, AJ. You got potential, but you gotta stay alive long enough to reach it. You feel me?"

AJ answered with his defeated eyes.

The shark looked at Prince. "Now, if anybody's killing Prince, it's me." He looked at Prince a few seconds. "You haven't once asked what this is about. Tells me you know what it's about. Where's my special hoe?"

"I don't know."

The shark bent over in his chair, resting both elbows on his meaty legs. "You're not knowing a lot tonight. My disciples are looking at me, wondering how I'm going to handle a nigga taking my special hoe. Now, Prince, this is the last time I'm going to ask you. If you tell me you don't know where my hoe is, I'm going to shoot you in the chest." The shark looked past Prince. "One of you get the block."

Prince's eyes couldn't conceal his fear. A couple of days ago he had asked Samira to shoot him in the chest. He had even tried to help her do it. But he had been a different man then. A desperate man eaten up by guilt, and convinced that he could free himself and Samira by letting her kill him. That insane moment was gone.

He couldn't see it, but he heard someone pushing the block into the room. He had seen it before. It was a big rectangular block of wood on wheels that they used to catch bullets that went through the people who were shot while sitting in the chair.

The shark pointed the gun at his cousin's chest. "Where's my hoe?"

"I took her home."

"You took *my* hoe to your house?"

"No. I took her home to her family. She's back in Chicago."

The shark's fat face suddenly took on the look of an animal's head mounted to a wall. Finally, his jaws jiggled. He lowered the gun, then raised it again. "You did what?" he yelled.

"I took her back home. It was my fault what y'all did."

"Y'all?" The shark looked around at his bodyguards. "Y'all? Nigga, you were first in line. What you mean y'all?"

"You right," Prince admitted sadly. "What I did was wrong. This whole thing is my fault. I did this to her." Prince looked into his soul, remembering her as she was before this. He remembered what she told him in the hotel room.

I shared my dreams with you, Prince. Do you know why? I knew you were a criminal. I knew you did bad things. But I shared my dreams with you because I saw something in you. I saw something more than a criminal. I saw a handsome, smart guy who had potential to be good. I saw someone worth saving.

The shark looked at Prince's gaze. He wasn't there. The shark's mouth opened on his full face. "What the—? This nigga in love. He's in love with my hoe." His big body bounced up to its fat feet. He walked back and forth looking at Prince as though he had two heads. "Prince? A hoe? A junkie? My *junkie* hoe? How in ghet-to hell did this happen?"

Prince left his memories. He looked up. His fear was gone. He had done the right thing in taking Samira home. He'd never forget the looks on her parents' faces. He'd never forget how Samira's sister fell to her face on the front lawn and cried while holding onto her sister's ankles.

Prince's fear was gone because he remembered the Voice in the dope house. *I will send you. You will help the others. Be strong and of a good courage. Do not be afraid, nor be dismayed, for the Lord your God is with you wherever you go.*

"You're not going to kill me," said Prince.

The fat killer stopped pacing. "Not until you tell me how a player fell in love with a dope hoe. How does something like that happen?" He looked at his bodyguards in the back. "Told you she was special," he jabbed his finger in the air. "District one. Grande Champagne." He looked at Prince. "What got you? The big words? How she enunciates? Those strange eyes? Those pouty lips? The hair?"

Prince looked up.

The shark cussed. "The hair? Prince!" he yelled, knowing that he had to kill his cousin. "You stupid—what were you thinking?"

"I went to yo' Oliver house to preach the gospel. I didn't know Samira was gone be there, but she was. When I saw her, God started talkin' to me."

"God started talking to you when you saw my hoe?"

"She's not yours, Sonny. She belongs to God. The other junkies belong to God, too. And Samira's not a hoe. And you're not going to kill me."

"I'm not?" He tapped the gun against his thigh.

"No. No one's going to kill me until God is through with me."

Sonny stood there percolating in anger. "I think God's through with you." He lifted the gun.

"God called me to save his junkies. The Lord is with me. You can't kill me." Prince's voice was low, without bravado, but without fear. He had heard from God. He knew he did.

The bodyguard who had stood on his other side walked over to the shark and whispered in his ear. Sonny bobbed his big head. "The Lord? I knew you were doing Bible studies with those church dudes. But nobody told me you had gone crazy." He paused. "The white dude's got a daughter. A pretty little thing from what I hear. They say her face is white, but from the neck down she's as black as Beyonce. That true?"

Prince's eyes flashed a murderous look. "Keep yo' hands off her."

He had no sooner gotten the words out of his mouth before his cousin's gun came down hard on the side of his head. "Does it look like you're in any position to be telling me what to do?" he yelled. "You better listen to me, Prince. "You took my hoe. You better give me another one. Just as white. Just as fine. And she better be from district one. Or I swear to the God who told you to take my hoe that I will kill you, cousin or not.

"Another thing, *Octavius.* You and God want my junkies? You can have 'em. You think that Bible you preach can change these dope addicts? Go right ahead. Matter of fact, I'm calling you to the ministry. You work for me. You're now my dope house preacher." Sonny looked at him with hatred. "You like junkies, huh? Here's the deal. You want to stay alive? I'm putting the word out that if anyone sees you anywhere other than one of my dope houses or on your way to one, you're dead. Ten thousand dollars to anyone catches you straying from your calling. How's that for ministry? Is that what you and your God had in mind?"

Sonny Christopher sat down hard on his chair. "Get the sticks and show my cousin we mean business."

Prince knew what *the sticks were.* They were short. About two-feet long and two inches in diameter. The Vice Boys used them to beat people into submission. They usually didn't hit you in the head unless they were planning to beat you to death. They'd take their time beating you. Sometimes they'd do this several times over several days.

Oh, God, I did what You told me to do, he prayed.

The four bodyguards stood around Prince.

Sonny looked at his cousin and saw only a nigga who had crossed the line. "I want to make sure we understand one another. You live in my dope houses from now on or you die. You bring me my Brandy. District one. Or you die. How you get my new Brandy without getting yourself killed for leaving your new ministry is your problem." He hit him again with the gun and sat down. "Now give this nigga thirty seconds of school. Don't hit him in the head or face. He gotta replace my hoe. He can't do that if we put him on the block looking like Frankenstein."

AJ started the thirty seconds across Prince's back.

Chapter 13

The angel's intense light went before him and cleared the room of its ugly trespassers. He landed beside the bed and stood over the daughter of God. She had only recently left the kingdom of darkness. She was a babe in Christ. Yet she had already distinguished herself as a mighty warrior of intercession.

The angel looked at the damaged shell of flesh in which this warrior was trapped. He noted the irony of the woman's broken condition and her value to the kingdom of God. Truly, the Creator had chosen the weak things of the world to confound the mighty. He gently put his hand on her head. *You are more loved and more valuable than you know, dear Rosa. You have answered God's call of intercession. You have entered labor with God.*

The angel pulled his hand back. He looked at her intently. *Never stop, dear Rosa. Never stop.* He walked around to the head of the bed. He placed each hand on a shoulder and pressed down. "The burden of the Lord," he said twice. Then he bent down to her right ear. "Kim," he whispered, and left.

Rosa had been feeling heavy all day. It began the moment she awakened. *Kim!* The name had echoed in her mind like it had been shouted in a valley and was bouncing off a surrounding wall of mountains.

She had prayed for her for fifteen minutes. The heaviness didn't lift. She prayed again. The heaviness increased. She prayed more. But the more she prayed, the heavier she felt the burden to pray for Kim. She could feel it in her shoulders.

After her mother gave her some water, she sat in her wheelchair and cried. "I don't know what's going on with Kim, Lord, but whatever it is, help her. I feel like she's in great danger. I feel like the devil's trying to steal the will of God for her life. Precious Jesus, whatever the devil is planning, stop it. Make it blow up in his face."

***

"In the devil's face? The devil? She's threatening the very face of our lord Satan?"

Contemptus saw in the rookie's face that he had no idea how stupid his question was. He was actually waiting for an answer. "Annus," he began, with all the excitement of a man who had to find a way to carry a buffalo, "do you remember your dance with the fireball?"

"Yes."

"Do you remember the scorching?" He looked at Annus's wounds. They were no longer raw, but he was still a burnt mess.

How could I forget it, you pompous peacock of a demon? "Yes."

"Think, Annus. Whose face is threatened?" He crinkled his lips and tilted his head a little. "Hmm?"

"Me? Why my face? How did my face get in this? She said—"

A demon standing before them turned around in a sneer. "I'm sorry. Our master, Annihilation, is talking too loud for me to clearly hear your gibberish. Maybe you should tell him to shut up, or perhaps you can talk louder."

"Shut up, Annus," Contemptus demanded in a whisper.

Annihilation's countenance was fattened with the fresh death of a toddler who had been killed by a stray *Mayhem* bullet. But how could he savor the taste of the child's death when there were Christians like Rosa around? It took everything in his massive body to not spin on his heels and simply stare at the wretched saint in morbid fascination. How had she become such a menace in only a month or so? *She's in a wheelchair. Why doesn't she just watch television?*

Then there was the humiliation of the sudden appearance of that blasted angel and his hideous light. What were the rules of this war anyway? One moment it was hand to hand combat. Demon versus angel. Army versus army. Sometimes the darkness won. Sometimes the light won. But then there were the so-called Christian weapons of warfare.

He didn't agree in the slightest way with the favor the enemy afforded his dirt when they used what he called the weapons of their warfare. *Prayer. Fasting. Acts of righteousness. Walking in love.* The next thought twisted his mouth in scorn. *Forgiveness.* Why should such power be released on their behalf just because they forgave someone?

The whole premise of the so-called weapons of warfare context was unfair. A context created to give the enemy's dirt the advantage. But unfair though it was, it was something Annihilation understood. Keep the dirt from their weapons—win. Don't keep them from their weapons—lose.

But this all went out the window when a single angel could show up and clear his army without so much as even acknowledging their presence. The whole thing was a charade. A farce. Another proof of the enemy's deceitful nature.

The general snapped out of his thoughts and focused on the demons before him. "For some unfathomable reason, the dog of heaven has chosen this pathetic," he searched for the word, "jelly fish to take Kim. What makes my dark blood boil is not so much that the enemy wants Kim. That's what he does. He interferes." Annihilation yelled, "It's that he's using such a weak vessel. He's trying to humiliate me! He's sending a message. He's trying to show that the weakest child of God can defeat the greatest dark power. We cannot let this happen. Do you hear me?"

"Yes, master," the army bellowed in unison.

"This is the second time I told you Rosa must be stopped." He glared from one end of the hundred-demon army to the other. "I will not tell you again." With that, he left.

***

Annihilation's demons looked hungrily at the house. They had to come up with some way to get her. The angel with the prayer burden had left, and there were no others on the premise.

"What are we waiting for?" asked Annus.

"You're right, Annus," said Contemptus. "You still have some hair left from your scorching. Why don't you show us how they do it in San Francisco?"

"I was just—"

"You were just assuming that the enemy's not there because you can't see them. But God's not like us. He doesn't show his hand. He deals with us the same way he deals with his own children. It often looks like he's nowhere around." He sucked his teeth, making a popping sound. "They have to walk by faith. We have to walk by faith. Everybody has to walk by faith."

"Demons don't walk by faith. I don't understand," said Annus.

"Of course, you don't."

Contemptus was correct. Surrounding Diane's and Rosa's little house in a cloak of invisibility was an army twice their size. They weren't there to keep away the tempting demons—they had a right to be there. The angels were there for those demons who would take things further than mere temptation.

On the opposite side of the home, directly across from the demonic army, but out of their sight was Adaam-Mir and Myla.

"Is this true, what Annihilation says? Is the Lord sending him a message?" asked Adaam-Mir.

"Yes."

Adaam-Mir pondered the implications of this action. "Why do we do this? Why do we tell Satan what we are doing?"

"Part of it is to prove his impotence."

"Impotence?"

Myla knew what thoughts occupied Adaam-Mir's silence. "He doesn't look impotent, does he?"

Adaam-Mir didn't want to say anything complimentary of the devil. He didn't answer.

"Adaam-Mir, this is not a contest of equals."

"I know this." The angel's words were full of conviction. "But he has done so much harm."

"And he will do so until the time appointed. Until then, the Creator will continue to patiently display His eternal plan to His creation. Angels. Demons. People. Everyone must see His works until the times of testings are over."

"But does this not give Satan an advantage? Rosa and Kim. Annihilation knows that Rosa is praying for Kim."

Now Myla allowed a slight smile. "What advantage does the tree have by knowing it will be cut down?"

"The enemy is not a tree."

Myla nodded. "In the Garden of Eden, the Lord told Satan that the time would come when he would bruise our Lord's heel, but that He would bruise Satan's head. How did that help Satan? Was he able to stop this from happening?"

"No."

"The Lord promised Abraham that He would make of him a father of many nations. He told him that his seed would be in bondage for four hundred years and afterward be delivered. Was Satan able to stop our blessed Creator?"

"No."

"The Lord declared openly that the Savior would be born in Bethlehem. Was Satan able to stop His birth?"

"No."

"Was he able to stop His resurrection?"

"No."

"Is he able to stop His second coming?"

"No."

"Adaam-Mir, the blessed book tells us in Revelation that at the time of the end one angel will lay hold of the dragon, that serpent of old, who is the Devil and Satan, and will bind him with a great chain and cast him into the abyss until the Great White Throne Judgment."

"One angel," said Adaam-Mir, thoughtfully. After a long pause, he asked, "Then how is this imposter able to cause such harm?"

"With human authority. Usually, he gets his way by what his servants do or by what God's servants fail to do. It's rare that he can use raw power to do anything. He depends on delegated or leftover authority."

"And Rosa and Kim?" Adaam-Mir asked.

"It doesn't make a difference what the devil knows or doesn't know. You recall in the blessed book where it says of the servants of God, "We see through a glass, darkly. And we know in part and prophesy in part?"

The angel brightened under the load of their discussion. He loved the blessed book. "Yes. That is 1 Corinthians 13."

"Adaam-Mir, think about it. God's children have the Holy Spirit, and *they* know in part and *they* see through a glass darkly. If the glass is dark for those with the Holy Spirit, how dark must that glass be for the *prince* of darkness? He's not as smart as he thinks he is, and he's not as powerful as people think he is.

Adaam-Mir looked at the ferocious army of demons peering at Rosa's house. They were like hungry beasts waiting for the slightest opening. "My brother, I know the Creator is all powerful. I know we win in the end. But look at them, how they're looking at the house. What about now? What will happen to Rosa and Kim *now*?"

Myla gripped the angel's shoulder. "This is war, Adaam-Mir. We will know when we know."

***

Kim seethed in silent fury as she walked toward the *Mayhem* parking lot. One side of the lot belonged to the Vice Boys. It had an assortment of late model cars and shiny, older cars that had been restored. The Vice Boys liked chrome and big rims. Even the late model cars were made up like this.

The grown man riding the little kid bike circling her was the reason Kim was boiling. What was it about black men that made them so disrespectful of women? They felt like they could just say anything to you. If you tried to smile them off, they interpreted the smile as giving them some play. If you ignored them— Then you got a nappy head, raggedy mouth dude with sleep in his eyes riding a kiddie bike in circles around you as you walked.

"Yeah, girl, I think I seen you in a video."

I seen you. Kim huffed at the bad grammar. The parking lot seemed to be a mile away. She looked at it and wondered what new comments she'd get from the crowd of guys standing around their cars. Already she saw that a few of them were looking at her like she was a piece of meat on a buffet table. *I hate this place,* she thought.

The guy stopped circling Kim. He sat on the low seat and walked the bike as he admired her butt. "I know you didn't put those pants on without help. You greased yo' legs, didn't you? I know you did."

Kim kept walking, but when she didn't hear him say anything else, she glanced over her shoulder. The last thing she wanted was him touching her. He smiled a bad smile. She sped up her gait.

"Girl, oh, girl. Yo' name Kim, ain't it? You need to slow down. 'Cause that lil' wigglin' action you got goin' on when you walk fast make me wanna bite 'cha."

Kim was no stranger to this kind of behavior from black men. She was from Baltimore, and they acted a fool up there, too. But she was a stranger to being in a place like *Mayhem*. There was something about this place that made her feel like she was in an alien land that just happened to be in Atlanta.

It was run by drug dealers and killers, and there was always something going on. People shooting up heroin on the steps, or even in broad daylight. Prostitutes earning money in the darkness of the stairwells. Fights. Shootings. But the worst thing was these people acted like this stuff was normal.

She thought of her having to step over a passed out man—he didn't look dead—at the bottom of the steps to get out of the building. Then she runs into this fool on a bike. What a choice, stay in Baltimore with an abusive boyfriend or stay with her cousins in a place named *Mahem Courts*.

"J-Dawg, I got this." The man in the parking lot motioned to the man on the bike to get lost. The man turned the little bike in the other direction and started trying to ride it on one wheel. He wasn't good at it.

Kim watched the man who sent away the guy on the bike. She watched the man get up from leaning against a car. It was on the Vice Boys' side of the lot. He walked towards her car. When she committed to coming his way and not trying to get in through the passenger door, he leaned his back against the door.

Kim kept walking toward her car. What else could she do?

"Kim, right?"

The guy wasn't like the guy on the bike. He at least didn't have to look in a dictionary to find out what a comb and soap and water was. His shirt was unbuttoned all the way down, but it did actually fit. His muscles pushed against his t-shirt, and she could see that his waist was small. Lord knows she didn't try to look inside his mouth, but she did. His teeth were pretty and straight. Were it not for how he had approached her, she would've thought he was good-looking. No, she would've declared him good-looking.

Kim folded her arms. She tilted her head in irritation. "Yes. My name is Kim. Are you going to let me get in my car?"

"I'm Tony. Some people call me Pretty Tony. Some people call me P.T." He chuckled confidently. "But you can call me tonight if you want to."

Kim had seen it all before. Actually, she'd seen it in her boyfriend. Pretty face. Hard body. Cruel heart. Not interested. "Can I get in my car?"

"Lot of brothas been talkin' 'bout you. I told 'em to chill 'cause I was gone holler at you."

Fine or not, Kim couldn't believe the audacity of this guy. Her expression showed what she was thinking. "Okay, I'll consider myself hollered at by Pretty Tony. Can I get in my car now?" She reached for the door.

His hand slid around hers. She was going to yank her hand free, but this pretty face had eyes of ice. Her boyfriend had the same kind of eyes. She knew Tony's friends were watching. It probably would not be a good idea to disrespect him in front of them.

"Tony, can I please get in my car? And will you please tell your friends to not accost me any more? I have a boyfriend. I'm just here for a few weeks until I take care of some things."

He looked down at the hand he held captive. It was soft. Weak. He could break her hand just by squeezing if he wanted to. "That's cool that you got a boyfriend. But we got rules in Mayhem, Kim."

Kim was not only humiliated. She was afraid. She felt like she was standing before her boyfriend, Richard. Helpless. Wanting to say no, but knowing there was a painful price to pay for saying no. She tried to not let her fear show on her face. Richard could seemingly smell her fear. She imagined this guy Tony had the same gift.

"What rules?"

"You gotta get yo' lovin' from Mayhem, baby."

Now she knew she had to get in the car. "I have a boyfriend, Tony. I don't want another one. Please let me in my car."

"That plan's not on the menu."

She pulled her hand from his and called upon every ounce of strength in her body to look him in his eyes. But that's as far as she could get. She couldn't say anything.

"Plan A is Pretty Tony."

She looked up at him and shook her head. Kim found her voice. "I have a boyfriend." She was proud of herself. Her voice was stern. More stern than it had ever been with Richard.

Tony stood up straight. She didn't know he was that tall. He casually pulled his shirt to the side. Kim tried unsuccessfully to not be terrified at the gun.

"Plan B's not a good one, Kim. You need to make up yo' mind whether you family or not. Family get treated a whole lot better than visitors."

How did these kinds of guys always find her? Was there something on her that attracted abuse? *No,* she told herself, *it's not me. There's nothing wrong with me. It's these people. There's something wrong with them, not me.*

Kim wanted to be strong. A blanket of fear dropped on her when she remembered the last time she stood up to Richard. She ended up beaten senseless, raped, and in the hospital. Her courage dropped to the broken asphalt ground beneath her trembling feet. She had to find a way to get away from this man. "Can you give me some time to think about it?"

"Kim, look at me." She saw the monster behind the mask. "Look at those niggas behind you."

She looked behind her. Maybe ten guys were looking at them as though they were at the movies.

"You know what they waitin' on? They waitin' on you to make up yo' mind. If you don't want Pretty Tony...." He shrugged his shoulders and flashed those pretty white teeth. "Well, if you don't want Pretty Tony, Pretty Tony can't help you."

Kim was so afraid and confused she could've passed out. But where would that get her? She shuddered at the thought and tried to will the queasiness from her stomach, chest, and head.

Tony had been through this before many times. He knew exactly what he was doing. He knew exactly what the frightened woman in front of him was thinking. He spoke softly, reassuringly. "Kim, all you gotta do is show we cool. We can get to know each other better later."

Kim knew if she asked this man what he wanted her to do, he would see this as weakness. It was Richard all over again. She looked around. She was in the middle of *Mayhem.* They could gang rape her right here in the parking lot and no one would help her. No one would call the police.

She looked into his eyes, trying not to look submissive. "What do you want me to do?" She was sickened at the sound of her question.

"Not a whole lot, baby. Just press that body up next to mine and put my hands where they belong. Let Pretty Tony taste that tongue fo' a minute. Everything be cool. You go on do what you have to do, and we can holler later."

Kim felt what little world she had left after Richard being pulled from her like a roof in a hurricane. She was totally vulnerable. She had to do this to save herself. She closed her eyes and opened her mouth.

"Get away from my car."

Tony looked at the crowd of dudes looking at them. "Really?" he said. He stared at her for several long seconds, crazy thoughts going through his mind. "I was hopin' you was smarter than that. I'll be seeing you."

Kim thought the moment he walked away, she'd jump in her car. Instead, she stood there with her trembling hand on the handle, tears rushing one after the other down her cheeks and across her closed, trembling lips.

Finally, she opened the door and gently sat down. She locked the doors and doubled over. She was proud of herself that she had stood up to this man. But she was terrified at his threat. What did he mean by he'd be seeing her again? And what was Plan B?"

***

He had been watching Kim from the blue mist she and Tony had been standing in. The demons around the man talking to her knew the danger of the mist. It was like a foreboding sky full of potential lightning bolts. A remote chance one would hit them. Most likely, it wouldn't.

The children of Adam didn't let dark clouds keep them indoors. The demons of *Mayhem* couldn't let a blue mist keep them out of the parking lot. Besides, this was *Mayhem*. They weren't used to restrictions. But they were careful to not let the mist touch them. No need in being reckless.

But they weren't careful enough.

Lightning jumped out of the mist. Its name was Enrid.

The servant of darkness towered over the terrified woman. Enrid saw and felt her fear. It tore at his heart. His task restrained him from answering the righteous anger that rose within him.

He looked at the man with fiery eyes, thinking of the day when the Lord and His angels would appear in the sky in flaming fire to take vengeance upon the ungodly. This man who called himself Pretty Tony had no idea of such a day. He had no idea that he was the angel who killed King Herod when he accepted praise worthy only of the Creator. He also had no idea that, like Herod, his sins could demand payment now. The Lord owed mercy to no man.

The angel had seen the man's intention when Kim had told him to get away from her car. The scene was horrible, disgusting. He couldn't let that happen. Rosa's prayers had sent him there to stop it. That's when he made his move.

Enrid shot out of the mist with his sword and dagger in hand. His dagger found a belly, a neck, and two backs before the demons knew they were under attack. Pride, Violence, Hatred of Women, and Rape lay on the ground. Hatred of Women was the last of the four to go.

He put his hand to his neck and looked at the black liquid. "I hate women," he gurgled, and dropped his face hard on the ground.

Task accomplished.

But the element of surprise was gone. The demons had rushed to the fight from behind Enrid, cutting him off from the mist. They fought him farther away from the safety of his exit into the mist. Suddenly, the fighting stopped.

Enrid was surrounded inside a thick circle of demons. He looked up. The sky above him was thick with the blackness of Mayhem's evil spirits. He was trapped inside a dome of vicious evil.

***

This was the moment Rosa's prayer burden for Kim had gotten its heaviest. It's the moment she prayed, "Lord, whatever he's planning, let it blow up in his face."

***

Enrid turned in a tight circle. Hundreds of eyes peered at him.

Out of the top of the dome two spirits descended. They weren't close, but close enough for him to see who they were. Slavery and Annihilation.

"Slavery, is this who I think it is?"

"Yes, Annihilation. It's the great angel, Enrid. The Lord's *special* warrior."

"That job comes with great hazards. He seems to have gotten himself into a special mess," said Annihilation.

An angel stood up out of the blue mist. He hurled the golden object at the demons. It was a small container that held the precious mixture of Rosa's prayers and tears for Kim. The concentration of evil was formidable, but Rosa's tears added potency to the bomb.

BOOM!

The force of the blast hit the dome, scattering demons in every direction. The lucky ones awakened to find that the extent of their injuries was ringing in their ears and damaged hearing. Those not as lucky would have to learn to get by with one or more less limbs. And those not lucky at all were scattered in parts like the aftermath of a trailer park hit by a tornado.

Enrid heard the explosion, but felt none of its effects. Prayer was a friend, not an enemy.

"Enrid."

Enrid turned.

"Trin," he said, excited not only that he had been rescued, but that he hadn't seen Trin in a while.

"Come. Quickly. It's Sharon. She needs us."

Chapter 14

A second blue mist flowed out of Rosa's bedroom and down the streets like a new river that wouldn't be denied. For some reason, the thought of a second attack had never come to mind. The demons hadn't anticipated that she would pray for someone else. A couple of demons followed the new mist until they were certain and relieved it was going out of their neighborhood.

"Somebody else's problem. Let's get back," said one demon to the other.

The mist separated into two rivers of blue. One stopped at the Styles'ss home.

***

Barbara looked at Sharon's plate. "Is that all you're going to eat?"

Today Sharon had completed her first three-day fast ever with only water. "Yes. This is it," she answered with a smile. "Jonathan said once you hit the three-day mark in a fast, you need to be careful coming off."

"Wow, Sharon, I can hardly believe you went three days without eating," said Andrew.

"Neither can I," said Barbara. "Surely you can at least have some more salad?"

Sharon got a little more for her mom's sake.

Barbara smiled, and Sharon smiled, too.

"What did you fast for?" asked Andrew.

"That may be private," said Edwin.

"No, it's okay, Dad. I can talk about it. I was fasting for more revelation. Jonathan said if I wanted to develop my prophetic gift, I needed to spend a lot of time in prayer and fasting and deliberately listening for God's voice."

"Well, I hope you don't go overboard with not eating," said Barbara. "I'm sure God would rather have a healthy prophetess than one sick from malnourishment."

Her statement didn't come across as critical, just motherly. Sharon posted a little smile and chewed on a cherry tomato. She glanced at Edwin and lowered her head again as she chewed. "Dad, I did get something."

Edwin stopped chewing, then resumed. He dabbed at his mouth with a napkin. "Oh."

"Yeah, I had a really vivid dream."

"Tell us about it," said Edwin.

"I saw two white sheep with a big, hypodermic needle hanging from both of them wandering in thick bushes. A pack of wild dogs jumped on them. Suddenly, another sheep, a black one, fought off the dogs and carried the sheep to safety. Then the black sheep was tied to a chair by dogs. The dogs beat it with sticks and put it in a filthy house."

Barbara dabbed her mouth. "Edwin?" she said, with bright eyes and the slightest trace of a grin.

He arched an eyebrow and tilted his head. "Well...."

"Then a bloody lamb carrying a big sword rescued the black sheep from the filthy house and put it in a beautiful mansion."

"Wow, Sharon. Cool. Can I give it a shot?" asked Andrew.

Barbara's eyes crinkled a *Saved by your son* message to Edwin. She was sure there was a huge grin under her husband's expression of thinly veiled gloating.

"Okay," said Sharon.

"Jesus is the Lamb of God," said Andrew, and stopped.

Sharon waited. "That's it?"

"That's all I got."

She poked out her neck. "Really? Jesus is the Lamb of God? *Okaaaay.* What a remarkable gift of interpretation you have," she joked.

"Hey, I never said I was a prophet."

"That's okay. You're still on my *I love you* list." Sharon looked at Edwin.

"Oou!"

"What?" said Sharon to Andrew, who looked like he had just discovered the cure for cancer.

"The bloody one with the sword is Jesus." He looked at Sharon, shaking his head with raised eyebrows. "The *blood* of Jesus."

Sharon tilted her head to one side, then the other, and nodded. "There may be room on the king's payroll for you after all, Andrew. I was thinking of that. But what about the other sheep?"

"What about Prince?" said Barbara, then put a piece of gravy covered veal into her mouth and chewed without looking at anyone at the table.

"Prince?" said Sharon.

"Don't you recall his story, Dear? When he and Holly joined us for dinner? He rescued that poor girl from those awful men. They certainly were acting like animals."

The room went silent as everyone thought about how much sense this made.

Barbara pushed her fork through a bit of her salad and dipped it ever so lightly in the small spot of dressing on her plate. "There was a black sheep and a white sheep. The black sheep rescued the white one. Octavius is a black man. He rescued a white girl. The hypodermic needle could represent dope. There is that element in his neighborhood. Seems to add up to me," she added as an afterthought. She put the salad in her mouth and tightened her lips in a quick smile to her daughter.

Sharon sat up straight on her chair. Her mouth didn't drop open in surprise, but it almost did. Edwin's did, however. Andrew looked at his dad. Edwin closed his mouth and looked at Sharon.

"Mom, I think that's it," she said, excitedly. "I had forgotten about Prince's story. Dad, what do you think?" she asked in a rushed voice.

"Sounds like you've got yourself an interpreter."

"Whoa, Mom, you hit it out of the park," Andrew gushed. "Sharon, you've got some competition."

"Sounds more like she's got herself a new team mate," said Edwin, looking at his wife with a soft smile.

Barbara looked around the table and tried to simply smile politely in response to the praise. But she felt something happening to her heart, like a casing was being cracked off of her, exposing a deep thirst for acceptance and affirmation. It was silly.

"Lucky guess," she said.

Sharon's eyes watered. "It wasn't a lucky guess, Mom. It was the Holy Spirit. God spoke to you."

"No, Sharon, God wouldn't talk to me like that. It was just a lucky guess." She felt her face fill with the emotions of the possibility that God may have spoken to her.

Sharon looked tenderly at her mom. She got up and went to her and wrapped her arms around her from behind, resting her face against her mom's. "You're such a good mother. I love you. God loves you."

"I love you, too, Sharon. What a sweetheart."

Edwin and Andrew were used to Sharon's spontaneous gushings. They both were periodically on the receiving end of them. Yet Andrew still sat there wondering if he was supposed to do something now. Hug his mom? Say something nice? Smile?

Barbara looked at Andrew. He smiled.

Sharon sat down.

"Something bad has happened. Or is going to happen," said Barbara.

"What?" said Sharon.

Barbara took a tentative step. "I mean if the dream...." She smiled apologetically. "I'm probably wrong."

"What, Mom? Say it," said Sharon.

"The black sheep was beaten and confined to a filthy house. I'm sure those guys he stopped from assaulting that girl are still angry with him."

Sharon turned in alarm to Edwin. "Dad, you and Jonathan haven't heard from him in weeks. Something's wrong. We have to do something."

"Wait a minute, Sharon. Let's make sure there's a problem before we try to fix it," said Edwin. *And if there were a problem, what could they do?*

"I can call him," said Sharon.

Barbara remembered her sniffing Octavius's chest. "That's not a good idea, Sharon."

"Dad, you can call him."

"That's a better idea," said Barbara.

"We've been calling him. He doesn't answer."

"That could mean anything," said Sharon, her alarm had now turned to fear, and it was in her face.

"Calm down, Honey," said Barbara. "It could mean he doesn't want to talk."

"Or that he can't," said Sharon. "Dad."

"Okay," he said. He called. Everyone watched him, waiting anxiously. No answer. He looked at Sharon. "Sorry, Honey. If he doesn't pick the phone up, we can't talk to him."

"God has spoken to us about him. What are we going to do?" said Sharon.

"We're going to pray for him," said Edwin.

"Pray?" said Sharon.

"Yes. We're going to pray for him. Jonathan will be back from London in a few days. If we can't reach him by time Jonathan returns, he and I will go down there and look for him."

In a few days? I hope he's not dead by then, thought Barbara. *For Sharon's sake, I hope he's not already dead. The poor girl has been through enough with Holly.*

In a few days? thought Sharon. *I led him to the Lord. He's my responsibility.* She thought about Holly. Holly had been in trouble and she didn't see it. If she had helped Holly, she'd still be alive. *I can't stand by and let Prince be hurt. I have to find him. I have to warn him.*

***

Prince sat in a tortured heap against the wall in the hallway of the first floor of his sister's building in *Mayhem*. It was dark inside and smelled like urine. He could've done without the urine. Its pungent assault was tearing his nose apart. But he welcomed the darkness. He didn't want anyone to see him like this.

The only part of his body that didn't hurt was the right side of his face. The Vice Boys had beaten every part of his body except his face and head with sticks. Sonny Christopher, his fat, muscled, Al Capone wannabe cousin, had hit him in the face twice with his gun. And some invisible nigga had tried to break his head back in the dope house.

It was a miracle he had made it from Sonny's building to his sister's building. *The pain was so bad.* Everything ached. He wondered if he had any broken bones. It felt like he did. It felt like his whole body was broken. He didn't know if he could make it up the stairs. And now that he could think a little more clearly, it probably didn't make sense to try. He needed to get away from *Mayhem.*

***

Kim's heart pounded against her chest. Her breaths were short and rapid. She told herself she wouldn't be afraid. She was tired of living like a victim. She had told that Pretty Tony dude off, hadn't she?

This didn't stop her from parking the car a block from where she needed to park. She could see the parking lot. It was full of people dancing to music coming from cars with speakers as large as refrigerators. She shook her head. What had she expected? *This was Mayhem.*

She could park her car as far away as possible from the Vice Boys' side of the parking lot. It was night, and only one of the four lights in the parking lot worked. Maybe they wouldn't recognize her. But probably they would. There was something about a car parking in the lot that mesmerized the Vice Boys. They'd stop whatever they were doing and study every approaching car until they knew it wasn't the cops—not that cops ever came into *Mayhem*.

From what Kim had been told, cops didn't sneak into *Mayhem*. Too dangerous, even for them. Their choice was a full invasion. But that line of reasoning did little to persuade Kim that the Vice Boys would ignore her car.

Oh, I wish I could just go home, she thought. But her crazy boyfriend had almost killed her the last time he beat her. She knew that if she ever returned home, her next beating would end with her in a coffin. She rubbed her left side, remembering the broken ribs. It was crazy Richard or Pretty Tony.

Kim lowered her head. Instant tears rolled down her face, a contrast of dark beauty and raw pain. "Oh, Lord, I don't know what to do. I don't have anywhere to go. I'm so afraid." She put her trembling hands on her lap and sat, looking anxiously into the darkness of *Mayhem's* night.

***

Playboy looked at the fatter of the two sisters. His nickname didn't belong with his face. Even he knew and admitted he was ugly. But in his mind, that's part of what made him awesome. Pretty Boy was Pretty Boy because he was pretty. But he was Playboy because even though he was ugly, he had tight game. More than once a fine girl had underestimated him because he was ugly. Then a little while later she was waving that white flag and begging for ugly love.

His lip turned up in an unattractive, confident snarl.

Shanice looked at the money on the wood and glass coffee table that had never seen coffee, but had seen a lot of weed. Playboy had tossed the money on the table and spread it out for effect. Fifty twenty-dollar bills.

"What you think, pretty girl?" said Playboy. "Get that hair done up fresh. Wrap a new skirt around that big booty. Like that red one you got."

She looked at him.

His ugly snarl turned into an ugly smile. "Yeah, I seen you. Long, red and black wrap-around skirt. All that leg showing when you walk." She had never waved the flag. But Playboy knew that was only because he had never given her the opportunity. He didn't ever see that happening. He wasn't against loving a big girl, but he wasn't into mountain climbing. "Saw you wearing that skirt one day. The wind whipped up and God have mercy, girl!" He turned his face from side to side a few times. "Flames were shootin' out. I almost called the fire department."

Shanice almost smiled involuntarily. But the sight of a thousand dollars in twenty-dollar bills on the table kept her face straight. "Why y'all paying so much if y'all not gone turn her out? I don't want my cousin to be no junkie."

"Girl, we ain't gone turn her. We just gone train her for a couple of days. That's all."

Shanice knew Playboy was lying. The Vice Boys wouldn't pay this much money if that's all they were going to do. They were going to make her cousin a junkie hoe. And they were asking her to set Kim up for a thousand dollars.

She looked at the extra-large, thick cloth bag and its drawstring. That's what they were going to put her in. She looked at the drug.

"Keep the bag here. Put the *E* in her drink. Call us. Somebody'll come get her." Playboy didn't like the way she was looking at the drug. "What you thinkin' 'bout, Shanice? What you want me to tell Sonny?"

The mention of Sonny's name tightened the vise on Shanice's egg shell of morality. What could she do? She could say no. They'd take their money back, raise her taxes, and beat her down. Then they'd take Kim and dare her and her sister to say anything. Or she could take the money. Either way, they were going to get her cousin.

She starting gathering the money, straitening the bills in her thick hand.

***

Kim's mother used to joke darkly that she didn't have a problem with depression. Her problem, she said, was the twenty minutes every other day that she wasn't depressed. What was she supposed to do with twenty minutes of daylight every other day?

Kim didn't want to end up a basket case like Mom. That's why she was irrationally afraid of the tight band of darkness she felt descending over her head. She looked out her left window and gasped.

An exceptionally white dove was flying in place at her window. Its feet gripped a piece of paper. The bird stared at her.

Rosa.

Kim was leaning as far to her right as possible without getting in the passenger seat. She watched the large, white bird clutching the paper close the remaining foot or so and fly right next to the window. Kim leaned upward. *Rosa?* Why had that name popped in her mind?

She and the bird stared at one another several seconds until it landed on the front of the car and looked at her through the windshield. Kim's mouth opened in astonishment when the bird spread his wings. They were way too large for a bird its size.

The bird screamed.

Kim screamed, covering her face and hiding her head between the steering wheel and the door.

She was shocked to hear a scream come from a dove—and she was sure it was a dove. But that's not why she screamed. She screamed because when the bird screamed, she saw it turn into something vicious and fly through the windshield.

Kim broke a nail trying to open the door to jump out. Her escape failed miserably. It would have been comical had she not been so terrified. She grabbed and clawed at everything on the door, but was too disoriented by fear to let herself out the car. Suddenly, the quietness of the inside of the car brought sense to her mind and tamed her fear. *How could a bird fly through the windshield?*

She looked up.

The dove looked at her through the thick glass, standing perfectly still on the car's hood.

Her head turned slowly around the car. She looked in the back seat. Then on the floor behind both seats. She looked up. The bird was still there and still clutching a piece of paper. It took off into the night. Kim watched it briefly, then looked curiously, then astonishingly, at the paper the bird had left.

Chapter 15

Inside Kim's car, the spirit of depression that had been pulling a tight band of darkness down over her head was in the fight of his life. He hadn't heard the angel's scream until he was all over him.

Thick, razor sharp claws. Long, pointed, penetrating beak. All ripping, tearing, puncturing the hapless demon with speed and ferocity that he had only heard about from others who had been butchered by angels looking like doves.

The evil spirit never considered for a moment to fight. What was it that was written in the cursed book? *He who seeks to save his life, the same shall lose it?* This was one of those moments. In a burst of dark adrenaline, the evil spirit tore itself from the creature that was stabbing and shredding him. It disappeared into the darkness of night, desperately hoping the blood-thirsty bird wasn't following.

***

Kim opened the car door without taking her eyes off the piece of paper that was pressed against her windshield. Her mouth was wide open for good reason. She picked up the paper, looked at it, reading some of its writing and looking up into the dark sky. She sat down in the car and shook her head.

"What...? Can't be," she said, when she read the underlined writing. *God scattering the enemy?* What were the odds that a bird would land on her car carrying a page from the Bible with this verse underlined? Was He telling her that he was going to scatter the enemy? She put the gear in *Drive.*

***

Pretty Tony bounced coolly to the strong bass that blasted from the *Alpine* speakers in his shiny, spotless, black *Classic Camaro.* Cool meant you didn't move too much. Just enough to get your groove on. His head bounced a little, turning from side to side. He slowly lifted both palms upward and motioned with his fingers for his long leg to catch up with where he was going.

The leg followed the magic that came from the palms of his hands. Pretty Tony glided in a tight circle. He always swore that with this move his feet never touched the ground. He dipped a shoulder, froze a pose, and gave three quick dips of his shoulder in the direction of a girl with more clothes off than on. She bounced herself next to and around him.

Pretty Tony put on his dark shades and crossed his arms loosely as the girl danced around him. They danced their way about a third of the way down the two lines of people. J. Cole was laying it on thick about what he was doing when he was up in New York. When the *Alpines* blasted out that the rapper was asking the Lord to follow him, it happened.

Pretty Tony snatched off his shades and looked up into the black sky and spread his arms wide. It was over. The crescendo. Sistah No-Clothes was on one knee, with an arm wrapped around one of his thighs. The small crowd went crazy.

SPLAT! SPLAT! SPLAT!

Eye. Eye. Nose.

Three heavy wads of nasty, white bird poop hit Tony's pretty face like mushy cruise missiles.

"Daaaaaaaaamn!" said a dude on the line, and broke out laughing hysterically.

Pretty Tony shook his head, then put his hands to his face. At first he didn't know what had happened. Then he heard the laughter and one of his boys call him Pretty Nasty. He scraped his face with both hands and slung the thick, warm liquid to the ground. "What the hell?"

The girl on his leg looked up, then hopped up. She backed away with a frown. "Aawww man, it ain't pretty, Tony."

SPLAT!

A wad exploded on her bare shoulder. She looked at it and cursed and stormed to a car.

SPLAT! SPLAT!

Two more found her before she cursed again and jumped inside the Charger.

Pretty Tony instinctively looked up into the sky.

SPLAT! SPLAT!

He screamed out a curse word and slung the mess to the ground and wiped his face with his shirt.

The revelers' laughter changed into astonished chuckles as they wondered at the powerful wads of bird poop that were finding dodging targets.

"Look!" somebody said.

Hundreds of white birds filled the sky, and it seemed that each one had diarrhea. Then the birds swooped on the partiers, chasing them to their cars. Those without cars ran towards their buildings.

Pretty Tony and the other Vice Boys sat in their shiny, restored cars. A Thunderbird. An Impala. A Cadillac De Ville. Two Mustangs, one a 1968 GT. A Cutlass. A 1980 Corvette. Others.

It was only a matter of seconds before it became apparent to the Vice Boys that these crazy birds had every intention of covering every inch of their cars in mess. The thing that sparked the squealing of tires was when a small rock dropped from the sky onto the windshield of the Cadillac. It tore out of that parking lot and every car followed hard.

The dove landed upon one of the nonworking light posts. The bird spread its wings and transformed into an angel. He looked in the direction of Kim.

***

Kim watched in awe as the crowd scattered. She put her hand to her face as the Vice Boys raced past her car. She approached the abandoned parking lot and parked. It was as though she had driven into some kind of energy field. Something was all around her. Something good. Something *good* in *Mayhem*.

Kim pressed the torn page of the Bible to her face, then kissed it. It didn't make sense, but somehow she knew that that lady Rosa had something to do with this. She had asked her to pray for her safety. *I guess she did. That has to be it,* she thought. *That's why her name popped into my mind when the bird appeared.*

Her phone rang.

It was Shanice. "Girl, where you at?"

"Almost there."

"Okay. What you gone drink? You want some of the root beer?" asked Shanice.

"I'm surprised there's some left. Yeah, that sounds good."

Shanice held the Liquid E guiltily in her hand. "Okay, girl."

Kim opened the car door and walked across the parking lot.

***

Prince grimaced and let out a pained breath. He opened his eyes and looked up into the beautiful face of a startled woman. He hadn't seen her before.

Kim looked into the dark corner at the man. It wasn't the guy she had seen earlier, slumped over and smelling like he had been baptized in liquor. This guy was younger, and good-looking. He was in the corner, but he didn't appear to be drunk or on drugs. His eyes were clear and lively. And, more importantly, he didn't look to be up to no good. He looked hurt.

You okay? Those were the words Kim heard in her mind. Then she heard some more words. *Are you some kind of T.V. fool? You are in Mayhem. You better get your behind up those stairs.*

"Hey, what's yo' name?" the man pushed the words out.

The man may as well have said, "Drop your pants." Kim rushed up the first short flight of stairs. She heard the man say, "What's yo' name? Don't go up there. Talk to me." Kim hurried up the second set of stairs and was halfway up the third set.

Her leg froze in the air. She looked at the white bird standing at the top of the stairs. It looked like the bird that was on her car. Kim slowly lowered her foot to the concrete. The bird spread its wings and looked at her.

What...is going on here? Kim tried to shoo the bird away.

It rose a few feet off the ground and flew in place. Slowly it made its way toward her in the air. When it was within four feet, it stopped. Its wings beat furiously, but its eyes focused intently on hers. It flew closer.

Kim went down one stair backwards.

It flew closer.

She went down another.

It flew closer.

She went down another.

This happened until she was back at the top of the first flight of stairs.

Kim looked inquisitively at the bird. *This could not be happening!* She turned and looked down the stairs. She couldn't see him, but she could hear him. That guy was still there. Or *someone* was there. She turned back to the bird. It was gone.

Kim went to the top of the second set of stairs. The bird was nowhere around. She stood there thinking. Connecting dots.

The bird at her car. Birds chasing away the Vice Boys. Now, a bird trying to keep her from going upstairs. *At least that's what it looked like.* She took tentative steps back down toward the bottom of the first set of stairs. She stopped on the middle step.

"You still there?" she asked nervously.

"Yeah. I'm not gone bother you. I just got a situation, that's all."

Kim could hear the pain in his voice more clearly now. "What's wrong?" she asked, on that same middle stair.

"Is yo' name Kim?"

Kim shook her head to herself. Partly in disgust. Partly in fear. *Every man in Mayhem knows my name.* "Yes."

"I thought so. Kim, you can't go upstairs."

"Why not?"

Prince pushed himself up and leaned heavily on the wall. He held his left side and came out of the dimly lit corner. "Because some bad people want to hurt you."

Kim felt her legs get wobbly. "Who wants to hurt me?"

"Same people who hurt me."

Whatever awe and elation Kim had felt when she parked her car in the Vice Boys abandoned parking lot was gone now. The torn Bible page that had warmed her face when she had pressed it against her face in the car now felt in her hand simply like debris.

"Who hurt you?"

"Help me, Kim. Please. I know you're a good person."

Kim went all the way to the bottom of the stairs. "Who hurt you? Who wants to hurt me?"

Prince knew he deserved the pain he felt. He deserved to be beaten with sticks. Hell, all the people he hurt, he deserved to be beaten with baseball bats. But this girl, she hadn't done anything to anyone. She didn't deserve what the Vice Boys had in mind. "You're a good person, Kim. I can see it in your eyes. I can hear it in your voice. It's why you came back downstairs. You didn't have to come back. You don't know me."

"Why does someone want to hurt me?"

"That's *Mayhem*, Kim. It doesn't like anything good. It doesn't like anything with life in it. It needs the Lord."

Kim's ears were sure this *Mayhem* man said *Mayhem* needed the Lord. But her mind had a hard time reconciling those words coming from this body. A ridiculous question bubbled up inside. "Are you some kind of preacher?"

"Yeah. *Some* kind."

Even in the darkness, Kim could see a little smile when he answered. "You have a church?"

"Lot of 'em." His shadow of a smile left. "Kim, you can't go upstairs. Yo' cousin done flipped you."

"But—"

"I heard the Vice Boys talkin' about you."

"My cousins wouldn't do that. We're family." Then the possibility of such a betrayal challenged Kim's idealism. "Family wouldn't do that."

"Kim, you're not family. You're not *Mayhem*. That's why they want you. Anyway, you can't really blame yo' cousins. They ain't got no choice. They stand in the way, they'll be cut down. That's *Mayhem*."

Kim stepped backward and leaned against the wall for support. What kind of place was this? Her mind raced at her non-options. She looked at the man, hoping he was wrong. Hoping he was for some sick reason making this up.

Prince saw fool's hope in her eyes. "Kim, if you walk upstairs, somebody's gone carry you out."

Kim was horrified. "Carry me out?"

"If you were ugly, somebody'll just put the glove to you."

She didn't know what this meant.

"Somebody with a glove on would knock you out. But if they fine like you, we," he paused, hating his old life, "*they'll* put you to sleep."

She stared at him as though he were a hooded executioner.

"Drug you, Kim. Put something in yo' drink. I know you heard of date rape drugs?"

"Put something in my drink?" She thought of Shanice's phone call. *The root beer.*

It was dark outside. It was dark in the hall where she was standing. It was suddenly getting dark in her soul. Kim felt her throat get tighter. She tried to pull air into her now constricted nostrils and throat. She opened her mouth and breathed. *Her cousin was trying to drug her.*

"You go upstairs, Kim, and *Mayhem's* gone have his way with you."

She looked at him with tears and a sick expression. "How do you know this?"

"I heard 'em talkin'—"

"No," she interrupted, "*how* do you know this stuff? Do you hurt people like this, too?" Her question sounded like she was expecting him to say yes, but hoping with all her heart that she was wrong. She thought she had heard kindness in his voice, but she had a PhD in being wrong about men. Could she be standing in a dark hallway talking with a violent rapist?

Prince hesitated. "Kim, I've hurt a lot of people. I deserve whatever bad comes my way. I can't take back none of the bad I've done. But...."

"But what?" she asked, feeling slightly less threatened by his honesty and remorsefulness.

"But then God saved me. Got filled with the Holy Ghost, too."

"The Holy Ghost? You got filled with the Holy Ghost?" She didn't know what to say to this. "I gotta get out of here?"

"You don't have nowhere to go."

"How do you know that? I have a car."

"Cause you in *Mayhem*. Anybody come to Mayhem don't have nowhere else to go. This the end of the world. Last stop."

She looked at him, shocked at the dark power of his words, and hopeful that they weren't true. At least not for her. *Call Rosa. She can help you.*

"Give me a ride out of here, Kim. I know some people who can help you." He saw she was hesitant. "I saw the Vice Boys leave. We gotta get out of here before they come back."

That's all he had to say.

"Come on," she said in a hurry.

Chapter 16

At first Prince couldn't believe it. His Mercedes SUV was still there. Parked in front of a crack house for a full day and no one had taken it. Then he saw the paper on the window.

That's why nobody took it. Vice Boys.

The paper read: Touch it, get smoked. VB

So they were good for something other than selling dope, kidnapping girls, and terrorizing their own community. But Prince knew that was just Sonny making sure he had a way to get him another girl.

He opened the door and got in. He shook his hurting head and smirked like a death row inmate who had found a way to cheat the warden out of an extra last meal before his execution. *Wait till that fat clown find out I took Kim.*

Then he smiled because he hadn't cheated the warden out of an extra plate of food. He had saved another woman from being ruined. Saving Kim was the best thing he had ever done. Better even than saving Samira. For he hadn't really *saved* her. He had merely picked up her barely-breathing body after he had pushed her in front of a truck. *His hero act was three years too late.*

It still felt good, though. He was showing God by his actions that he meant business. He hadn't just said a prayer. His heart had been changed. And he'd spend the rest of his life trying to show God that he loved Him for loving him and giving him another chance.

Prince looked out his window at that crack house the way Jesus had looked at His cross. He wasn't going to run away. *That fat fool made me a dope house preacher,* he defiantly thought. *You gone be sorry you ever did that. I'm gone preach like I'm John the Baptist, nigga.*

Prince reached for the door.

He never made it.

***

The great host of privileged angels surrounding the throne of God watched with great anticipation. Closest to the throne were seven mighty angels. Their might was in their knowledge of God, and their knowledge came from their closeness to His throne.

Another angel came and stood at the altar, holding a golden censer that hung from a golden chain. Much incense was given to him, so that he might add it to the prayers of those in Atlanta who had been groaning and crying out to God for deliverance. The angel lowered the golden censer onto the mercy scale without allowing the chain to touch it.

Another angel approached with a tiny, golden container, with a jewel for a top.

The great crowd of angels seemed to lean forward, focusing intently on the container.

"The prayers of the servant, Ebony Monroe, and the flock she serves at the Worldwide Apostolic Church of International Deliverance and Glory," said the angel with the tiny container. He poured its contents into the larger container on the mercy scale. The scale moved.

Booonnnggg!

The smoke of the incense, with the prayers of saints, went up before God from the scale.

"Apply the prayers," an angel yelled.

The first angel lifted the censer by its golden chain and flung it to the earth. Another angel who had been waiting for this moment for thirty years raced behind the scorched path to Atlanta.

Specifically, Oliver Street in *The Bluff.*

***

"Son of God."

Prince heard the words, but he felt them more. Deep inside of him, inside his soul and spirit. He felt as though the words were an actual person. The Person who had created him. He wanted to fall. He slumped to the right, across the stick shift.

Suddenly he was standing on a mountain and looking down into a valley of dry bones.

"What do you see, son of God?" asked the angel.

Prince turned toward the voice. His eyes widened.

"Do not be afraid. I have come from the presence of God. The prayers of your mother and the church she serves, and the prayers of others have reached the throne of He whom you serve. They demand an answer."

Prince looked intently at the angel before he was able to turn away. He looked to the left and right, then down into the valley. There were bones everywhere. Mounds and mounds of bones. "Bones. Nothin' but bones," Prince answered.

"This is *Mayhem*," said the angel. "Can these dry bones live?"

Prince looked more intently at the bones. Somehow he literally *felt* the dryness of the bones. That was his neighborhood. Where he had grown up. He knew how bad it was. And now he could feel how dry and lifeless his community was. He looked sadly at the angel. He said with tears, "No, Lord. These niggas too dry. They too dead. They can't live."

Suddenly, prince and the angel were passing through every home in *Mayhem*. Or every home was passing before them. He couldn't tell whether he was going or the pictures were coming. What was clear, however, was the spiritual condition of the people.

Prince fell to his knees under the weight of its sin. He heard cries and shrieks and groans. "What is that?" he asked the angel.

"It is the pain of sin. Look, man of God, what do you see?"

"I see some kind of monsters. A lot 'em. Everywhere. They're all over the people. They're all over my friends. They're eating them," he cried, his heart tearing in him. "I know these people."

"These are the two ruling spirits over *Mayhem* and *The Bluff*. Annihilation and Slavery. They must be stopped."

"How, Lord? How can those things be stopped. Can you stop them?"

"Come with me, son of God."

In a moment, Prince and the angel were inside a house in *The Bluff*. A girl sat on a sofa with her baby. She was rocking it in her arms and making funny faces at it. The girl couldn't be any more than fourteen or fifteen.

Something resembling a large bat descended through the roof and landed on the girl. It started biting her in the chest.

Prince jumped back. "Lord, do somethin'!"

Then dark shadows whizzed past him and the angel and entered the baby.

"What's goin' on? Can't you do somethin'? Lord, please!"

The angel looked solemnly at the son of God. "The bat spirit wants to eat away Aisha's heart. He wants her to lose the little hope she has left that she can find a way out of here. God planted a seed in her to become a doctor."

"A doctor?" Prince was surprised.

"The Creator has planted many good seeds in the hearts of your people. Prostitutes, addicts, criminals, thieves—God has put seed in all of them. But *Mayhem* eats the seed." The angel waited for that to sink in. "The spirits that entered the baby have an open door because of the weakness and despair of the mother. Spirits of anger, rage, rejection, and hopelessness are already at work within the child. She calls him Ray-Ray."

"What's going to happen to Aisha and her baby?"

The angel's eyes held no anger or accusation, but they were nonetheless intimidating because Prince knew nothing was hidden from his sight. The angel's eyes bore into his soul when he answered. "Tell me, son of God, what is going to happen to Aisha and her child?"

Prince didn't have time to ponder the puzzling question before he and the angel were back on the mountain looking into the valley of dry bones.

"Son of God, can these dry bones of *Mayhem* live? Can your friends and family and neighbors live? Can the prostitutes and addicts and criminals live? Can Aisha get out of *The Bluff*? Can she become a doctor? Can her child escape the demons who have claimed his soul?"

Each question pounded the foundation of everything Prince had believed about *Mayhem*. It wasn't hopeless. Its people weren't forgotten by God. But this new rising hope hit the turbulence of reality.

He had seen the demons that were destroying *Mayhem* and *The Bluff*. What could stop these creatures? Maybe somehow *The Bluff*, bur *Mayhem* needed a miracle.

"Lord, I believe these dry bones can live. But how? How can bones these dry live?"

"Prophesy to the bones, son of God. Command the bones to live, and your great God will be with you. He will give you the stage."

***

Prince was still slumped over when he heard the last of the angel's words.

"Prince, are you a son of God?"

"Yes."

"Your words have power. You must never curse yourself again. Do you speak life or death?"

"Life."

"Then you must never speak death again."

When he came out of the trance, he knew he had to do two things. The first was he had to stop thinking like nigga and calling himself a nigga. He wasn't a nigga. He was a son of God. The second was he had to prophesy. He had to speak life over his community.

And since God was with him, he was going to do it big time.

***

Sharon wiped the tears from her eyes. They were bubbling up from a heart torn in half. She was deliberately disobeying her father, and breaking God's commandment to honor her parents. But what was she to do? Let Prince die?

***

The demon tripped over himself getting to Heroin. Heroin turned just in time to see the clumsy spy reaching for the sleeve of his cape. He snatched his arm back, both hands now raised and palms facing the happy-faced demon. "Don't—ever—touch—my—cape."

"It's Sharon. The thorn. I think she's going to *Mayhem.*"

"Mayhem?" said Heroin, in shock. "Now? Who's going with her?" Heroin's smile turned sour. "Do tell me that dagger isn't going with her."

"Heroin, she's going alone."

"Alone?" Heroin didn't know what it felt like to get high, but something nice rushed up from his feet through his torso and was now in his head making it rock the blue brim hat in euphoria.

"For Prince. She's sneaking out the house."

Heroin smiled. "Sneaking out of the house for Prince. I thought I saw something when she was sniffing all over him. Looks like our little thorn is tired of holding that big Bible."

"Maybe she wants to hold something else."

Heroin looked at the demon with a surprised look. "That's pretty good. I'm impressed." He and the demon laughed. "Maybe she does want to hold something other than that Bible. Well, I've got something I want her to hold for me." He headed for Sharon's house. "Oh, Mama, what I'm going to do to that tender, white meat of yours." He looked at the other demon. "I can tell she's got good veins."

***

Sharon wiped her eyes, but the tears were stubborn. "I love You, Lord. I don't want to hurt my parents. I don't want to hurt You. What should I do?"

"Oh, no," said the demon.

"What?" said Heroin.

"She's asking God what to do. She's not going."

Heroin shook his head in harmless condescension. "Baby, that's why I'm Heroin, and you're you. Thorn or not, she's going. She's going to hear God tell her to go. You know why? Because she wants to go. Christians have a way of hearing the Spirit tell them what they want to hear. Check, check, check it out." He pointed at her with drama.

"I should've saved Holly."

"You're not God, baby," said Heroin.

"I don't want Prince to die." She wiped her eyes. "But even now, I'll stay. I'll go back in the house this very moment if You want me to. I'll trust You with Prince. Just tell me what You want me to do."

"This is the part I like," said Heroin. "When they pretend to submit to God's will. It's like my man, Balaam the prophet. The cursed book talks about it in Numbers. God clearly told him not to go with them cats. What he do, little man?"

"I don't know," said the small demon.

"What he do?"

"I don't know."

"He prayed about it. God said, 'Don't go.' Balaam prayed, 'Should I go?' 'Don't go.' 'Should I go?' You feel me? OG doesn't play that. He can get an attitude on you. This girl here, as much as He loves her, I guarantee you He's not going to answer."

"Why?"

"Because He already made Himself clear. He doesn't like to talk about His commandments. He just wants you to obey them. That's why we had to go."

"Heroin?"

"What, little man?"

I'm not a man. I wish you'd stop calling me that. "Who is OG?"

"Who is OG?" Heroin didn't know what the demon was talking about. "Oh, original gangster."

"Ohhhh, you were calling God the original gangster."

"Yeah."

"Why?"

Heroin let out a heavy breath. "You wouldn't understand. It's something they say." Heroin's eyes lit up at Sharon. "Here we go."

"Lord, when the apostles were ordered to no longer preach in Jesus's name, they said they had to obey You instead of the authorities. They had to break the law to remain true to You. You told our family about the danger Prince is in so we could save his life. Dad and Mom aren't going to do anything. So I have to."

Heroin listened to the rest of Sharon's prayer with closed eyes and a big smile. "Told you, little man. The big guy doesn't like to talk about His rules. That's why she's a thorn and not a dagger. Daggers don't pray about God's commandments. They obey them."

Sharon drove into the night.

Heroin looked at the admiring demon. "It's party time, baby."

***

More than once Sharon checked her doors. She looked around the dark streets. It was nearly two in the morning. Didn't these people sleep? She looked at how badly the homes had deteriorated. *Lord, help them. I'm sure they'd do better if they could.*

She stopped at a red light. Black men rushed her car on both sides, tapping on her windows, asking her what she wanted. Some had handfuls of little balloons. One pulled on the front passenger door. Another pulled her door handle.

Sharon sucked in a breath of fear as she scanned her doors. Her mind exploded with thoughts and conflicting emotions. She looked at the faces that were clamoring for her attention. She didn't want to fit the image of the stereotypical white person. She wasn't afraid of black people. She wasn't a racist. She wasn't—

Her tires squealed as she left a trail of rubber burned into the ground.

***

Heroin snatched off his hat and threw it on the ground. He watched Sharon drive away like she was in a drag race. He grabbed his hat and put it back on his head. He licked his thumb and index finger and rubbed them over his brim from left to right.

"These things happen, Heroin. You can't help it if drug pushers scared her off."

"What's your name?" Heroin's usual calm, amicable demeanor was gone. He was furious.

"Nosey," he answered.

Heroin looked at the demon's nose for the first time. It was long. It was hideous. It was not right. "Nosey," he shook his finger angrily by his own face, "those aren't drug pushers."

Nosey turned and looked at them. "They aren't? They look like drug pushers."

"Go take a closer look." Heroin spoke through clenched teeth.

"Okay."

The drug pushers were a block away. Nosey got within one block and the criminals all turned and faced the oncoming demon. *There was something peculiar about them.* Nosey was intrigued. He had to investigate further. He got within fifty feet. He clutched his chest when he saw their eyes.

All six *criminals* pulled out their swords.

One of them was Enrid.

Chapter 17

"Why do you think Annihilation is calling us off Rosa?" asked Annus.

"Oh, I don't know, Annus." Contemptus was feeling feisty. "Because we can't get within a hundred feet of the house? You think maybe that's it?"

"If that's it, we're in trouble."

"Brilliant assessment, Annus. Nothing gets past you."

Geez. He's in a terrible mood. I was just— The sight stalled his thought. "What do you think happened?"

Contemptus's eyes locked on one demon, then another. He couldn't help himself. Every demon looked worse than the one just before it. "They were attacked."

"Brilliant assessment." The words slipped out of Annus's mouth before he could stop them.

Contemptus looked at him. "Really?"

"Sorry," said Annus.

A demon came limping toward them. Contemptus stopped him. "What happened?"

"What?" said the demon in a loud voice.

"What happened?"

"What?" the demon yelled.

Contemptus looked at Annus, then at the other demon. He yelled, "I said what's wrong?"

The demon stuck his fingers into his ears and poked around. He opened his mouth widely a few times like he was trying to pop his ears. "My ears are ringing," he yelled. "I can't hear you. There was a bomb."

Someone blew a bugle.

Officers scurried around, screaming at banged up demons, trying to get them into formation. It was obvious that some of them couldn't even hear the shrill sound of the horn. These were slapped or kicked into attention.

Finally, two much smaller armies were assembled. Slavery faced his. Annihilation faced his. They delivered the same message. The enemy was planning an existential attack. He was planning the unthinkable. He was going to try to take *Mayhem* from them. Angelic scouts were everywhere. Communications were being cut. Mercy angels were in the area. The blue mist was going in and out of every building. And it couldn't be traced back to a single earthly source. There were too many sources.

"At least we're not in trouble," Annus whispered to Contemptus.

Contemptus closed and opened his eyes in irritated disbelief. "Did you not hear a word our lord said? Or are you as deaf as these ear-ringing cripples? If we're not in trouble, what are we in?"

"We're not all deaf," said a demon behind Contemptus.

Contemptus looked at the demon leaning heavily on a crutch, with a leg lifted up behind him and a socket where an arm used to be. "But you are a cripple, are you not?"

"Contemptus, you're going to get in trouble," Annus whispered a warning.

"Oh, shut up, Annus."

"I was just trying—"

"Annus, would you please shut up?" said the crippled demon behind them.

"Really," murmured Annus. "A crippled demon shouldn't talk to anyone like that." Annus looked up. "Contemptus, is that an angel standing in the sun?"

Contemptus looked up, as did everyone else. "What is he doing?"

Slavery and Annihilation followed the eyes of their soldiers.

"To your positions! No retreat! Fight to the death!" yelled Slavery.

Annihilation barked out much of the same and joined fast with his comrade, glancing nervously and defiantly into the sun. It seemed that the angel had fixed his eyes on him. Couldn't be. In any event, he hoped not.

"Do you see who that is?" said Slavery, his words carrying the venom of bad memories. Memories birthed by bad experiences with this particular angel.

Annihilation's contorted expression of anger and concern showed that he did. "Captain Rashti."

"That traitorous puppet," said Slavery.

"A *lethal* puppet," added Annihilation.

"Yes," the word was filled with contempt and slid slowly and out of Slavery's mouth. He looked at the angel's brilliant glow against the sun. Both hands rested on the angel's waist. "Such arrogance."

"The arrogance of one called *The Sword of the Lord.*" This was Annihilation's realism getting the best of him. "How long before our reinforcements get here?"

"I don't know. Hopefully soon. Any time before they attack would be nice." This last statement was Slavery's stab at Prince Krioni. Sure, the Mighty Bashnar had a huge ego...and he was arrogant...and he was insubordinate, but the prince didn't have to publicly humiliate him. He could've simply sent him sent to *The Dark Prison.* Now any time they requested the assistance of warrior spirits, there was always some reason they couldn't make it. Or if they did, it was always coincidentally a moment after the battle was lost. *Curse you, Prince Krioni!*

"Why?" Annihilation demanded of himself. "Why attack now? After all these years of uncontested rule." His bloodthirsty eyes scanned the perimeter. Their armies had been decimated. One-third blasted away by that prayer bomb—where'd they get so much prayer! And the rest, barely hanging on with various injuries. He twisted his face. Crippled, deaf, one-eyed demons. What were they supposed to do with this hodge-podge of demon parts?

"Annihilation, look!" said an uplifted Slavery. "They're here. A whole regiment of them. Demons of Hopelessness. Yes, my friend! This will kill any chance of a revival breaking out in our beloved *Mayhem.*"

"I don't believe it," said Annihilation, with a wide smile. That idiot prince has come through for us."

"Look over there!" said Slavery, with enough excitement to border on silly. "Oh...my...darkness. Warrior spirits! It's at least a hundred of them." He grabbed Annihilation's shoulders. "Warrior spirits."

Annihilation grabbed Slavery's shoulders. "Warrior spirits."

Slavery looked up at the angel in the sun. He pointed his sword. "Come, mighty *Sword of the Lord*. Come taste my blade." He pointed the blade toward the angel for several seconds. He smirked. He knew the legend wouldn't answer his taunts. Angels rarely responded to them.

"I will come for you, Slavery," said Captain Rashti.

The brash, shocked demon lowered his sword to his side. *The Sword of the Lord is coming for me!*

Annihilation looked at Slavery and was happy his name was Annihilation and not Slavery. He patted him on the shoulder. "It's okay, my friend. Look around you. We have your back."

Slavery did. *Couldn't they send more warrior spirits?* he nervously thought.

Annihilation made up his mind that from this point on, he would stay as far away from Slavery as possible.

***

Reinforcements had arrived. The darkness around *Mayhem* was thick, and more evil than it had ever been. One hundred warrior spirits. An entire regiment of spirits of hopelessness. Spirits of fear in abundance. And for added measure, Prince Krioni had not only sent demons of rebellion and lawlessness. He had sent several detachments of demons that showed he understood the battle as few did.

The demons of hopelessness would convince these slaves that God's freedom wasn't for them. But if they failed, that's where the prince's surprise support would make up the deficit.

He had sent spirits of fear. These would magnify the threat of the Vice Boys.

He had sent spirits of suspicion. These would cause them to focus more on the real or imaginary sins of the white race against minorities.

He had sent spirits of anger. These would inflame their passions and cause them to think illogically.

He had sent spirits of prejudice. These would cause them to judge all white people as bad.

He had sent spirits of racism. These would cause them to see themselves as superior to the white people who would come to *Mayhem* to help them—if it did get this bad.

He had sent spirits of error. They'd work closely with spirits of prejudice and racism to convince them that the Bible was a creation of the white man.

It was the final line of defense that was sure to kill any thought of widespread deliverance from sin in *Mayhem* and *The Bluff*.

Unforgiveness.

The prince had sent a horde of demons of unforgiveness. Before this threat, they had not been a pressing need. Most of their slaves had been so distracted by the hardness of poverty, fear, sin, and the virtual world created by rap music that forgiveness wasn't an issue. Who cared whether they forgave or didn't forgive? They would've still been slaves.

But if this threat of a gospel invasion was real, then unforgiveness could well become their last line of defense. That was the enemy's line in the sand. If their slaves weren't willing to forgive, they'd remain under their control.

Slavery smiled.

It was still surprising to him that American blacks had so easily forsaken the God who had delivered them from physical slavery—just like the Jews. If they had forgiven their oppressors and diligently served the Lord, He would've blessed them beyond anything they could've imagined. Instead, they had settled for the freedom to sin without the restraints of physical slavery.

I would rather have you on a plantation, thought Slavery. *But you haven't become the threat we thought you'd become. Hard to believe that we thought you'd be so grateful to God that you'd become a great testimony to the world of His power and love. A missionary people who'd bring deliverance to the world.*

A short burst of laughter erupted from Slavery. The more he thought of the rebellion of this ungrateful people, the more he imagined God's humiliation.

"Nothing good can come of this dirt," he spat, wishing that God could hear his words.

***

"Lord, sometimes I feel like dirt," said Prince. He had pulled over at a liquor store near Mayhem to pray before he entered his Jerusalem. "I've done so much bad that I...I...I know you love me. I know I'm not the man I used to be. I'm not the slave I was. I can never repay you fo' what You've done fo' me. I guess the best I can do with my freedom is to be grateful, and to live like I'm grateful. To live like I love You.

"I saved that white girl, Holly. And I saved Kim." Prince could almost hear the breaking sound of his heart as he thought of the one he didn't save. "Oh, God!" Tears rushed guiltily from his eyes. "Why am I so evil? How could I do that to someone like Samira? To anybody? Besides Sharon, she's the nicest, most good person I ever met, and I—I can't believe I did that to her.

"I owe Samira my life. I owe You my life." He raised his head and took his hand from his face. He didn't wipe away the tears. They felt good on his face. Monsters didn't cry. Maybe the tears were proof that he was no longer a monster.

He looked out his window at several faces beat up by alcohol and dried out by cigarettes. "Is there something else I can do to help that woman?" He knew there wasn't, but he needed to ask.

Prince prayed until the guilty anguish in his heart turned into determination driven by love. He pulled out of the liquor store's parking lot and headed toward *Mayhem*.

***

"He has no cover," said Adaam-Mir. "Why do we not hide him? Is there not enough prayer?" He spoke of Prince.

Myla answered the angel without taking his eyes off Prince's Mercedes. "There is no need to hide him. All they see is worthless dirt."

Adaam-Mir watched how the demons either looked at the son of God with contempt, or saw him and quickly turned away in disinterest. Myla was right. The ruling spirits had fortified the defenses and then let their greatest threat enter without so much as spitting in his direction. *Oh, Lord, how great is Your wisdom, and Your ways past finding out!*

"Hallelujah! Hallelujah, to our great God!" the angel's thoughts could remain silent no more.

Myla was now more accustomed to the angel's passion. He smiled inwardly, but kept his eyes on Prince.

***

The black Mercedes rolled slowly as Prince looked at the crowds of people, wondering, then wondering why he was wondering. *Sonny's party.* He grinned.

He will give you the stage. That's what the angel had said.

A curse word entered Prince's mind, but it didn't make it to the living room. He killed it in foyer.

He sent His word and healed them.

This time praise entered Prince's mind. He shook his head slowly in amazement. How had he just noticed? All of the pain was gone. He touched the back of his head. The side of his face. His side, arms, legs. Everywhere. The pain was gone!

"Jesus, I love You." The words came out as a whisper only because Prince was in spiritual shock. *How could he have lived so long without this amazing God? This God, who for some crazy reason, loved him?*

Prince looked at the stage. He listened to the music. Only God could make Sonny throw a *Mayhem* party so he could preach to everybody at once. He parked and leaned his head against the headrest, thinking about what he had to do. Thinking about Sonny and the Vice Boys.

How many times could one man die? He had died in Christ when he got saved. Sonny had a hit on him if he was caught away from his dope houses. Now here he was at a Mayhem party—thrown by Sonny. And he was going to bum rush the stage and try to preach.

Nigga, you must be crazy, was the thought that came to mind. Prince's next thought was, *Nigga, I ain't no nigga. Got ain't got no niggas. I'm a man of God.*

He thought on the crucifixion of Christ. He thought on what Jesus said about persecution. He thought about the resurrection. He thought about how little of the Bible he knew. He thought about how Jesus had promised His disciples that they didn't have to worry about what they would say to their enemies. They'd get what they needed to say when they needed to say it.

"Well, I ain't gone get it sittin' in here."

He opened the door and walked towards his Jerusalem.

***

Barbara picked the phone up. She turned and looked toward Sharon. "Really? Something unexpected came up and you're cutting your London trip short. The queen isn't a good conversationalist. Uh huh. You sure that's the only reason you're coming back soon?" She looked at Edwin. "Oh, you're actually at the Atlanta airport *now?* What a coincidence." She looked at Sharon. "Oh, nothing. It's just that your timing is impeccable. Uh huh. I'm sure the suit you picked up in London is impeccable. I'll be sure to tell Edwin about your suit."

Sharon walked toward the door leading to the garage.

Edwin kept the newspaper up before him. "That's some kind of coincidence—"Sharon kept walking—"isn't it, Sharon?"

Sharon stopped, saying nothing, her head lowered.

Edwin said nothing for several seconds. Finally, from behind the paper, he said, "It's like that uncle of yours can read your mind." Pause. "Must be a prophet thing."

"Dad, Mom," said Sharon, weakly, "I have something to tell you."

"No, Sharon," Edwin brought the paper down, "have a seat. I want to tell you about a frightening and strange thing that happened this morning."

Sharon took the slow death walk to the chair her father pointed to. She tried not to blink so the water in her eyes would stay in her eyes and not run guiltily down her cheeks.

Barbara sat next to Edwin. "First, your mother gets the interpretation to your dream. I was surprised. I think we all were surprised. Weren't you surprised, Sharon?"

Sharon grunted something her parents interpreted as yes.

"Well, if you think that was something, imagine my surprise when your mother awakens me a little after midnight, terrified because of a nightmare she had that you were held somewhere in *The Bluff* or *Mayhem* being sexually abused by half the neighborhood."

Sharon was horrified. "Half the neighborhood?"

"Give or take ten or twenty," said Edwin.

Sharon's wide eyes looked at her lap and refused to look up.

"I assured your mother everything was okay. We went to your room and peeked in. It was silly, I know. But parents, well, parents aren't rational when it comes to their children. All they care about is their safety. And when you have a daughter as precious as you, it makes them doubly irrational. Of course, we prayed together for your safety."

The tears rebelled and rolled down Sharon's face. She didn't look up. "Dad—"

"Wait a minute, Honey. There's more," he said.

Sharon's chest bounced with emotion. She swallowed the shame that had been caught hard in her throat.

"We went to bed. Then some time later I dreamt that I heard the garage door open and close. Twice. Can you imagine that?"

Sharon's lips were trembling so hard that Barbara squeezed Edwin's hand to get him to stop. He didn't.

"Dad."

"Sharon, that dream has come and gone and you're sitting here." His voice almost broke. He held his emotions in check. "Sitting here before us. Safe. As beautiful and as precious as ever. Now, we're going to put these dreams behind us. We don't need to talk about them. We know your heart. Look at me, Sharon."

She wiped her eyes and looked up.

"We know that you love us, and that we don't have to worry about you putting yourself in harm's way. Right?"

"Yes, sir."

Barbara squeezed his hand. This time from relief.

"Now, you're going to go spend some time with Diane and Rosa," he said.

"Yes."

"They live in *The Bluff,*" he said.

"We're meeting at Starbuck's off of Powers Ferry Road."

"Have a wonderful time, Dear," said Barbara.

"Tell them I said hello," said Edwin.

Sharon walked to the door.

Barbara whispered to Edwin, "That was wonderful, Edwin. You handled that perfectly."

Sharon got to the door and stood still for a moment. She turned. "I'll never again put myself in harm's way through disobedience to God. But as his disciple and prophetess, I'm willing not only to be abused for Him. I'm willing to die for Him. I love you both. I'll tell Diane and Rosa you said hi, Dad."

The door closed behind Sharon.

When Barbara recovered her balance, she asked, "What do you make of that?"

Edwin stared at the door. Part of him wanted to scream, "Hey, you get back in here!" Part of him wanted to say, "That's right, Sharon! He's worthy!" He turned to Barbara. "I don't know."

"Edwin, she called Jonathan in England. You know that, don't you?"

"Of course."

"Do you think she has a crush on Octavius?"

This question snatched Edwin into a whole different frame of mind. "What?" he asked. This was ridiculous. Barbara looked at him with an expression that conveyed more than concern over a silly crush. "What? You think there's something more? Barbara, really. We—"

"You think she's in love with him?"

"What?" he yelled. "That's absolutely ridiculous."

"Why else would she risk her life to go see him?" They both silently pondered these words. "You know how easily she loves."

Edwin's face turned into an expression that resembled reluctant enlightenment. "She does love easily, doesn't she?"

Chapter 18

His patented move.

Pretty Tony glided in a tight circle. He bent to the side and dipped his shoulder three times. Two girls broke out of their slow, sensuous moves into full, frenzied shaking of everything that could be shaken. One of them did her very best to defy physics with her body. The other sensing that she wasn't getting the attention she deserved, tried to make up with sexuality what she lacked in skill. *That was the trick.* The men started barking like dogs.

Suddenly, the music stopped.

Octavius "Prince" Monroe, son of Prophetess Ebony Monroe, pastor of *Worldwide Apostolic Church of International Deliverance and Glory*, and adopted son of God, stood on the platform with the DJ's mic in his hand.

The hush wasn't merely from the music stopping. Some were quiet because they knew Prince. They'd heard that this killer had been acting strange. Some said that he had gone crazy on his own drugs. Others said that he had gotten religion. But others had heard that he wasn't cool with the Vice Boys any longer.

Rumor was that he and his cousin, Sonny, had a falling out because that white girl, Samira, had flipped Prince. Word was that she had put something on him that stole his mind and made him send her back to Chicago.

It had also gotten out that the Vice Boys had put the sticks on him. That had a few people shaking their heads in confusion. They had seen people who had been put to the sticks. Why didn't Prince look messed up? Where were the bruises? The knots? The broken bones? Why wasn't he limping? And why did he look so cool?

A few dudes from *The Bluff* were there—no friends of Prince. Seeing him reminded them of when he had busted into the dope house and took that white girl from them. The one who had shot him that night was in this mad group.

The freshest rumor was that the Vice Boys were going to train that new, fine, white-girl talking sister, Kim. But Prince had gotten to her first and had put her somewhere. Somebody needed to stamp his forehead *Kill Me. I'm Crazy.*

The most shocked of the muted crowd were those who didn't see Prince holding the microphone. It was those who knew about Sonny's contract on Prince. They saw ten thousand dollars holding a microphone. This group was also nervous. Their nervousness came from knowing that if one of the Vice Boys killed Prince before they did, that was ten thousand dollars down the toilet.

A few in the large crowd patted themselves just to make sure their guns hadn't disappeared at this ten-thousand-dollar moment. A few others took off for their cars or their houses. Every second counted. They wouldn't be surprised to hear *Pop! Pop! Pop!* while they were late trying to get in the game.

Prince looked down at the crowd. He knew what was going on. There were a lot of people here. It was still bright outside. But this was *Mayhem*. Lot of folks in *Mayhem* had abruptly left this world during the day with a lot of folks watching.

"Ten thousand dollars is a lot of money," he said to the crowd. "That's what my cousin, Sonny Christopher's payin' to have me killed. Y'all wanna know why he wants me dead?" Prince moved his head to the side. "AJ, that you? Not like you to be so far away from Sonny."

AJ glared, but said nothing. He looked around the crowd for other Vice Boys.

"Word's out that I ran off with Samira. I did. I took her home—where she belongs. Where people love her. I took another white girl, too. One they was training. Got shot for that one, but it's all good. Wasn't a real gun. Double deuce." Prince looked at AJ. "You ain't got no double deuce, do you?"

"Naw, nigga, nine mill. Beretta," AJ snapped.

"Beretta? How *you* get a Beretta?" Prince asked like this was an impossibility for someone like AJ.

"Don't worry 'bout it, nigga."

"Least it's a real gun," said Prince.

A few people laughed.

"That's another thing," said Prince. "I ain't no nigga. I'm a son of God. Ain't no *niggas* out here. God didn't create no niggas. He created sons and daughters of God. What I see is people who don't know who they are, and they lettin' people like my cousin tell 'em who they are."

AJ moved closer to the platform.

***

Annihilation and Slavery and the armies of demons watched the trail of what appeared as fire race across the sky. It took a sudden turn and headed in their direction.

"Is that thing coming here?" Slavery said out loud to himself. He glanced back at the sun to make sure *The Sword of the Lord* was still there. "It is coming here." He was about to scream, "Sound the alarm!"

No need to. The siren was blaring.

The demons looked at the fire trail, then looked at where it appeared to be going. It was going to the crowd of people dancing. Wait. They weren't dancing. They were standing around listening to somebody talk.

Octavius?

Before they knew what had happened, the fire trail sped up and landed on Prince. The warrior spirits first instinct was to do what they did best. Fight! But there was nothing to fight. How do you fight fire on a man?

The angel of anointing in the fire was unseen to the demons. He was unseen to Prince. But Prince felt something strange happen to him. Something out-of-this-world strong, but impossible to describe. The thought that came to Prince was that God was in his mind and mouth.

"In Jesus's name, I bind you, Satan!" said Prince. "I take authority over you. You ain't gone stop these people from hearing me. And you ain't gone kill me until God is through with me."

The Sword of the Lord left the sun.

***

Prince rebuking Satan loudly over the mic brought a lot a funny looks. It also caused some people to shake their head because it felt like something had left them. They felt lighter, like a heaviness that they didn't know was there had been pulled up and out of them.

"Some of y'all know me. Some of y'all don't know me, but you know about me. You know that Sonny's my cousin, and that I used to be a VB before I went independent. I made my way."

Everyone understood what "made my way" meant—crime.

"Y'all know that I proved my point when necessary."

"Proved my point" was *Mayhem-speak* for shooting someone.

"Went permanent on two"—he deliberately did not say *niggas*—"dudes."

If someone in Mayhem *"went permanent,"* on you, you were dead. *Permanent.*

"That was somethin' I had to do then." Prince looked at different faces. "But that's not who I am now. I'm standing here because somethin' happened to me. Me and my boys were out shoppin. We hooked up with some white folks and jacked them. Thangs turned on us. The folks we jacked could've put me up for good. They didn't do that. Instead, they forgave me. Told me that Jesus loved me. They said that God brought us together so they could keep me from going to prison.

"I was like, cool, I ain't going to prison? I'll pray to Jesus, repent, whatever. But later on the dude and his friend started coming to my crib for Bible studies."

Murmuring broke out in the crowd.

"Wait a minute," somebody said. "You telling us the dude you jacked came to yo' house for Bible study?"

"Yeah," said Prince.

"Hell naw!" said the man. He knew nobody would do that.

"Serious, Dawg," said another man. "That nigga straight, Man! I seen 'em. A white dude and a brother. They came here a couple of times."

Prince continued. "That's when I really knew there was somethin' to this Jesus talk. They weren't like any Christians I ever heard of. I was high as a"—the *MF* word came to mind, but that's not who he was anymore. He left the sentence hanging. He paused.

"Those cats didn't let it stop 'em. Tell the truth, I did that"—the *s* word came to mind. That wasn't him any more.—"*stuff* on purpose. I wanted to see if these cats was legit. Then my little nephew peed all over the pastor. The white dude. Edwin. That's the one we robbed. He didn't let it bother 'em. His friend, Jonathan, even laughed about it. Said somethin' about God didn't like ugly pants, and that He had used my nephew to prophesy against 'em by peeing on 'em."

Laughter broke the near silence.

AJ wasn't laughing. He never did like Prince. Didn't like the way Prince looked at him. The way he always had something smart to say. The way he disrespected Sonny. The way women acted a fool for him. The way people talked about him like he was some kind of gangsta celebrity. He wasn't no real gangsta. He wasn't a Vice Boy no mo'.

Go ahead. Crack yo' jokes. I'm gone go permanent on yo' black—thought AJ.

"I started readin' the Bible again. I used to read it every now and then, back when my mama was out there. Some of y'all know my mama. She got a church now. But a long time ago she was strung out on that *stuff*. I can still remember her believing God to free her. I thought she was crazy, shooting up and reading the Bible. But then one day the Lord did His thang, and *bam!*, it was gone. Now she a prophetess, kickin' it with her church.

"When I took Samira—"Prince saw the looks. They were with him until he had said this. They thought he was crazy.—"I'm not crazy. I met God. I know He's real. Those people who been doing Bible study with me, I listened to what they had to say. But I read the Bible for myself. Not all of it, but enough for it to make sense. I asked God, I said, 'Jesus, if You real, do somethin.' Do somethin' now and come into my heart.'"

For a second, Prince's mind wandered back to that moment, reliving it. He looked in the crowd. Aisha. And her baby. She wore the same clothes she had on in the vision. His face didn't carry the smile, but his heart did. He looked away from Aisha.

"Then somethin' happened. I don't how to explain it except that I knew all my sins were washed away. It was like my eyes were opened for the first time in my life. I knew that I was a new man. That's why when I saw Samira, I had to do something."

The DJ saw a couple of Vice Boys looking menacingly at Prince. "Gimme the mic, man." He acted like he was going to get up.

"You better slow yo' roll, brother," said Prince.

The dude looked into Prince's eyes. He may have been talking about Jesus, but he still looked like a killer to him. He sat back on the bench and made sure he didn't look into the crowd. He didn't want some Vice Boy volunteering him to get shot.

"Samira didn't belong in no dope house. What we did to her was wrong."

"That ain't the Prince I know," said a girl in the crowd loud enough to cause similar comments from others.

"This the new Prince," he said. "I'm God's prince now." He winked at the girl. It wasn't meant as a flirt, but that's how she took it. She smiled.

AJ saw the wink. He heard the laugh and the girl say something about Prince being fine. This was almost enough to make him cap Prince right now. But he was talking so crazy, he had to listen. *What had that white girl put on him to make him go crazy?*

"God told me to rescue Samira," he said boldly. "So I did it. God told me to rescue His junkies, and his drunks, and his hoes."

"Oh, girl, he talkin' about you, Shameeka," a girl said loudly.

The girl affectionately cussed at her friend in response. "He ain't talkin' 'bout me, you fat heifer."

"He said hoes," her friend said, laughing.

"He did say hoes, Shameeka," a dude said. "The man said *hoes.*"

Shameeka laughed and told them both to go do something to themselves.

"Shameeka's not a hoe," said Prince, looking at her with a tenderness that had suddenly dropped upon him.

"The hell she ain't!" said another dude.

Prince heard the crowd's loud laughter, but it seemed as a distant whisper. He looked at her. "Shameeka, that's not who you are. That's not who God created you to be. There's more."

That sounded odd coming from him. He was part of the reason people were laughing and calling her a hoe.

***

Sonny Christopher looked out his top floor window. He could see everything. His fat face limited his range of expressions, but his fury found a way to show murder. He stormed his big body to a back room. He came back with a rifle with a scope on it. An AR-15. A rifle used by law enforcement and militaries around the world. One of its bullets could travel 3,200 feet a second. Prince's big mouth was only three hundred yards ago. He'd be down before anyone heard the shot. And even if someone saw him, they knew better than to open their mouth.

An enraged Sonny Christopher looked through the scope. There was the prince who thought he was a king. The bullet couldn't get there soon enough.

***

"Hold the line! Hold the line!" screamed Annihilation. "Shut that dirt up! Octavius is sending them after the demons of hopelessness!" He looked at an officer of the warrior spirits and jabbed his finger in the direction of Sonny's house. "Get some demons up there! Quick! They're going after Sonny!"

The warrior spirit looked at the ruler spirit without the respect customarily given to this class of demons. It may not have risen to the level of disrespect, but it definitely was not respect.

"Well?" demanded Annihilation. "What are you waiting for?"

The thick, muscled demon wasn't as massive as Annihilation. But there was an intimidating presence about him. He looked like he'd fight Satan if he crossed him. He took a few steps forward and stood within a sword's thrust of the general.

"I knew the Mighty Bashnar."

Is this what this is about? You arrogant son of an angel. He got what he deserved. "So did I. He was a great warrior. It was a shame what happened to him."

The warrior spirit looked unconvinced.

Annihilation didn't want to provoke a fight with him—they were so unpredictable!—but a war was raging all around them. "Not that I don't enjoy discussing the news, but can we skip the weather and sports and fight these angels?" Annihilation knew his tongue had gotten the best of him.

The warrior spirit was as uninterested now in protocol as he was before the general spoke. "Of course. That's why we warrior spirits have come—to fight your battle."

There was nothing but contempt in the way this demon spoke. But this was hardly the time to get distracted with the petulant nature of warrior spirits. They were a necessary evil. "The top floor. There. That's him in the window with the rifle."

Annihilation watched the warrior spirit and three others of his kind go toward Sonny's place. Four warrior spirits. That should be enough. Annihilation jumped back into the fray, hoping that nothing jumped out of the blue mist that was all around him and his demons.

***

Sonny's finger rested lightly on the trigger. He held his breath.

The bird came from Sonny's left, sharp, oversized talons outstretched, digging deeply into his fat cheek.

Sonny screamed and grabbed his face. The rifle twirled butt over barrel twelve floors until it hit the dirt.

Enrid turned from Sonny to face the four approaching warrior spirits. When the warrior spirits saw the angel's alarm turn into a smile, they turned and looked at what the angel was smiling at.

The Sword of the Lord!

***

Prince looked at Aisha. She was bouncing her baby on her hips and kissing him. She looked up. Their eyes met. He seemed to be looking directly at her, as though he knew her. She looked to her left and right. That dude was looking at *her*.

Prince smiled at her and turned in another direction. "I'm gone say somethin' now that ain't gone mean nothing to nobody but the person I'm talkin' to. You young. By yo'self. Ain't got nobody, really. When you was little, you used to wanna be a doctor." Prince scanned his curious audience. "How does anybody livin' down here get it into their head that they can be a doctor?

"Ain't no doctors down here. All we see is gangstas and drug addicts and hoes. All we see is people being shot." Prince looked into his mind and recalled the wonder of the vision. "You wanna know where you got that idea to be a doctor? You got it from God. He put a seed in yo' heart to be a doctor. He did it before you was born. You ain't crazy to think you can get out of here.

"But you got yo'self into a situation. Now it's not just you. You got another responsibility. Sometimes you get so frustrated. Sometimes you just cry and pray, wondering why you had to be born into this mess. Wondering how come you weren't born into a family where things ain't crazy all the time. I saw some kind of monster birds eating yo' heart out of yo' chest. The angel told me that was yo' hope they was eatin'. But I want you to know God has heard yo' prayers. Don't worry 'bout what it look like right now. He's gone get you out of here. You gone be a doctor. You gone help people."

One Vice Boy said to another, "This nigga seein' monsters and talkin' to angels. He crazier than Sonny said he is."

It was this crazy talk that was so fascinating to those who wanted to kill him that kept them from doing it immediately. How could they not want to hear more from a former Vice Boy who had gone independent with his own crew and now had flipped on Sonny? This dude knew Sonny had a contract on him, and here he was in broad daylight on Sonny's stage talkin' 'bout taking Samira. Talkin' bout he wasn't no nigga no mo'. Talkin' bout seein' monsters and talkin' to angels. Everybody wanted to hear what this crazy fool would say next.

But not everybody thought he was crazy.

Aisha's face was wet with the last drops of water of a lake of irrational hope that had been scorched dry by *Mayhem's* merciless sun. How could this man know what was in her heart? How did he know that sometimes just before she got really depressed and started thinking about killing her baby and herself, that she felt like something was eating her heart and taking every drop of hope from her? How did he know she wanted to be a doctor? How did he know she had asked God over and over why she had been born in her family?

Aisha didn't want to leave the party, but she had to. She was only seconds away from bursting into tears. She didn't want these people to see her break down like that. She put Ray-Ray in his stroller and navigated through the crowd, looking down, hiding her face as she walked.

Aisha left the last of the crowd.

God has heard yo' prayers.

Don't worry 'bout what it look like right now.

He's gone get you out of here.

You gone be a doctor.

You gone help people.

She was about fifty feet away when her dry soul heard a clap of thunder. The rain of hope began to fall. A torrential rain that turned into a flash flood, sweeping away her fears of the future and every doubt of God's love.

Aisha's wet face smiled as she bent over the rickety stroller as she walked. "Come on, Ray-Ray. Momma's going to be a doctor."

***

"Dad," Sharon sounded frantic on the phone, "I'm with Rosa and Diane and Kim at Starbucks. They're going to kill him, Dad. Prince.

Kim said he went back to Mayhem. She said he was talking like he knew they were going to kill him."

Chapter 19

Prince pointed at the crowd. "God showed me that He put seeds in all of us. Things that we supposed to do. People we supposed to be. But He said *Mayhem* eats the seed." Prince swept his arm. "This is what's left when you eat yo' seed. Nothing but violence. Hopelessness. People acting a fool. Like we animals. One of the reasons why people think we animals."

"You got some kind of nerve, Prince." This came from a heavy girl who had angrily herself near to the front of the crowd. She wore half a strapless sundress that revealed several tattoos on her calves, arms, and back. There was one that went from shoulder to shoulder. It was *Luck You!* But luck was spelled with an F.

Prince grimaced under the heaviness of shame when he saw her.

"My brother still can't see out his left eye. How you gone beat my brother blind and get yo' black a— up here and call somebody an animal?" LaQueesha grabbed a guy's bar-b-que chicken breast off his plate and hurled it at Prince. It hit him in the chest.

When the chicken fell at his feet, her adrenaline of anger vanished. She stared at the chicken, too terrified to look up into his face. The crowd was silent, except for various people giving one-line commentaries on what Prince was going to do to her.

LaQueesha knew what was next. He was going to beat her like she was a man. He had to. This was *Mayhem.* He couldn't let a woman disrespect him like this. She stared at his black boots, visibly trembling.

"LaQueesha, come here," said Prince.

Her wide body didn't move. She kept staring at his boots. She felt like she was about to throw up.

"LaQueesha," he repeated.

A woman said, "You better get up there, Kwee. Don't make that nigga get off that stage."

LaQueesha's physical size didn't translate to courage. He probably wouldn't kill her—she had been cool with him before he beat her brother down—but she didn't want to be beaten half to death on a stage, either. Nonetheless, she found herself obeying the voice. She stood in front of him. Not once had she looked him in the face since her chicken found its mark.

Prince's voice was neither soft nor hard. "LaQueesha, look at me."

It was like her head weighed a hundred pounds. She lifted slowly, with great difficulty. She looked at one of his cheeks, but not his eyes.

"LaQueesha." This time his voice sounded soft. Not angry soft, but like he really wasn't mad.

She looked into his eyes. She was hoping her fear wasn't making stuff up. *He didn't have killer eyes any more.*

"I'm sorry, LaQueesha. I was wrong. I didn't have to do business like that." He paused. "Don't worry 'bout the chicken."

Her eyes were two big question marks.

Prince smiled a little. "Now had that been a pig's foot...."

She was too afraid to catch the humor. Her face screamed the question. Then after a few awkward moments, her mouth gave it voice. "You ain't gonna hit me?"

Prince opened his mouth and released his shame in a short breath. He looked at her with a pained expression and shook his head. "LaQueesha—I—the Lord Jesus has changed me. I don't do that any more. God didn't create you to be a doormat. No man has a right to put his hands on you like that."

Their eyes connected like the lines that connect telephone poles. Nothing was spoken, but much was heard.

"You're not gonna hit me. I can go." LaQueesha wasn't asking. In wonderment, she was stating it. The zebra looked at the lion. "You're not the same Prince. Only God could've done this."

Prince's heart was heavy for his victims. He had hurt so many people. If everyone he had hurt confronted him today, he'd be on this stage forever. Guilt was pulling at him like an anchor. He knew that he had been forgiven by God. But there was a forgiveness he'd never get. He'd never get Samira's forgiveness. He'd never get LaQueesha and her brother's forgiveness. He'd never get the forgiveness of all the others.

He watched LaQueesha step off the platform. He read her big *Luck You!* tattoo. She turned and looked at him, unafraid. Prince saw she was unafraid. This helped his heart some.

"What happened to you, it's real, Prince. You not the same. You must've seen God." Then she said something that made him fight hard to not cry. "Everything cool."

Everything cool.

Or, *I forgive you.*

A man with a black patch over his eye pushed himself up to the edge of the platform. "How everything cool?" he said angrily. "I'm the nigga who blind."

***

Sonny and eight Vice Boys stood outside his building next to the bike pole. After that crazy bird ripped his face, he had looked down to where the rifle landed. Now it was gone. How'd somebody get his rifle that fast?

It had to be somebody in his building. Somebody on one of the lower floors. But the Vice Boys had gone house to house and searched them all. No one had been fool enough to say no. Wouldn't that have meant they had the rifle?

Sonny stood next to the bike pole with his hands on his hips. He looked up at his window. Then he looked at the crowd at his party. Prince was still running his mouth. Why hadn't someone capped him yet? Better that they hadn't. He'd keep his money in his pocket. "Come on. Let's go shut this nigga's mouth."

***

The crowd watched the confrontation of Lil' Johnny and Prince end with those two and LaQueesha praying together. Prince had asked both of them to forgive him, and they had. This was some of the best entertainment *Mayhem* had ever had. It certainly was the most bizarre.

Prince wiped the tears from his face. He'd have to get used to this crying business. He was doing this a lot lately.

"Sonny coming," someone said, her voice mixed with excitement and warning.

Hundreds of sober eyes looked toward the entourage of Vice Boys coming. Sonny was leading the pack, wearing a white suit and a white derby. Even from this distance, Prince could see that even his cousin's shoes were white. He never did learn how to dress without making himself look ridiculous.

"Look at me," Prince told the crowd. Some turned, but others were fixed on the approaching Vice Boys. "I said look at me," he said more forcefully.

Nearly everyone looked at Prince, or at least gave him their divided attention. *This was like something from a movie!*

"Jesus Christ is real. He ain't something some white man cooked up to get over on black people. Ain't no white man smart enough or dumb enough to come up with the Bible. It's the Word of God." Prince looked earnestly at the faces in the crowd. "How do I know it's His Word? Because of its power.

"That book talks about a God who loves us so much that He died for our sins. It says He rose from the dead on the third day and went back to heaven. It says He's coming back again to make thangs right. It says we don't have to go to hell. It says all we have to do to escape His punishment for sins is to repent. He's just looking fo' us to do what makes sense—get right with 'em.

"I told y'all about that seed He put in you. You know you ain't come from no monkeys. Now if anything's a lie of the white man, that's it. A monkey? I came from God. You came from God. But our sins have messed up everythang. We gotta make that right."

"What you talkin' 'bout, man?" a guy yelled.

Anthony.

"I'm talkin' 'bout eternal life, Anthony."

"How this nigga know me?" Anthony said to the girl he was with.

"I'm talkin' 'bout you turning from yo' sins and making it right with your Creator, Jesus Christ. You know it's real. You know *somethin'* done happened to me. You know what that somethin' is? That somethin' is Jesus Christ."

Prince looked at Sonny and his posse. It looked like Sonny had sped up his white shoes. "Listen to me," he urged. "I'm telling you that Jesus Christ is God, and He died for your sins. I'm telling you that if you ask—I mean right now—He'll prove it to you. Ask Him to forgive you. Ask Him to wash away your sins. Ask Him to change your life, to give you power to live the way He wants you to live. Ask Him to fill you with His Holy Spirit."

Sonny was dangerously close, almost there.

"Do it now," Prince demanded. He knew he didn't have much time. "Do it now and see what He does." He looked at the anxious faces. It looked as though his words had hit home with a lot of people.

What now? What now? His mind raced.

Sonny and the Vice Boys were there.

"God, now!" Prince shouted. "Show your power now! Holy Spirit FALL!"

Sonny reached inside his left holster. His hand touched the gun. His foot was about to touch the ground when everything went black. He fell forward like a big, fat log. His arms appeared pasted to his sides until his face slammed onto the hard dirt. His white derby rolled several feet before stopping upside down. A white bird swooped from the air and landed on the hat. He dropped an insanely big load on it, shrieked, and flew off.

Prince and everyone else watched Sonny bite the dust. Then they watched the other Vice Boys with him fall over on the ground and lay there motionless, as though they were dead. No one said anything.

Prince snapped himself out of his gaze. This was an answer to his prayer. He felt like he had been put into the championship game after begging the coach to let him play. But now what?

"Everybody, look at me. Don't worry 'bout them. Look at me." Most did. Prince looked at the body on the ground to his left. *AJ.* He shook his head. "What did I say to you? Didn't I say Jesus Christ is alive? Didn't I say He's real?" Prince started pointing in the crowd. "He's real, LaQueesha. He's real, Lil' Ricky. He's real, Asia. He's real, Jamal. He's real, Marquis. He's real, DeShawn.

"Now what y'all gone do with this? The Lord done showed you He's legit. Make up yo' mind right now what you want out of life. You want what you got? Or do you want eternal life? Everybody who wants to serve Jesus Christ, raise yo' hand."

Prince was shocked when he saw so many hands go up. *More than half?* He knew he saw what he saw, but he blinked hard and looked again. *So many.* "Okay," *Lord, what do I do?* he thought, "Okay, look, just cry out to God and ask for mercy. Ask Him to forgive you. Ask Him to save you and fill you with His Holy Spirit."

Prince was shocked again when so many people began to pray. Some people had their hands in the air. Some were on their knees with bowed heads. Others were on their knees with outstretched arms, their faces wet with tears and seemingly reaching for the heavens. What was this? How could this be happening? This was *Mayhem*.

Prince smiled in awe at the God Sharon had introduced him to. That crazy girl would be proud of him. He had called on the Holy Spirit to fall the same way she had done when he was at her house. The same power that had come upon him had come upon his brothers and sisters in *Mayhem*.

Who would've thought it would be so easy? thought Prince.

The DJ's mouth dropped open. He looked at Sonny and his crew. They were standing now, looking confused and talking to one another. Sonny grabbed his hat and pressed it hard on his head. He snatched his gun out. So did the others.

"Awww," the DJ cursed and dove off the stage.

Prince's eyes narrowed in curiosity at the sight of the man jumping on the dirt. He watched the man dig his elbows into the ground one after the other and drag his body as though he were in army training, crawling under barbed wire. *What?*

"Prince."

The earth-filling, soul-filling sound of his name came from everywhere, but Prince's attention was drawn toward the heavens. He looked up and died to everything this world had to offer. He pointed to the sky and yelled, "Look, I see the heavens open and Jesus standing at the right hand of God."

Pop! Pop! Pop!

Pop! Pop! Pop! Pop! Pop!

Pop! Pop!

Pop! Pop! Pop!

Pop!

Pop!

Pop! Pop! Pop!

Sonny stood over Prince's body and looked into his ungrateful, dead cousin's eyes. He looked up at the scattered crowds. They were running away. *Away from Sonny Christopher.* They were terrified. *Terrified at Sonny Christopher.*

"Any nigga opens his mouth is dead," he yelled. "You hear me? Dead."

Annihilation and Slavery stood on both sides of Sonny.

"What?" said a shocked Sonny to Prince. "Nigga, you ain't dead?"

Prince's mouth moved. A pained, suffocated whisper fought the blood in his mouth to be heard.

Sonny pointed the gun at his head. He looked at his moving mouth. He shook his head in irritation and smacked his juicy lips. He lowered his gun and got on one knee. He put his ear next to his dying cousin's mouth.

"Mayhem...belongs...to Jesus. You...you can't stop...God."

Sonny looked at Prince like he had just been dropped from a dog's butt onto his white, patent leather shoes. "What? I don't have to stop God, nigga. I just got to stop you."

He stood up and pointed the gun at his bloodied chest. *Pop! Pop!*

***

The two massive demon rulers looked down at the bloodied, still dirt. Their smirks and body language showed their satisfaction. But there was obviously something about the limp body interfering with their moment.

"The warrior spirits were fantastic, were they not?" said Slavery, pondering the mystery of Octavius.

"If you can ignore their arrogance, they're worth their weight in misery," said Annihilation. "They saved your butt." He sounded distracted. He was. It was this Octavius dirt. "The Sword of the Lord, he almost got you."

Slavery put his finger into the slice across his wide chest and traced the wound to where it ended at his waist. "The Sword of the Lord is better than this."

"What do you mean?"

"The warrior spirits didn't save me. Rashti held back. I saw him fight in Hong Kong once. At the walled city. It was because of him that it was torn down. Scattered my slaves."

"He is a legend, but even legends fail. They surrounded him. He fought through the weak flank and fled." Annihilation's explanation sounded unlikely, even to him.

"Trust me, Annihilation, he held back."

"Why would he hold back? He said he was coming for you."

"He will." Slavery's attention went back to the body before them. "There's something else going on. Something bigger than *Mayhem*."

Annihilation stood more erect. "Bigger than *Mayhem?*"

He looked at the dirt at his feet. It made sense. The reinforcements had made *Mayhem* stronger than it had ever been. Yet God could send wave after wave of angels to finally overrun them.

Of course, it wasn't merely a case of who had superior numbers. If that were the case, the darkness would have lost eons ago. There were spiritual dynamics of prayer, righteousness, freewill, and other arbitrary, so-called *rules* of the enemy that had to be considered.

"This dirt," said Annihilation of Prince, "how did this happen? How did *he* happen? He was such a good destroyer."

"A wonderful slave," said Slavery.

"*How...did...he...happen*?" Annihilation obviously had his own answer in mind. "If this can happen to dirt of this quality...."

Slavery nodded.

"Did you see how quickly the slaves dumped us for the Christ?" said Annihilation. "It was like they were waiting for this moment. The ungrateful vermin."

"I must admit, I am surprised how quickly they discarded us. I didn't see any signs of such treachery." Slavery's dark mind tried to connect the dots. "You can't always go by how bad a sinner looks or speaks. That cursed gospel seed could be growing beneath the surface."

"But this is Octavius." Annihilation's words were angry and full of regret.

"*Was* Octavius. A disappointment certainly, but he was a threat. Now the threat is dead. Our dirt will come back home. Mark my word, Annihilation. I've seen it all before. They prayed their little prayers and cried their little tears. But when they see how demanding the Christ is, when they see that He wants more than words and tears"—a genuine, untroubled expression resembling a smile finally found a place on his face—"they'll give up this sons and daughters of God foolishness." He patted his friend on his shoulder. "Haven't they always been their own worst enemies? Haven't they always been good niggers?"

"Yes."

Slavery patted his friend again. "And good niggers they shall remain. You'll see. Today it's Christ. Tomorrow sex, drugs, and dancing."

Annihilation was worried, but he couldn't pass up the opportunity to say something insulting about the people he hated with special hatred. "And basketball." He chuckled darkly. "And rap music."

"Yes, basketball and our beloved rap music." Slavery pointed to Prince. "The threat is dead."

Annihilation's worry killed the hopeful moment. "Octavius is dead. But something tells me he's more of a threat now than when he was alive. I don't know how, Slavery, but what you said about *The Sword of the Lord's* retreat being phony. I think this dirt's death was all part of some master plan."

***

Adaam-Mir looked at Myla with wide eyes. "Demons are liars, I know. But, Myla, is this true? Is this why we pulled back?"

Part of him wanted the answer to be yes. Part of him wanted the answer to be no. If it were yes, it would put Octavius's death in perspective and take some of the sting out of this tragedy. If it were no, well, it was difficult thinking that there were times that children of God were abandoned—even if it were for some mysterious good.

Myla looked intently at Adaam-Mir. "God never abandons His people."

Adaam-Mir watched with surprise as his mentor left him standing there alone with his thoughts. That was it? No further explanation? When he saw his mentor's image disappear into the horizon, the answer became obvious. He'd have to do what every son and daughter of Adam was expected to do when they didn't understand God's actions. He'd have to trust in God's goodness, wisdom, and love.

Adaam-Mir got on one knee and lowered his head. He raised his right hand to heaven. "Blessed be God my Creator. You are good. You are wise." He lifted his face toward heaven. "You love me, and I love and trust You." A cool, refreshing breeze blew across the angel. His insides danced. *Blessed Holy Spirit,* he thought.

The angel took off in the direction of his mentor. Captain Rashti's retreat made sense now. A slow smile formed as he flew. Octavius's death wasn't the end. It was the beginning. Of what, he didn't know. But whatever it was, it was big.

"Hallelujah," he screamed.

Chapter 20

Jonathan laid his suit bag across their bed. He unzipped it and started pulling suits out. "Didn't even get to wear this one," he said. "Good thing I didn't."

"Why not?" asked Elizabeth.

"Liz, God is perfect. I don't deny that. But I think he made a mistake with me. You know, a man can be too good-looking. You couple that with intelligence, wit, and that cologne you got me when you and Ava went to France"—he stopped and looked at her seriously—"wearing that suit would've taken me from almost irresistible to absolutely irresistible."

Elizabeth folded her arms and dropped her head a little, smirking at him with a raised eyebrow. "Really?"

Jonathan still wore his serious face. "The danger of beautiful, hungry females was everywhere. But never fear, my dear. I fought them off with the strength of Samson. I told those bobcats that I had a tiger waiting on me at home."

Elizabeth shifted her weight to the other leg and smiled. "Is that right? Beautiful, hungry females everywhere?"

She didn't wear midriffs outdoors, but she did around the house. Jonathan noticed that the little top inched its way up when she shifted. His eyes dropped to her shorts. Then a slow journey to her bare feet.

"I haven't been gone a week"—his eyes made it back to her shorts and stopped—"and I see the devil has been busy."

Elizabeth moved closer. "Has he now?"

Jonathan loosened his tie. "That top is backslidden. It's lost material." His voice was dry, strained. "Totally unholy."

Elizabeth pressed into her husband. She kissed him on the neck. "And what about my pants?"

Jonathan felt her hot breath on his neck. "Help me to be strong, Jesus," he said. "Help me to tell this woman the truth."

Elizabeth fought back the laughter that almost exploded out of her.

"Sister Banks, those aren't pants. And they'd need at least four more inches to be true shorts. They're hypocrites."

Elizabeth kissed him on the other side of his neck. "God doesn't like hypocrisy, Jonathan."

"Neither do I, Sister Banks. And since I'm a holy man of God, I'm willing to help you get rid of your unholiness and your hypocrisy. I'm willing to help you get rid of the sin and the weight that doth so easily beset you."

She bit his ear. "Even though I'm not British?"

He didn't say anything.

Elizabeth looked up into her husband's face. His eyes were wide and intense, as though he were looking at something she couldn't see. She was used to this. It was part of his prophetic calling. Spontaneous visions, trances, and weird experiences were as much Jonathan as the color of his eyes. She hugged him and rested her head on his chest until he came out of it.

"Liz."

She looked up. Tears rolled down his face. "What? What is it?"

"The young man, Prince. The one me and Edwin's been having Bible study with. I saw him get killed. He was shot. Over and over. I saw several people shooting him. I couldn't see their faces."

Elizabeth grabbed her face. "Oh, Jonathan. What? Has it already happened? Can we stop it?" She was already rushing to get changed.

"I don't know, Liz. I don't know." Jonathan was shaken.

"We have to go, Jonathan."

"Yeah. You're right," he said, trying to shake off his shock and sadness. He shook himself. "We gotta go."

His phone rang. He answered. He heard Sharon's scream and sat on the bed.

"*Jooonaathan!* I had a vision. I saw Prince murdered. Pleeeeeeeeeze, pleeeeeeeeeze, Jonathan what do I do?" she cried.

***

Jonathan's car drove past the Mayhem sign first.

Edwin and his family was second. Their full car was a product of a hysterical and heartbroken daughter, a mother who wasn't going to let her daughter anywhere near Mayhem without her own eyeballs watching her, and a son who happened to be with his parents when they received Sharon's call.

Kim's car was next. She was scared to death to go back into Mayhem. But she was at a crossroads in her life—again. These all too frequent crossroads normally gave her the option of driving off a fifty-foot cliff or a hundred-foot cliff. This time, however, it looked like at least one road led to something good.

Live with Diane and Rosa? Where had this offer come from? One moment she was sitting in a Starbucks with them and their friend, Sharon, telling them about her life, and the next moment these strangers were playfully, but seriously fighting over who she was going to live with. Sharon had lost the contest because her parents knew nothing of their daughter trying to move in a stranger.

Kim had participated very little in the unbelievable conversation. Actually, when she saw that these strangers—nice people, but strangers, nonetheless—were serious about helping her in this way, she simply sat back and listened in amazed silence. She had never met Christians like these. *People who would sacrifice to help someone they didn't even know.*

So as terrified as she was of going into Mayhem, how could she not go with Sharon? She was there when Sharon had dropped her drink, saying through tears that she had just seen in a vision a new baby Christian murdered. And when she said that the baby Christian's name was Prince....

The caravan rolled slowly.

Jonathan, Edwin, and Kim noticed something strange. No one was outside. No loud music. No groups of people in the parking lots. No children running around. Nobody being cursed out. A warm May evening, and no one was outside at Mayhem?

There was something else strange. It seemed like there was someone in every window looking out. They were all looking toward a platform.

Jonathan first saw what looked like a body on the stage.

But it was Sharon who was first out of the car. It hadn't come to a complete stop before she had kicked off her shoes and was out and running across the hard dirt toward the body, screaming, "Prince."

The sight of her screaming daughter running across a large field in Mayhem toward what looked like a body was a shot of adrenaline to Barbara. She jumped out and ran protectively behind her impossibly impulsive daughter, calling her name.

Sharon knew the moment she saw the body from the car that it was Prince. She ran as hard as she could. *Why was it taking so long to reach him?* But she didn't really want to reach him. Not like this. Not like Holly. She wanted to see him as she had seen him the night he was filled with the Holy Spirit. The night he clutched his chest and cried for an hour because he was overwhelmed by the presence of the sweet Holy Spirit.

She jumped on the stage and got on her knees over him. Blood was everywhere. She looked up at Jonathan who was almost there, and the others who were only several yards away, except Kim. She was still in her car with locked doors.

"Jonathan, he's dead." Her words were long and filled with the grief of his and Holly's deaths. She dropped her head. "I failed again. I let someone else die." She gripped one of his hands with both of hers. "I'm sorry, Prince. I should've been here for you. I should've warned you. Oh, God," she cried, "I told Prince that you'd take care of him. I told him that if he trusted in You, You'd use him to spark a mighty revival in Mayhem. Now he's dead."

Barbara looked at the body. *The body.* This wasn't a funeral. It wasn't a body whose murder had been professionally hidden by morticians and a beautiful casket. It was the raw, freshly bloodied body of someone who had eaten dinner at her home. It was someone whom her husband had risked his life to make a disciple. It was someone whom her daughter loved. But she saw now that it wasn't the kind of love she feared. It was that Sharon kind of love. That God kind of love.

Barbara willed her eyes from the blood on the platform and from Prince's chest. She looked at his face. His smile was a stark contrast to the pool of blood that surrounded him. It was a stark contrast to the horror and regret on Sharon's face. She got on her knees and hugged her, laying her face tenderly across her shoulder.

Edwin looked down at Prince. He saw the smile, but he got no comfort from it. It was the smile of a young Christian who had been brutally murdered. No one in this hellish place had even had the decency to call the cops or an ambulance. He tried to swallow and couldn't. It was like all the air was gone. He gulped hard and looked around at the innumerable peering faces. He pulled out his phone.

Jonathan got on his knees and faced the top of Prince's head. He put his hand under Prince's neck. He looked at the young man whom Satan had murdered.

"Why did God show us this? Why, Jonathan?" Sharon pled. "Why give us visions of something like this? Something that can't be stopped?"

Jonathan's heart was torn by the desperation in Sharon's voice, but he didn't look at her. He cupped Prince's face in both hands, closed his eyes, and lightly pressed his forehead onto his.

Suddenly, something snapped in Sharon. She stood up and looked intently at Sonny's building.

"Honey?" said Barbara.

Sharon's attention was drawn to the top floor of a particular open window that framed a man wearing a white hat. She took slow, but determined steps toward that white hat.

Barbara watched in silence until it became clear that Sharon wasn't stopping. "Sharon," she said, with a mother's authority.

Edwin turned and saw Sharon walking away from them. "Sharon," he called, with a father's authority.

Sharon took off in a sprint toward the white hat.

***

Sonny and a couple of Vice Boys watched the girl run toward their building like she was being chased by Po-Po. Their curiosity kept their mouths shut.

***

Sharon stood about twenty-five yards from the entrance to Sonny's building. She pointed her fingers at the man in the white hat. She wasn't sure he could hear her, but she knew that a lot of the other people on lower floors looking from their windows could hear her.

"Who killed him?" she yelled.

Edwin caught up to her and stopped about ten feet from her. Something told him to give her this space, that she'd be okay. But he watched her carefully. There was no way she was going up those stairs. And why had she chosen this building? There were others that were closer.

"Who killed Prince?" Sharon demanded again. She pointed her finger at the white hat. "Was it you? He was my friend. He was God's friend. You won't get away with killing God's friend."

Sharon dropped to one knee and held her face in her hands and cried. *Holly. Prince.* Her heart hurt so badly. She stood up and felt her father's hand on her shoulder and heard him say softly, "Sharon."

She looked up at the white hat. "You won't get away with this. In the name of my Lord Jesus Christ, you—won't—get away—with this! Revival is coming to this wicked place. You killed Prince, but you can't kill the move of God. The blood of the martyrs is the seed of the church. This is not the end. It's the beginning. You in the white hat, did you hear me? It's the beginning. Prince is gone, but we're going to take his place. I'm going to take his place."

Edwin flinched.

"My father's going to take his place. My mother's going to take his place. Jonathan and Elizabeth and Ava are going to take his place. Our church is going to take his place. We're going to get others. Other churches. You can't kill us all. Prince's death is not in vain. We'll be back. Mayhem belongs to God—and you can't stop God!"

Barbara and Elizabeth watched Edwin and Sharon as they got closer to them. "Jonathan," said Elizabeth, "they're back."

His forehead was still pressed against Prince's forehead. "You're a lie, Satan," he whispered again. "You can't have him. I rebuke you, Death. Let him go."

"Sharon," said Barbara, clearly exasperated by her daughter. "What were you thinking?"

Sharon heard her mom, but she answered all of hell. "You can't kill the revival." Her voice was flat and determined, and she didn't look at her mother when she answered.

"Sharon, you're right," said Jonathan. "There's a reason God gave us visions of Prince's murder. He wants us here." He stood up and held out his hands. "We gotta pray over him."

Sharon was confused at his words, but quickly took his hand. She looked at the searching expressions of her mother and father. "We're going to hold hands and pray, Mom."

Edwin was obviously also trying to sort out why they were going to pray over a dead body. But he had learned that Jesus Christ was alive and among His people. He only knew of one person who had claimed to have participated in raising someone from the dead, and that person was asking them to hold hands and pray over Prince.

"Andrew needs to be in on this," said Edwin.

"And get Kim, Dad. She needs—" Sharon looked at Kim getting out of her car.

Edwin went to get Andrew from the car—where Sharon would have been had her emotions not gotten the best of her.

Jonathan broke the circle of prayer and joined his wife's hand with Sharon's. "Rebuke the spirit of death until I come back."

"What? Me? Where are you going?" asked Sharon.

"I have to deliver a prophecy."

"A prophecy? To who? Right now?" said Sharon.

"Especially now. God even gave Pharoah a chance to repent."

Sharon's eyes got big. "Repent?" She looked at Prince's body. "A chance to *repent*?"

Jonathan knew the war that was going on in Sharon's heart. "They won't repent. God has shown it to me."

"Then why go to them? Jonathan," she looked at him with pleading eyes, "they killed Prince. They're dangerous people." Sharon looked at Elizabeth, but they had obviously already had this conversation.

"I'll be back, Sharon. Lead everyone in prayer. Remember my Haiti story about the dead woman?"

She nodded.

"Just do that. Keep doing it. I don't know how long it takes ambulances to come to a place like this. They're probably waiting to get police protection. Let's hope something happens before they come."

She watched him walk towards the same building she had gone to. *Let's hope something happens?* She looked at the body and the blood. *Something like what? This isn't Haiti. And the Haitian lady had a heart attack. Prince was shot. A lot of times. Does he actually think we can fix this?*

***

Sonny's binoculars magnified up to one hundred and forty times. He looked through them at the black man walking across the field. He shook his head. It was still nuts, but it made more sense. Prince had gotten hooked up with some crazy people.

He connected a couple of more dots.

He looked at the white girl and cussed. She was badder than Samira. Maybe Prince was only half crazy. Maybe he just liked fine white girls. He looked at the other people circled around Prince. "What the—?" It was that new sister. Kim. What was she doing with *them*? He looked at the black man with new irritation. "Anybody know this nigga?"

"Yeah," said a Vice Boy, "he and that white dude the ones been coming down here having Bible study with Prince."

"Figures. See what happens when you get too nice? People take advantage of you." He watched the black man enter his building.

"Now this nigga think he can walk around Mayhem like he owns the place. He knocks on that door, teach that nigga some respect."

Jonathan knocked hard on the door.

***

Sharon prayed as hard as she could. She prayed in English. She prayed in tongues. She bound death. She loosed life. She commanded healing. She quoted Scripture. She did everything she knew to do.

Prince was dead.

A mustard seed of faith was a lot larger than Sharon had ever imagined. She pulled her hands from Elizabeth and her mom. She held her nauseated stomach as she took a few steps away from the circle. "I'm okay. I just need a few moments."

"It's okay, Sharon," said Elizabeth. "Everyone pray. This is something we all have to do. It's not Jonathan or Sharon we're trusting in. It's Jesus Christ. The Resurrection and the Life. The One who raised Lazarus from the dead after four days. Come on. Everyone cry out to God. I'll start, but everyone needs to pray."

Edwin spoke up. "Elizabeth's right. We've seen God work miracles. We don't have to be in church for God to work a miracle. He told His disciples to heal the sick, cleanse the lepers, cast out demons, and raise the dead." He looked at everyone with a confidence he didn't yet feel. "Well, Prince is dead. Let's do like Jonathan said. Let's command death to leave until either Prince comes back or the ambulance comes."

"Death, let him go!"

"God, bring Prince back for Your glory!"

"You are the same yesterday, today, and forever!"

"His work isn't through. Don't let the devil steal his ministry!"

"Remember his mother's prophecies that he'd preach around the world!"

"Show Mayhem that You are Lord over life and death!"

"You said, 'Verily, verily, I say unto you, he who believes on Me, the works that I do shall he do also. And greater works than these because I go unto My Father!"

"God, you said if we had faith, we could speak to the mountain and it would be removed. We speak to this mountain of death to go!"

Commands, petitions, tears, and praise went up with renewed energy. Even Kim found herself doing something as unbelievable as praying over a dead body to a God she didn't know, but had always wanted to know. Tears rolled down her face, as much as for her as for Prince. *Lord, I'm dead. I need to know a God who raises the dead. I don't mean to tempt You, but I need You to show me Your power. So I can live, too.*

***

A Vice Boy opened the door. "What you want?"

"I got a message for Sonny," said Jonathan.

The man snickered. "Sonny's got a message for you, too."

"I thought so," said Jonathan.

***

Jonathan walked toward the flashing lights of several police cars and an ambulance. He pulled his hand down from the gash above his right eye. His hand was full of blood. He tried to guess how many stitches this time.

The closer he got to the area, he wondered at the indifference of the police officers. Most were standing around laughing and talking. Someone was taking pictures. Another was walking around and looking at the ground. The ambulance folks had either viewed the body and had gotten back into the ambulance, or had never gotten out. They didn't seem too interested in what was going on around them.

Edwin and Barbara were talking to a police officer.

Sharon and the others were holding hands and praying their hearts out near the cars.

Jonathan went to the ambulance. It was a man and woman team. He knocked on the passenger window. She looked at his head, then at his clothes and rolled down the window. "I sure hope you're in a good mood tonight. He smiled and pointed toward

Edwin and Barbara. "I'm with them. I ventured off a little and ran into a stick. A club, really."

The woman jumped out the front. "Sir, you're in luck. My divorce is final today."

"Uh oh. You don't have any anger issues, do you?" asked Jonathan.

She smiled. "Not any more. Come on."

Jonathan looked at Sharon, Elizabeth, Kim, and Andrew. He could tell by their movements that they were praying hard. He looked at Prince's body. "What's going on with the body?" he asked the woman.

"He's got at least twelve bullets in 'em. Cops know 'em. Drug deal gone bad. Live hard, die hard. We're waiting on the medical examiner. Busy night. Hope he gets here soon. Counting tonight, I've been in Mayhem one hundred and fifty-one times. I still get the heebie-jeebies coming in here, even with a cop escort."

When the lady finished helping Jonathan, he said, "I don't know why your ex-husband divorced you. You do good work."

"You were smart to not say that until I patched you up," she said with a smile.

"I'm smarter than I look. Thank you." He turned toward the praying group. He was immediately heavy. He had to help them pray. This guy could show up any moment.

***

Forty minutes later the three car caravan prayed harder and louder in a circle, holding hands, as they watched the paramedics roll the body bag toward the ambulance. They rolled the gurney into the ambulance and shut the door.

Barbara gasped.

Sharon turned to Edwin. "Dad." Her voice was low and full of defeat. "It didn't work."

Jonathan looked at Sharon. "Keep praying." He glanced at Elizabeth. "Come with me, Liz."

"Dad, what is he doing?"

"Let's keep praying, Sharon," said Kim.

Jonathan jogged to the ambulance and waved his hands at the driver. He rolled the window down. Jonathan started talking. After a few minutes, he motioned to the others. They hurried over.

"Why not? We got nothing better to do? Right, Glenda," said the driver.

"Don't make me hurt you, Jimmy. You look a lot like my ex-husband. The cops are still here. It's not going to hurt anything. You don't believe in prayer."

"Since when do you believe in prayer, Glenda?" he mumbled.

"Never mind him. He's just hungry," she said to Jonathan. Glenda got out the van and opened the back door. She got in the back and unzipped the body bag. She took Prince's pulse. Her eyes popped wide. "Danny," she screamed, "I think I got a pulse!"

***

Slavery glared at the Christians jumping up and down at the ambulance. Sharp teeth protruded from his frown. "I had hoped my suspicions were wrong."

"Raised from the dead on my watch? I have never lost one like this. Never in all my darkness," yelled Annihilation.

"It is not the *one* we must be worried about," said Slavery. "You heard that winch of a thorn, Sharon. It's her. It's the others. It's the church. That's what this whole thing is about. The dog of heaven is at it again."

Slavery didn't want to admit it, but their enemy was a brilliant strategist even if He was unjust and arbitrary. "We thought this was about Octavius. The enemy saving one slave." He slapped his palms together. "It never was about saving one slave. It was about using that slave to save the church!"

Annihilation's eyes went wide with horror. First, this plan was big. Huge. It wasn't an attack to save a few people from their stronghold. It was a bold plan to destroy their stronghold. This could well turn out to be cataclysmic. As bad as that was, there was something else that was deeply insulting about the enemy's plan. He was using a black man to light a fire under the church's butt.

"I've had it with this *'God chooses the weak things of the world to shame the things which are strong'* crap," said Annihilation. "I know we are at war, but there are some lines that shouldn't be crossed."

"That's what He does, my friend. He crosses lines. And this one, He takes particular pleasure in crossing."

"Using the weak, the poor, the despised." Annihilation's anger exploded. "I know this. I know this. I know this. But I will never accept it. It's too much. It's wrong, Slavery. Everything about it is wrong."

Slavery understood the ruler spirit's angry outburst. He felt the same anger. "I have come to grudgingly accept this tactic of the enemy." He smirked with contempt. "It's his way of humiliating us, of showing the sons and daughters of Adam that the weakest of their kind is stronger than our greatest strength when they trust in him." His simmering hatred bubbled to a full boil. "What I cannot and will not ever get used to is how he loves them."

"I have dedicated myself to destroying black dirt, to getting them to destroy themselves—and now this!" said Annihilation.

"If this works, if the church rallies around this...this...fiasco—"

"Look," Annihilation said sharply, "the last thing we need is for the church to start acting like Jesus. Can you imagine our beloved Mayhem being invaded by an army of people who are doers of the word and not hearers only?"

Slavery recalled how in 2004 his friends had been run out of Manchester, Kentucky when sixty-three churches prayed together and marched through the city declaring that his friends had to leave. He shuddered. "Yes, unfortunately, I don't have to imagine it. Do you really think there's a danger of the church leaving the comfort and security of their buildings to come here?" He was hoping his friend would say something encouraging.

"Sharon. Jonathan. That blasted Holy Spirit," was his answer.

Slavery grimaced as though he'd been shot. "Oh, Annihilation. We can't let this happen."

Chapter 21

Glory Tabernacle hadn't had what could've been called a regular church service in over a year, if regular meant one that wasn't punctuated with dramatic healings, demons being cast out of people, and the altar flooded with people crying out to God for salvation.

Edwin opened his Bible on the pulpit and looked out over the congregation. Their transformation from a church that basically served a historical figure—even if they called Him Lord—to serving a living Christ who was active among His people had been about as calm and orderly as a tsunami.

There had been nothing negotiable or incremental about it. It had been all or none. He had found that despite the popular saying among charismatics that the Holy Spirit was a gentleman, He was no gentleman. He had found that actually He was quite stubborn and pushy. The Spirit had one agenda: lift up Jesus.

Perspectives, schedules, agendas, traditions, beliefs, education, family, friends, jobs, reputations, goals, fears, anything that stood in the way of lifting up Jesus had to be put on the altar as a sacrifice—a dead sacrifice. Compromise and half-hearted efforts to commit one hundred percent to what the Holy Spirit wanted to do were dead on arrival.

Gentleman? No.

God? Yes.

But although Edwin had found this new relationship terrifying, he had also found it exhilarating and liberating. The boredom and sense of stagnation was gone from his walk with the Lord. Every dangerous day was exciting and worth living.

Danger.

He flipped the pages of his Bible. That's what was different about this service. He had to talk to his congregation about danger. Serving God dangerously.

"Jesus Christ was brutally murdered."

Pause.

A very long, awkward, now some were thinking, *embarrassing* pause.

"Jesus. The Lord we adore. He was brutally...murdered. This was a horrifying event. Something so barbaric and difficult to fathom. The Son of God is tortured to death. His death was many things, but one thing it wasn't was tragic. As bloody, as cruel, as unbelievably gruesome—and if you consider it was His own people who delivered Him to the Romans—as treacherous as His death was, it wasn't tragic.

"A tragedy is an exceedingly bad event that leaves you crushed with sadness and despair. Something precious and irreplaceable is lost. This does not describe the death of our Lord. Bandits didn't jump out of the bushes and shoot him for his money. He wasn't arrested in his carpenter's shop and falsely charged for a capital offense and killed by the state. He wasn't hit by a stray arrow. Nor did he lose his footing and slip off a cliff to an untimely death.

"Our Lord, the Lord we adore and follow, was not the victim of bad circumstances. He was not at the wrong place at the wrong time. Jesus Christ was murdered because of His own deliberate conspiracy. A conspiracy of love."

Edwin closed his eyes and raised his hands to God while he quoted Romans 5.

"For while we were still helpless, at the right time Christ died for the ungodly. For one will hardly die for a righteous man; though perhaps for the good man someone would dare even to die. But God demonstrates His own love toward us, in that while we were yet sinners, Christ died for the ungodly."

He opened his eyes and didn't bother wiping away the tears. "Brothers and sisters, Christ died at the *right* time, and He did it for those, you and I, who were helpless in their ungodliness. I suppose He could have died on another planet for us, but He chose to die where the need was. This tells me that love is attracted to need. The need was on earth; so He came.

"There is a young man who is in Grady Hospital as I speak. I don't know whether he will live or die. Honestly, I don't know how he's still alive. Well, I do know how he's still alive." Edwin's voice got stronger. "My daughter and my son and Jonathan and Elizabeth and the young lady seated next to Sharon raised him from the dead. He was shot twelve times on Thursday at close range, and he is alive today because somebody believed that the God who raised Lazarus from the dead after he was dead four days could give life to a man who had been shot down by thugs."

The congregation erupted in praise.

Edwin did nothing to stop them. It was a great thing God had done, and He should be praised. He continued amidst the last spattering of clapping hands and hallelujahs. He told them how Prince had robbed them, and how Sharon had scared the man so badly with her suicidal driving that he threw his gun out the window. He told them how Prince prayed for salvation right there on the side of the highway once they stopped the car.

When the next round of praise died down, Edwin continued. "Jonathan and I started having Bible studies with this new convert, where he lives. He lives in a place they call *The Bluff*. It's known for its violence and for being a capitol of sorts for heroin distribution.

"There's another place not far from there that's even worse. It's aptly called Mayhem. The young man in the hospital grew up in Mayhem. He was in Mayhem, and Mayhem was in him. Until light swallowed darkness. The reason he has twelve bullet holes in him is because the darkness wanted to stop his light. Satan's attempt to stop this man failed because the church was there to raise him from the dead. I think there's a larger message here.

"Not too long ago, when Sharon's friend died of a drug overdose, I promised my daughter that our church would start an inner city ministry. We started one, but while we were praying and analyzing and organizing and praying and analyzing and organizing and praying and praying and praying, Satan was shooting down our new convert in broad daylight."

Sharon bent over onto her lap and cried into her hands.

"That's how they do things in Mayhem," said Edwin. "They shoot you down in broad daylight. I've never been to a place before where the evil can be felt in the air. You can feel it in Mayhem. But I believe it's time to change the atmosphere in Mayhem. I believe the prophetic message behind Prince being raised from the dead is that God wants us to see that we can raise Mayhem from the dead."

The auditorium was silent.

"Our Lord knew He could change our Mayhem. But He knew He couldn't do it from the safety of heaven. He'd have to make Himself vulnerable to save others. He'd have to give His life to save life.

"I'm asking everyone here to search your heart. Ask yourself what you're willing to do to save others. Ask yourself what does it mean for us as a church to leave the ninety-nine and to go after the one who is lost. Ask yourself what kind of Christian you are, and what kind you want to become. Ask yourself how you want to face God on that great day.

"I ask you these hard questions without wanting to manipulate you. I *want* to persuade you, but I do *not* want to manipulate you. Jesus said no king goes to war without counting the cost. Count the cost. And be honest. Please, be brutally honest. Because I'm going to ask you to follow me as I follow Christ into Mayhem."

The church again erupted into praises and shouts of "Hallelujah."

This time Edwin held up his hands to quiet the crowd. "I don't believe— Listen to me, please. Heaven may have broken out in praise when the Word announced that He was going to earth to save sinners. But I think the celebrations stopped when He announced that He would be killed for His kindness."

A slow somberness came over the congregation. Here and there, the expressions on some faces, and the energetic whisperings of others, showed that it was dawning on the church that they weren't being asked to watch a movie about Daniel in the lions' den. They were being asked to go into the lions' den.

"Good," said Edwin, at the serious mood. One by one, he looked at his family and Jonathan and Elizabeth and smiled. "Now I have to be honest with you. I have a confession to make. I'm afraid. No, I'm terrified." He waved his hand. "Not of going to Mayhem. Not of dying in Mayhem. I'm terrified of not being willing to die in Mayhem for our Lord. I'm terrified of not being willing to die for my Lord anywhere."

Kim was crying. *How could this man be willing to give his life for people in Mayhem?*

Sharon was beaming. *How could she be so blessed to have such a courageous father?*

Elizabeth was fuming. *How could he be so irresponsible and presumptuous?*

"Those of you who are interested, there's a new Mayhem tab on the church website. Read about Mayhem. And read about what God did in Manchester, Kentucky in 2004. How He changed that community when the church counted the cost and got serious about running the devil out of town.

"Now we're going to have two teams. The first team are the frontline evangelists. You and I will work side-by-side in Mayhem. The second team are the intercessors. You will provide round the clock intercession for the evangelists.

"Tomorrow at 7:00 p.m., we will meet here to be baptized in water—the evangelists. It's critical that it's fresh in our minds that we have been buried with Christ. And if our bodies have died to the world and its sinful passions and its fears, there is nothing left for the devil to use."

Edwin exhorted the congregation further. Afterwards, Jonathan gave a short exhortation. He told them what he knew about the Vice Boys and how they probably were the ones who tried to kill Prince. He also told them how one of them had used a club to burst a pimple on his forehead.

A special treat was Elizabeth's adoptive mother, Ava, sharing how God had used her for the past thirty years to save girls from prostitution and forced sex trafficking. She emphasized how you had to go into that ministry with your eyes wide open and your faith firmly in God.

At the conclusion of the service, Edwin told his congregation that they wouldn't be alone. He was sure that Atlanta could have the kind of revival that God had given to the churches in Manchester, Kentucky. He'd start calling pastors for their participation once he saw what he was working with in his own church.

Edwin knew that challenging the dark powers over Mayhem was going to be the fight of his life. Just before he gave the closing prayer, he glanced at Barbara. He saw in her face that the fight was going to begin tonight as soon as their bedroom door closed.

Chapter 22

The bedroom door closed.

"Edwin, how long have you known about this suicide mission?"

Edwin got on his knees facing the side of the bed. He held out his hand.

Her head jutted out. "What? Pray? Are you serious? We need to talk about this."

"I agree. We need to talk about this. And we're going to pray first," he said.

"Edwin, this is—"

"Or we're not going to talk," he said.

Barbara briefly went blank. She looked into his eyes. They looked calmly determined. "Edwin, this is not like you. What's gotten into you?"

"The Holy Spirit."

She stood there, watching him with the stillness of a statue. "Okay, Edwin." But they weren't going to bed before talking this out. She walked over to him and put her hand out.

He took her hand as she kneeled beside him. He took his other hand and placed it on the side of her face, digging his fingers into her hair. He pulled her head forward and kissed her deeply.

Barbara didn't respond. That is, she didn't respond outwardly. She was angry, furious really. Edwin had no right to make such a dangerous, life-changing decision without discussing this with her. This kiss was inappropriate. Its odd timing, however, didn't stop her insides from catching on fire. It had been two days since they had last made love.

Just when it felt that mercifully his kiss was ending, and she could recover herself so they could get to the bottom of Edwin's insanity, he overpowered her lips again, sucking and pulling on them and exploring her mouth.

Barbara felt herself weakening, forgetting her anger. She yanked back. "Edwin, what are you doing," she demanded. She snapped a palm to her chest and panted. "This isn't prayer." She jumped up and hurried to the bathroom and splashed cold water on her face and returned.

Edwin was still on his knees. He reached for her hand.

"Do *not* kiss me, Edwin."

"I won't."

She gave him her hand and got on her knees.

"Lord, thank You for saving me and calling me to Your ministry. Thank you for trusting me with Your church. Thank You for my wonderful family, and especially my beautiful—lovely wife. She has given me her youth. She has given me three wonderful children. She is my friend, my lover—"

Barbara blushed. It felt funny talking about being lovers in the presence of God.

"—my partner in life. She's everything I always imagined a perfect wife would be. She and my beautiful family are my Isaac. I love them. I always will. But I put them on the altar. I place myself on Your altar.

"Lord, I ask that You give to my wife the spirit of wisdom and revelation in the knowledge of You. I pray that you open her eyes to Your great love for her, and that you'll open her eyes to my great love for her. Help her to understand me, and why I must follow You, even if it's to the cross."

He opened his eyes and kissed her on the forehead. "Sorry, I said I wouldn't kiss you." He sat on the edge of the bed.

Barbara's eyes were still closed. Tears rolled down her face. Her husband's prayer was both beautiful and terrifying. She knew he loved her. He was a Christian. How could he not love her? But how could he feel so tenderly about her? It had been only a little over a year ago that she had been unfaithful to him.

And she knew the story of Abraham and Isaac and the altar. This is what terrified her. She joined Edwin on the bed.

"Saturday evening," said Edwin. "That's when I decided to take the church to Mayhem. When I looked at Prince hooked to those machines. When I realized that had we not gone to Mayhem, Prince would be dead. When his mother told me that the devil couldn't kill Octavius because she was a prophetess, and that God had told her that her son would preach the gospel around the world, and he hadn't done that yet."

"God told Abraham to kill Isaac." Barbara spoke just above a whisper.

"Yes, He did."

Barbara stared straight ahead of her. "God didn't want Abraham to put his son before Him. He won't permit idolatry in our lives."

"He had waited a long time for that son," said Edwin.

"Twenty-five years," said Barbara.

Edwin's eyes crinkled curiously.

"Why'd you kiss me like that?" she asked. "Why'd you kiss me like you were going away?" She still stared straight ahead.

"I kissed you because I love you."

"You kissed me like that because you know the same people who tried to kill Prince may kill you. Isn't this the truth, Edwin? You know that I may soon be a widow and our children may be fatherless."

He got on one knee beside Barbara. Everything within him wanted to assure her that she was wrong. That he would challenge and vanquish a dangerous enemy for the Lord and come out of it unscathed. But his mouth wouldn't move to speak such lies. The threat was real. Barbara had spoken the truth.

"Please answer me, Edwin."

"Yes. That could happen. I could be hurt."

"Not hurt. Murdered. At least say it, Edwin. Murdered."

"Yes. I could be murdered."

"What about us? What about your family? Do we matter in all this? My need for a husband? Our children's need of a father? Does any of this matter?" She wiped an eye. "You can put us on the altar like Abraham put Isaac on the altar, and free yourself of whatever idolatry you feel we are to you, but you can't put your obligation to your family on any altar. If a man does not provide for his family, he has denied the faith and is worse than an infidel."

Edwin was surprised at Barbara's use of Scripture. She certainly wasn't biblically illiterate, but she wasn't one to use non-popular Scripture verses often. Yet, in the past minute or so she had mentioned that Abraham's wait for Isaac was twenty-five years, and she had quoted Timothy.

"Barbara, I'd like to answer you."

"The floor is yours, Edwin."

"First, you're not my idol."

"Obviously not." Her words were soft and thoughtful, not angry.

"I thank God for my family. You're not a burden or an anchor to me, Barbara. I don't see you like that."

"I'm not a burden to you, but you put me on the altar. Altars are for sacrifice, aren't they, Edwin?"

"Honey, I love you. You know I do. Don't misinterpret what I'm saying. What I'm talking about is commitment to Christ, not lack of commitment to you and the children. Loving God with my whole heart does not mean I love you any less. It simply means that I can't let my love for you and our family keep me from obeying God."

"So, God told you to go to Mayhem? To lead the church into Mayhem?" said Barbara.

Edwin looked into his heart. He recalled the words of Jesus. He recalled Prince hooked up to tubes, barely clinging to life. "I believe He has."

"And you have counted the cost?" she asked.

"Yes."

Barbara's eyes and voice changed. "All of the cost, Edwin?"

He wondered at her shift from resignation to a challenge. "Yes," he said, not knowing what to expect next.

"You could die."

"Yes."

"The people who follow you to Mayhem could die."

"Yes."

"Are you allowing women to follow you into Mayhem?"

Edwin stumbled mentally. He hadn't thought about it. He had been so caught up in the urgency and magnitude of the call that it just never came to mind.

"You announced this to the entire church. You're going to have women show up," said Barbara. "You know Elizabeth will be right there with Jonathan. And Ava's always itching to rescue somebody. She's going to show up. She'll probably bring some of her female workers."

Edwin's mind was spinning at the new troubles. They hadn't even gone to Mayhem yet and already things were getting out of control.

"Amy Carmichael was a wonderful evangelist and missionary for the Lord, wasn't she, Edwin?"

Amy Carmichael was a sickly woman who had gone to India as a missionary in the early 1900's. She established a work that saved hundreds of girls from forced temple prostitution.

"Yes, she was," said Edwin, wondering what Amy Carmichael had to do with this. And how did Barbara know about her?

Barbara could tell by his tone that he was surprised. "Amy Carmichael is my mother's favorite girl hero. Besides Margaret Thatcher." She studied her husband's thoughts. They were as much on his face as in his head. "You are going to have a male and female army."

He was forced to agree. "I guess I am."

"The church has always had female martyrs, as well as men," said Barbara. "You could have females killed for the Lord."

Edwin got off his knee and stood up. He walked to the window, rubbing his hand through his hair.

"Some of them could be mothers," Barbara added. "How do you feel about this? How does the Lord feel about this?"

Edwin looked out the window for several thoughtful seconds. He turned and faced Barbara. "I think it breaks His heart."

"But He has commanded them also to go into all the world and preach the gospel?" said Barbara.

"Yes, He has." Edwin's voice was heavy with this admission.

"And what about you, Edwin? How do you feel knowing you may be leading some mother to her death?"

Edwin searched his wife's face for the sarcasm he didn't hear in her questions. He found none. Nor did he find the sword in her mouth that was slicing through him. Honesty was brutal and took no prisoners.

"I pray that this doesn't happen."

"But if it does?" Barbara pressed. "If some child loses her mother, if some husband loses his wife?"

Edwin's watery eyes mirrored the sickness he felt in his pastor's heart. "Honey, if this happens—"he shook his head—"if this happens, I honestly don't know what I'd do. I'd be crushed. Devastated. I'd hope that the family could somehow find a way to forgive me. I'd hope that I'd somehow find a way to forgive myself."

"Edwin, knowing this, will you call it off?"

"No," he said, wiping his eyes. "I can't. Love goes where the need is. I have to go. Those who are baptized tomorrow will have counted the cost. I'll go over it with them again, in detail. I'll make sure that everyone knows we are counting all things loss that we may evangelize Mayhem. I pray that no one is hurt, but I know no way to rescue Mayhem without going into Mayhem."

Barbara went to her husband and looked into his eyes. "Do you believe this with all of your heart? I need to believe in you, Edwin. I need to believe that this is not some hero or insecurity or 'I want to be like Jonathan' phase you're going through."

He shook his head. "No. No. It's nothing like that, honey. It's the call of God that's driving this. It's my fear that I will stand before God on Judgment Day and be exposed as a coward. As someone who had been given so much and had given so little."

"Good," she said softly, so softly Edwin wondered whether or not he'd heard correctly. It was her turn to walk to the window and look out. "Behold, I send you out as sheep in the midst of wolves."

"What?" said Edwin.

"Jesus. He told that to His disciples," said Barbara, still gazing out the window. "He who seeks to save his life, the same shall lose it. But he who loses his life for My sake, the same shall find it." Barbara couldn't see her husband, but she knew his expression was displaying full shock.

Edwin's head tilted in thought.

"Edwin, I study the Bible all the time. I've memorized Scripture since I was a little girl in Sunday school. I'm not as ignorant of the things of God as people think I am." She let that sink in a bit. "You remember when I surprised you with the announcement that I wanted to go into politics?"

Do I remember? How could she ask such a thing? Even the memory of that evening was enough to threaten that he'd throw up. "Yeah, I do. I most certainly do."

She turned around and looked at Edwin. "I never wanted to go into politics. I know I've got strong conservative values, and I know I get riled up whenever we talk politics. God knows someone ought to get riled up. This nation has lost its way. When you look at—" Barbara took a deep breath. "That's another conversation."

"You never wanted to go into politics?" Edwin was befuddled.

"No, Edwin, I never wanted to go into politics. What I wanted, what I *want* is my life to count for eternity."

Edwin's mouth dropped open. He snapped it shut when he realized Barbara could probably see his tonsils.

"Surprising, isn't it?"

Edwin stammered for an answer that wouldn't qualify as a lie.

"It's okay, Edwin. I haven't done much over the years to make anyone think otherwise. But when I'm alone, when it's just me and the Lord—"*me and the Lord?* thought Edwin—"I read and study and pray. Sometime for hours."

Sometimes for hours? Did I just hear her say hours? Edwin would've commented had he been able to stop his mental conversation with himself.

"I never *wanted* to go into politics. I gravitated to it by default. What I wanted was to be like Amy Carmichael."

"Amy Carmichael? *You* wanted to be like Amy Carmichael?" He waved his hand apologetically. "I'm sorry. I'm not saying—"

"Yes, you are saying, and it's okay."

Edwin's eyebrows stretched up and down, saying what he said he wasn't saying. "It's just, honey, this...this is, well, it's new. I've never heard you talk about her." He stepped out a little further. "Or about eternity. I mean, I know you love the Lord, and want to go to heaven. But, I mean, the part about making your life count for eternity. I've never heard you talk like that."

"Edwin, I'm a senior at Regent University. I'm finishing up a BA in Biblical and Theological Studies. Dad has been paying the tuition so I could keep this secret."

Edwin's mind wasn't blank. But his perfectly frozen body had stopped receiving instructions from his brain, except to not collapse. And the deluge of competing words and blurred thought fragments had not connected in a coherent way to allow him to answer.

Barbara looked more closely at him. "Edwin?"

He shook his head, as though he hadn't been listening. "Huh? You...are a senior...in Bible school? What? I mean—"

"All of my general education courses transferred. That left me with seventy-one credits. The degree's totally online, and it's regionally accredited. I've been working on it for a year."

Who was this person impersonating his wife? *I've always wanted to be a missionary, and I've been secretly going to school for a year. My school's accredited?* "What a minute," he shook his hands downward. "Just wait a minute, Barbara. Back up for a moment." He palmed his face with both hands and tried to rub away some of the shock. "I knew you used to want to be an attorney. But I had absolutely no idea you had any spiritual aspirations other than being a wonderful wife and mother. And school? A secret Bible degree? Barbara, what is going on?"

"Edwin, I know this is a shock."

"Why the secrecy? Why'd you feel you had to keep this a secret?"

She sat on a chair.

He hesitated, then sat on the bed. He saw her face crinkle out an expression somewhere between embarrassment and a loss of words.

"The best I can come up with, Edwin, is I've been heartbroken most of my life."

Edwin wanted to be a good husband. *Don't try to fix everything,* that's what the Christian books said, *just listen.* He kept his face straight, but it was hard to do it while he was inside of a tumbling dryer. *Barbara—what are—you talking about?*

"I betrayed the Lord. I didn't answer His call. Ever since then, my heart has been sick. Broken. Closed to God's voice."

"Ever since when, Barbara?" Edwin asked tenderly.

Guilty tears rolled out of her eyes. She knew this would hurt Edwin, but she had held this suffocating burden for so long. It was time. "Ever since I married you."

The tumbling dryer sped up.

Barbara knew Edwin's silence was filled with pain and questions. "I was supposed to go to the mission field. I didn't go. Instead, I got married."

Could this dryer speed up any faster? Edwin felt sick.

"I was afraid to obey God. I was afraid that I might not ever get married. I was afraid that I might not ever have children. I was afraid that I might die on the mission field. Fear." Barbara said the word as though she hated it. "I used to have vivid dreams from the Lord. Yes," she answered his look, "Barbara Stowell, the on-fire Christian teenager used to be a little Sharon. Well, maybe that's pushing it. But I did have a sweet relationship with Jesus. He used to talk to me so often. I'm going to tell you something else shocking."

Oh, Lord, no. I've had all the shocking I can stand, thought Edwin.

"Dad used to call me Little Joan."

Edwin recalled once hearing her father call her that. He also recalled the look that Barbara gave him. That was the first and last time he had heard her father call her that.

"It was Joan of Arc. The prophetess. Imagine that, huh? Me being called a prophetess."

"A prophetess? A *prophetess*, Barbara?"

"I used to get a lot of dreams. Some of them eerily prophetic. Helped Dad make a killing once in a business deal. I was only fifteen, too." The light in Barbara's eyes went dim. "Everything stopped when I got married. No more dreams. Precious few words. I know the Lord loves me, but something changed when I disobeyed Him."

Edwin didn't know whether he felt sadder for her or for himself. He was the pastor. He should have something to say. And he would say it—as soon as the dryer stopped, or at least slowed down.

"I know I'm not making much sense," said Barbara, "but I think that's why I didn't tell you. Living without the intimacy I used to have with my precious Jesus has been so absolutely devastating to me, Edwin." She shook her head. "Our Sharon. I love her so much. God knows I do. But every day I look at her, I die because I was supposed to be her. And now she's having dreams and visions." Barbara burst into tears.

Edwin rushed over and hugged her. He was still in the mental dryer, but at least now he understood why he was being pummeled.

"I'm sorry, honey."

"It's not your fault, Edwin. The fault is all mine. I could've told you, but I never gave you the chance to say yes or no. I was just so afraid of losing you that I said no to God. I only went back to school to try to stop the pain. I think it was my way of telling God that I'm sorry."

"Oh, He knows you're sorry, honey. He knows your heart."

Edwin held his wife tightly. Holding her helped him keep his spiritual guts from falling onto the floor. *He had been an idol to her, and had cost her a lifetime of unhappiness.*

"Edwin, I have something else."

How much more was there? He waited for the dryer to speed up again.

"I'm going to Mayhem with you. So is Sharon. So is Andrew. We go as a family or no one goes."

This was no dryer's tumble. This was a tornado.

He jerked back. "What do you mean?" It wasn't a question. It was more a *No you are not!*

"I missed God once because of fear. I'm not going to do it again." She met his resistant eyes. "I'm not, Edwin." She was resolute. "I'm not living another day letting fear dictate what I do for my Lord."

"Barbara, you *can't* be serious. And our children? Sharon? Andrew?" He shook his head. "Honey, I know you've had it hard since you—"

"Since I chose having a family and being safe over following the call of God," she finished. "Edwin," her lips trembled during the pause, "you remember when I helped to interpret Sharon's dream?"

"Yeah." His answer was rough.

"It wasn't just an interpretation. I had a dream, too. For the first time in nearly twenty years, I had a dream, Edwin. It was about Prince being in trouble. That's why the interpretation came so easily." She rubbed her wet eyes, shaking her head with a happiness she didn't think she'd ever feel again. "It's like I'm Samson. With my eyes wide open I put my head on Delilah's lap, and she shaved me bald." Barbara coughed out a laugh. "But God has caused my hair to grow back. He's giving me another chance."

Edwin's body was tense with defiance. There wasn't an inch of him that was going to stand for this. He was not putting his family in harm's way. But how? How was he going to stop his wife a second time from following her heart? Where could a disagreement like this end?

Oh, God! he screamed in his mind.

Honestly, he had to admit that he didn't know how this conversation would end. But one thing he did know. Come what may, Sharon and Andrew were not going to Mayhem.

Barbara wiped her eyes and looked at Edwin with a calm smile. She closed her eyes and inhaled and exhaled deeply. She seemed totally at peace. She opened her eyes. "Edwin, we've been through a lot, and I've put you through a lot."

He looked at her questioningly. He dropped his eyes when it became apparent she was referring to her infidelity a year ago.

"I don't blame you for my life. You've given me a good life. You're a wonderful husband and father. And how much you've grown in the past year or so is amazing. You're not weak any more, Edwin, and I like that."

He smiled.

"I'm not weak any more either. God is giving me another chance to put my Isaac on the altar. This time there's no question as to my allegiance. I've already slashed his throat. I'm serving God alongside you and Jonathan and Elizabeth and Ava...and Sharon and Andrew."

"Barbara—"

Barbara shook her head slowly and put her finger over Edwin's lips. "You said you are willing to send other children's mothers to their deaths for the call of God. You said you are willing to make other men widowers for the call of God. If you protect your family from the very danger you are leading other people into—I know you don't mean to be a hypocrite, Edwin, but...

"And at what age should our children begin to serve the Lord?" she continued. "There's no question about Sharon. She wants to serve God. Let her. Let her be a light in that dark place. She'll not be alone. There will be enough men to make sure no woman is alone. And Andrew is young, but he has a heart for God. Let's expose him to Jesus outside of the walls of a church building."

Edwin the husband and father was repelled by the thought of his precious family going into Mayhem. What those people did to Prince in broad daylight. Edwin the man of God, more specifically, the man of God he had become, knew that although every carnal bone in his body was put out of joint by this talk, his wife was right.

It wasn't a questions of whether or not his family was going to die. Death was appointed unto everyone. The questions to ask were, How would they live before they died? And would they glorify God in their death as well as their life?

Oh, God, you have to help me. I want to do what's right, thought Edwin. *Lord, give me a sign, please. I don't want fear to stop us from doing what we're supposed to do as a family.*

Barbara reached up and pulled Edwin's face toward her. She kissed him deeply. "I love you, Edwin Styles. I love the man you've become. I know you won't let fear stop us from doing what we're supposed to do as a family."

He looked up. "Thank you, Lord." He smiled at Barbara. "I think Little Joan is back."

"How do you think we should celebrate?" she asked, with a twinkle in her eyes.

Edwin wasn't a prophet, but he interpreted that twinkle correctly.

***

It was late. Very late. It had begun with a twinkle, and had ended with Barbara lifting her resting head off of Edwin's chest and pecking him lightly on the lips. "So what do you think about Sharon's idea to move Kim in with us?"

Edwin didn't open his heavy eyes. He had been had. What was it about mice and peanut butter? Or men and sex? "It's not nice to take candy from a baby, Barbara."

He didn't see her smile, but he felt the kiss on his cheek. "I paid well for this candy."

He smiled with closed eyes. *Can't argue with you there?*

Chapter 23

Edwin punched the numbers into his phone and exhaled an angry breath. He had gone through three churches. Every pastor wanted to donate money and equipment, but no one was willing to actually do anything.

Correction.

The Victory World Outreach Center was willing to, in the exact words of the pastor, "Pray and open the heavens over Mayhem. We'll bind the strong man so you and your people can go in and rescue the captives."

Edwin pressed the pastor for a commitment of boots on the ground. He had reminded him that God had told Joshua that He would give Israel every place that the soles of their feet would tread. The pastor's answer was that he and his people did that in the spirit. But Edwin had been assured by this "full gospel" preacher of a thriving church that he and his people would "release the angels to go before you."

It had been hard for Edwin to not say something sarcastic to a preacher who thought he had power over God's angels, but who would not help them any more than to cut a check or let them use some equipment.

Pastor number four came to the phone. "Edwin, how are you brother? What can I do you out of?" The jovial voice on the other end of the phone matched the full waistline and plump cheeks of the preacher with the everlasting smile and full arsenal of jokes.

Edwin braced himself for Reverend Johnny Carson. It was a mystery to him how a minister who at times came across as a frustrated comedian could have such a large church. "Hopefully, nothing, Paul."

"Aww, you're no fun. I bet you pay your taxes only once a year, too. Am I right?"

"Yeah, that's right," said Edwin.

"What a stiff," said the happy preacher. "Charlene tells me you got something wild going on over there at glory land."

After three failed calls, Edwin figured he'd try a different approach. "Probably not as wild as what I hear you have going on in Africa."

"*South* Africa, young man. *South* Africa. There's a world of difference in South Africa and the rest of the continent."

Edwin recalled some of Jonathan's stories about ministering in South Africa. Extreme poverty disproportionately represented in the black population. Unbelievably high murder rates and rapes of women and children. A deplorably high rate of HIV-AIDS. A general sense that the country had imposed upon itself an apartheid of self-destruction.

Edwin's heart warmed because here was someone who, though irritatingly silly at times, was leading his church to take light into dangerously dark places. He'd understand what Edwin was trying to do. "I hear it's really dangerous over there," said Edwin.

"It can be. You gotta be careful."

"Have you lost anyone?"

"What do you mean?" asked Paul.

"I've got a friend who's done a lot of work over there. He's had some bad encounters."

"Probably veered off the *beaten* path. You do have to be careful. Lots of dark places in South Africa," said Paul.

The beaten path? Edwin wondered.

"We've been ministering in South Africa for years, and we've never had a single problem. Not a one," he added.

Edwin thought of Jonathan's work over there. "That's amazing. How have you managed to work in such a dangerous place and not have any safety issues?" Edwin perked up and slid a paper tablet closer to him. He tumbled the ink pen between his fingers, waiting for this man's secret.

"Get ready, Edwin. Here it comes. I'm going to tell you the secret to staying safe in South Africa, and because I like you, I'm not going to charge you extra."

"I appreciate that," Edwin said, masking his impatience.

He chuckled. "Oh, don't get too happy. I *am* going to charge you. Just not as much as I would if you were on the list. 'Thou shalt not muzzle the ox that treadeth the corn.' So put your hand on your wallet, my friend."

Edwin shook his head and rolled his eyes.

"You ready, Edwin?"

"Yes."

"Here's my secret to staying safe in South Africa."

Finally, thought Edwin.

"Stay out of the dangerous places. That'll be one hundred Euros, my friend. Wait a minute. I said I like you, didn't I? I'll take one hundred American dollars. You have a Pay Pal account, don't you?"

Edwin's teeth clenched.

"Don't feel taken advantage of, my friend. You don't pay me for my effort; you pay me for my knowledge."

"Paul?" Edwin wasn't sure whether he cared or not if his anger was coming out. "Where does your church minister in South Africa?"

"Oh, Edwin, we're all over. We're in Cape Town, Johannesburg, and Pretoria. What an absolutely gorgeous country. We have a trip coming up soon. You should seriously think about coming with us. Edwin, there are nearly forty-seven thousand millionaires in South Africa, and I know seven of them. They've got some billionaires, too." He added sadly, "But I don't know any of them." He perked up. "But I'm believing God. The wealth of the wicked is laid up for the just. And I've already put the paperwork in to change my name from Paul Winston to Paul The Just."

"What exactly does your ministry do over there?" asked Edwin.

"Oh, Lordy, Lordy, Edwin," the happy preacher squeezed his eyes shut and shook his head thinking about the glory, "it's a good thing we're not face to face. I'd have to put a blanket over my head like they did Moses so the glory wouldn't blind you. We have some of the most powerful worship—and intercession—and prophetic ministry. Lots of salvations, too. Incredible conferences."

"Where do you have the conferences?"

The happy preacher shook his head again. "Sometimes we do them at a church, but mostly we do them at a hotel. The one coming up will be at The Michelangelo Hotel. Absolutely magnificent. Boating, fishing, horseback riding, tennis courts—hot air ballooning, Edwin. You name it. It's there."

"Doesn't sound like you'll be able to help me," said Edwin.

"Sure I can. Ye must be born again," he said, laughing at a joke that he had apparently found hilarious."

Edwin grimaced. "I was hoping you'd be able to tell me some things about inner city ministry. About ministering in dangerous places. About reaching the poor."

"Edwin, you've got a thriving ministry. Why'd you want and go do something like that? God is blessing you."

Edwin pulled the phone from his ear and looked at it, frowning in disbelief.

"Edwin? Edwin? You there, brother?"

"Yeah, I'm still here."

The preacher wiped his forehead with the back of his hand. "Whew! That was a close call. Thought I had missed the rapture." He laughed. "Now, what's gotten into you, Edwin? I don't understand why you'd take a perfectly good ministry and start acting like some desperate minister just out of seminary trying to do something for God. You and that Jonathan fella's got some good stuff going on. Don't go mess it up."

Neither man said anything for several seconds.

"I'm almost afraid to ask you what form of suicide you're contemplating, Edwin."

"Our church is starting a ministry in Mahem Courts."

Silence.

Reverend Paul Winston reached over and grabbed—grabbed—the little fancy bottle of frankincense oil he had picked up in

Jerusalem. He dabbed a little on his forehead. He spoke calmly. "Do you mean Mahem as in May—hem Courts?"

"Yes."

"Mayhem?" the preacher yelled. "Mayhem? Are you crazy? Edwin, I got three guns. If you're just a itchin' to leave this world, you can use one to shoot yourself. If you don't have the heart to do it yourself, come by the house and I'll put you out your misery. Gua—ran—tee, when I tell the judge why I did it, he'll send me home in a limousine."

"Paul, isn't this what Jesus told us to do?"

"Uuh uh, brother. He may have told you to feed the sharks, but that's not what He told me."

"Feed the sharks? Paul, Jesus said 'Go into all the world.' Mayhem is part of that world."

"And so is Capetown. And so is Johannesburg. And so is Pretoria."

"Jesus said He was anointed to preach the gospel to the poor," said Edwin.

"News bulletin. This just in. I'm not Jesus. My name is Paul, and I don't mean the apostle Paul, either. What's gotten into you? Where'd this come from?" Paul made himself calm down. "Edwin, I don't mean to be so hard on you. I know you mean well. Really, something had to bring this on. It didn't come out of nowhere. Have you watched some documentary? One of those liberal demons at CNN jump on you?"

"Paul," Edwin was exasperated.

Paul shook his head. "Edwin, I'm going to be frank with you. Hear me out, brother, okay?"

Edwin rolled his eyes. *Why can't I just hang up right now?* "Sure."

"White guilt—"

"It's not—"

"Just hear me out, Edwin. White guilt will kill you just as surely as smoking cigarettes or running across the highway during heavy traffic. One is slow. One is fast. Both are dead. I may not be a poet, but I'm telling you the truth. Jesus said, 'The poor you have with you always.' You are not going to fix poverty by getting yourself killed. And you can't fix it with handouts either."

Edwin was too tired emotionally to listen to any more of this. "Paul, how much did you pay for your salvation?"

"Not a red cent. Salvation's a precious gift."

"So it was a handout?"

"Now just wait a minute, brother. Salvation's different," said Paul.

"Of course, it is, Paul. Our handout is always different from the other guy's handout."

"That's not—"

"Goodbye, Paul."

Click.

Edwin closed his eyes and tried to think of nothing. It didn't work. "Lord, forgive me, but I have to be honest with you. I don't like that man."

Edwin made nine more phone calls. Each conversation was some variation of the one he had with Paul.

"Lord, looks like it's just our forty people and You."

In the beginning God created the heavens and the earth.

Edwin wondered at the thought that popped into his mind. He smiled when the meaning became clear. "You didn't need an army to create the world, did You?"

***

Myla looked at Adaam-Mir, knowing his thoughts and anticipating the conversation. "You don't like him."

The angel's eyes popped wide. He was instinctively going to deny this. He had been promoted because of his great love for the sons and daughters of Adam. But Myla had spoken truth. Adaam-Mir pondered what this meant.

In his heart, he knew that he would fight to the death for this Paul Winston. He would serve him a million years if sons of Adam lived that long. But it was true that there was nothing spiritually attractive about this man. There was nothing there for him to like.

"Our blessed Creator loves the world, but He is not pleased with it," said Myla. "He loves the church, but there is much about it He dislikes." He knew the next revelation would be difficult for Adaam-Mir. "Some things about it He hates. There are some things about some of His children that He hates."

Adaam-Mir knew that Myla's words were weighty and difficult, but something about this revelation snapped into place. "The Creator is light. In Him is no darkness at all. He hates anything contrary to His nature."

Myla nodded. "This is a great mystery to many in the church, but it shouldn't be. Many of His children walk in extremes of misunderstanding His love. Some sadly don't see His love clearly enough to free them from the heaviness and guilt of sins they have repented of. Some don't see His love clearly enough to let it help them overcome sins that try to hang on to them. Others tragically see His love through a dark glass of impurity and presumption that convince them God's love for them is so great that He doesn't hate the sin they tolerate, and that there is no penalty for refusing to let it go."

"But that is contrary to who He is." Adaam-Mir's voice raised with passion. "From where do they get such reasonings? The blessed book, my brother. The blessed book is there for all to read. Tell me. Where do they get such reasonings?"

"Human flesh has the ability to believe anything it desires to believe, with or without a logical reason for doing so. Sons and daughters of God are no exception," said Myla.

"I do not understand. They have the blessed book and the Holy Spirit. How can a child of light walk in darkness? How can a child of righteousness not understand God's hatred of unrighteousness?" Adaam-Mir's intense expression pulled at his mentor for an answer to the great mystery.

"Adaam-Mir, you heard the conversation between Edwin and the man, Paul."

"Yes," the angel urged.

"The man, Paul, has exempted himself from his obligation to the poor and suffering, and hard places of service. There are things that the Lord requires that he finds unacceptable. So he rationalizes them away, as did the Pharisees."

"The Pharisees?" Adaam-Mir was in one spot, but his short, agitated movements seemed to be arguing about which direction to go. He lifted his hands to shoulder level and shook his head energetically. "No, my brother," he said, swooshing his hands down emphatically, "not like the Pharisees. Like that traitor of all that is good, Satan—the serpent! Is this not why we are at war at this present moment? Because there were things about walking in the light he found *unacceptable?*"

"It is," Myla answered somberly.

Adaam-Mir looked at his mentor and softened his expression. He exhaled. "I am sorry. I do not mean to get beside myself. I mustn't let my passion for the Lord's honor get the best of me."

"Do not apologize for having passion for our Creator, Adaam-Mir. It is why you are here, with me." Myla let that thought grow. "It is why you are *here,* with the Lord, in the eternal light, and not on the side of darkness." He squeezed the angel's shoulder. "It's understandable that you find it difficult that many who call our blessed Creator their Lord do not obey His commands."

Adaam-Mir's insides trembled in holy anger, but he limited his response to staring at the ground and shaking his head. *Lucifer was kicked out of heaven for this,* he thought.

"This condition—"

"This hypocrisy—" said Adaam-Mir.

Myla paused. "This *hypocrisy,*" he agreed, "will be dealt with at the proper time."

"When is it ever proper to dismiss the commands of the Almighty?"

"Never," said Myla.

"'Let all who name the name of Christ depart from iniquity.' That is what the blessed apostle Paul instructed Timothy," said Adaam-Mir.

"That is true, my brother. But he also said, 'The Lord knows those who are His.'"

Adaam-Mir looked at him with a question on his face.

"You remember in the blessed book when our Lord explained the mystery of the wheat and tares?" asked Myla.

Energy replaced the question on Adaam-Mir's face. He loved the blessed book. "Yes."

"The devil sowed tares among the wheat," said Myla. "But when the owner of the field was asked by his servants should they remove the tares—"

"The Lord said no," Adaam-Mir cut in, pondering the Lord's response. "He said that if they tried to separate the wheat from the tares too early, they would damage the wheat."

"Adaam-Mir, listen to me."

Adaam-Mir locked eyes with his mentor.

"Never forget this. The Lord is more concerned for the safety and growth of the wheat than the hypocrisy and presence of the tares. The Lord in His wisdom gives the tares freedom to demonstrate they are not worthy of the coming kingdom—just as He did Lucifer and his angels."

"And the wheat, my brother?" asked Adaam-Mir.

"When they are young, the wheat and the tares look alike. That is why it is unwise to go after the tares too early. If we thrust in the sickle of judgment before the time, we will hurt the wheat. Adaam-Mir, the church community has false Christians, weak Christians, carnal Christians, and strong Christians. A weak or struggling saint may for a time resemble a false saint. A strong saint may for a time resemble a weak or false saint. A false saint may for a time resemble a strong saint. You understand?"

"I think so," said Adaam-Mir. "It is troubling, but I think so."

"Judas Iscariot was a thief from the beginning," said Myla.

"He was phony," Adaam-Mir punctuated Myla's statement. "He betrayed the Lord."

"Yes, he was phony, but he appeared genuine. And Peter also betrayed the Lord, but he was wheat. He was weak wheat, but he was wheat, nonetheless. Do you see, Adaam-Mir? It can be dangerous to condemn too soon."

Adaam-Mir took slow steps in a wide circle, his intense eyes squinting with new understanding. He spoke as he walked. "The blessed book says, 'Who are you to judge another man's servant? To his own master he stands or falls. Indeed, he will be made to stand, for God is able to make him stand.'" The angel stopped and spun and looked at Myla. "The Lord was speaking of the weak."

Myla said nothing. It would be better to let the revelation unfold in the way the Holy Spirit had chosen.

Adaam-Mir thought of the bewildering tenderness and forgiveness of the Lord. It was a mind-blowing mystery—even for most angels—that the Creator, who hated unrighteousness so intensely, and who judged unrepentant sinners so severely, was so infinitely gracious, patient, and longsuffering to those who had genuine faith in Him for salvation.

"I think I see now how the sons and daughters of Adam are able to deceive themselves into believing the Almighty overlooks their sin." The angel thought of something from the blessed book. *Because sentence against an evil work is not executed speedily, therefore the heart of the sons of men is fully set in them to do evil.* "It is the same mistake that Lucifer made. They mistake His kindness and longsuffering for acceptance. So they continue in sin until it is too late to recover."

"And what of the wheat? The weak wheat?" said Myla.

"God is able to make them stand," he declared. "It doesn't make a difference how weak they are, if they have repented of their sins, if they love righteousness and trust in the Lord for victory, they shall have it."

"The victory that overcomes the world is their faith," said Myla.

"And the Lord knows the difference in true and false faith," said Adaam-Mir, speaking out the revelation as it was being revealed to him. "He knows the difference in a weak, struggling child of God and a pretender."

Myla nodded approvingly. "This is why the Lord spoke so many parables about the true and false existing alongside one another for a time. It is a reason why He chose Judas Iscariot. He was prophesying to His church that there would be pretenders in their midst."

Adaam-Mir considered the conversation between Edwin and the pastor. "And the last man Edwin spoke to? What of him?"

Myla didn't hesitate. "He is either wheat or tare. This is the Lord's business. He will deal with Paul in the manner and timing of His choosing."

Adaam-Mir knew the conversation was over. "This church is alone for such a dangerous work. They have so few." His words and hanging head reflected his disappointment.

"That's right," said Myla. "So few. Like Gideon's army."

A slow grin overtook the concerned look on Adaam-Mir's face and turned into a wide smile. He pumped his large fist toward the sky. "Gideon's army! Samson's jawbone! David's sling!"

"The Lord doesn't need a lot to do a lot," said Myla, his countenance darkening as his fingers rolled across the jeweled handle of his sword.

***

Barbara ended the call with a satisfied smile. This was wonderful. Senator Abbie Lockhart had agreed to assist their church in addressing the needs of Mayhem. "Thank You, Lord," she said. "Thank You for a second chance." She wiped a tear from her eye.

The demon watching her smiled. She had immediately accepted his thought to call the senator for help.

Ironically, the angel that watched Barbara and this demon also smiled.

Chapter 24

The attack was no secret. How could it be? That blue mist had coursed its way down Mayhem's main street and stopped at one of the parking lots.

Sonny Christopher looked out the window through his binoculars. He didn't see the blue mist. He didn't see the ferocious fighting of angels and demons in hand to hand combat. But he did see a long line of vehicles coming into his Mayhem. He watched everyone park and gather into three circles, holding hands. They were praying.

He searched the faces. That crazy, fine white girl was there. She made him think about Samira. He shook his head and cursed Prince. That smart-mouth, clown preacher who they had beat down was there. That new girl, Kim, wasn't there. But the other people who had prayed over Prince's dead body were there. And a bunch of other people were there.

When they finished, he watched two flatbed trucks drive across the dirt and park where his platform had been. On one of the trucks was a forklift. On the other was a big square box-looking thing. Sonny watched with intrigue as the forklift picked up the box and carried it off the truck.

What are you crackers doing?

***

"A portable baptism pool, Dad?" said Sharon. "I didn't know there was such a thing."

"Neither did I until Reverend Winston said we could borrow theirs."

"Reverend Winston. I like him. He's funny," said Sharon.

"Yeah, he's hilarious," said Edwin.

Jonathan, Elizabeth, and her mother, Ava, approached Edwin once the baptism pool and audio equipment was ready.

"You ready to rock Satan's world, Edwin?" said Jonathan.

Sharon's face radiated as she looked adoringly into her father's face.

Edwin looked around at the tall buildings that surrounded them. It was only nine o'clock on a Saturday morning, and apparently, with the exception of a few people, Mayhem liked to sleep in on the weekend. "Yeah, I guess so."

"I know so, Dad. This is why we're alive—to make a difference in the world," said Sharon.

Edwin smiled at his daughter. "Yeah, I know."

She smiled because she knew he really did know. "I love you, Daddy."

"I love you, too, Sharon."

"Oh, for crying out loud you two," said Jonathan. "We can only stand so much of this mushy talk." He twisted his face and bobbed his head. *"I love you, Daddy,"* he mimicked Sharon in a girly voice. He stuck out his chest. "I love you, too, Sharon," he said in an exaggerated deep voice, mocking Edwin.

Sharon looked mischievously at Jonathan. She wrapped her arms around his waist. "I love you, Jonathan."

He hugged her and closed his eyes. "I love you, too, Sharon." He kissed her on the forehead.

Edwin looked at him with a tight, smileless smirk.

"What?" said Jonathan. "She took advantage of me. Got me at a weak moment. I'll be ready for her next time."

"Sure you will," said Edwin.

"The Lord said I'd be persecuted," said Jonathan.

"Jonathan, you're up first, right?" said Ava. She had always been a holy terror, but her intensity had grown since her brain aneurism and coming out of the coma a couple of months ago. "It's time."

Jonathan looked down at the little dynamo, probably the bravest woman he knew. "That's right, my beloved mother-in-law." He kissed her on the forehead. "I'm up first."

"Let's get with it," said Ava.

Jonathan looked at Sharon. "Don't grow up to be a pushy woman."

"Get, Jonathan, or I'll show you pushy," said Ava.

"Just for that," he kissed her again on the forehead.

"Jonathan," she said, with mock irritation, "get out there."

He walked to the microphone and bowed his head.

***

Sonny snatched the binoculars from his eyes, shook his meaty face, and put the binoculars back to his eyes. *I shut one stupid nigga's mouth, and here's another one. What? Is there a factory around here making stupid niggas and nobody told me?*

He looked at one of his crew. "Trey, get out there and make sure everybody in Mayhem knows that we haven't run out of bullets. This nigga is about to do a Prince on us. He's about to preach." He pointed his finger at Trey. "We're not having any more Jesus up in here. That Jesus crap makes people crazy. Let everybody know that if they listen to this clown, they're going to get the sticks."

Trey took a few guys and left the apartment.

Sonny hurried to the door and yelled behind them. "And find out what that nigga's doing with that box thing."

***

Jonathan opened his eyes from fresh recollections of Prince's bloody body lying in this same area with twelve bullet holes in him. He stretched forth both hands towards the buildings and pivoted in a circle while he said, "In the name of Jesus, I bless you and bring you the good news of the gospel. My name is Jonathan. I'm a minister, and I'm here with a message from Jesus Christ to all of you."

Jonathan looked around at the dismal buildings. Even the buildings looked sad in this place. "I don't know what you know about Jesus Christ, so I'm going to start with the beginning. The world's a mess. Everything. It's all a mess. But it wasn't always a mess. In the beginning God created the heavens and the earth, and everything was good. But you know people. We have a way of messing things up.

"God's first man and woman rebelled against Him. They did their own thing. When that happened, death entered the world. First, it went into their spirit, the part of them that lived forever. Then it showed up in their flesh. That's where death came from—the first sin.

"From that point on, every child born into the world arrived with a sin nature. You've seen it. Something in every human that wants to do evil. It's that *something* that had made the world the way it is. It's that *something* that has caused us to be enemies with God, with our Creator. And it's that *something* that God has taken it upon Himself to fix. Because nobody else could fix it but Him.

"God is holy, without fault, morally perfect. But He's more than that. He's so morally clean that He can't stand sin. He can't and won't tolerate it in His presence. That's the problem that needed to be fixed. He created people who turned on Him and became the very thing that He hates."

Jonathan noticed as he spoke, a man wearing a long, white t-shirt and a baseball style cap turned sideways walking towards them. About thirty or forty feet from the man, a woman holding a little girl's hand was also walking towards them.

Then Jonathan saw something that narrowed his eyes in anger. A man wearing baggy clothes and a red scarf around his head confronted the man first, then the woman. He couldn't hear the conversations, but it was definitely a confrontation—a one-sided confrontation. The man and the woman with the little girl turned and went back to where they had come.

The little girl looked over her shoulder twice in Jonathan's direction before breaking from the woman and running toward him. The woman screamed something at the little girl, but her little legs didn't stop. The woman ran and swooped the child up and carried her off.

Jonathan felt a deep spiritual pain in his heart and upper abdomen. He had just watched a man snatch a life preserver from a drowning child. The little girl stretched her arm out to him until she and the woman disappeared into a doorway.

Jonathan pulled his horrified gaze from the doorway and glared at the minister of Satan. Satan's minister looked at Jonathan in defiance, grabbing his crotch and jabbing his finger at him as he mouthed things Jonathan couldn't hear.

What Jonathan couldn't hear was, "What? What you gone do, nigga? You in Mayhem. You in Mayhem, nigga, and we gone show you wassup in Mayhem. This the last time yo' black a— gone come up in here. You better be ready to die coming up in here with that cracker Jesus."

Jonathan felt something like a warm blanket drape over him. Suddenly, his eyes were opened. Beside the man stood a demon at least a foot taller. Oddly, the demon looked nearly identical to the man. He was dressed like him and even wore a red scarf on his head. The demon and the man did everything exactly the same and at exactly the same time.

Jonathan wondered at this and looked around. Angels and demons were everywhere. He wondered greatly at the oddness of what he saw. In some places angels and demons were locked in battle. In others, they weren't fighting even though they appeared to be surprisingly close to one another. In one of these non-fighting close encounters, he somehow knew that the demons weren't aware of the angels.

His attention was drawn upward. He gaped at what he saw. Armies of angels of every kind were in a half circle around Mayhem. In dead center of this arc of angels stood an angel with a long sword in his hand.

He was large, but not the largest. Yet, there was something about him besides his position that identified him as special. A light came from him that Jonathan knew represented righteousness. He also knew that this angel was a great hero of many significant battles, and that he and his angels were somehow limited or empowered by the prayers, faith, love, and action of him and the other saints.

Jonathan heard Ava say something before she took off toward the man and the demon with their red scarves.

Edwin saw this and hurried to join her. *Hadn't they agreed that there would be no running off like The Lone Ranger?*

Jonathan watched her, Edwin, and three angels approach him. By the time they got there only one red scarf was present.

Ava was in red scarf's face, and he was in hers. Edwin was doing his best to figure out what to do next. They had covered nothing in seminary about what to do when a feisty five-foot-tall woman threatened a thug in his own backyard with the wrath of God for keeping people from coming to Jesus.

Sharon and Barbara watched intently. Sharon with a warm glow; Barbara with growing concern. *Why was Ava pointing in that man's face?* she thought anxiously.

Jonathan watched Edwin walk Ava away from the man. Elizabeth joined her mother about half-way back.

"You saw that precious little girl, Elizabeth?" Ava was steaming. Hot, angry tears rolled down her olive colored cheeks. "I will not stand by and watch someone keep a little girl from coming to our precious Lord."

Elizabeth was immediately overcome with emotion. She knew there was a deep love in her mom that drove her to save girls. She helped women, too, but her soul belonged to little girls. It was that same love that had driven her adopted mom to risk her own life to save her from that sex-trafficking gang in Argentina. "Yes, Mother, I saw. What did you say to that guy?"

"I told him that I saw what he was doing, and that if I saw it, Almighty God saw it. I told him that God had killed people for far less than that, and that he was provoking God to cast his miserable soul into everlasting hell."

"You told him that?" Elizabeth asked.

Ava didn't answer. She rubbed more tears from her eyes and joined the group. There were little girls to save.

***

The curtain to the spiritual dimension closed.

Jonathan looked around at the tall buildings with a modified message. “Two thousand years ago God became flesh and lived among us. His name is Jesus. He was born to save you from your sins—the sins you know you’ve committed. He did this by living a sinless life and dying on a cross as a sacrifice to break the power of sin over your life. He did this to save you from dying in your sins and going to a place of everlasting punishment. That place is hell.

“The only way you can escape paying for your sins yourself in hell is by trusting in and submitting to the mercy of God. But this mercy only comes one way. It comes through Jesus Christ. There is no other way to escape God’s anger for your sins but to believe and obey Jesus Christ. There is no other way to know God than to come through Jesus Christ.

“There is no other way to be free from Satan’s power than to come through Jesus Christ. If you come to the Lord, the Lord who loved you so much that He gave His own life to save you, He will give you eternal life.”

Jonathan waited and looked at the many heads that were now looking out of a lot of open windows.

“Repent!” he said. “Turn from your sins. Turn from your drugs and alcohol. Turn from your crimes. Turn from your hatred and fighting and cursing. Turn from your sexual sins. Turn from your adultery. Turn from everything that separates you from Jesus Christ your Creator.

“A little while ago my friend,” Jonathan stretched out his arm towards Edwin and Sharon, “our friend, Prince was shot down.” He pointed to the ground. “He was shot down right here, like a dog. And I think a lot of you saw it happen. I think a lot of you know who did it. The cops think it was a drug deal gone bad, but we know better, don’t we?

“I don’t know exactly what happened here, but I have a good idea. We found Prince dead on a platform. There were a bunch of scattered plates of food and soda cans with stuff in them all over the dirt around the platform. I think you were all out here having a good time when Prince took the stage. I think Prince got on that stage and told you how Jesus Christ changed his life. He may have told you about how he robbed my friends here and they forgave him.

"He may have told you how the man he robbed—that man right there—came down here to have Bible studies with him. He may have told you how the sweet girl he pistol whipped—that's her right there—how she afterwards invited him to her home for dinner. He may have told you how she prayed for him to be filled with the Holy Spirit and he was.

"I think Prince got up here and bravely told you how he had become a child of God. That's what I think. And I think what happened to him so unnerved Satan, the devil, that he shot him dead." Jonathan bounced his finger in the air. "But Satan doesn't pull triggers. He uses puppets to pull his triggers. I think the puppet he used to kill Prince lives right up there." He pointed toward Sonny's place.

"I think that man works for Satan. I think Satan rules Mayhem and The Bluff through Sonny and his so-called Vice Boys. I think they are greedy thugs who are worse than the KKK. The KKK killed black men and raped black women. They terrorized them and made them live in constant fear. Isn't that what we have in Mayhem? Isn't that what Sonny and the Vice Boys do to you? The only difference in some KKK grand wizard fool and Sonny is the wizard wears a white sheet and Sonny wears a white suit."

Jonathan preached some more and turned it over to Edwin. Edwin spoke, then Ava.

"Ava, I want to say something," said Sharon.

Ava handed her the wireless mic and patted her on the shoulder. "Good girl," she said.

Sharon wore pants and a long pink t-shirt—all the females wore the same shirt. Her long hair was draped over one shoulder. She looked at the people in the windows and loved them. They needed the Lord so desperately. She smiled softly at them.

"I don't know you, but I love you," she said.

Sonny's eyebrows pressed hard against the high-powered binoculars. He looked at her shirt and cursed. "I love you, too, Wonder Woman."

For several minutes Sharon told them of the Prince she knew. She also told them about her friend Holly who had died of a drug overdose. "The more I think about my friend, Holly, the more I see that she could have been saved. She could have been saved, but she was too ashamed to reach out for help. Please, don't make that mistake. The Bible says, 'How shall we escape if we neglect so great a salvation.' Salvation has come to your house today. Reach out and take it. Please."

Sharon turned. Barbara's heart raced with nervousness as she looked at the mic. She watched indecisively as Sharon handed it to Jonathan.

Jonathan looked at several men stationed around the Mayhem buildings. *Must be Vice Boys,* he thought. His heart became heavy. It was easy for him to come into Mayhem and speak so boldly. Sonny wasn't going to kill anyone from the church. They were outsiders. He'd be locked up for life.

But what would happen once he went back to his big house in the suburbs? And that was the bottom line. This was a good, necessary work. But the truth was as good as it was, it was an event. *Lord, please help these people,"* he pleaded. *Sonny's not going to let them serve you.*

"I know that many of you want God," said Jonathan. "I know that many of you want to turn from the life you're living. You want what changed Prince's life." Jonathan searched his heart and waited for a different prompting. Perhaps he had heard wrong. After several excruciating moments, he grimaced. "Jesus said anyone who confessed Him before men, He would confess that person's name before His Father. But He also said that if you wouldn't confess Him before men, He would deny you before His father."

He waited a minute or so.

"You're in a difficult position," he said. "Satan and Sonny don't want you to serve God. But I believe God is requiring you to make a public declaration that you are submitting your life to Jesus Christ."

He exhaled a deep, responsibility-filled breath. "Behind us is a baptism pool. Baptism represents death and life. Jesus Christ voluntarily gave His life for you and went to the grave and rose again on the third day.

"When you are baptized in water, it represents you dying to the world. When you come up out of the water, it represents you receiving a new life in Christ. I'm asking you to search your heart and to decide whether you want Jesus Christ and eternal life—even if it means you are beaten. Even if it means you are killed.

"For those of you who want to start a new life in Christ today, the worship team from our church is going to sing while you make your way down here. When you get here, we're going to dedicate you to the Lord and His service, and we're going to baptize you. I want you to think about what they did to Prince before you come. Count the cost."

Jonathan put the mic down and joined the others in prayer.

***

Lil' Johnny's version was that he lived with his sister. LaQueesha's version was that he lived *off* his sister. Big sis' had it right. He was a trifling, lazy something. Half player, half drug dealer, half thug, half thief. Half everything. Except whenever he infrequently got a job. Then it wasn't half. It was zero. Full zero. Nigga was just sorry.

But that didn't stop LaQueesha from being crazy about him. He was as funny as she was fat, and as nice to her as she was mean to everyone else. He loved his big sister. That's why she was so traumatized when Prince had beat her brother into a limp, groaning pool of blood.

Everybody knew Lil Johnny couldn't fight. King Kong was in his mouth, but marshmallows were in his fists. He couldn't fight a lick. Prince knew this. But when Lil' Johnny stole two joints from him—two joints!—something came over Prince, uncontrollable rage, that wouldn't let him stop beating her brother. She had begged him to stop, and was going to push him off her brother.

Prince's eyes.

Prince had turned and looked at her with such evil eyes. "You touch me, and I will kill both of you right here, right now."

Her big body had gone rigid with fear. All she could do was helplessly cry as he started back to beating her brother.

Now LaQueesha and Lil' Johnny both looked out the window at the people Prince had told them about before Sonny killed him.

***

Aisha was only on the third floor. She could see everyone clearly. They weren't far away. *But they were far away, in another world.* A world of privilege and possibility and hope and...God. She stared at them. They had a glow, every one of them. Especially the girl who had spoken. She was so pretty, and she seemed so nice.

Aisha followed Sharon's movements and wondered what kind of life she had. What kind of family did she have? What kind of school did she attend? Was she a cheerleader? What college was she going to attend? She knew the girl was going to go to college. What was she going to be when she got out of college? *I bet her parents make her study,* she thought. *I bet they talk to her about college.* How large was her bedroom? What kinds of friends did she have? Did she have her own car?

Aisha didn't know she was smiling as she wondered about the pretty white girl. She thought of the girl's friend who had died of a drug overdose. She had said she could have saved her friend had she only told her what she was going through. Aisha thought how blessed the dead girl had been to have a friend like her. Aisha didn't think this; she felt it. *I wish I had someone like her to talk to.*

Dante's hand slid up the inside of her thigh. His shirtless chest more near her than she wanted. She pushed his hand off her in irritation.

"Stop it," she said, her face showing the irritation she felt. She turned back to looking out the window.

He stood over her with a frown and looked at the top of her head. His sagging pants covered only half his butt. He reached over her shoulder and squeezed her breast.

"Get your hand off of me," she said sharply, pulling away from her baby's daddy.

"What the — wrong with you?"

"Nothing is wrong with me. Something is wrong with *this*."

Dante backed up and grabbed his sagging pants with one hand. He frowned in angry confusion. "Wrong with what?"

"With this," she said, pushing her hands out.

"Girl, what I look like to you? You need to talk English to a nigga."

"And *that*," she said.

"That what? What the hell you talkin' 'bout?"

"And *that*? Cursing, and you putting your hands on me like we're married."

He looked at her as though she were crazy.

"And nigga this and nigga that. Dante, I don't want my baby to grow up calling himself a nigga. It's bad enough white people call us that. We don't have to run around calling ourselves niggas."

"What? He is a nigga. Look at him." He picked him up and started bouncing around the small living room, jutting out his neck, and making up a spontaneous rap.

Call me what you want.
Call me what you will.
I'm yo' nigga.
I'm yo' thrill.
Got gold in my mouth.
Gotta a golden grill.

He pressed his nose against the baby's nose. "Sing it, Ray-Ray."

"Just stop it, Dante," she said sharply.

He put Ray-Ray down. "I thought we done talked about this already. We gone get married one day. When things right."

"You didn't hear me, Dante. I'm not talking about getting married. I'm only fourteen. I am too young to get married. I'm talking about us carrying on like we're married. We shouldn't be having sex. It's wrong."

"Wrong? When it get wrong? It wasn't wrong two days ago."

"It was wrong two days ago," she said.

"Oh, so it was wrong? Why you do it then?"

"Because you wanted me to do it, Dante. That's why I did it."

"That's the only reason you did it?" He grinned. "Didn't sound like that was the only reason you did it. Sounded to me like you liked it."

Aisha shook her head, partly from frustration, partly from shame. "I do like it, Dante, but we're not married. It's a sin. It's fornication. You can't just do something because it feels good. We're not animals." She looked out the window at Sharon. "God didn't create us to act like animals."

Dante frowned and looked out the window.

***

Sonny was shocked at what he saw. He grabbed his binoculars. His face hardened in rage. After Prince, he had thought these niggas would've learned that he wasn't playing with them. He was going to have to send Mayhem another message.

Chapter 25

Rosa hadn't been feeling well since Friday evening. Kim coming to stay with them had come out of the blue. But as extraordinary as it was to ask a stranger to live with them, Rosa had done so, and her mother, Diane, had agreed. Kim was in a desperate situation, and they were Christians. How could they say they loved God, and not help a woman in danger?

And the fact that she was absolutely adorable didn't make it any more likely that they could ignore her need. But this arrangement, which had turned beautiful the moment Kim entered their home, lasted only a few days until she went to live with Sharon.

Rosa wasn't angry at Sharon for offering her home, and she wasn't angry for Kim accepting Sharon's offer. Sharon was right. *The Bluff* was dangerously close to *Mayhem*. And it was only wise to assume that some of the thugs in their neighborhood were Vice Boys. If this were true, Kim would be in constant danger of being kidnapped.

Nonetheless, Kim's departure had left her with a sick heart. Kim would sit and talk to her for hours. She'd rub her lifeless, numb arm as they talked. And she'd so often kiss her on the forehead. When she entered the room, before she left the room. Any excuse to show affection.

Rosa's mother loved her, she knew. And God knew her mother had sacrificed so much for her, and she was grateful. So very grateful. But she was Mom. Good moms loved their daughters, even if they were paralyzed and needed constant attention. But Kim wasn't her mom. She was a stranger. And, yet, she showed such love for her.

It wasn't the love of pity, either. It was like what Sharon had. It had nothing to do with what was wrong with her body, but everything to do with what was right with Kim's heart. But surprisingly, though Kim was loving and knew some things about God, her own sad confession was that she was not a Christian.

It was in this state of mind and sickness of heart that Rosa prayed for Glory Tabernacle's Mayhem outreach this Saturday morning. She had never been in Mayhem, but she lived close enough to it to see its towering buildings, and to know it was a terribly dangerous place. She pressed past her deep sense of loss and pushed the prayers out of her hurting heart.

"Oh, God, save Mayhem," was how she began.

Satan's constant lies to her that she was a worthless cripple would have lost their agonizing potency had she seen her intercession ascend as a request to the throne of the Almighty as a light blue mist and descend back to her and into Mayhem as a darker blue mist.

***

A blue mist entered the C building doorway and went up the stairs and into the home of LaQueesha and Lil' Johnny. Immediately, spirits of fear swarmed them both. Some focused on sending powerful thoughts into their minds. The others focused on manipulating their bodies to exaggerate the physical feelings that come with fear.

Do not fear him who can destroy your body and nothing else. Rather, fear Him who after He has killed has power to cast your soul into hell. Neither LaQueesha nor Lil' Johnny knew one Scripture, but they both heard this one in their heart.

Pretty Tony didn't say anything to LaQueesha and Lil' Johnny when they walked past him out the doorway of their building. They could've been going anywhere. But in a minute it was obvious they weren't going *anywhere*. They were going toward those church people.

"Where y'all goin'?" he yelled after them.

Pretty Tony was a Vice Boy. His words chilled them both.

They abruptly stopped.

"I said where y'all goin'?"

Lil' Johnny would've sworn under oath that he felt his bones trying to tremble away from his flesh. He fought through his chattering teeth to answer. "We goin' over here."

"Alright, Lil' Johnny," Pretty Tony said, with a tone that said it all. But just in case he was too stupid to get the message, he made it plain. "You get yo' skinny a— in that water, you better hope the Lord comes back before you get out."

He turned and joined his still sister. They both stood motionless, backs facing Pretty Tony, and looking nervously at the church people looking at them.

Sharon begged them with her expression to ignore the man's threat. She took a couple of steps toward them.

"No, Sharon," said Jonathan.

She looked anxiously at Jonathan. "They're scared, Jonathan."

Jonathan looked her in the eyes. "This is their cross. You can't help them carry it, and you can't carry it for them. You're going home today. I'm going home today. This is their home. They have to live right here with whatever decision they make. We can sacrifice our lives for the Lord, but it's not right to make someone else a martyr."

Sharon's face turned into a mess of tears. She looked at Edwin and Barbara and Elizabeth, then Ava. She turned and walked away and knelt alone on the hard dirt and prayed. It was too much to watch people being intimidated away from the Lord.

LaQueesha and Lil' Johnny took a few timid steps toward the church people.

Pretty Tony yelled out, "You hear me, Lil' Johnny? A dry nigga's a live nigga."

The terrified brother and sister froze again.

"I can't do it," said LaQueesha.

Lil' Johnny took his big sister's hand. "Yes, you can, Kwee. You gotta do it."

"Lil' Johnny, you saw what they did to Prince. If they do that to him, what you think they gone do to us?"

Lil' Johnny had never seen his sister scared. She was so mean, he didn't even know she could get scared. She looked more scared than he was, and he was so scared he was about to pass out.

"A wet nigga's a dead nigga," yelled Pretty Tony.

Lil' Johnny looked at his sister. "Just what PT said, Kwee—kill us."

LaQueesha shook her head like she was trying to shake off a wig. "I can't do it, Lil' Johnny. I can't do it. You can't either. These niggas gone kill us if we get baptized."

"Kwee," Lil' Johnny's voice was deep with conviction. His unpatched eye carried a courage that was often in his mouth, but rarely in his heart. He shook his head from side to side, with an imploring look on his face. "Don't you see? We already dead. Look at us. Look at this place. Ain't nothin' good about it. Ain't nothin' good about my life, and it ain't gone get no better. You know that, Kwee.

"I can't do nothing right. I'm as dumb as they come. In my world, two plus two is five. Always have been. Always will be. You know I'm dumb. Probably retarded if I tell the truth. But I know that for once in my life I don't have to be dumb. I got to get my black a— in that water, Kwee."

She stomped her foot in desperate frustration. "Why you talkin' like this? You ain't got to get in that water, Lil' Johnny. You can ask God to forgive you without gettin' in that water and getting' yo' self killed."

"I don't know a lot, Kwee. But I know Jesus didn't die in the basement for me. He gave it up right there in front of every d—body. He wasn't ashamed to die for me. Why should I be ashamed to live for Him?"

"Because it's gonna get you killed."

"What? Like Prince?" asked Lil' Johnny.

"Yes, —," she cursed. "Like Prince!"

Lil' Johnny's mind was made up. He looked at his sister with a determined eye, the only good one he had left. "Kwee, Kwee," her name came out in two short, powerful bursts, "like Prince? You know what kind of person Prince was. Look at this patch on my eye." He tapped it. "You know I know what kind of person he was. Something happened to that nigga, Kwee. And I ain't talkin' 'bout him getting' smoked. What's gone turn a crazy nigga like that into the one they killed, Kwee? Huh? You tell me."

"I ain't sayin' it ain't real, Lil' Johnny. I know it's real." Something happened in LaQueesha's heart that made tears roll down her cheeks. That something was she realized she was letting fear keep her from Jesus Christ and eternal life. "I saw his eyes," she said sadly.

"Who eyes? Prince?"

"Yeah, I saw it in his eyes. He wasn't a killer no mo.' He had good eyes."

Lil' Johnny stepped closer to his sister. "I saw somethin', too, Kwee. Right before they shot Prince, he pointed to the sky and said, 'Look.' I looked, Kwee. I looked. You know what I saw?" His one eye widened with excitement. "I saw Him. I saw Jesus standing next to a throne."

Lil' Johnny was getting caught up in the exhilaration of having seen God. Why had God opened the heavens for someone like him? Just a dumb nigga who couldn't do anything right? He could've talked to his sister for an hour about this. His mouth opened—and stopped. "I gotta go, Kwee."

"I'm begging you, Lil' Johnny, don't do it."

"Everybody's gonna die, Kwee. I'd rather die like Prince than live like I'm livin'." He kissed her on the cheek. "Bye, Kwee."

Bye, Kwee. Bye, Kwee? LaQueesha looked at her brother walking away. If he got in that water, it would be *Bye.* She ran behind him and let loose a right hook to the side of his face that put him down.

Lil' Johnny hit the dirt and was momentarily out. It wasn't that his sister hit so hard. It was that, among Lil' Johnny's many deficiencies, he also couldn't take a punch.

LaQueesha grabbed both his collars and started dragging her skinny brother away from getting himself killed. She was also keeping the one true friend she had.

Lil' Johnny's face rubbed and bumped hard on the dirt. A hard rub woke him up. He flailed his arms and found a way to his feet.

"You ain't goin,'" said his sister.

"I'm goin', Kwee."

"No, you ain't!" She rushed him like a mad bull. He dodged her like a matador. She rushed again and this time grabbed him. He tried to spin her outstretched arm off of him. She wouldn't let go. "Nigga, you ain't goin'," she screamed.

"Let me go, Kwee!" Lil' Johnny tried desperately to shake his big sister off of him, but it was like tangling with an octopus. She just wouldn't let go. "Kwee, I'm gone knock yo' fat a— out if you don't let me go," he said, twirling and ducking and pulling.

His threat wasn't much of threat, however. He had never won a fight, and there probably wasn't a six-year-old anywhere in the world that Lil' Johnny could knock out on his best day. They tussled and tussled. The more they tussled, the farther away from the church folks they got.

"You ain't doin' it," his hefty sister said, as she manhandled her undersized brother.

Then something happened.

On one of the twirls, as Lil' Johnny's sliding feet lost more ground, he caught a glimpse of the baptismal pool getting farther away. Eternal life was today. If he didn't do it today, he would probably never do it.

Lil' Johnny turned and swung his soft, little fist at his sister's big face. It connected. He watched in shock as her big body fell backwards like a slow-falling tree. An angel's hand guided her head gently to the ground.

He ran to the stunned church folks. "She gone be alright," he said to Jonathan. "I want what Prince had."

Jonathan had been all over the world. He had ministered in some of the most dangerous places in the world. He had seen people killed for Christ. He had nearly been killed for Christ more times than he could accurately remember. But he had never seen someone literally fight to die for Christ.

Jonathan's face formed an admiring, questioning half-smile. "Looks like you've counted the cost."

"Everythang, Rev. Gone cost me everythang. I'm good as dead."

Jonathan looked at this living martyr. Several scriptures came to mind. How many times had the Bible said Christians were to consider themselves dead? He recalled how after His resurrection, Jesus had instructed the church in Smyrna through John the apostle that Satan was going to cast many of them into prison for their faith that they may be tested, and some of them he was going to kill.

Jesus didn't offer them an easy way out. Instead He had said, 'be faithful unto death, and I will give you the crown of life.' Here was a man who was valuing the crown of eternal life more than earthly life. This sure wasn't the prosperity gospel.

"This doesn't bother you?" asked Jonathan.

Lil' Johnny's one eyebrow moved down. "Yeah, it bother me. Look at my hands." He held them out.

Jonathan looked at the man's hands. They weren't trembling. They were shaking. His whole body was shaking. This man was having his own earthquake. "And you still want to do this?"

Lil' Johnny smiled wide. "Gotta do it, Rev. I know what I saw."

"Call me Jonathan."

Sharon had joined them. "What did you see?" she asked.

That one eye lit up. "Right before they shot Prince, he pointed to the sky and said, 'Look! I see Jesus standing next to God.' I looked up and..." Lil' Johnny looked into the sky. He relived the moment. Tears rolled down his face. "He was looking right at me. Right at me, man." Lil' Johnny looked at Sharon. "Why would Jesus look at me? I ain't nobody. Just another po' *Mayhem* nigga. That's all I am."

The terribleness of his words hit Sharon hard. She gasped, clutching her chest with a hand.

"You may be poor in this world's goods, but you're rich in faith and courage," said Jonathan. "What's your name?"

"Lil' Johnny."

"Lil' Johnny, huh?" Jonathan looked at the big girl who he had knocked out. "Lil' Johnny, you got a mean punch."

He looked at his sister. He didn't want to smile. He loved his sister. But he had never knocked anyone out before. A little man-grin came to his face. "Yeah, I didn't put as much into that punch as I could've. She my sister. I didn't want to hit her. She was trying to keep me from the Lord. You can't let nobody keep you from the Lord. Momma, daddy, sister, brother—"

"Vice Boys. Sonny," added Jonathan.

"Vice Boys, Sonny, nobody. You can't let nobody keep you from eternal life," said Lil Johnny.

Jonathan smiled largely and pulled Lil' Johnny to him in a tight hug. He let him go. "What do you have against food, Lil' Johnny?"

"Aww, naw, it ain't like that. I likes to eat. I've always been this skinny. I can eat a cow and won't gain a pound."

"Is that right?" Jonathan rubbed his belly. It wasn't big as it used to be, but he could've still used another long fast. "I got that same problem," he said smiling.

Lil' Johnny laughed. "Oh, alright, Rev. I can see that."

"You can?" said Jonathan.

"Yeah. Pretty soon they gone be calling you Lil' Jonathan."

"Lil' Jonathan? I think I like you," said Jonathan. "You ready for eternal life?"

"Been ready all my life. I just didn't know it until I saw what happened to Prince."

"You knew Prince?"

"Oh, yeah. I knew him."

"Edwin, this is Lil' Johnny. He's a good guy. He sees me as I really am—slim and trim. Take good care of him."

Lil' Johnny was sucked into the crowd of cheering and brave Christians who had gone down to the most dangerous place in metropolitan Atlanta to win souls. It wasn't yet noon, and already they had a convert. A convert who had literally fought to come to God.

There was no way they could have understood how deeply this moved Christ. And no way they could have understood how furious this made Sonny.

***

Lil' Johnny looked around at the smiling faces. There were around thirty or forty people, white and black, a few more whites than blacks. Some people were so excited they were hopping up and down. They seemed more excited than he was, if that were possible.

It was possible.

Lil' Johnny tried to not think about Pretty Tony and the three other Vice Boys who were near his building's doorway, staring at him. But it was impossible to ignore being slowly beat to death with the sticks. He'd rather be shot like Prince than to go out with the sticks.

"You better go home with 'em, Lil' Johnny," a Vice Boy yelled across the field. "Sticks waitin' on you, baby."

Lil' Johnny didn't just hear those words; he felt them. They were like ice sickles that froze his head as they tore through his ears. He felt the cold go down his neck and lodge in his chest before expanding into his lungs. His fear felt alive.

It was alive.

It was a demon of fear. He specialized in two things.

One, he influenced and controlled people. But nearly every demon did that. Where his expertise came in was in getting people to either do or not do things because of fear. How many dreams, ministries, and relationships had he prevented or destroyed by getting someone to focus on a lie—or a truth. It didn't make any difference to him. As long as they focused on something other than the word of God!

Two, he opened the door for other spirits. The most routine way of doing this was by getting a person to fear a thing. When the fear became sufficient, the *thing* entered. One of his favorite and most successful tricks was to mimic a physical symptom of a sickness or disease. He'd then tell the dupe that he had that condition. Almost always, the person would embrace his lie like the embrace of a lover. Then in came spirits causing the actual condition.

And the pathetic sons and daughters of God were no wiser than children of darkness. They'd walk all over their own angels to turn a symptom into a disease or a rumor into a reality.

Then there was this Lil' Johnny dirt. Slavery had put him on his case the moment Prince asked him for forgiveness. The general had told him to not underestimate the power of forgiveness. There was no telling what kind of crazy thoughts it might put in his head. How right the general was.

Fear saw the exact moment Pretty Tony's words found a home in the dirt's heart. He followed the words from Pretty Tony's mouth. He reached both hands across his body and whipped out two short daggers. The daggers weren't for angels. They would have been of little use against their long swords. The daggers were for Lil' Johnny. He had a right to him, and he was going to have him.

He took long strides toward the stupid nigga. When he was halfway to Lil' Johnny, he stopped like he had hit a wall and dropped both daggers in horror. He quickly picked them both up and shot back to Pretty Tony. He stood next to him, panting as though he had just run a grueling race.

What are You doing here? thought Fear.

***

It had begun as a twirling fire, the size of a man. It resembled a tornado. Suddenly, it burst into a brilliant light. Out of that light came the Lord God Almighty, Jesus Christ. Once He was clear of the light, it collapsed into Him.

He stood next to Lil' Johnny and placed his hand around the back of his neck, squeezing his shoulder supportively as Lil' Johnny talked with Edwin.

"That's not fair," the demon of fear protested in fury, but not loud enough to provoke the Lord. "That nigga belongs to Slavery."

Too late.

The demon saw the Lord's head turn in his direction. *He heard me? Time to go.* But he didn't go. His tremoring body didn't respond to his panic. What he saw next confused and terrified him. *How...?*

The question was how could the Lord stand next to that dirt and walk toward him at the same time? Two of them?

The Lord was draped in fire. This fire flowed around and behind Him like a long, loose cloth blowing in the wind. The spirit futilely fought the force that held him still. Frantically, he wondered what could have possibly caused the Lord to single him out. He hadn't broken any rule of engagement. He was simply following the fear. These were His rules. He couldn't punish him for following the Lord's own rules.

Jesus stood before His cursed creation. He looked into his evil, yellow eyes. "You have cursed what I have blessed."

Everyone in the dark kingdom knew that just because the Lord called Himself the Word, it didn't mean you could count on a long conversation before He judged you. The angelic rebellion was a perfect example.

Commandment.

Long, bewildering silence that makes you think you got away with the sin.

Sudden, calamitous judgment that proves you were wrong.

The demon sensed that the couple of seconds that had elapsed since the Lord's last word was the silence before judgment. He had to do something, say something, to save his life. "But Jesus, we always curse what You bless. And, besides, Lord, Lil' Johnny—"now he was Lil' Johnny—"calls himself a dumb nigga. I didn't make this up. I'm only saying about him what he says about himself. You can't—"

POOF!

The incineration was instant.

Lil' Johnny lifted his hands above him without any prompting. He confessed every sin he could remember without any prompting. He screamed out, "Jesus, save me!" without any prompting. He dropped to his knees, then rolled over onto his side in a fetal position and cried harder than some of those watching thought was possible.

Jesus got on both knees. The fire was gone. He had a large, golden bowl in one hand and a towel in the other. He pushed the towel into the bowel until it couldn't be seen. He brought it out without wringing it and placed it atop Lil' Johnny's head and began washing. He washed every part of His son's body.

The Lord then took part of His own robe and made another out of it. He slipped it over His servant and adopted brother's head and watched with a large smile as it draped to his ankles. He tenderly placed His hands on the sides of Lil' Johnny's face and kissed him on the forehead.

"What I have blessed, is blessed. What I have cursed, is cursed. Let no corrupt communication come out of your mouth. Say only what I say about you."

The Lord kissed His servant's forehead again and disappeared in a burst of light.

***

"Did you see that hideous display of affection?" said Slavery.

"Did I?" said Heroin. He put his hat back on. "That was worse than bad dope. Makes you just want to throw up, doesn't it?" He looked anxiously at Slavery. "That was the *Lord,* baby. We better have a Plan Z. 'Cause something tells me that Plan A through Y just went down the toilet."

Annihilation spoke up. "I have a plan. A plan that will chase these weekend warriors back to where they came from."

***

Sonny Christopher had the same plan.

Chapter 26

Annihilation's plan was no surprise to Slavery. After all, he was Annihilation, wasn't he? Annihilating is what he did. Nonetheless, what the plan lacked in originality, it promised in effectiveness. Murder always worked.

Slavery was not going to be outdone, however. The truce and partnership between him and Annihilation was going surprisingly well. But that didn't mean they had stopped competing with one another. Murder was still like swallowing a steak whole. No chewing meant no tasting. The truce hadn't changed Slavery's preference to taste his victory—over and over again. That's why he had summoned Heroin.

Slavery looked at Heroin's ridiculous human outfit. This time it was bright red. Clothes. Shoes. Hat with feather. Was that a black satin stripe going down the side of the pants? And then there was the cape. Always a cape. Oh, the theater of it all.

You're a demon, Heroin. You're not human.

Slavery wisely and perfectly masked his derisive feelings. It never helped anything to question the insanity of this brilliant demon. One wrong question or comment was known to put him over the edge. It could take an hour to get the hypersensitive demon back to his brilliant self. *What had the fall done to this demon?*

Heroin listened to Slavery's plan. His mouth watered hideously with excitement. He wiped the dripping at the corner of his mouth with the back of his hand. "I like it, Daddy-O."

Slavery held his tongue.

"I'll start working on this right away." He left with images of veins in his mind.

***

Senator Abbie Lockhart looked out the window as she drove deeper into *The Bluff* and nearer to *Mayhem*. Her naturally upturned nose turned up even more as she looked at the blight and the sight of criminals and low-lifes everywhere.

What a drain? she thought. A black woman walking with three young children caught her attention. *Our tax dollars at work. Wonder what size television she watches all day while America's at work?*

The marked police car she followed had two officers. It was the only reason she was venturing into this third-world, above ground replica of hell. She was still miffed at herself for not protesting more strenuously to the assistant police chief to provide at least one more police escort car. He had assured her that the officers he had chosen to escort her had worked the Mayhem area for several years, and had established a great relationship with them. They were the only cops on the force who could go into Mayhem without fearing for their lives, he had said.

Yeah, tell me anything," she thought bitterly. The fact that the assistant police chief was an outspoken proponent for the Democratic Party made her even angrier. *If I were democrat, I'd be following a SWAT escort, not a patrol car.*

Senator Lockhart looked in the rear view mirror at the news reporters following them. A half-smile lifted the little mole on her right cheek higher. She wasn't always going to be just a state senator. The nation needed people like her in the highest offices. Her smiled deepened. *Perhaps the highest office.*

Senator Lockhart's smile was on her face long after it had left her mind. The White House, if that ever happened, was decades away. But that didn't erase the significance of what she would say this evening.

For her more immediate journey to become a U.S. senator would be the culmination of a thousand carefully orchestrated steps.

Establishing herself as a strong, no-nonsense conservative was one of those steps. Getting the right audio sound bites and video footage circulated was another.

In a little while, present state senator and future U.S. Senator and future U.S. president, Abbie Lockhart, stood in a large field in Mahem Courts. Again, she was upset. She wasn't miffed. She wasn't angry. She was furious. Those cops had left her alone and disappeared into one of the buildings.

A thousand carefully orchestrated steps. With special emphasis on *carefully*. She would have to be a master of managing surprises and making on-the-spot changes. Changes which looked like non-changes.

Abbie looked into the camera. She knew it liked her. All cameras liked her. She was blessed with beauty, but fortunately the Creator understood politics and didn't make her so astonishingly beautiful that it became distracting. No, her beauty was just enough to be a powerful political tool.

The man holding the camera knew that the station manager would be ecstatic when he saw this clip. This woman was something else.

"In the truest sense of the word, there is no way a place such as this, a place that has through its violent crime, illegal drug trade, and regular murders, a place that has blatantly lived up to its infamous name of Mayhem Courts, can be considered a community. By what stretch of the imagination would anyone dare call this dungeon of despair a community?

"Our great nation is experiencing remarkable economic growth. Look around. Where are the signs of that growth? Why hasn't it reached this placed called Mayhem?"

U.S. Senator Lockhart saw the explosion of light in her mind. *What a brilliant idea!*

"And Brenda," she said to the reporter, with a new twinkle in her eyes, "we must ask ourselves who benefits from this arrangement?"

"Arrangement?" asked Brenda.

"Yes, Brenda. This arrangement. This ghetto. What we're looking at is not the aftermath of a tornado, hurricane, or earthquake. It's the wreckage of failed democrat policies that herd people together under the naïve socialistic assumption that misery plus good intentions plus other people's money minus common sense equals prosperity."

The interviewer asked several other questions. Which would be aired? Who knew? (She certainly hoped that last statement made the cut.) So the senator answered each as though it was a step toward the U.S. Senate.

The last question asked was, "Senator Lockhart, you're well connected. You have the governor's ear, and you have friends on the Atlanta city council."

"I have many wonderful partnerships, yes."

"What is the answer? How do you tame such a stubborn societal beast?"

U.S. Senator Abbie Lockhart looked confidently into the camera. "You don't tame it. You starve it. Stop feeding it old, moldy democrat answers. The answer to poverty is not more poverty. The answer to a picture this ugly is not to use taxpayers' money to purchase a new frame. There's a reason Mahem Courts is the last public housing project in Atlanta."

"And that is...?" Brenda prodded.

"Manipulation. Cruel, heartless manipulation of the poor for political expedience. This concentration of Mahem residents is for one purpose only—democratic votes. My answer isn't simple, but it is morally right and economically progressive. Rescue Mahem from the democratic machine. Close down this death trap."

"Where would residents go?" the interviewer asked.

"People move all the time. Changing one's residence isn't a new idea. Mayhem is the last of forty-four public housing projects. It is the only ignoble survivor of the democratic experiment of getting rid of poverty by concentrating it and making it worse. Where did the residents of Techwood Homes go? Where did the residents of Capitol Homes and Grady Homes go? Where did the residents of Bankhead Courts go?

"That's where they'll go. They'll move into neighborhoods with decent schools. They'll move into neighborhoods where hearing gunshots isn't the norm. They will move into neighborhoods that are serviced by commercial businesses. They'll leave this fabricated ghetto and assimilate into the mainstream of American society."

Brenda knew she had a good story. She'd squeeze for more. Her experience dealing with politicians told her she wouldn't have to squeeze hard. The senator was a fire hydrant doing her best to come off as a water hose. "And do you feel there is the political will in Atlanta to shut down Mahem?"

"Absolutely not. There is neither the desire nor the courage to dismantle this prison of hopelessness and despair. As long as the Democratic Party can depend on Mayhem to deliver its votes to them, nothing's going to change."

Answers. Answers, Abbie. Anyone can rail about the problem. Give them an answer.

U.S. Senator Lockhart looked into the camera as sincerely as she could. "Something must be done in this dangerous neighborhood that transcends politics. Something that stops the blatant crime and frequent murders. I think what this place needs is a strong police presence. Mini police precincts have proven to work. Can you think of a more deserving place than *Mayhem* to have its own police precinct?"

Once the interview was aired on local television, it was the senator's last statement about a police precinct in Mayhem that prompted a number of phone calls. One of those calls was to Sonny Christopher.

It was someone speaking for his unseen boss.

***

Officer Crandal held his personal phone to his ear as his partner, Officer Brown, drove, leading the senator out of Mayhem. He listened to the voice and nodded his head. "Yes, sir. We'll take care of it."

"What was that about?" asked Officer Brown.

"Our good senator said something that someone doesn't like. We need to help fix it."

The other officer glanced at his partner. After brief eye contact, he turned back to looking straight ahead. They had fixed or helped fix a lot of things. The other officer continued.

"We need to escort the senator home. Check her house. Seems someone has seen a prowler on her property."

Officer Brown smiled at Officer Crandal. "Well, let's go protect the senator."

The officers followed the senator and didn't stop her car until they were within a mile of her home. She had wondered why they were following her, and had reluctantly concluded that they were going out of their way to protect and defend a lady driving alone at night. A prowler? Of course, they could go in and check her home.

State Senator Lockhart was relieved when they approached her car and told her all was well. She closed the door and turned around and let out a breath. It was a good breath. She smiled and stood there for a moment thinking about her performance tonight. It had been good. No, it had been stellar. She would have to find more ways to get in front of the camera.

She walked to her bedroom and sat on the bed and removed a shoe. She put her foot across the top of her thigh and massaged her foot. She did the same with the other shoe and foot. Why hadn't she gotten rid of these shoes?

Abbie took off her suit jacket and tossed it on the bed. She did the same with her blouse and skirt. She went to the kitchen and poured herself a little cranberry juice. A couple of cool gulps and it was gone.

U.S. Senator Abbie Lockhart.

She smiled and let her hair down. She shook her head and ran her hands through her hair. She went back to the bedroom with light feet, almost floating, nearly dancing. "U.S. Senator Abbie Lockhart," she said, and closed her eyes. She twirled once and opened her eyes. Her mouth parted wide with a scream that never came out.

It wasn't the masked man's finger to his lips that muted her scream. It was the gun he pointed at her with his other hand.

Abbie's arms shot up halfway. Her whole body shook with terror. She stumbled backwards until she fell onto the bed.

No. No. Abbie, get off the bed.

The fear that had taken over her body wouldn't let her stand up.

I'm going to be raped. The power of this thought wrapped itself around her mind like a strait jacket. There was nothing she could do to stop it. All she had ever told herself about fighting off her attacker or outsmarting him disappeared into that gun's dark barrel.

Abbie's mouth widened to match the new level of fear that was tearing at her bones. Two other men stepped into her bedroom. Three men. She was going to be raped by three men. Her mind descended deeper...deeper...deeper into a depth of fear she hadn't known existed. She looked at each man. They all wore ski masks, gloves, and shades.

Abbie struggled to make her mouth form the question she knew was unnecessary. But maybe talking would save her life if not her body. "What do you want?" Her voice was so low she could barely hear the question herself.

A man sat next to her. He put his arm around her and whispered in her ear. "If you want to live, do exactly what I tell you. You understand?"

Her answer followed her tears. "Yes," she said softly. This was it. Abbie's mind raced everywhere, but fixed upon nothing except fear and hopelessness.

The man who spoke to her motioned to a man with a pouch. This man opened the pouch. She couldn't see what he did once the pouch was open because they tied her blouse around her head and eyes.

"Remember our agreement," she heard the whisper in her ear. "Act a fool and we'll stop being nice. Okay?"

Abbie was too scared to answer.

"Okay?" the man asked again.

"Yes," she answered.

Someone pulled her hand up. He made her touch what felt like plastic bags. Then something that felt like bundles of money. Then they pulled her arm forward and turned her palm up. Something was tied around her arm.

Heroin's chest heaved up and down in excitement as he watched. His face was involuntarily drawn toward the needle as it got closer to the woman's arm. Heroin and the man looked for a good vein. In a moment, they smiled together.

"Pop it, baby. Pop it," said Heroin.

Abbie was horrified when her fear finally allowed her to realize that they were about to give her a shot. *Oh, my God, they're going to drug me and take me somewhere.* This opened a whole new world of cruel possibilities.

"What are—?"

"Sshhhhh," said one of the men.

Abbie felt a prick, but dared not move.

"Aaawww, baby," said Heroin, as he mimicked pulling something out of the air, "there it is. Paradise."

In a few seconds, State Senator Abbie Lockhart was in paradise. Her head bobbed one way, then the other. She mumbled a curse word. This caused four smiles. One belonged to Heroin. "I'm good, ain't I, girl?" he asked.

In a little while, State Senator Abbie Lockhart was led out of a car and coached to walk. When the men finished recording her with a stolen phone, they drove off. One of the Vice Boys in the car called Sonny.

Abbie smiled and floated her way to a large tree two blocks from her home and got on her side and laughed softly.

***

The television reporters got to the senator first. That's how it had been designed. Shortly thereafter, a cop car arrived. Besides the fact that State Senator Lockhart was lying on her back next to a tree wearing only a bra and panties, she had a piece of rubber tied around her arm. When her home was searched, police found a lot of interesting things. Things that were actually even worse than being found nearly naked and passed out under a tree from heroin use.

Police found an assortment of drugs. Marijuana, oxycodone, and heroin. They found drug paraphernalia and what appeared to be drug money. Ten thousand dollars wrapped. They even found something that showed the senator had taken precautions against overdosing. There was an Evzio kit so she could inject naloxone to counteract an overdose. By all appearances, the senator was a dealer and user of illegal drugs.

The senator's desire to be known nationally had finally come true, and years earlier than she had planned. Since she had just come out with such a scathing rebuke of the Mayhem community and the Democratic Party's purported manipulation of this community for political purposes, it was only natural that her political opponents aggressively helped her desire for fame to come true.

The Atlanta Journal and Constitution couldn't get enough of writing about the senator. And like clockwork, the Associated Press got a hold of the story and published it in thousands of newspapers and on hundreds of television and radio stations.

One peculiar effect of this exposure of the senator and the way the stories were reported was that Mayhem was now national news.

What was *Mayhem*?

Was it really as bad as that drug-pushing senator described?

If it were that bad, why hadn't Atlanta done something about it?

And why had the Atlanta Housing Authority closed only forty-three of its forty-four public housing projects? Why was Mahem Courts still standing? Who was keeping this place open?

***

Annihilation was impressed at Slavery's successful, although secret, mission against the senator. She had been thoroughly discredited, and all that talk about a mini police precinct had gone up in a puff of black tar smoke.

But he was as angry as he was impressed. Everyone was congratulating Slavery and talking about his strategic "brilliance." Why even Annihilation's own demons were talking about Slavery like he was a human rock star. Slavery hadn't commented much on his success, but the few comments he had made were like long fingernails scraping a chalkboard.

It was nothing really.

Well, yes, I guess it was brilliant.

A general above generals? That's the opinion of many, yes.

It was that last comment that got under Annihilation's crusty skin. A general above generals? Above what generals? Was he included in this lofty self-assessment?

"Annihilation, I don't think there is any longer a need for your plan," said Slavery.

"Oh," said Annihilation. "And why is that?"

"The senator. This has gone much better than I imagined it would."

"Really? How could such a brilliant strategist and general above generals not anticipate the results of your secret mission?" Annihilation peered at his colleague. "I don't see how this is possible?"

Slavery swung his arm upward as though he were swatting a fly. "Is that what this is about? I knew you were acting funny. Oh, Annihilation, stop behaving like an angel with a broken wing."

Annihilation stepped forward. "And now the great general not only issues orders, but he insults me."

Slavery felt a slow-rising burn going from his belly to his chest. For the sake of the truce, he pushed his ugly face into an expression that Annihilation saw as a smile. "I'm not giving you orders, and I didn't mean to insult you. We are partners, are we not? Our enemies are those who want to take away our beloved Mayhem."

Annihilation looked unconvinced.

Oh, my darkness! If it's not Heroin acting like an idiot human, it's a ruler spirit letting envy get his eyes off the target, thought Slavery. "Annihilation, maybe I did get a little full of myself with the senator thing."

"A little?"

Slavery pushed his bottom lip up. "Okay, maybe just a tad bit more than a little."

"How about a tad bit more than Niagara Falls?"

"That bad?" said Slavery.

"Yes, that bad," Annihilation answered gruffly.

"Hmmm, I guess you're right." Slavery chuckled a little, then laughed. "Okay, Annihilation, I admit I'm no angel."

The slighted demon joined Slavery's laughter. He knew what had just occurred, but rather than feel manipulated, he felt vindicated that the general had shown him respect. Nonetheless, when the laughter ended, he stated forthrightly, "I will have my murder."

"It was a brilliant idea you had, my friend. But the situation has changed. It is now a bad idea," said Slavery.

"You and Heroin got your senator. I'm going to have my murder. I'm going to taste the warm blood of one of those new Christians."

"It's going to backfire on us, Annihilation. I don't know how, but something tells me this is going to be Prince all over again."

"Well, something tells me you conducted a secret mission that has gotten you another slave. I'm not going to stand outside looking through the window as you and Heroin go through the buffet line. I will have my murder. A Christian murder."

"Why Christian?" Slavery demanded, with a raised voice.

"Two reasons," Annihilation snapped, with his own raised voice. "I'm hungry. And I want that church to know that Mayhem is off limits."

Slavery watched him fly off toward Sonny's place.

Chapter 27

Annihilation was furious with the foreplay. "Get on with it!" he screamed.

"Kwee, you never been up here," said Sonny, looking at the trembling woman. He looked her up and down. "You got some meat on yo' bones, don't you, girl?"

"Uh huh," was the frightened reply. Her eyes darted from one man to the next. She had heard about what happened to people who were "invited" to see Sonny. She glanced nervously at the man who stood behind her with a short stick. She hadn't gotten in the water. So why had she been invited up here?

"Don't worry about him. I'm the one you need to worry about," said Sonny.

"What I do, Sonny?"

"What I do?" Sonny said, glancing at his Vice Boys. "What I do?" He pushed an irritated breath out of his nose. He looked up at a tall man. "Tell her what she did, Pretty Tony."

"I told you what would happen," said Pretty Tony.

LaQueesha's eyes were locked on Sonny.

"Why you looking at me?" Sonny snapped. "PT's talkin' to you."

LaQueesha's head snapped to Pretty Tony. "Pretty Tony, you saw me. I didn't do nothin,' Pretty Tony. I tried to stop my brother from getting' in that water. You saw what happened, Pretty Tony."

Pretty Tony frowned. "Pretty Tony. Pretty Tony. Pretty Tony. How many times you gone say Pretty Tony? He looked around at the other Vice Boys while he rubbed his face. "I know I'm pretty."

Sonny shook his head and rolled his eyes.

AJ laughed.

"Nigga, what you laughin' at?" said Sonny. AJ stopped laughing.

"You right. You didn't get in the water, but you started to." Pretty Tony bounced his finger at her, with a pretty smile. "I saw that, too, now didn't I?"

She shook her head to save her life. "But I didn't get in, Pret— I didn't get in."

"That clown preacher say something you like?" asked Sonny.

"Uh uh. I don't want nothin' he was talkin' 'bout, Sonny."

"Eternal life. Forgiveness of sins. Go to heaven," Sonny sang. "All that crap my aunt talks about?"

"Prophetess Monroe?" asked LaQueesha.

"Yeah, Prophetess *Ebony* Monroe. You know who I'm talkin' about. Why you acting stupid up in here?"

"Man, when she gone bring some more of them ox tails up here?" asked a Vice Boy.

Another perked up. "Yeah, man, when we gone get the hook-up. She ain't been up here in a while."

Sonny looked at both of them with the crazy look. "How long Prince been dead? Where'd he die? Who do you think she thinks did it? Me. There goes your ox tails. Better learn how to cook 'em yourself." Sonny looked at LaQueesha. "Where's Lil' Johnny."

"I don't know."

The man in back of her swung a wide arc and came down hard on her collar bone with his oak club. She screamed and fell to her knees, grabbing her shattered shoulder.

Sonny wiggled his lips and looked at the crying, moaning woman. "Get up. Have a seat in the chair."

LaQueesha moaned and moaned. She was in a silo of pain. She didn't see or hear anything. Nothing else in the world existed, but this throbbing, tearing pain in her shoulder.

The chair.

Those two words tore through her silo and slapped her to attention. Everyone in Mayhem knew about the chair. She lifted herself to her knees. "Sonny, please, no."

Sonny looked at the begging woman. He looked at the man behind her. Down came the stick on the back of her head. When she awakened, she was tied to the chair.

***

Adaam-Mir clutched his chest in a deep agony. Not because of the cruelty of these sons of darkness, but because of the woman's testimony to God that she didn't want eternal life. She didn't want forgiveness of sins. She didn't want to go to heaven.

"Her words, Myla...." Adaam-Mir took a few unsteady steps. "The Lord said that if any person denied Him before men, He would deny that person before His Father."

"It is a tragedy," said Myla.

Adaam-Mir looked at his mentor, shaking his head. "She was so close to eternal life. Why did she turn back? Why did she let fear of man keep her from what she knew to be true?"

"Fear keeps many from what they know to be true," said Myla.

Adaam-Mir winced with each blow of the sticks upon this coward who had denied the Lord. He remembered with great sadness the words of Christ in the blessed book. *He who loses his life for My sake shall find it. But he who seeks to save His life shall lose it.* "She tried to save her life," he said.

"The sons and daughters of Adam do not understand that whatever they do not give to the Lord will be lost forever," said Myla.

"And yet they struggle and strive and scheme to get or hold onto what they are sure to lose. What does it profit a man to gain the whole world and to lose his very soul?"

Myla's mouth tightened as he watched Annihilation licking the blood of the broken and battered woman. What kind of a monster found pleasure in such misery?

Adaam-Mir looked at the ruler spirit. He turned to Myla. "I have *seen* enough. When can I fight?"

Myla felt God's fury in him as he watched Annihilation feast on a woman who had come close to the kingdom of God, but not close enough. "I agree. Let's join Enrid."

***

Dante had thought about running when he heard that Sonny had invited him to his crib. But where would he go? And what did he want with him anyway? A stupid thought popped into his head. *A JVB? Naw, that's crazy. Why would he all of sudden make me a Junior Vice Boy?* Another more scary thought popped into his head. *What if Sonny blames me for Aisha getting into that water?*

Dante's nervous eyes bounced back and forth from the ground to the two Vice Boys sitting on the cement slab to the opening that led to Sonny's stairwell. Everything in Dante wanted to run. But he had nowhere to run, not unless he wanted to stay gone forever. Then what about his family? They'd go after them.

"What up, gangsta?" said a man wearing a red scarf around his head.

Dante wasn't a gangster. He was a wanna-be rapper. But it sure sounded good being called a gangsta by a real gangster. "Everythang cool."

"Is that right?" said Red Scarf.

"Yeah."

The other Vice Boy didn't say anything from behind his dark shades. He beckoned Dante by quickly curling his fingers a few times. Dante stepped forward, one hand holding up his pants. The man motioned with his hands and Dante put both hands in the air. Dante had to widen his legs to keep his pants from falling to the ground.

The man patted him down and sat back on the concrete slab without saying a word.

"Where's that little lady of yours, Player?" the other Vice Boy asked.

Dante's eyes tightened with curiosity. "I don't know. She ain't been by today."

The man smirked. He lit up a joint. "Don't know, huh?"

Dante didn't have to be a prophet to figure out something was as wrong as he had earlier thought. He summoned enough courage to ask a question without his voice cracking. "Uhh, you know what Sonny want me for?"

The man blew out some smoke. "Yeah." The smirk was back. He watched Dante stare at the ground, then look toward his own building, then drop his eyes again. He didn't like what he knew Dante was thinking. He lifted his shirt and pulled out a gun and sat down. He took another hit off the joint and looked at him with squinted eyes.

Dante's thought of sprinting away sprinted away. He climbed the dark staircase with the other Vice Boy behind him. When they reached the top floor, a metal slot opened the fortified door. The door opened.

There stood Sonny Christopher in a baby blue suit and what had to be gold shoes.

Dante had seen Sonny before, but his open mouth revealed his awe—and fear. Sonny was a killer who had killers working for him. He was a pimp who had pimps working for him. He was a drug pusher who had drug pushers working for him. He was the king of Mayhem.

Sonny looked at the young dude gawking at him. He smiled and pulled his big head back. "I ain't Jesus, man. Come on in."

Dante stepped inside and the other Vice Boy went back downstairs.

"Jesus walked *everywhere*. I'm not walking *anywhere*," he said, laughing.

Dante walked deeper inside. His eyes widened. He wasn't merely in the presence of the king. He was in the presence of the king's army. Being locked in a house with them—how many were there...eight or nine?—wasn't the same as seeing them stationed or walking around Mayhem.

Dante's eyes opened wider. A bloody woman was tied to a chair. Her busted head hung with her chin resting on her chest. He couldn't see past all the blood to recognize who it was.

"You know who that is," said Sonny.

"I don't...I don't...I can't see who she is," said Dante.

"Show Player who she is," said Sonny.

AJ pulled the woman's hair up.

Dante jumped. "That's Kwee."

"You're probably wondering why you got the invitation to come visit," said Sonny.

Dante answered with nervous eyes.

"First," said Sonny, with both palms up facing Dante, "I need to tell you something about Kwee. I invited her here for a simple reason. Well, two reasons actually. First, I put the word out that there's not going to be any more Jesus up in here. My aunt, Prophetess Ebony Monroe's the only somebody who's authorized to talk about Jesus in Mayhem.

"Kwee, I don't know," Sonny hunched his shoulders, "I guess she went crazy. Maybe she smoked some bad K2. I don't know. What I do know is she disrespected me. Saturday she and Lil' Johnny crossed the line. Lil' Johnny jumped his narrow behind in that water. Kwee didn't get in the water, but she started to. She went halfway to Jesus. Halfway obedient is not acceptable to me. It's not acceptable to the Vice Boys. And from what my aunt says, halfway is not acceptable to Jesus either."

Sonny looked at her for a long, thoughtful moment. "Ain't that a shame? She in that chair for pissing off me and Jesus. See, in this world, Dante, you got to make up your mind who you're going to serve. No man can serve two masters." Sonny looked up at Pretty Tony. "Now I know that's Scripture. Am I right?"

Pretty Tony laughed. "Yeah. Yeah. Yeah, Sonny. You right. I bet you can't quote another one."

AJ appeared to be about to laugh. Sonny looked at him. "Nigga, what is so funny?"

AJ started stammering.

Sonny smiled. "I'm just kiddin'. You too nervous." Sonny looked at Dante. "You'd think I was a stone cold killer the way they treat me up in here. Oh, you still trying to process this Kwee thing. The second reason why she's in that chair is because I asked her a question and she gave me the wrong answer."

Sonny looked at Dante as though he was trying to pull some particular words out of him. Dante saw that Sonny wanted him to ask him something. "What did you ask her?"

Sonny slammed a pointed finger in Dante's direction. "That's it. That's what I'm looking for. I asked her an easy question. But it must not have been that easy, 'cause I got the wrong answer. I asked her just like this"—Sonny spoke in a low, calm voice—"where's Lil' Johnny? You know what her answer was? It was I don't know."

Sonny let that hang in the air for a while.

A Vice Boy with a stick got in back of Dante.

"Don't worry about him. He's just a mind reader. He reads my mind and does what I'm thinking. You feel me?" said Sonny.

On the third try, Dante got the words. "Yeah, Sonny."

"Now, I'm going to ask you a question."

Dante swallowed hard.

"Your girlfriend got in that water. Where is she?"

Dante whipped his head around and looked at the man with the stick. He turned to Sonny. "I can find her."

***

Aisha had never cried so hard. She had never cried so long. It had been six days since she had met Jesus. Six days since she had been baptized in water by the people from Glory Tabernacle. It was still hard for her to believe she had spontaneously gone down there and gotten saved and baptized.

It wasn't like she had had a change of clothes with her; she didn't. And she had just gotten her hair done, but that didn't matter. She hadn't even thought about the fact that she'd have to walk home with bad hair and wearing soaking wet clothes. All that mattered that moment was that the warmth in her heart that started the day the Vice Boy preached at the picnic had turned into a fire when she heard those church people preach.

Aisha's chest heaved as she gushed out more tears. She wasn't concerned about waking her naked mother—as far as Aisha was concerned, that little thing her mother wore, and with no underwear, qualified as naked. Her mother's customer had left early this morning. But not before stopping by Aisha's room.

Furious disgust rose freshly in her chest. She could've spit on the memory of the man's unshaven face. She had known he was going to try something as soon as she had seen him. The way he had looked at her with those big bubble eyes, licking his nasty, orange fish lips.

Aisha was only fourteen, but these were in hard ghetto years. The ghetto had exposed her to cruel realities that had stolen her childhood and had accelerated her maturity and survival skills.

Beautiful fourteen-year-old black girl with a fully developed body living in *The Bluff* with her thirty-year-old junkie whore mother.

Survival skills.

Aisha had a sign on her door.

WARNING!

§ Georgia Code 16-6-4
I am fourteen years old.
Prison bait.
The penalty for child molestation for a first
offender in Georgia is 5 – 25 years in prison.
You put your hands on me
and you will go to prison.
I will testify.

She hated having to live like this, but it was the world she lived in. Her instincts had proven correct again when her bedroom door opened at 3:00 a.m. The man's bubble eyes bubbled even more when he saw her fully awake and sitting against her headboard with her arms folded across her chest.

"Aaa—eee—sha, right?" he said, as he stepped in softly and turned to close the door.

"I figured you couldn't read," said Aisha.

"What?"

"Look at the sign on my door."

His full, dark cheeks pulled those big fish lips up into his version of a mack daddy smile. He read the sign. He looked at her. "Ain't no way you fourteen."

"There's something else I didn't put on the sign. I didn't want it to be used against me when we go to court."

"Court? You talkin' crazy, girl. Ain't nobody goin' to court," he said softly. He faced her as he slowly pushed the squeaky door closed behind him.

"The part I left off the sign is that the additional charge of sodomy increases the penalty to life, or a split sentence of not less than twenty-five years and probation for life. That's what I'm going to tell the jury you did to me. You put your mouth all over my fourteen-year-old body. Get out of my room or you'll be sorry."

The man pulled out his wallet. "I ain't lookin' fo' no freebie. I'm gonna pay," he said, as he thumbed through some bills.

Angry tears marched out the corners of Aisha's eyes. She whispered, "You are going to pay."

The man smiled when he heard that. He looked up with a twenty-dollar-bill in his fingers. His smile left when he saw the knife in her left hand. Her other hand was still folded across her chest. "Aawww, girl what you gonna do with that little knife?"

"My boyfriend gave it to me for niggas like you who can't read."

The man stepped forward. "He should've gave you a bigger knife."

"That's unnecessary," Aisha answered calmly. She pulled her right arm from across her chest. "My momma gave me this."

The man stepped back with his hands up. He turned his head to the side. "What you got there, girl?"

"Double deuce."

For some stupid reason, this made the man feel brave. "A 22? Yo' boyfriend give you a little knife. Yo' momma give you a little gun—"

"And God gave you a little brain. You better use that half an ounce of brain you have and get out of my room."

"Yo' momma in there sleepin'. Yo' baby right there sleepin'. You ain't gonna shoot nobody, Aaa—eee—sha." He rolled his tongue across those juicy, orange lips and stepped forward.

POW!

The little bullet tore through the palm of the man's hand. He grabbed his hand and fell to the floor on his knees, cursing and looking back and forth at her and his bleeding hand.

Ray-Ray jumped in his crib and started screaming.

"It's okay, Ray-Ray. Momma just had to shoot a dumb nigga who can't read." She put the knife on the bed, and without taking her eyes off the moaning, cursing man, she squeezed Ray-Ray's fat stomach. "That's why momma's always reading to you. So you can learn how to read early."

The man's watered eyes peered at her with an anger that could've strangled Aisha. "You black—"

Aisha pointed the gun at his face.

His words went back down his throat like poop being pushed down a toilet with a plunger.

"Take whatever memories you bought from my momma and the one I gave you for free and get your sorry self out of our house."

She had followed him to the door.

As Aisha thought about the incident, she recalled that the saddest thing about it wasn't that a man had tried to rape her. It wasn't the first time, and it wouldn't be the last. Rather, it was that her mother was so strung out on drugs that she could sleep through a gunshot in the next room.

Nothing had changed with her momma. She was still a whore. She was still a junkie. She was still a shell of a parent. Yet Aisha couldn't stop crying for joy. The joy? It was unexplainable. She couldn't put it into words. All she knew was that something strange and beautiful happened when she made up her mind to ignore Sonny's threats and to turn from her sins and to give her life to God.

She had literally felt something rise through her body from her feet and leave through the top of her head. It felt like garbage and smelled like a sewer. *She smelled whatever had left.* Then something beautiful and warm entered through the top of her head and filled her entire being.

She didn't actually hear the words. But she felt them press against her soul. *You are my daughter. I will take care of you and Ray-Ray.*

Aisha didn't know how or when she would be delivered from *The Bluff* and into a new life, but it would happen. She knew it would.

Her phone rang.

It was Dante.

And Annihilation.

Chapter 28

"What's wrong with you, Dante? You sound funny?" said Aisha.

Dante put his hand to his forehead and shook his head. He opened and closed his mouth with a grimace. He didn't know what to do. Aisha was his baby's mama. This baby's mama. He had another baby's mama. That was Shantrell. But Aisha was his favorite baby's mama.

"Are you there?" said Aisha.

Dante couldn't get the gruesome picture of Kwee out of his mind. The blood. Oh, man, the blood. She was busted everywhere. How could they do that to a girl? The sound of her moaning had tormented him the whole two days he had slept outdoors trying to figure out how to save Aisha without him having to sit in that chair. For all he knew, he was probably already just as good as being in that chair for disappearing.

But as he thought about what he had seen, the worst thing wasn't what the Vice Boys had done to Kwee. It was what they had made him do to her. Thinking about it brought back the taste of his vomit as it had left his mouth and poured onto Kwee.

Sonny had laughed and said he'd hold onto Kwee's dress in case the police wanted to know who took part in putting Kwee to the sticks. "They got some people who can put this vomit right back in your mouth, Player," he had said to Dante. "Sixteen years old, huh? Those crackers," Sonny shook his head, "sometimes they don't understand the rigors of our business. Every now and again they want to send a message. And a young player like you—you came up here to put Kwee to the sticks trying to become a Junior Vice Boy. Probably won't get the death penalty. They don't care too much about black folks killing black folks. But they gotta do something. What you think, PT?"

"LWP, baby," Pretty Tony had answered.

Sonny pretended to be shocked. "Life without parole?" He smiled. "No doubt. Little nigga like you—LWP. Bam! Just like that. Next," he said, playing the part of the sentencing judge.

Dante's sad, tired, red eyes looked unenergetically on the broken sidewalk. *LWP? I'm only sixteen.* Every good thought he had ever entertained about Sonny and the Vice Boys and people like them now rose up like an orchestra of shameful truth and challenged his dreams of being a rapper.

Kwee sitting in that chair looking like a zombie got a hold of her wasn't a video. Him walking the streets for two days jumping like a scared cat every time he thought he saw a Vice Boy wasn't a video. His baby's mama sitting in Sonny's chair—

"Dante," Aisha said louder, "I said, are you there?"

"Yeah." His voice was as weak as his will and as unsteady as his courage. *Aisha's only fourteen, and she got a baby. Kwee was grown. They wouldn't do that to Aisha,* he told himself.

"What do you have to say to me that can't be said over the phone?" she asked.

Sickness rumbled in Dante's belly. "I haven't seen you and Ray-Ray in almost a week. I miss y'all."

Aisha pulled the phone from her ear and looked at it. "You miss us?"

Annihilation said, "Yes. We miss you, Christian."

Dante answered as slowly as possible for a one word answer. "Y...e...ye...ye..."

"Why are you grunting like a cave man, Dante? Can't you answer a question as simple as that about me and your son?"

This is wrong.

This is wrong.

This is wrong.

Dante had never killed anyone. But this was just like killing someone. Killing his own baby's mama. "I need to see you, baby."

***

The angel had tried everything to get Rosa to pray for Aisha. Rosa didn't know her, but that was unnecessary. The most powerful prayers were those that were directed specifically by sons and daughters of God. Nonetheless, all acceptable prayers were useful for the work of the kingdom.

The intercession angel understood—to a certain degree—why Rosa wasn't responding to his promptings. She was having a horrible day physically, and an even worse day emotionally. Her mind kept going back to when she was shot. There had been so many opportunities to not go to the club that night. Each one played vividly and cruelly on the screen of her troubled mind.

The two demons who had been assigned to get Rosa to focus on her troubles so she'd stop praying looked smugly at the intercession angel.

"She's busy," said Self-Condemnation.

"Yeah," said Torment, "she's busy. She's got stuff to be sorry about."

Self-Condemnation knew he was well within his rights. He was sure that they wouldn't be attacked. Well, as sure as he could be dealing with a God who changed the rules whenever it suited His purposes. He looked at the angel, with a smile meant to dig under his skin. "I've made a sorry mess of my life."

Rosa said, "I've made a sorry mess of my life."

"I'm so young to be paralyzed. I'm going to be like this the rest of my life," said the demon.

Rosa repeated his words.

"It was my fault for being there. I should've left when I got that feeling that something bad was going to happen." The demon continued in a mocking voice filled with fake sniffles. "But I wanted to stay around long enough to go to bed with someone."

Rosa shamefully recalled how lustful and vain she had been before she had gotten shot. She was chained to this chair because she had been determined to sin against God. An uninvited chuckle happened in her mind. *I didn't see it as sin back then. It was just doing whatever felt good.*

Self-Condemnation repeated his words exactly.

"It was my fault for being there," said Rosa. "I should've left when I got that feeling that something bad was going to happen. But I wanted to stay around long enough to go to bed with someone."

"That's disgusting," said Self-Condemnation.

"It's so disgusting," said Rosa. "How many men have I gone to bed with without even knowing their last names?" Another wave of guilt rolled over her. "Some of them I didn't even know their real first names."

It was Torment's turn. "I'm paying for my sins."

"I'm paying for my sins," said Rosa. "The only thing keeping me from living like a whore is this chair. I'm no different than what I was."

Torment pulled back his head, looking at the angel, then looking at her. "Now that's good, Rosa. I'm impressed. Didn't even have to give you that one." Torment looked at Self-Condemnation. "We better watch it. We could find ourselves unemployed."

The demons laughed as they watched the saddened angel leave. Torment yelled out after him, "Aisha's on her own."

***

It didn't make a bit of sense to Aisha that Dante would call her and act so mysteriously heartbroken that he hadn't seen her and Ray-Ray for a week, then insist that she not take her baby with her when they met.

Aisha let out a long, exasperated breath. She was one of about a dozen people who were baking in Cool Mike's Laundromat. There was nothing cool about Mike's laundromat. She wiped the sweat from her brow. She wished she could wipe the stifling heat from her body.

A young woman sitting on a table tried to satisfy the itch under her purchased hair by furiously tapping the side of her head. "I hate that Chinaman. Why don't he do something about this heat?"

"And fix this stuff," shrieked an older woman who wore a scowl made permanent by a stroke. "He's about one tight Chinaman. Half these machines don't work. He gone gimme my money I lost in this dryer or I'm gone slap those slants out his eyes. I tell ya that. I ain't playin, either."

Baking or not, Aisha let out a laugh. Mike wasn't a tight Chinaman. He was a tight Laotian. She knew this because she had spoken with him before about his country. But that didn't make a difference in her neighborhood. Mike had slanted eyes. He was a Chinaman.

As usual, Dante was late. Aisha tried to ignore the heat by daydreaming about college. Then it was about what it was going to feel like owning her own washer and dryer. Then it was back to college. Were there Christian colleges? Finally, Mike's sauna had taken its toll. Being born black was one thing. Being baked black was unacceptable.

"I'm getting out of here," she said, and went outdoors and started walking back home. She didn't notice the car that followed until it suddenly stopped alongside her, and she saw the gun pointing at her. She was going to run until one of the hooded men mentioned Ray-Ray and her mama.

***

A lot of prayer had gone up to prepare the way for Glory Tabernacle's second Saturday in *Mayhem*. The first Saturday had produced two salvations and two subsequent baptisms. Eight thousand residents. Two salvations. A little by man's standard; a lot by God's standard.

These weren't seeker friendly, "Every head bowed. Every eye closed—no one looking, please. I see that hand," salvations. No, these were public declarations of faith in Christ despite the threat of death. Lil' Johnny and Aisha had literally counted all things loss that they may gain Christ. If there were two willing to follow all for

Christ, there were more. The Glory Tabernacle caravan rolled into Mayhem full of faith and ready for the harvest.

Sonny looked down from his perch with his binoculars and smiled. He looked around at the other buildings. Word was out: anyone caught looking out the windows at those church folks would answer to the Vice Boys.

"Yeah," he said, looking at all the closed windows and feeling his power, "you niggas bet not look out them windows." Sonny's big cheeks pushed up into a cocky smile. He couldn't wait for those church folks to find his present.

Jonathan wasn't the first to see it, but he was the first to get out of his car. He walked slowly, shaking his head, not wanting to believe what he saw. He started trotting toward— She was unrecognizable. Whoever had done this was a monster, and if there were a doubt as to who was responsible, the crude cardboard sign next to the woman's body told Jonathan all he needed to know: *No Jesus in Mayhem!*

Sonny stuffed a fork with four pieces of cooked frozen waffles into his mouth and immediately followed that with a big hunk of sausage. He chomped on the mouthful as he watched from his window. "What I say?" he shouted in glee to his crew. "Told you. They got good sense. They gettin' out of here."

And they were doing just that—getting out of there. Not all of them, but out of thirty-five people who had come this morning, the only ones left were Edwin and his family, Jonathan and Elizabeth, and Ava and two women.

Soon the police showed up. Then the local television reporters showed up.

The Glory Tabernacle saints were in stunned silence. What kind of place was Mahem Courts that someone would savagely beat a woman to death and try to use her death to stop the preaching of the gospel?

No Jesus in Mayhem!

Sharon looked at her father and Jonathan. It was obvious to them both that she was struggling to say something. She had to suppress the horror that was making it impossible to speak. "We know who did this."

Both men wore grim expressions.

"Yes, we do," said Jonathan. He looked at a man who wore a suit and hat. He must be a detective. He went to him. "Have any idea who did this?"

The man gave him a thinly veiled looked of annoyance. "And who are you?"

"I'm Jonathan Banks. I'm with the people over there. We're from—"

"Glory Tabernacle," said the detective.

"Yes," said Jonathan with surprise.

"We know who you are. All of you." There was nothing warm about this statement. "Your wife, Elizabeth. Reverend Styles and his family. Sharon and Andrew." The detective seemed to be trying to recall another name.

Something about this didn't seem good to Jonathan. He waited.

"Ava," said the detective. "Your adopted mother-in-law, Ava. She's recovered well from her aneurysm. How's her work with the girls going?"

Jonathan hesitated. This was a power play. The detective was sending a message. But what message? "Fine. She's helping a lot of girls with their pregnancies. Helped another baby get adopted just last week."

The detective's face was expressionless. Nonetheless, his body language betrayed him. He was enjoying himself. "Not those girls, Reverend Banks. The other girls. The prostitutes. The girls she snatches from pimps and hides in Stockbridge until she figures out what to do with them."

Jonathan returned the detective's expressionless face with one of his own. Yet, he knew that the detective saw through this like a sheer curtain. "That's going well."

"Yes, it is. There's a lot of mad pimps in Atlanta, Reverend Banks. They'd love to get their hands on the lady who is messing with their business."

"Good thing we have the police to protect us," said Jonathan.

The detective smiled. "Exactly, Reverend Banks. As long as the police are on your side, she and the rest of your friends here are safe."

Jonathan pondered the detective's words. "We believe Sonny is behind this girl's murder."

The detective looked icily at Jonathan.

Jonathan got the distinct impression that this *detective* was capable of operating on the other side of the law.

The detective's cold stare ended with a smile that would've fit perfectly on a snake. "I want you to meet a couple of cops who work this beat." He walked Jonathan over to them. "Officer Crandal, Officer Brown, you know who this is. Reverend Banks, you heard of that state senator who was found nearly naked outside? The one who was busted for drugs?"

"Yes," answered a wary Jonathan. "She said the drugs weren't hers, that someone broke into her home and framed her."

The detective chuckled. "Well, these are the two fine officers who personally checked her home just before she says this crazy story happened." The detective looked intently into Jonathan's eyes. "Now if there were someone waiting for the good senator in her home, these two fine officers would have seen them."

Jonathan felt as though a dump truck had just dropped its load onto him. It all made sense now. There was no way this kind of *Wild Wild West* behavior could go on without Sonny having protection.

"I'm going to leave you with Officers Crandal and Brown." The detective looked at the officers. "The reverend believes that someone named Sonny Christopher is behind this girl's murder. Reverend," he said, patting him on the shoulder, "please share everything you know with them. They'll take care of you—and anyone else who's concerned with this Sonny Christopher guy."

Jonathan encouraged himself in the Lord. "Detective, what is your name?"

"Detective Arnold."

"Detective Arnold, do you know who Sonny is?" asked Jonathan.

"No. Never heard of him."

"How did you know his last name?"

"What?" said Detective Arnold.

Jonathan looked intently into the detective's eyes. "I said Sonny, and you said Sonny Christopher. How'd you know the last name of someone you never heard of?"

The detective knew he had slipped on the ice of his own carelessness. He got to his feet and looked at Jonathan with a grin that was inadequate to mask his anger. "Lucky guess." He looked at the officers. "Make sure you take care of Reverend Banks."

"We'll be glad to," said Officer Crandal.

Chapter 29

It had been a little over an hour since Sonny's friends on the police force had strongly encouraged Jonathan and Edwin to leave Mayhem.

"We can't guarantee your safety," Officer Crandal had said. "It would be in all of your best interests to leave this place and never come back."

Officer Brown answered Jonathan's raised eyebrow with, "Things happen."

Jonathan looked briefly at Officer Brown and lowered his head in thought, then silent prayer.

"You understand?" asked Officer Brown.

Edwin wondered at the officer's words, surprised at how threatening they sounded. Certainly, the officer didn't mean how he sounded. After all, he was a *police officer*. "We'll be careful."

Officer Brown looked at the naïve preacher with eyes that communicated the danger his words were meant to convey. "Reverend, careful is staying away from Mayhem."

***

Now everyone was gathered at Edwin's home in silence, sitting in the large living room, contemplating the horror of finding the woman's body, and of being subtly but clearly threatened by the police. There were also two people present who had not gone to Mayhem to win souls. Kim and Lil' Johnny.

Kim had stated without hesitation that she was never going back into Mayhem. Besides, there was nothing she had to offer that crazy place. But she had been spending a lot of time at Grady Hospital offering her services there.

And Lil' Johnny hadn't thought twice about Jonathan's offer to stay with him and Elizabeth for a while. Would a drowning man think twice about grabbing the life preserver thrown to him? But Kwee hadn't been so lucky.

Lil' Johnny hadn't spoken a word since he had heard of his sister's death, and although everyone tried to comfort him, no one tried to make him say anything.

"Jonathan, you know what we have to do," said Ava.

"Yeah, I know what we have to do," he answered.

Sharon opened her mouth, but someone beat her to it.

"We gotta pray," said Lil Johnny.

Everyone looked at him and then shared looks with one another.

"He shot Prince. He killed Kwee. That man is Satan. The only thing can stop Sonny and the Vice Boys is God," said Lil Johnny. "I saw Jesus in the sky right before they shot Prince. You think He'll do something 'bout Sonny if we pray with our whole heart?"

Sharon's eyes were instantly wet with tears. She exhaled deeply. "Yes," she said with a punctuation of emotion. Sharon looked at her father and Jonathan. "If we pray with all our heart, God will stop Sonny."

Lil Johnny wiped his wet face. "I can't bring my sister back. She gone. But if praying with all my heart will stop that man from killing someone else, I'm gone pray 'til I die."

It was sudden.

A thousand-pound weight of remorse dropped onto Lil Johnny. He fell to his knees and wailed. "Oh, Kweeeeeeee, you didn't make it in. You didn't make it in, Kwee. Oh, God, my sister in hell."

Sadly, Lil Johnny was correct. For just four days prior…

***

The mercy angel had appeared out of nowhere in the midst of the gleeful demons. Actually, he jumped out of a blue mist. He erupted in a fury of large swinging fists that connected to every targeted face. That was every face there. When the large angel's fists stopped swinging, seven demons were sprawled across Sonny's floor. There would have been more had the others not shot out of there when they saw what kind of angel was attacking. Only a fool would voluntarily tangle with a mercy angel.

Had the mission been merely to destroy the demons surrounding the bloodied woman, other angels would have been used. But this was a mission of mercy, not one of destruction. The Lord had seen LaQueesha's intention to come to Him when her brother had done so. She had cowered in the face of persecution and had betrayed Him and rejected eternal life. But Johnny had asked Him to have mercy on his sister. That's why the mercy angel was here.

The big mercy angel looked around at the panicked, fleeing demons, then at those laid out on the floor. He found the one he was looking for. He got on one knee over one with a pointed head.

Palm *slap!* Backhand *slap!* Palm *slap!*

The demon didn't move.

The mercy angel looked toward the heavens.

"Get up," the demon heard, although the mercy angel heard nothing.

The antichrist spirit opened his eyes. When he saw what was kneeling over him, he had the equivalent of a human heart attack. He clutched his chest in morbid fear.

"Do what you do, demon. If you refuse, or if you try to escape, I will rip your head from your vile body." The angel stood.

The antichrist spirit was afraid to stand. It could be seen as provocative. He looked into the big angel's narrowing eyes. Perhaps he should stand. He stood. He looked at the woman in the chair.

"You *want* me to tempt her?" This must be some kind of trap. "God does not tempt anyone with evil," he said, his voice a mixture of a statement and a question.

Angels detested talking to demons. The mercy angel's large jaws clenched at this unwelcome necessity. "You tempt the sons and daughters of Adam to keep them from the kingdom of God. The Lord God Almighty tests them to prepare them for the kingdom of God."

"But—" began the wary spirit.

The big angel lifted a thick finger. "Not—one—more—word." The mercy angel glared at this enemy of God and added, "Demon."

"Look at me, Kwee," said Sonny.

A scrambled thought rose to the surface of LaQueesha's mind like debris in the aftermath of a tsunami. It was crowded and bumped by other thoughts made nonsensical by the unimaginable pain she felt all over her body.

Look up. Look up.

LaQueesha couldn't look up. She couldn't do anything but slump heavily in the chair. And even if she could find the strength to raise her blood-soaked head, she couldn't see him anyway. Both eyes were swollen shut.

Sonny smiled. "Last chance, big girl."

The last chance of which Sonny spoke had nothing to do with Lil Johnny. Brother or no brother, he knew Kwee would've flipped on him after only a few minutes of the sticks. She had been in the chair what? Three, four days? No, LaQueesha's last chance had come from the pointy headed antichrist spirit who had been unwittingly invited in by Sonny.

When LaQueesha didn't look up at Sonny, he turned to Pretty Tony and said, "See what I mean, PT? Some girls, no matter what you do to them, they still won't listen."

Pretty Tony pulled back his arm to come down hard on her swollen head.

"No," said Sonny, grabbing his arm. "She's going to come around." He looked at the pitiful sight, yet without any pity at all. "Aren't you, Kwee? You want to walk? You wanna get out of this chair and go back home?"

LaQueesha's lips moved ever so slightly. No words came out.

Sonny saw her lips. "See," he exulted, "there it is. "There—it—is. Kwee's got good sense."

"Sonny, how long we gone play with this girl? We got other business to take care of," said Pretty Tony.

The angel Enrid leapt from the blue mist. His mission was confusion and strife among the enemy. He turned and looked intently at Sonny before palming his head in his large hand. He said something to him, then jumped back into the mist.

Sonny's mouth responded faster than his brain. His words came out quick and carried an obvious threat. "Only room on the throne for one nigga at a time. Unless you plan on sittin' on my lap."

AJ's eyes got so wide they could have fallen to the floor. The other Vice Boys had similar responses. Sonny was the king. But as it was in every kingdom, there were some things even the king couldn't do, and some people even the king couldn't offend. Unless he was going to decisively deal with the repercussions.

For every king stayed in power because of two things. Fear and loyalty. He could exist without one or the other, but not in the absence of both. When a king lost both fear and loyalty, unspoken thoughts and hushed whisperings became loud protests and demands for change. Civil war was next.

Pretty Tony wasn't Pretty Tony just because he was pretty. He was Pretty Tony because he was also smooth and smart. At least, smarter than the rest of the Vice Boys. He did exactly what everyone expected him to do with Sonny's sudden and uncharacteristic—at least toward him—public humiliation.

After an awkward silence that seemed much longer to everyone than it was, Pretty Tony said, "You got a lot on yo' mind, Sonny." He spoke softly. His words were like a train on the right track, but carrying a dangerous load.

It was only a few seconds after the words left Sonny's mouth that he knew he had made the worst mistake of his criminal life. PT wasn't some kiss-butt nigga like AJ trying to get a reputation by being a Vice Boy. He was an original Vice Boy. He and PT had started the Vice Boys. He couldn't treat him like this and not have to deal with it.

Sonny had made a stupid move, but he wasn't stupid. A stupid man could never have ruled Mayhem the way he had. PT had moved his piece on the chess board. True to PT's form, his move couldn't readily be seen as offensive or defensive. But this was Mayhem. Every move was offensive.

Sonny didn't look around the room. He didn't have to. He knew what was going through their minds. They were nervously wondering whether he or PT would make a move against the other. That was a scary thought. But scarier than that was that if this happened, the others would have to make a move, too. They'd have to shoot those whom they felt were loyal to Sonny or Pretty Tony. Otherwise, the survivor would kill those whom he felt were loyal to the dead enemy.

The problem was, a situation like this had never come up or had even been secretly discussed. So although everyone knew they had to shoot someone, no one knew who that someone was. Everyone looked anxiously around the room, hands inching closer to their guns.

Sonny answered without looking at any Vice Boy. He didn't want some nervous nigga to start indiscriminately blasting away. "Yeah, we got business to take care of." He would've killed LaQueesha right then, but the antichrist spirit pressed him. Sonny peered at her. "Tell Jesus right here and now that you don't want Him."

The antichrist spirit rested his hand on LaQueesha's left shoulder. The mercy angel rested his hand on her right shoulder. Her body was nearly dead, barely clinging to life. But her mind received the opposing thoughts, clearly and forcefully. She still could not lift her head, but each thought was like a strong whiff of ammonia. She was as alert inside as she was battered outside.

"No," she whispered.

"No what? Do you deny the Christ, the Son of the Living God?" the demon in Sonny screamed.

This outburst made a few Vice Boys wonder at his behavior. It was understood that they couldn't have people in Mayhem disobeying them. But it seemed like Kwee was in the chair because Sonny had something going on with Jesus?

"Yes." Her answer was mixed with a labored groan.

Antichrist's eyes widened. "Louder," he yelled, his craving for a denial of Christ temporarily causing him to forget the presence of the mercy angel. "I want to hear you deny the Creator."

"Louder," yelled Sonny. "I want to hear you deny the Creator."

More peculiar looks from Sonny's Vice Boys.

LaQueesha gurgled her answer in isolated words that sounded like verbal islands separated by waters of silence. "I..."

"Come on. Come on," said the antichrist spirit and Sonny.

"De..." LaQueesha's lungs were sharing the shock of the rest of the body. It hurt to breathe.

"Come on."

"...ny. De...ny..."

Sonny got on one knee besides LaQueesha. His knee rested in blood on the floor. Pretty Tony and the others stared at the unlikely sight of Sonny deliberately dirtying his clothes. He was obsessive about his clothes and appearance.

"Come on. Say it. Say it. Say it." He cursed her.

He and the antichrist spirit had to wait excruciating seconds before it came out.

"Chr...Chri...Christ," she said, sealing her eternal doom. Eternity began before her lifeless head tilted to a fateful stop.

***

LaQueesha opened her eyes. Surprisingly, the pain that had only a moment before consumed her whole body was mysteriously gone. She looked to the right at Sonny. He was on his knee next to her, howling like a dog, celebrating something.

That last thought jarred her like she was in a car wreck. She heard a loud sound like a lock snapping into place. It startled her. She looked down from where the sound had come. Then her head whipped up and toward Sonny. She knew why he was celebrating.

For the briefest moment, she saw what she instinctively knew was a mercy angel. A mercy angel sent to give her a final chance to submit to Him as Lord. Before she could say, "Thank God," he turned and flew away.

"It would be a waste of time, LaQueesha."

She turned to the voice. The voice belonged to a hideous creature. It had features like a man, but it wasn't a man. It wasn't human. It was tall. About the height of Pretty Tony. Its face was reddish-orange and had deep lines. Its narrow lips or absence of lips revealed long, sharp teeth. Its head long and pointed. But it was the creature's eyes that magnified the fear that bore through her soul like a power drill's bit. There weren't words to describe their evil.

"I am antichrist."

"What do you want with me?" asked LaQueesha out of desperation. She knew why he wanted her. The moment she saw Sonny celebrating, she knew why a creature like this would want her. Why such a creature would feel they had something in common.

Somehow the creature found a way to smile. "Because we both are antichrist. Our hatred of the Christ is mutual."

"But me and Lil Johnny—"

The demon cut her off. "You and Johnny were offered eternal life. He accepted; you rejected. I saw the fight, LaQueesha. We all saw the fight between you and the Christ lover." The demon was enjoying the conversation, but he knew it would suddenly end. "Say what you must, coward. You haven't much time." He was surprised that she was still there.

"I was afraid. Sonny said—" LaQueesha stopped and looked down.

"Feels like something around your ankles?" asked the demon.

She looked at him, eyes full of terror, remembering what she had heard about hell. *I'm going to be tormented forever for rejecting Christ?* "Yes," she said, the word trembling out of her mouth.

He shook his head a couple of times. "Those are your sins. The Christ paid for them. Offered you mercy. You said no. God is righteous. Somebody's got to pay for every sin. Since you rejected God's mercy," the demon smiled, hoping he'd be able to get in this last torment before it happened, "who do you think that someone is?"

"Me?" she asked, with a face filled with the horror of her eternal mistake.

The demon clapped his hands together as he answered. "Yes. Exactly. You."

"But I was scared."

Immediately, LaQueesha was violently snatched downward by her sins.

The antichrist spirit watched her disappear into the floor. He closed his eyes and rocked his head from side to side. This had been a good day. For him.

LaQueesha, however, was hurtling downward through another dimension in thick darkness like a shooting rocket. At first the darkness was similar to what she had experienced prior to dying in her sins. But the darkness grew thicker as she traveled. Soon she could actually feel the darkness. Somehow she knew the darkness wasn't the absence of God. It was God. It was a manifestation of His wrath.

If I make my bed in hell, behold, You are there.

The thought had come out of nowhere, and she knew it was a Scripture. *Then why did some preachers say hell was separation from God? I can't get away from Him no matter where I go. Everything and every place is His.*

The uncomfortable heat LaQueesha had been feeling was now more than uncomfortable. It was stifling. She wasn't in a fire, but it felt like she was standing next to a huge open furnace. She began to moan.

"Save me, Jesus," she pled.

Despite the tangible darkness, she saw a fast approaching fire that was one moment fiery red, then blacker than the darkness that surrounded it.

How…what? she wondered. *He's going to put me in that fire?* LaQueesha fought through the heat and screamed, "How can you do this? You're a God of love. What about grace?" She shook her head violently as she repeated the futile question. "What about grace?" she screamed into the darkness.

LaQueesha entered the fire knowing that her fate was forever sealed, and wondering what would happen when the Vice Boys caught up with her brother and that girl that was baptized.

Chapter 30

Lil Johnny listened as others in the Styles's home prayed for Mayhem, quoting Scripture after Scripture. He felt bad that he didn't know any. He waited for a lull in the loud praying. There wasn't one. The prayers were constant, growing in intensity and eloquence.

Jonathan was walking the floor and jabbing his finger in front of him as he prayed. He had an angry look on his face. One moment he was praying in English, shouting about some walls of Jericho coming down, whatever that was, or some dude named David killing a giant. The next moment he was shouting some of that tongues stuff he had gotten too when Jonathan had laid hands on him the day he had received Christ.

That girl, Sharon, and the short woman named Ava, were walking around almost screaming stuff at the devil. *They talk smack like that to the devil?* thought Lil Johnny. Every now and then they'd point into the air and say something about taking land from the Canites, the Jebudites, the Mackalites. Everybody must've been related because all their names ended in *ites*.

Lil Johnny looked at the others in the room with their hands lifted in prayer, their eyes closed. Some with tears flowing. Some praying in English. Some in tongues. Some quoting Scriptures—mentioning those *ite* people. But everyone praying strongly.

He jumped in. "Lawd, I don't know about no Megabytes, and Termites and Highlights. I just got saved. I don't know no Scriptures. All I know is Sonny gotta be stopped. And you the only one can stop 'em. You gotta stop that crazy nigga, Jesus. He standin' in the way of the gospel."

Lil Johnny's words cut through the holy raucus and found Barbara's shocked ears. She looked at him on the sly. *Stop that crazy nigga, Jesus?* It was all so confusing. She agreed that the word was offensive. But if black people found the word so offensive, why did they use it so much? Octavius routinely used the word. This black man *prayed* using the word. The short time she had spent in Mayhem, she had heard people there use the word. Was this a word that only white people weren't supposed to use? It just didn't make sense. Either the word was bad or it wasn't.

Edwin saw her looking at Lil Johnny. He prayed his way next to her and whispered in her ear with a slight smile. "I know. I know. God knows his heart."

She shook her head at the irony of hearing a black man ask Jesus to "stop that crazy nigga." She went back to crying out to God and asking Him to save Mayhem.

After nearly three hours of desperate prayers something remarkable happened.

***

The command went forth from heaven's throne. "Gather my people for the great battle."

***

The divine knowing descended lightly on the intercessors. The battle for Mayhem wasn't over, but this prayer session was. Edwin looked at Jonathan. "We have to go back, don't we?"

"We have to go back," he answered.

Everyone was thinking it, but no one was going to say it. Sonny Christopher and the Vice Boys were cold-blooded murderers. They had shot down Prince in broad daylight in front of everyone, and no one had been arrested. They had beaten Lil Johnny's sister to death, and had thrown her naked body out into the field for them to see it. No one had been arrested. And the police had all but threatened their safety should they return.

But they had to go back.

Sharon spoke up. “Gideon started with thirty-two thousand soldiers, and God sent him out to fight the enemy with only three hundred.”

“How many were they fighting?” asked Lil Johnny.

“I don’t know. The Bible doesn’t say exactly,” she answered. “Just that they were fighting at least three nations, and that their armies were as the sand on the seashore. Too numerous to count.”

Lil Johnny made a face like he was computing figures in his head. “That’s a hell of a lot more than three hundred.”

Barbara’s mouth gaped in surprise. She closed her mouth almost immediately. Edwin was right. This man had only been saved a few days. His mouth hadn’t caught up with his heart yet. Besides, despite his rough speech, he was practically a martyr for the faith, and he had lost his sister. She wondered whether she would have the same courage and faithfulness if she faced similar circumstances. She smiled admiringly at him when he looked at her.

Edwin, Sharon, and Jonathan smiled at Barbara as she smiled at Lil Johnny.

“Samson killed a thousand Philistines with only a jaw bone,” said Andrew.

Lil Johnny’s face twisted at Andrew’s words. He didn’t see how a dude could beat even one man by swinging his face at him. He shook his head. *Whatever,* he thought.

Ava chimed in. “And the words of Jonathan, “There is no restraint to the Lord to save by many or by few.”

Lil Johnny looked at Jonathan with an expression that said, “Cool.” Jonathan gave him a “What can I say?” look.

Edwin shook his head at Jonathan. “Really?” he asked with his eyes.

Jonathan exhaled in submission. “It’s another Jonathan, Lil Johnny.” He looked at Edwin. “But had I been there, that is exactly what I would’ve said.”

“That’s good, Jonathan,” said Edwin. “Because it looks like if Mayhem’s going to be won, it’s going to be won with a few.”

“That’s a few more than the devil has,” said Jonathan.

Sharon lit up. "What's the plan?"

"Same plan God gave Moses," he answered.

"What's that?" asked Edwin. "Show up and say let my people go?"

Jonathan smiled. "You got the showing up part right."

"You're kidding, right?" asked Edwin.

"Ohhh, Lawd," said Lil Johnny.

***

Aisha didn't know where she was. They had put a hood on her and pushed her head down onto a man's lap for the whole drive. She didn't like the way he rubbed her, but what could she do?

It was a short drive, so she knew she wasn't far away from home. But a short way from home was a long way from home when you were tied to a chair, your mouth was gagged, you had a hood on your head, and your kidnappers were joking about having their way with you.

Right now she was alone. The men were in the next room. The door opened. It closed. Ominous footsteps sounded off the hardwood floor. They stopped behind her. Hands draped over her shoulders and onto her chest. She closed her eyes under the hood and cried.

God make him stop, she begged.

"I know you ain't cryin'," the man said angrily. He looked at her with a sneer. "Like you some kind of virgin queen. I know you got a baby. You ain't get that baby by playin' checkers." He smiled a nasty smile as he thought of the cleverness of his words. "I think you know a lil' somethin' about playin' chess, don't cha, girl?"

Jesus, please make him stop. I'm Your daughter, Aisha pled.

The door flew open.

The man who opened the door looked at the man behind Aisha. He looked at the man's hands. A bad look came to his face.

"What?" the man with the dancing hands snapped.

"What? What? You need to hear it again, nigga?"

The hand man looked at the dude at the door. He didn't appreciate the drama. "Don't front me like that, nigga."

"Stick to the script," the man pushed.

The man with the hands bent down and whispered to Aisha before he left. "I hope you ain't smilin' under that hood. We gone finish what we started." He walked past the other man provocatively slow.

"If you know what's good fo' you, nigga, you best keep walkin."

He smiled defiantly, but he kept walking.

The man who had run off dancing hands looked at the bound girl up and down for a long few seconds before slowly closing the door.

Ten minutes later dancing hands opened the door and hurried to Aisha. "We got company coming. If I hear one sound from this room, I'll put my foot up yo' behind. You hear me?" He smacked the hood hard. "You hear me, girl?"

Aisha grunted.

The man pointed at her hooded face before hurrying out the room.

***

The four men looked at the pots and plastic containers. If there was a way for them to smile larger, it hadn't been discovered yet. Prophetess Ebony Monroe laid it all out while getting on all their cases for not serving the Lord. The men did what they always did when she got on them about their heathen ways. They politely agreed and said they knew they needed to change and would one day.

Prophetess Ebony Monroe had a sort of dual citizenship in the hood. In her younger days she had done everything a hard ghetto girl could do. Correction. Everything a hard Mayhem girl could do. And though Mayhem was definitely anybody's definition of ghetto, there was a world of difference in basic ghetto and Mayhem. Basic ghetto was simple addition. Mayhem was advanced calculus.

She had tricked. She had tracked—shot up heroin. She had boosted—stolen for a living. She had even shot a dude to teach him a lesson. But it was for a good reason. He had sold her some bad dope. The judge felt obligated to follow her logic and teach her a lesson. That's where her five years free room and board at the Georgia Women's Correctional Facility (GWCF) came from.

Unlike many women there, she made it through without being sexually assaulted by a prison guard. In most prisons, sexual assaults committed by guards were rare. Not so at GWCF. Prison guard philosophy there was that prisoners had no rights. *No* rights.

Pre-Prophetess Ebony Monroe was five-feet and seven inches. Sixty-seven inches of dark caramel beauty. When Ebony showed up in GWCF, it was like God was doing the Garden of Eden thing all over again with the Tree of Knowledge of Good and Evil. Adam and Eve couldn't resist biting the forbidden fruit. Neither could the guards of GWCF.

Yet pre-Prophetess Ebony Monroe had managed five years without doing or being done by one of GWCF's horny guards. That was not to say that it was five years without certain sexual humiliations. But those humiliations didn't rise to the level of actual sexual assault.

Pre-Prophetess Ebony Monroe knew she wasn't just lucky. No female at GWCF who looked like her could be that lucky. She knew that there was only one reason her fruit hadn't been plucked by a guard.

Jesus.

Not *her* Jesus. Her sister's Jesus.

Her sister, Sonny Christopher's mother, Aliya, had enough Jesus for herself and her. All she had to do was to ask her sister to pray away whatever guard that was becoming sexually aggressive toward her and in short fashion something *coincidental* would happen.

One guard who had more than once allowed his imagination and hands to get the best of him, and the best of her, killed himself after he came home one night and found that his wife had taken their two little girls and had left him for another woman.

Another who had never gotten the courage to put his hands on her in a sexual way, nevertheless had no problem describing in detail what he wanted to do to her. That guard transferred to another prison because his wife got an out-of-state promotion.

The last, the scariest of the three—because of his well-earned reputation—had a heart attack and died shortly after another inmate, a white girl from a family with money and connections, hired an attorney and pressed charges against him for repeatedly raping her.

But that was all so long ago. Prison days. Pre-prophetess days. Ebony was now, and sincerely so, Prophetess Ebony Monroe. She had gotten out of prison, walked the straight and narrow path of a drug-free lifestyle for thirteen days before she and Heroin resumed their old love affair.

Finally, a year after her sister died, she hit the bottom of life so hard she landed in the basement. Suicide seemed the only honorable thing to do. But as much emotional pain as she was in, she couldn't do it. Octavius needed her. And her nephew, Sonny, needed her. She couldn't abandon her obligations as a mother and aunt.

So although she was too weak to put down heroin, she couldn't put down the memories of how her sister's Jesus had protected her in prison. It was out of these memories that a persistent and foolish thought captivated her imagination. If Jesus could protect her while she was *in* prison, maybe He could free her *from* prison. The prison of drug addiction.

It was due to this strange thought that Prince got his memories of seeing his mother shoot heroin with a big Bible on her lap and going into a stupored nod while calling on Jesus. He had cynically wondered at this ridiculous picture of a drug addict with a needle hanging from her arm, and saying things like, "Don't worry 'bout this needle, Octavius. Jesus gone free me from this—"and she'd finish the statement of faith with a cuss word. "He gone free me. And I'm gone preach and tell the world about it. You gone preach, too. God showed me you gone preach around the world."

Time had proven that the Spirit of God had been resting upon a criminal whore ex-con junkie and feeding her the nourishment of irrational hope. Hope, not only for her, but for her son.

Prophetess Ebony Monroe's conflicted thoughts rose from her heart like the smell of the ox tail stew that rose from the pot on the stove. Her own nephew, the boy she had raised alongside her own son when her sister was killed by a stray bullet, had tried to murder her son. And at least two of the Vice Boys who had reportedly shot him were sitting at the table waiting for her food, and smiling like chimpanzees, thinking that she was too stupid to know they had tried to kill Octavius, or that she knew but was too scared to say or do anything.

Prophetess Ebony Monroe wasn't stupid.

Nor was she afraid.

Her sister's Jesus was now her Jesus. She had her own testimony. The God who had saved her from the prison guards, and the God who had saved her from the prison of heroin, was giving her the power to do what she needed to do. Didn't the Bible say, "If your enemy is hungry, feed him"?

Prophetess Ebony Monroe fixed the three men large portions of ox tail stew, rice, hot water cornbread, and salad. When the meal was over, she didn't ask, she directed them to stand for prayer.

The men stood immediately and lowered their heads. After she prayed for them, two of the three Vice Boys followed her onto the porch. One wanted to tell her about how he had been healed of his skin disease when another preacher had come to the house looking for Prince and prayed for them. The other wanted to tell her how sorry he was that Prince had been shot by a rival gang. He was also sorry that Prince had been cremated. He would've gone to the funeral had she had one for him.

The third of the three Vice Boys said he had to go to the bathroom. But he didn't go to the bathroom. He went to see Aisha.

She had to fight to keep her bladder from releasing when she heard the door open. *Oh, Jesus,* she thought.

Talik entered the room with a bowl of ox tail stew. He pulled up a chair and placed it next to her, but it faced the opposite direction. His face showed that he had just remembered something important. He looked around the room. He was relieved when he saw a bed pillow. He snatched the pillow case off, twirled it, and stood behind Aisha.

"Don't turn around—" he called her a name.

She continued to look straight forward when the hood came off.

Immediately he wrapped the folded pillow case around Aisha's head and eyes. He smiled and looked her over. This made his smile widen. "You hungry?"

Aisha heard the words. She understood them at one level. But at the level where her brain would allow her to answer, she couldn't. She was like a car whose starter was unsuccessfully fighting to start the car. Turning, turning, turning. Enough current to make noise; not enough to make the engine start.

"You can't talk?" Talik challenged.

Aisha clamped her muscles to keep the urine from coming out. Mercifully, the engine of her mind turned over. "I can talk," she answered compliantly.

"I said, you hungry?"

"No."

Talik's brows furrowed in anger. "No? Open yo' mouth," he demanded.

"I'm not hungry." Her answer came out with a tremble.

The Vice Boy glared at her. He sat the bowl on the floor.

Slap!

He turned around and looked at the door, listening to see whether the loud sound of the slap had gotten anyone's attention. Nothing. They were still on the porch talking to Sonny's aunt. He turned back to Aisha. He sat down and picked up the bowl.

Aisha's face burned from his heavy hand slapping her almost sideways onto the floor. She didn't want to be a baby, but began crying like one. Suddenly, she felt hands around her throat. She couldn't breathe.

"Shut the — up," he cursed in a whisper. He released her neck. "You gone shut up?"

Aisha nodded her head.

"Now, you hungry. You hear me?"

She nodded submissively.

"Open yo' mouth," he said.

She did.

He put his hand in the bowl of stew and pulled some of the tender meat off an ox tail. He put it in her mouth, rolling his index finger along the inside of her bottom lip before putting his hand back in the bowl. He watched her chew. He looked down at her lap and was angered that she wore pants.

Talik listened again for the others and was confident that he had a little more time. He reached in the bowl and used his fingers to scoop up some rice. "Open yo' mouth."

She did.

He put his dripping fingers into her mouth and pulled them out ever so reluctantly. He dipped a finger back into the stew. "You need some gravy, girl." He didn't tell her to open her mouth this time. He didn't want her involvement. He wanted to have his way. He frowned as he stuck his finger into her mouth. "You bet not leave a drop of juice on my finger."

This feeding lasted only a few disgusting minutes. Her tormentor heard the others wrapping up the conversation. He put the hood back on her head and hurried out of the room, leaving a thoroughly traumatized fourteen-year-old girl tied to a chair, with a bottom wet with the evidence of her terror.

***

Prophetess Ebony Monroe left the Vice Boys. She had one more ox tail stew stop to make. She had to go to Sonny's. She didn't smile as the Scripture rolled around inside of her. Her soul was too troubled for that. But she did get strength and comfort from it.

Do not be overcome by evil, but overcome evil with good.

Chapter 31

The demon shook his head. There had to be a mistake. He walked quickly and tightly, trying but not really wanting to keep up with his superior. "Contemptus, this just can't be correct. I'm from San Francisco for crying out loud. We don't have these kinds of battles back there. What good am I on the front lines? I don't *know* anything," Annus pled.

His superior's backhand was across his face before either of them knew it was coming. Contemptus glared at the irksome demon. He had not meant to smack him, but he was under a lot of pressure. The armies of God were rousing the saints from their spiritual sleep and becoming much more aggressive in their attacks. Slavery and Annihilation was threatening, no, promising, punishment for any failures. He was not in the mood to listen to Annus whine. "You may be from San Francisco, but are you a demon?"

Annus instinctively responded to the surprise smack by crouching and baring his claws at Contemptus. He hissed at his superior, knowing that his reactions, though in response to being struck, could be seen as gross insubordination, and thus cause for severe punishment or even death. Yet something deep inside of him pushed him further into this dangerous territory.

Contemptus looked at the humiliated and enraged demon with a dark smile. He nodded. "Yes. Yes, you are a demon after all." He got into Annus's face. "You are from San Francisco, but you are a demon." He paused. "And *that*, Anus, is all you have to know." Contemptus turned and resumed his brisk walk.

Annus didn't move. He watched Contemptus, his anger lessening with each of his superior's steps. He slowly raised to his full posture. He wondered at how he had responded to being slapped. It was not like him to feel such murderous rage—although foolish under the circumstances. He contemplated the foreign feeling. It felt dark. It felt good. It felt demonic.

Annus started walking quickly toward Contemptus. But not too quickly. He needed a few more moments of uninterrupted time to savor this discovery of self-darkness. *Could there be a fighting demon inside of me after all?*

He saw a demon with an anxious face approach and stop Contemptus. Whatever he told him wasn't good. The spirit left Contemptus and hurried to another team of demons.

Contemptus turned and looked hard at the straggling demon who had begun as an irksome, yet comical forced side-kick, but who had become, due to worsening battle conditions, a weight around his neck. Annus did appear to hurry it up a bit. This, however, didn't improve Contemptus's mood.

When he got to him, Contemptus said, "Nice to be able to take a leisurely stroll during a badly developing battle that could send you and I to the Dark Prison."

Annus didn't know where the old Contemptus was, but the Contemptus who slapped him and who glared at him now was not him. There would be no repeat of his insubordination. Annus lowered his head and said, "I beg your forgiveness." He did not raise his head.

Contemptus looked at the demon's lowered head. This show of good behavior removed a little of his irritation. "The Spirit of God and that wretched blue mist of His is nearly everywhere, Anus. Angels are using it like it's a highway. They're jumping in and out of it with near impunity. Our lords have designated everyone as frontline soldiers. If we lose Mayhem..."

If we lose Mayhem? thought Annus. He hadn't been in Atlanta long, but he didn't have to be to know that a loss of this magnitude would send shock and fear through the dark kingdom. For if a place like Mayhem could fall, what was next? San Francisco? Hollywood?

"Perhaps the church will resist the Holy Spirit," Annus offered tentatively. "They've rejected Him in so many other areas. The gifts of the Spirit. Holiness. Repentance. Separation from the world." Annus got a short burst of enthusiasm, just enough for the next word. "Homosexuality. Maybe they'll just say no to the Holy Ghost."

Contemptus thought of the significance of what he had just heard, and wondered how it had come out of the mouth of a San Francisco demon. The saints *were* famous for kicking God's plans to the curb. Maybe, just maybe, they'd do it again.

Then again, maybe not.

How bad had things gotten that the continued glory of Mayhem had been reduced to hoping that the saints would disobey God. Contemptus snapped out of his musings. "Annus, report to the armory. We're going with a strike team."

The brave thoughts that had warmed Annus's dark heart only minutes before were gone. He tried to hide his fear. "Strike force? What are we striking?"

"Not what, who?" Contemptus answered curtly. "Get to the armory. You'll find out when we get there."

***

Captain Rashti was within the middle of a circle of standing angels. Enrid, Myla, Trin, and Adaam-Mir were among them. Adaam-Mir stood between Enrid and Myla. He looked at the legendary hero and tried to focus only on what he was saying. Yet despite his greatest efforts, he'd cast a quick glance to his left and right. What was he doing in a group like this? He didn't belong here.

Captain Rashti caught him in one of these self-contemplative glances. "Promotion comes from the Lord."

These out of place words jarred Adaam-Mir from his thoughts. He looked at the captain, wondering how he knew what he was thinking.

"The first shall be last; the last shall be first," said Captain Rashti.

"Blessed be the name of the Lord," said all of the angels.

Adaam-Mir smiled, a bit embarrassed to be the center of attention. "Blessed be the name of the Lord," he said.

The captain resumed his briefing. "Our mission, as usual, is difficult and dangerous. But its difficulty is not in its danger, but in what we must do. And what we must do in so short a period of time. We must free the church from fear, selfishness, and love of comfort. Those freed will be used in the great battle."

The captain's words weren't met with unbelief, but they were met with thoughtful silence and hard, unspoken questions. It wasn't that they were to free the saints from such immensely powerful forces. Many saints had been delivered from those monsters.

What caused this response in the angels was that although there were some saints who had been freed from these forces, they were few in comparison with the multitudes of saints who had never rid themselves of these things. Or at least not to the degree that they'd ever be able to powerfully and consistently demonstrate Christ through their lives. There simply was too much of their self-interests that had not been submitted to God. How were they to do in a short period of time what had not been accomplished in a long period of time?

"And we must get the church to work together to destroy the Mayhem stronghold," added Captain Rashti.

"Together, Captain?" asked an angel. "You mean getting *a* church to work together?"

"No. I mean getting *the* church to work together." The captain answered as though this wasn't in the same category of difficulty as freeing saints from fear, selfishness, and love of comfort.

"Captain?" said Adaam-Mir.

The captain nodded approvingly.

"This—how can such a thing be done? I have not seen as much as all of you. There is much that I do not know. It's just that from what I have seen, the church, it has lost its way. With few exceptions, it has been conformed to the world. How do we get it to see that it is here to serve, not to be served? How do we get the saints to stop living for themselves and to start living for others? And in a short time? It takes a long time to get saints to walk in love."

Adaam-Mir ended that statement feeling like he may have spoken with more certainty than his limited experience justified. But the other angels' expressions showed that he had spoken what was on their hearts.

"You have spoken truth." The captain spoke as he slowly turned, looking each angel in the eyes. "But there is another truth, an event. 'Who has heard such a thing? Who has seen such things? Shall the earth be made to bring forth in one day? Or shall a nation be born at once? for as soon as Zion travailed, she brought forth her children.'"

"That is the blessed book, Captain Rashti. Isaiah. The great prophet Isaiah," Adaam-Mir said excitedly. He listened to the silence around him and tried to calm down. It would be difficult.

Good-natured laughter filled the air.

The captain didn't laugh, but he did lift his back as he admired the angel. "Please, continue."

Adaam-Mir's eyes widened for a second at the thought of being asked by the captain to speak about the blessed book. "The Lord's inheritance. Israel. Israel was scattered to the four winds of the earth." The angel made large sweeping gestures with both hands. "But the Lord, our great God, He commanded Cyrus the king and gathered His people."

Adaam-Mir wasn't finished. He raised a finger and looked around at the angels. "Then He did it again. At the rebellion against Rome in the first century, when the emperor retaliated in his hateful anger and scattered Abraham's seed, and destroyed them as a nation, it appeared that all was lost. That the great promises God had made to Abraham would never come to pass. But my brothers," the angel's voice lifted as his body and mind were filled with the majesty of God, "on May 14, 1948 Israel again became a nation. In one day a nation was born." His eyes glistened as he finished.

"There is another fulfillment of the great prophecy," said Captain Rashti.

All eyes looked at him.

"Another nation was also born in a day." The captain allowed the quizzical expressions to remain before he went on. "The church, the Lord's holy nation of sons and daughters was born in a day."

Lots of heads started bobbing up and down, big smiles on the angels' faces.

"Much death and destruction preceded the fulfillment of this prophecy," said the captain. "Our Lord used His own death to bring life to many. He is doing this once more."

"Once more?" asked an angel.

"It will become more clear as the battle progresses." Captain Rashti looked at his angels with the determination of one called the Sword of the Lord. "Except a seed falls to the ground and dies, it remains alone. But if it dies, it brings forth much fruit."

Adaam-Mir whispered to Myla. "Who else is going to die? Can we stop it?"

The captain's back was to Adaam-Mir when he spoke. "For the glory of God and the sons of men!"

Every angel raised a clenched right fist. "For the glory of God and the sons of men!"

They went to the entry point of the blue mist of the Holy Spirit and entered with their weapons drawn. The Lord had spoken. Life would come from death.

Mayhem was to be born in a day.

Captain Rashti pulled his Special Forces angel, Enrid, off to the side. He had a mission for him.

***

Annihilation and Slavery were ready. More than ready. This time they were on the offensive. Their replenished armies—compliments of Prince Krioni—were perfectly positioned for ambushes. Once the angels entered the kill zones, two things would assure their destruction. The element of surprise and superior numbers. They'd be overwhelmed. Never knowing what hit them.

The plan had been concocted by Ferocious, the chief of the warrior spirits who had been assigned to the Mayhem battle by

Prince Krioni. He had become a legend by his brilliant use of ambushing the enemy.

He had ambushed the great king David and had taken the wives, children, and property of him and his men. He had ambushed the great king Uzziah at the height of his prosperity and power, and by the time he had figured out what had happened to him, he had leprosy and was banned from the temple. Similarly, he had ambushed Judas Iscariot, and later the twelve disciples.

Ferocious was still angry about the Judas incident. The dark master, Satan, entered Judas only because of the warrior spirit's masterful ambush. But he had taken full credit for the betrayal of Judas.

Ferocious looked at various individual soldiers as they went about their military business. He noted with disdain and pride the difference between his warrior spirits and those of these two ruler spirits. If he had his way, he'd dismiss their armies. He didn't need them. They weren't properly trained. They just got in the way of him and his warriors.

Ferocious looked at Slavery and Annihilation. They were talking to one another about who knows what. What did ruler spirits talk about? If wars were won through talking, he and his warrior spirits wouldn't be here.

Slavery saw the chief warrior spirit approaching. "Here comes Chief Butthead now," he said to Annihilation.

This insult wasn't without some basis of fact. Ferocious was built as a legendary warrior spirit would be expected to be. He was tall, large, and ugly. He had the permanent scowl and the expected scars that signified his great battles. But he also had a feature that made him the *butt* of jokes. His large face had plump cheeks that rose on both sides. They sloped downward and met where a deep line divided them in the middle. The appearance was unmistakably that of human buttocks.

Annihilation looked at his face and said under his breath to Slavery, "What did he say to Jesus to get a face like that?"

Ferocious approached and stopped before them. His heavy feet stamped his boots into the dirt.

"Ferocious—"

"Stealth. Surprise. Superior numbers mean nothing against Rashti if we don't have the element of surprise." Ferocious had cut off Slavery's words.

"You will have—"

He cut off Annihilation. "Speed. The moment they are detected, the attack begins. The moment, the very moment. Not one second more."

"Is there *anything* else you'd like to instruct us on?" said Slavery. "What would two ruling spirits know a butt warfare?"

Ferocious snapped his attention to Slavery, his eyes narrowed, wondering whether Slavery had just insulted him.

"Yes," said Annihilation, "who knows warfare butta than you?"

The warrior spirit's eyes rocketed to Annihilation. Had *he* just insulted him? He didn't see anything in the ruler spirit's face. Perhaps he was just being overly sensitive. "No indecision. The moment must be seized or it will disappear."

Annihilation opened his mouth to speak. He closed it as the surly warrior spirit spun and briskly walked away. "There'll be no *cracks* in the execution of the ambush," Annihilation yelled after him.

Ferocious stopped. He didn't turn around. He looked at the ground at his feet as he pondered.

"We're *behind* you one hundred percent," Slavery joined in.

Ferocious put both hands on both swords.

Fun was fun, but this was the chief of the warrior spirits they were making fun of. These unpredictable creatures couldn't be counted on to observe protocol or rank. Slavery and Annihilation pulled out their swords. They watched the warrior anxiously for the several seconds they knew he was contemplating whether or not to attack two ruler spirits. They were relieved when he walked away without turning around.

Slavery turned to Annihilation. "I don't want Butthead to have anything to say against us to Prince Krioni. We better make sure that we blast those angels the moment they're detected."

***

The angel scout came back to Captain Rashti. "We've cleared the area."

"Good," answered the captain. He turned to Trin, one of his most trusted leaders. "Gather the saints. I'll return shortly."

The angels approached the Atlanta television stations.

***

Enrid didn't have the benefit of hiding in the mist of the Holy Spirit as he stalked the company of demons. For although he would have been unseen to them, the mist was visible. Prior to the arrival of the warrior spirits, the demons had grown complacent by the presence of the Holy Spirit's mist, which seemed to be everywhere. But Ferocious had immediately remedied this by positioning his warriors in fortified groups in strategic places around Mayhem.

Fortunately, this mission wasn't in Mayhem. He didn't have to worry about the concentration of fortified strongholds of warrior spirits.

Unfortunately, this mission wasn't in Mayhem. He had to worry about the company of warrior spirits he was stalking.

Enrid had absolutely no chance to destroy such a large company of warrior spirits. But that was not the mission. He spotted the mission. The leader of this strike force company. He wore full body armor. The angel noted that they all wore this armor. But he identified the leader by the long, flowing red robe he wore.

Special Forces angels were designated as such because of their amazing fighting ability and resourcefulness, but primarily because of their predisposition to see the possibilities in impossibilities. He was outnumbered five hundred or more to one. And that was only part of the impossibility.

But that red robe...

Enrid crouched and moved with the stealth and steady patience of a tiger closing in on its unwary prey. He knew he had only one shot at success. He followed the red robe until it was far enough away from the others that he could make his move. The angel unconsciously thanked God that demons were so often blinded by pride. Why else would this demon, leader or not, wander away from the protection of his company. *Because you don't need protection, do you? You're a warrior spirit,* thought Enrid. *You've got your own company.*

Enrid stepped out from his hiding place.

The warrior spirit's swords came out without a discernible motion.

Enrid noted that the warrior's eyes looked around without him moving his head. They had a sense of awareness about them. Enrid put his finger to his own lips. "Don't be afraid, warrior spirit. I am alone."

The warrior spirit could've rushed the angel for this insult alone. *Don't be afraid?* Warrior spirits didn't fear. "I know you are alone, angel. I've been watching you watch me for several minutes now." The warrior spirit eyes widened in dark humor. "I hope I haven't hurt your feelings." The warrior spirit took two steps toward him.

Enrid concealed his surprised. He put up a hand. "Wait. You haven't much time. I want you to understand something before I sink my dagger into your heart."

The warrior spirit could hardly believe his ears. It was the only reason he didn't rush the suicidal angel. "I haven't much time? You are singlehandedly going to destroy me and my company of warrior spirits?"

Enrid looked into the red eyes of the armored demon. "No. I am only going to destroy *you.*" The demon looked at him questioningly. Enrid continued. "Captain Rashti has commissioned me to use your company for the kingdom of God. It sounded impossible when he first asked me to do this."

"And it is no longer impossible?" the demon asked, taking another step toward Enrid.

"Your armor and your robe, they make my mission possible," said Enrid.

The warrior spirit took another step forward. "You'll have to excuse me, angel. I don't follow your insanity."

"Once I destroy you in the name of the Lord, I will put on your armor and robe and command your company," said Enrid.

In a flash, the warrior spirit spun in a full circle, surveying the area. "There's no one but you, angel." The warrior bared his sharp teeth.

"I told you that. I work alone." Enrid put up his palm to get a few more seconds. "There are only two things that can stop me, and neither is you. The first is if you are fortunate enough that one of your demons see us. My discovery would defeat the whole purpose for me being here."

The warrior spirit wanted to kill the mouthy angel, but he simply had to hear what the second thing was. "Tell me the second thing before I gut you, angel."

"Your fear," said Enrid, knowing that nothing got under the skin of a warrior spirit like an accusation of fear. "You know I am alone. You know I have come for you. You know that Captain Rashti would only select me for this mission if he had confidence that I could defeat you."

The demon's eyes grew large with insulted rage. Protocol demanded that he immediately alert the others. There were several reasons why he and the angel knew he wouldn't follow protocol.

First, irrespective of protocol, the other warrior spirits would wonder why their leader had not made a quick and brutal example of a lone attacking angel.

Second, Captain Rashti thought so little of his military ability that he had sent one angel to take his company.

Third, and this was akin to the second reason. Captain Rashti had so much confidence in this one angel that he had sent him on this suicide mission.

Fourth, and this was the one that made it impossible for him to follow protocol, a solo angel with a big mouth had challenged him, and had told him to his face that he, a warrior spirit with his own company, was afraid of him.

"Obviously, the real reason your captain sent you after me is he has no use for insane angels," said the warrior spirit as he moved closer.

"So you are afraid of me?"

The warrior was about to rush him.

"Your armor," said Enrid. "Is armor not for heated battles? Army versus army? To stop errant swords and lucky arrows? But you come out in armor against a single angel who wears no armor? I would expect more from the demon who wears my robe."

That brought the response Enrid had desperately hoped for. The warrior spirit took off the robe and threw it to the ground without taking his eyes off his next victim. "Is this where you attack while I take off my armor?"

"As the Lord lives, I will not attack you until you have taken off my armor," said Enrid.

The warrior spirit had no use for the promises of a crazy angel, but in a few quick moments the armor was off.

Enrid pulled out his long sword. He moved to his right by slowly crossing his left leg over the other. He positioned and pushed his foot into the grass before stepping to the right with his right leg. He wanted to see the movements of the warrior spirit before committing to pulling out his dagger. The dagger wouldn't be of much use if the demon fought from the distance of a long sword. But it would be lethal and decisive if the fighting was close.

The demon lifted both swords.

Enrid felt a wind rush by his ear. He heard a sound come from the demon's chest.

Two swords fell to the ground.

Enrid looked at the swords and looked up at the demon. His arms were still raised. His face registered pain; his eyes a question. The demon appeared to be looking over Enrid's shoulder. Enrid turned and when he did, Captain Rashti swooshed by him and pulled a knife from the demon's chest.

"Captain?" said Enrid.

Captain Rashti put the demon over his shoulder.

"How did—? He knew I was watching him. He would have detected you from a thousand yards," said Enrid.

"Pride and anger. They blind humans *and* demons. Your brothers have killed a warrior spirit. No one saw it done. Complete your mission." He turned before he flew off with the demon. "I threw it from twelve hundred yards to make sure he wouldn't see it coming."

Enrid's mouth opened in awe.

"Complete the mission, Enrid."

***

The frenzied rage of the company of warrior spirits could barely be contained by their red-robed leader once news got out that a warrior spirit had been ambushed and killed by the ungrateful forces of Annihilation and Slavery. No one. Not even a ruler spirit could do such a thing without expecting immediate and devastating revenge.

***

Annihilation and Slavery looked over the carnage of demons. This wasn't the work of angels. They were brutal, but not obscene. And even for demons, the things done to these bodies were obscene.

But there had never truly been a question as to who had done this. There were survivors. Three of them. Well, three, but for all practical purposes, two. The third demon was too traumatized to talk. There was a demon named Contemptus and one named Anus.

"Which one of you is Anus?" asked Slavery.

When Annus didn't answer, Contemptus looked at him with a turned up lip.

"Well, are you or are you not Anus?" demanded Annihilation.

Annus looked at Contemptus.

Contemptus looked at him with a full scowl. "Why are you looking at me? The general has asked you a question."

Annus looked sheepishly at Annihilation, then at Slavery. "It's Annus, with a soft a."

Annihilation slapped him to the ground. "Get up, Annus with a soft a!" he yelled.

The demon's head was spinning. He made it to one knee and couldn't find his footing.

Contemptus didn't want Annihilation's anger to spill over onto him. He got on one knee beside the groggy demon and jerked him hard. "Get your sorry San Francisco—"

"San Francisco?" asked Slavery.

Contemptus looked up. "Yes, my lord."

Slavery turned up his face. "Soft a. Figures."

Contemptus got the terrified demon to his feet.

"Tell us everything you saw, Anus," Slavery ordered.

He did.

"But why? Why?" screamed Annihilation. "Why would they do this?"

"Who knows why a warrior spirit does anything?" Slavery answered angrily. "The priority now is to gather all of our forces and to hunt them down like the rabid dogs they are."

Annihilation agreed. What else could he do? But something told him that God was behind this civil war.

Chapter 32

Aisha had sat tied to her chair for over a full day. But although she had been sitting the entire time, she was exhausted, more mentally than physically. But the physical exhaustion was intense. Under the circumstances, it was impossible for her body to interpret sitting with resting.

Her situation had gone from bad to worse, at least in her mind. For her first thought had been that she had been kidnapped by the Vice Boys for sex. They would gang rape her like they had done so many others. Then her fear turned to a horror that nearly drove her insane. What if they made her a heroin addict so they could make her what they called Vice Boy property? But when she heard someone in the other room say something about her being put to the sticks, she died without actually dying.

Aisha desperately tried to move. She pulled her arms against the ropes. They didn't budge at all. She pushed her torso against the ropes that held her firmly to the back of the chair. Very little movement. Her legs weren't tied together. Nor were they tied to the chair. So she could stand with the chair attached to her, and she had done that several times. It didn't get her any closer to freedom, but being able to at least stand when she wanted to gave her momentary relief from the suffocating feeling of being totally helpless.

Survival skills.

Her little knife.

It was in her back pocket.

Her sudden hope sank. Her back pocket was a million miles away from her tied arms. Hopeless tears ran down the young girl's face. Her tears grew as her mind cruelly showed her graphic scenarios of her being raped by a room full of Vice Boys. Then they'd shoot her up full of heroin, and she'd end up like her mother, going to bed with anyone to get money for a fix. An offended thought pushed back at her for thinking that about her mother. Junkie whore or not, she had always been there for Aisha.

Aisha's tears followed her growing pain, but she wisely kept her crying low. She didn't want to attract attention.

Survival skills.

She was trapped. Totally helpless. Totally at the mercy of the Vice Boys. There was nothing she could do to help herself.

New survival skills.

Pray. She needed to pray.

"Jesus," she began softly, needing to hear her own words, "I know You love me. I don't know why this is happening, but I know You love me." She trembled as she summoned the courage to say, "No matter what they do to me, I'm going to serve You. I won't let them take my faith."

"We'll see about that," said the antichrist spirit who was anxiously awaiting Sonny to arrive.

***

The car was a sparkling red 1963 two-door Chevrolet Impala. Its *Impala* label rested iconically on the wide white accent that ran along its side from the back and stopped a few inches from its door. It had four wide, chrome, mag-rimmed wheels, and four men in the car. Two in the front. Two in the back. One of the men in the back was Sonny Christopher. Oddly absent was Pretty Tony.

The antichrist spirit in Aisha's bedroom of captivity had been joined by a demon of death. Both of their heads turned simultaneously in the same direction as they felt the evil in the red car approaching.

The antichrist spirit smiled evilly. "No matter what they do to you. Right, little Christian girl? That's what you said."

***

Something was wrong. Dante knew it.

Dante had been saving money for years for studio time and to make a demo. He was going to slam those rhymes all the way to the bank. And he was going to take Ray-Ray and Aisha with him. Get out of Mayhem. Go someplace nice. Maybe get a condo in the Buckhead area. But that was all gone now.

He shook his head at how stupid he had been to trust Talik. But what choice had he had? Sonny was going to get Aisha. He always got whatever girl he wanted. It was only a matter of time.

He had walked around for days trying to figure out how to save Aisha. So when Talik had run up on him with a gun drawn and gave him a choice at gunpoint to work with him to trick Sonny, he went along with it. It was crazy that a Vice Boy was trying to run a game like this on Sonny, but he didn't care about that. That was none of his business. Aisha and Ray-Ray was his business.

So in return for Talik's promise that after he gave him Aisha, he'd help her get away before they did anything bad to her, he gave Talik over seven hundred dollars. This way he'd be off the hook with Sonny, and Aisha would be free. He and Aisha would take Ray-Ray and go somewhere Sonny couldn't find her. He had kept enough money to buy bus tickets out of state. He'd get a job somewhere and take care of his family. It was a desperate plan, but it was his only plan. So he went with it.

Something bad is happening to her. He didn't think this thought. It had simply come on him like a midnight home invasion. Were they raping her? Were they making her one of those nasty hoes? Dante remembered Kwee and ran to the bathroom before his stomach emptied on the floor. He fell to his knees at the toilet in the tiny Mayhem bathroom and threw up everything.

Not everything.

The guilt wouldn't come out. It wasn't only in his gut. It was all over him. Aisha was smart. She wanted to go to college. Now she was in some house being trained by the Vice Boys. Or...or...maybe she was like Kwee. Sitting in a chair looking like something from a horror movie.

Some house.

They didn't have her at Sonny's place in Mayhem. He had heard that he had another house in the burbs somewhere. Maybe he had her there. No, he probably wouldn't do that kind of thing where white people lived. He'd stay in the ghetto for something like that. But where? Where—?"

Dante ran to his electronic tablet. He punched in the username and password to his iCloud account. He was so nervous that he had to strain to recall a password he had used a thousand times.

"Chill, Dante. Chill," he told himself, knowing that each moment lost was a moment the Vice Boys were doing something horrible to his baby's momma. He recalled the password and had to retype it three times before he got it right. "Okay. Okay. Okay," he said almost as one word.

His mind froze. Now what. He looked at the buttons.

Find My iPhone.

He knew he was supposed to push it. Tears went down his face. He closed his eyes. "Lord, help me to push this button."

His hand finally obeyed his mind. A map came up. His head jutted forward. He double-clicked the mouse. The map enlarged. He did this a few times.

"I know that house," Dante yelled to himself. He hopped to a closet and stuck his hand in a boot. He pulled out a Smith & Wesson .380. He frowned as he looked at the short grip. It only held seven bullets. "What difference does it make? I'm dead anyway. But those niggas gone let go of my baby's mama, I tell you that."

Dante chambered a round and put another bullet in the clip. Now he had eight bullets.

***

Aisha's face was cramped from its grimaced crying. She had been struggling to stay afloat, but she felt herself sinking fast in a dark sea of hopelessness under a full night moon that gave a light just bright enough to confirm all was lost. She could hold on no longer. A soft thought floated toward her like a feather riding the dark surface of the threatening sea.

Trust Me.

It was a whisper among shouts. Yet Aisha heard it. And she saw it. Riding the wave. Could something so light carry her in this dark hour? She didn't have enough faith to believe she wouldn't be hurt by the Vice Boys. But she had enough faith to believe God would give her strength to be faithful to Him as she suffered this trial.

Aisha stated to the Lord Scriptures she had never learned. "I trust in You, Lord, with all my heart, and I do not lean to my own understanding. I am Yours. I will not fear what man can do to me." Then she said in the weakness of her humanity, "Do You see me, Lord? Do You see what I'm going through for You?"

Something happened in heaven when God's daughter made this proclamation of trust and surrender. The Lord Jesus stood from His throne and said, "I know your works. See, I have set before you an open door, and no one can shut it; for you have a little strength, have kept My word, and have not denied My name."

The Lord started walking.

***

Talik made his way back into the room with Aisha. He'd have a little fun with her before Sonny arrived.

Aisha bounced emotionally back and forth between faith and fear under her hood. One moment, rest; the next, turmoil. One moment, held by the arms of the Lord; the next, held by the ropes of the Vice Boys.

The bedroom door opened with a slow creak. It closed with a slower creak.

Fear. Turmoil. Ropes.

"Jesus, help me to be faithful," Aisha said.

"What you say? Jesus?"

Oh, no. It was her tormentor. Aisha tried bravely to hold onto her faith, and was discouraged and ashamed when she felt the last of it drain from her soul. She didn't want to betray God. "Yes," she said.

Her answer should have been bold, courageous. Instead, it was like a water gun's squirt coming out of a firefighter's hose.

"You sure? You don't sound too sure."

"I'm sure," she said, with no noticeable increase in confidence.

Talik walked over and sat on her lap, straddling her. She gasped.

Her tormentor smiled. "Not yet, girl. You get excited easy."

Aisha wasn't sure whether she was still breathing. What was he going to do to her now? The others had left her alone, like she wasn't even in the house. But this one couldn't get enough of talking to her, of making her eat out his hand, of touching her, of scaring her, of smacking her.

She felt his hot breath on her ear. Then his disgusting tongue in her ear. She stopped her instinct to jerk her head away. He'd only slap her and do what he wanted anyway.

"I bet you a freak, ain't you?"

"No, I serve the Lord Jesus Christ." She was surprised—and pleased—at her answer and the courage that had risen from nowhere.

He jerked his head from her neck. His faced turned to a scowl. "You serve Jesus?" He stood up and popped her hard on the head. "When Sonny get here, we gone see who you serve. You gone serve the Vice Boys. We gone tear yo' butt up. Teach you some manners," he spat. "Yeah, put some of that good dope in you." He smirked, "You a be trickin' for VB just like that white girl. Just like Vette and Asia and Sha-nay. Jesus. Sonny sick of y'all talkin' 'bout Jesus. I'm sick of you talkin' 'bout Him. Where is He now? Huh? Where is He?"

***

Antichrist peered at Aisha for the slightest sign of betrayal. He wasn't impressed with the fear he saw in her. Experience had proven that their Lord could see even the tiniest speck of faith amidst their fears and weaknesses.

Well, at least that was heaven's official response to the accusation that God regularly gave His servants credit for having faith that no one but He could see. *Oh, how convenient! It's there because I say it's there.*

The death demon sensed a change in the room. "I feel myself being swallowed."

The antichrist demon was about to ask what he meant when the demon suddenly shot out of the room. *Swallowed? What did he—?*

He looked behind Aisha. His question was fearfully answered. *Jesus?*

There He stood. He was clothed with a garment down to the feet. A golden band was wrapped around His chest. His head and hair were white, and His eyes like a flame of fire. In one of His hands he carried a silver key.

The antichrist spirit pulled his eyes from the Lord for a fraction of a moment and looked at his servant, Talik. The fool had no idea that His creator and judge was standing behind the girl he was molesting. He had no idea that he was tormenting one of God's daughters.

A trembling request came from the demon's mouth. "Have you come to destroy me before the time?"

The Lord didn't answer.

A swallow got stuck in the demon's throat. "May...may I leave?"

"Go."

The spirit was gone before the Lord finished His command.

Eternity's eyes, filled with fire, looked at the man who was hurting someone who had put her trust in Him.

***

"Where He at?" Talik challenged again.

"He's here. He's here with me now."

"You must see Him behind that pillow case, 'cause ain't nobody in this room but you and me." He pulled something out of his pocket. He opened it. "And this," he said. He pressed its flat side against Aisha's cheek. "You know what that is?"

"No."

He gave her a little poke on the leg.

She jerked at the pain. "It's a knife," she said. "Why are doing this? Nobody else is treating me like this, but you. Why?"

"'Cause I want to."

"But why?" she asked.

He smiled. "'Cause I'm evil. I like hurting people."

Aisha had never heard anyone say something like this. When she got over the shock, she asked, "Why are you evil? Why do you like hurting people?"

"Way of the world, freak," he said.

The unseen Person in the room placed His hand on her shoulder.

Aisha and her tormentor heard her response with the same surprise. "The Lord is not only a God of love. He's also a God of judgment and wrath. Don't think that because it seems you've gotten away with so much evil that you'll go unpunished. He has given you a lot of time to repent. That time is almost gone. Turn to God before it's too late."

The room went suddenly silent.

Aisha's eyes would have been wide with shock and fear had the pillow case not been tied so tightly around her eyes.

Surprisingly, the long, awkward silence wasn't interrupted by him slapping her or popping her on the head. Instead, he chuckled. "You sound like Prophetess Ebony Monroe. She been telling us that crap for years. She told us that"—he cursed—"yesterday."

"He could come at any moment," said Aisha.

Talik snapped the large knife shut and put the hood over her blindfolded eyes. He felt the top buttoned pocket of his permanent shirt. He smiled at the bulge he felt. "You know who gone be here any moment? Sonny. That's who gone be here. Not Jesus."

Aisha heard the door creak open. He walked away. She didn't hear the door close. She waited for him to come back and close the door. He didn't. No one did. Then she heard the creaky front door open. It didn't close.

This was the first time this had happened. Aisha sat wondering what had distracted them.

The unseen Person in the room bent down and said something in her ear.

A wild and scary idea popped into her head.

***

Talik went to join the other two Vice Boys who were sitting on the porch steps smoking weed. He pulled out his knife and crept behind one of the sitting Vice Boys and put it under his neck. "Stop hogging the joint, crackhead."

The man didn't look back. He pulled up his other hand that was dangling between his legs. In it was a gun. "Go on and get all that ugly blown off yo' face." The man took a long hit of the joint and passed it to him.

The other dude on the porch added his two cents. "You a need a shotgun to get rid of all that ugly."

Talik ignored the comments. He took the joint and sucked hard. He used the open knife to rub the side of his own face. He looked down one end of the street. Crack hoes. Winos. A little dude named, Chuckie, popping a wheelie on another bike he had stolen. He looked down the other end of the street. Was that Dante?

***

Prophetess Ebony Monroe couldn't shake the thought. It had begun as an impression. She disregarded it. It came again. She ignored it again. It persisted to the point that she couldn't think of anything else except going back to the Vice Boys' house to get her dishes. She had lots of dishes and plastic containers; so it made no sense that there was practically a voice in her head shouting that she needed her dishes.

The angel left when he saw her actually make the turn to go back to where she had made one of her ox tail stew deliveries.

***

Aisha was reeling from what had popped into her mind. It was ridiculous. She was blindfolded and had a hood over her head. She was tied to a chair. They'd kill her if it didn't work.

Wait a minute. If what doesn't work? This is crazy. What if something is on the floor? What if I hit something and fall? What if someone else is in the house? What if he did this on purpose just to have some kind of sick fun? He said he likes hurting people. What if—?

"Trust Me."

Aisha's rapid breaths stopped. That wasn't a thought. It was a voice. A real voice. Someone had said, 'Trust Me.' She listened as though she were trying to find a ticking time bomb. Who said that?

"Who's there?" she asked in a whisper.

The door is almost closed, she heard in her mind. *Run, Aisha, run!*

She jerked her head blindly to the left and right, her breaths rapid with fear, indecision, and confusion, wondering whether she was really hearing what she thought she was hearing.

Now, Aisha! Run or die! The voice was urgent.

Aisha jumped up. She was hunched over. The heavy chair hung awkwardly on her back. Ropes crossed her thighs, preventing full range of motion. But she was free from the knees down. She could take only short steps at a time.

Aisha took off running, the top of her hooded head leading the way like a torpedo moving toward its target. Her target was first the bedroom door. Then, hopefully, the length of the long hallway. Then—it would have to be a miracle—the open front door. After that, she didn't know. The voice didn't give those kinds of details. He just said to run.

***

Prophetess Ebony Monroe turned left down the narrow street where the Vice Boys' house was just before Sonny's car made that same turn coming from the right.

"Sonny, I think that's yo' aunt in front of us, man," said a Vice Boy.

Sonny sat up. "What? Prophetess Ebony Monroe? What she doin' here?"

The prophetess was pulling the car over when it happened. Her mouth gaped at the sight.

A speeding, hooded torpedo had miraculously made it through one room, a long hallway, a living room, and out the front door. It was now flying through the air where there was no more porch. It hurtled over the stairs and hit Talik in the back, who had been standing on the fourth stair from the top.

He was no longer standing. The force of the human torpedo knocked him forward. He flew ungracefully through the air and landed face down on the concrete. His left hand lay still, stretched above his head like he was reaching for something. His right hand was under his heart. His long knife was in his heart.

Aisha landed first on a sitting Vice Boy, then flipped in the air and landed on the chair's four legs before the momentum of the fall pushed the chair backwards onto the concrete.

Prophetess Ebony Monroe was momentarily frozen at the sight. But in a moment, she was on one knee next to the screaming girl. "Baby, it's okay. Prophetess Ebony Monroe is here." She pulled the hood off the traumatized girl. The poor girl was also blindfolded. She took it off her. "Aisha?"

Aisha recognized the face, but she was in shock. Whatever calm she had miraculously shown when she was in that house was gone now. Absolutely gone. She screamed as though her life depended on it.

Prophetess Ebony Monroe worked frantically to get the ropes untied.

The two Vice Boys didn't know what to do. All kinds of people were on the street. And one of them was Sonny's aunt. So they did what usually worked in situations like these. They ran.

The guy driving Sonny slowed down.

"Keep driving. Keep driving," said Sonny as he put his head down.

Aisha's screaming unfroze Dante's legs. He ran to her and threw himself to his knees. He helped untie one of the stubborn knots.

"Aisha. Aisha, baby, I thought you was gone." He yanked away the ropes and threw it behind him. "Thank you, God. Thank—You—God." Dante hugged her to himself. She cried hysterically into his chest.

"What is this, Dante?" asked the prophetess. "Why'd they do this to Aisha?" The realization of the only reasonable answer poured over her the moment she asked the question. "Those dirty—"the prophetess stopped herself from cussing.

Did Sonny know about this? How could he have not known? He's out of control, she thought.

Dante's face rested on Aisha's head as he held her in his arms. He looked over her to Talik. There was a big pool of blood coming from the left side of him. Dante looked at curious eyes. Right now the curious eyes were staying put. They knew this was a Vice Boy situation. But sooner or later it would be too late to follow up on a longshot.

Talik had that same shirt on that he had worn when Dante gave him seven hundred dollars. He obviously hadn't kept his part of the bargain. He had played Dante. However, something had gone wrong, and Talik had fouled out. But the game wasn't over. Maybe Dante had one more play.

"Prophetess Ebony Monroe, will you pray for Aisha?" Dante guided his wailing girlfriend to her. She eagerly pulled her into her arms.

Dante kneeled and positioned his body between Talik's body and the people to the far left of him. He reached his hand under the body and felt for the top pocket. There was a bulge. He undid the button with that one hand and discreetly took what he knew was his money. He balled his fist and pulled back his hand. He stood up and looked around. "He's dead," he said, with a face full of fake sadness.

He wanted to make sure that version got back to the Vice Boys. He stuck both hands in his pocket and walked in a tight circle with a pained expression, shaking his head, and saying, "Thank You, Jesus," under his breath.

Prophetess Ebony Monroe knew she couldn't call the police on the Vice Boys. That's not the way things worked in The Bluff and Mayhem. But she and her church were praying harder than they had ever prayed for God to free their communities.

She knew that God had been listening. Soon He would act.

***

The moment the knife sank into Talik's heart, his eternity began.

Talik's spirit rose from his lifeless body. He hovered over it like a person about to hit the swimming pool's water belly first. He looked down at his body. A million questions rushed him at once. Slowly, his body repositioned itself, feet towards the ground, head towards the sky. The soles of his feet were just above the ground. How was that possible?

Suddenly, something tight and powerful snapped around both of his ankles. He looked down. Chains and shackles.

"Why do I have chains on me?" he said aloud.

"Really? You're asking why?" asked the death spirit with irritation and cruel humor.

Talik jumped in fear when he saw the creature. "Who the hell are you?"

"Hell. A most appropriate and timely topic," the creature answered. "You are guilty of sin. Your next stop is hell. You will suffer in this place until the great day of God's judgment. Then you will be cast alive into the lake of fire where you will be tormented forever and ever. That about sums it up."

"God?" said Talik.

"Maybe you've heard of Him," the spirit said, as though Talik was being ridiculous. "The creator? The judge? The savior?" The victim appeared dumbfounded. "Come on, you must've seen at least one Jesus movie. What about *Passion of the Christ?*"

"I don't understand," said Talik.

The death spirit moved closer. "Yes, you do," he said with a voice that had gotten harder with this last sentence.

Talik's panic magnified a million times. "Can I—?"

He was snatched downward before he could ask the question that nearly everyone who went this way asked. The question that was denied all who futilely asked. "Can I have another chance?"

Chapter 33

The blue mist had filled *Mayhem* and *The Bluff* to such a degree that new sightings, though abundant, were no longer reported. As Slavery had spoken with such eloquent disgust, "It's a storm. What's the use of counting raindrops?" The best they could do was to guess which of the streams of blue *may* produce an immediate attack.

But the mist hadn't only concentrated in *Mayhem* and *The Bluff*. It had also concentrated in various strategic places around Atlanta. Two of the largest concentrations were around the buildings of the Atlanta Journal-Constitution newspaper and CNN. Smaller concentrations were around other television, radio, and newspaper buildings.

Terry Night had been a CNN anchor for several years. He had been all over the world on assignments, some quite dangerous. He had seen with his own shocked eyes the carnage of the barbaric massacre of 800,000 Rwandans by the Hutus in 1994. He had interviewed serial killers and had seen the sick excitement in their eyes as they described their sordid exploits in gruesome detail.

It would've been a monumental stretch for him to say that the story he was about to report to millions of viewers was the most horrific story he'd seen. But it wasn't a stretch to say that he was shocked by the implications of the story.

Terry read the teleprompter:

> And now a most disturbing story. The story of a young African American woman brutally

> beaten to death, stripped naked, and left in a dirt field in Atlanta's last public housing project—Mahem Courts. A public housing project that has been described as one of the most dangerous places in America. This horrible death is made worse by the troubling and nearly unbelievable details that have surfaced concerning life in Mahem Courts.

Highlights of the anchor's story were truly shocking.

Woman beaten to death and left in a large field surround by several buildings filled with residents. No one sees who dumps the body. No resident reports the body. Strangers had to call police. No arrest. Apparently no investigation.

Then something bizarre.

A cardboard sign left next to the body: No Jesus in Mayhem!

Terry Night was intrigued by this story. He had been around long enough to know that a routine story hunch could lead to a startling *George Polk Award* revelation—his second *George Polk Award.* His first had been for national reporting. A second one for local reporting would be more than enviable.

Who needed a *Pulitzer* when you could get the only journalism award that really meant anything, the one that celebrated gritty, world-changing investigative reporting—the *George Polk Award?*

Terry Night had a *George Polk* hunch about this Mahem Courts murder.

***

Slavery was incensed at Annihilation. "Have you seen the news on television? It's bad."

Annihilation saw the anger on Slavery's face. He heard it in his voice. That was enough for him to get angry. "I don't watch much television these days, Slavery. I'm busy fighting a war against angels and a civil war against warrior spirits. If I want bad news, I don't have to watch television to get it."

Slavery's massive frame stopped within a foot of Annihilation's now equally massive frame. Slavery's usual slight advantage over Annihilation in size had been diminished ever since their decision to work together. The increase in murders, overdoses, and suicides had fattened him up.

"I told you that your thirst for Christian blood would backfire on us," said Slavery.

Annihilation's curiosity produced thoughts but no words.

"Did you hear me?" asked Slavery impatiently.

That brought a response. "You are standing fourteen and three-eighths of an inch away from me. You are foolishly and dangerously yelling in my face. How can I not hear you?"

Slavery shook his head. "You're right," he said. He turned and took a few slow, thoughtful steps. "I'm letting this war get to me."

"What is the bad news?" asked Annihilation.

"That girl you killed. LaQueesha. The enemy has put her on television. Pictures of her bloodied body with that blasted *No Jesus* sign next to her are on every news broadcast. They're all now wondering what's going on in Mayhem. He's shining light on our darkness, Annihilation. We need darkness if we are to keep our property."

"You remember His words?" asked Annihilation.

"Whose words?"

Slavery's tone could've gotten Annihilation stirred up again. It didn't. He was more concerned with his own thoughts than Slavery's sour mood. "His words. The Lord's words. 'If I am lifted up, I will draw all men to Myself.'"

Slavery's look of disgust increased. "How can any of us forget those words?"

Annihilation bobbed his head. "We thought we had Him. We crucified Him and hung His wretched human carcass on a cross. We had Him." He looked at Slavery and swung through the air as he said again, "We had Him!"

If Annihilation could've read Slavery's mind, if he could've felt the hot contempt that burned in his heart toward him for not listening to him, he would've pulled his sword. "And yet," spat Slavery.

"We never had Him," admitted Annihilation. "He had us. All the while that we thought we had Him, He had us. It was His plan all along to die. But we were so bloodthirsty that we couldn't see the trap."

Slavery's eyes burned with anger. They said what he knew would only cause one of them to die had he spoken them. *You blundering, foggy-minded idiot, I told you this would backfire on us. I personally sent Joseph to Egypt in chains. But it had been God's plan all the while to use the hardship for His own glory. Now it's happening again with LaQueesha. You killed her to satisfy your lust for blood, and to send a message. Now God is taking your message and using it as His own. What kind of a pea-sized, infantile, stunted brain rolls aimlessly in your large, hollow head?*

Annihilation continued, unaware that the more he spoke, the more Slavery was inflamed. He paced back and forth in front of Slavery muttering to himself and periodically speaking something loud enough for Slavery to make sense of what he was saying.

"Three days He was dead...we thought that was the end...the beginning, not the end...tricked us...looked defeated...wasn't defeated...somehow uses our plans against us...how could I have seen this coming?"

Slavery heard that last question. His burning eyes widened.

Annihilation was pacing away from Slavery when he said, "I shouldn't say this, but sometimes it seems like we're being played for fools, like the enemy has seen every one of our moves before we move. It's like no matter what we do—when we lose, we lose; when we win, we lose. It's like we're competing in a contest that has already been decided. Slavery, what do you—?"

Slavery's fury exploded in his chest and rushed down his right shoulder, down his arm, into his large hand. In a flash, before he knew what he was doing, he answered Annihilation's question by severing his large head from his body.

He watched it drop heavily onto the asphalt with a thud and wondered at his action. He felt anger pulsating in his hand. But had he acted entirely on his own, or had he somehow been manipulated? If so, how?

And what about the ambushments of the angels that never happened? Had Ferocious set him and Annihilation up? Had he dropped the idea of ambushing angels so they'd commit armies elsewhere while his own warrior spirits massacred their Mayhem army? Or worse, had this whole charade been nothing more than an angelic ruse? Another of their misdirections?

A long, slow growl of frustration gurgled through his clenched teeth. *Enemies in front, enemies behind...enemies of light, enemies of darkness,* thought Slavery. *"Who can you trust?"*

He caught something from the corner of his eye. It vanished. But not before Slavery got a full look at him.

That royal pain in the darkness. The angel Enrid.

Slavery hid Annihilation's body and head. He needed to get away, if only for a few minutes to think about his next move. Was there anywhere he could just relax for a little while? "Of course," he said, and headed for a liquor store.

It was when he saw a drunk try to lean on a wall that wasn't there and fall forehead first onto the ground that he made his decision. "Mayhem may be lost as a stronghold, but it's up to the people who live there whether some of us can stay. Those angels can only run us off if the people no longer want us. We'll let them decide."

Slavery left the liquor store to go find Heroin. They had work to do.

***

Reverend Paul Winston sat in the midst of a blue mist. The mist had come out of the sixty-five-inch television and filled the kitchen and living room, the latter was where he was sitting. He slowed down his chew of boneless ribeye steak as he looked at the blurred photo on the television screen.

"What kind of person would do something like that?" asked Jennifer, the reverend's fifteen-year-old daughter.

Paul didn't hear her. His attention was focused on the sign next to the girl. *No Jesus in Mayhem!* He sipped his red wine without tasting it.

The room brightened with the angel's presence who had come out of the television's screen with the blue mist. Its light was unseen in Paul's dimension. Nonetheless, the preacher looked around the room. Something was different.

"Dad, I don't understand," said Jennifer. "What do they mean no Jesus in Mayhem? Where's Mayhem? You think she was killed because she was a Christian? I didn't think things like that happened here."

"That's what it looks like, Jen," he answered without taking his eyes off the screen. *Edwin, what is going on down there in that ghetto?*

His daughter's blue eyes widened in shock. So did her open mouth.

Paul's eyes cut a glance at his daughter. Her expression was begging for answers. "It's a bad part of town in Atlanta. Projects. They got thousands of poor people stacked on top of one another. Drugs. Violence. Gangs run the place. Folks get killed down there all the time."

"But why would they kill somebody for being a Christian?" she asked.

"World's a mean, dark place, Jen," he said.

Jennifer's eyes were moist. "Dad, you remember what you said about Jesus leaving the safety of heaven to come to a place where He knew He'd be crucified, but He did it anyway because He loved us?"

Paul's answer was slow out of his mouth. "Yes."

"Can we pray that God will raise up Christians who love Him enough to leave their safety to save the people in Mayhem? There must be somebody there who wants God. You said there are thousands of people."

The expression on Paul's face was something between a burdened smile and a public fight against diarrhea.

Jennifer had been on fire for God for two years. The fire was lit when she had heard a lady named Heidi Baker with an apostolic ministry preach about what she was doing in Mozambique. After the sermon, the lady had called for all the teens who wanted to be used by God to come up to the front. Jennifer went up.

The lady laid hands on her and prayed. Jennifer fell backwards onto the floor and got up two hours later, full of the Spirit, and praying for everything and everybody who didn't pray for her first.

The on-fire teen grabbed her preacher daddy's hands and lowered her head. She waited confidently for his prayers.

The angel listened to his prayers with extreme interest.

***

A dangerous rumor had been making the rounds in *Mayhem* and *The Bluff*. Had anyone noticed that Sonny and Pretty Tony hadn't been seen together lately? Supposedly, this was because there had been a falling out between them. There had almost been a shootout among the Vice Boys in his Mayhem house.

This was almost too crazy to be real. Sonny and Pretty Tony had been together forever. They had started the Vice Boys. But something had happened that let everyone know that the supposed falling out was a real falling out. A deadly falling out.

Two Vice Boys had been mysteriously murdered. On the same day. In both cases, no one saw the shooter. Coincidentally, one of them had been staunchly and outwardly vocal about his loyalty to Sonny. The other had taken the same posture about Pretty Tony. Now both of them had been shot in the head.

Word was out that both Sonny and Pretty Tony were saying they had no idea who had killed either Vice Boy. But everyone in *Mayhem* knew better. Who else but a Vice Boy would kill a Vice Boy? And no low-level Vice Boy would be stupid enough to do that unless he had approval from Sonny. But now that the Vice Boys had apparently split in two, with Pretty Tony leading the other faction, that meant Pretty Tony had ordered the other hit.

The odd thing was that both of them were doing their best to make it appear that things weren't as bad as they were. They had been tight nearly all their lives, since being little kids. But things had gotten crazy fast. More crazy than either of them could have imagined possible. No one knew where this would end. Hopefully, there would be a peaceful resolution. But neither Sonny nor Pretty Tony saw how this was possible. So each continued to make power moves without wanting to provoke a full scale war.

There was one thing about this undeclared war that gave Sonny a panicky feeling. Pretty Tony would not have made a move against him without approval from Sonny's unseen boss—unseen, but not unheard from. Everyone had a boss. And it was only because of that unseen boss that he could do what he had done all these years.

His unseen boss had relayed a message to him through Officers Crandal and Brown that he was concerned at the publicity that he had generated by advertising to the world what he was doing.

Sonny knew he had only two possibilities before him. Fix or be fixed. He preferred to be the one doing the fixing.

Enrid was in the blue mist that flowed onto and around Sonny Christopher. He also preferred to be the one doing the fixing.

***

Rosa had had another excruciatingly lonely and hard day. The presence and kindness of her loving mother had been no match for the voices that raged in her head tormenting her for going out to the club and getting herself shot. They were also no match for the dark bleakness and hopelessness she felt.

She was paralyzed from the neck down.

She was a drain on her mother.

She was never going to be married.

She was never going to have children.

She was worthless.

All she had was the invisible God. The God who was so refreshingly and supernaturally real some days and so depressingly and painfully absent most days. Although it seemed a foolish thing to do, and at times a complete waste of time, she mustered the tiny bit of strength she felt and continued praying that God would move in that horrible *Mayhem* place, and that he would bless Kim.

She added to her prayers, "Lord, I pray that people who aren't as bad off as I am stop complaining about their problems. That they'd stop putting off the things they should be doing for you. And I pray that no one has to be put in a situation like this before they realize how blessed they are."

Chapter 34

An army of fear demons attacked Edwin, Jonathan, and the handful of others who had decided to go into *Mayhem*. In the unseen realm, the air was thick with the swarming spirits. The attack had begun at the house when they were discussing their plan.

There seemed to be no end to the evil variety and appearance of demons of fear. These that attacked the would-be stronghold killers looked like barracudas with wings, but they were black. Their mouths were long, narrow, and filled with rows of sharp teeth. On their sides were short wings. Under their long undersides were two sets of sharp claws.

They attacked in a frenzy. Their mouths snapping violently in a blur, too fast for the beginning or ending of the bites to be seen. They appeared to prefer the bellies of their victims. Those who couldn't press into the bellies because of the swarming crowd before them, went for the chests. If they couldn't get the chests, they went for the heads before trying again for the bellies.

Three vehicles under attack by swarms of spirits of fear left the Styles's driveway and headed toward *Mayhem*.

***

Adaam-Mir had finally tasted battle. It had been brief, and he knew in a controlled environment where their success had been all but guaranteed, yet he didn't mind. He was new. Love of God and devotion to the sons and daughters of Adam didn't automatically make one a formidable warrior. Like everything in the kingdom of

God, growth was fundamental. Nonetheless, destroying that courier demon had been immensely satisfying.

He looked at the swarm of fear demons biting chunks out of everyone in the car and two SUVs. As he looked closer, however, he saw that Jonathan, Sharon, and Ava weren't being bitten. The demons would go to clamp down on their spirits, then a fraction of an inch before their teeth made contact, they'd turn away as though something was distasteful. But this happened so quickly that one had to look really hard to see what was happening.

This was fascinating to Adaam-Mir. He turned to Myla, Trin, and Enrid. They were closest to him. But there were twenty other angels only yards away, and hundreds of others within ten seconds of them. "Jonathan and Sharon and Ava, why aren't they being attacked?" he asked.

Trin answered. "They are being attacked, Adaam-Mir, but faith tastes awful to demons of fear. It makes them sick. Sometimes they get into such a frenzy that they bite into it anyway." Trin pointed. "See that one? The red one flopping on the ground with the swollen belly?"

Adaam-Mir looked. "I see it. Why is it different from the others?"

"He bit Jonathan," said Trin. "Faith inflames the insides of fear demons."

"Cooks them from the inside out like a microwave," said Myla. "That's why he's red. He's been cooked."

Enrid pointed. "There's another one. He bit Sharon."

Adaam-Mir said, "You'd think they'd learn."

"Demons are two things," said Enrid. "Always persistent; often stupid."

"What about the others?" asked Adaam-Mir, speaking of the others besides Jonathan, Sharon, and Ava. "Shouldn't we stop the demons? They're eating them."

"No," said a voice that arrived before its owner. Captain Rashti walked over to them. "It is not necessary to get rid of fear to do the will of God. God is glorified when His servants serve Him in the presence of fear."

Adaam-Mir hadn't known that the captain was so close to them. Although he had been honored with the distinction to interact with the great leader, talking to the angel known as The Sword of the Lord was still a bit awe-inspiring. He wanted to ask him something, but kept it to himself.

"You have no questions about what I have spoken?" asked the captain.

Adaam-Mir looked at the captain for a couple of seconds before answering. "The blessed book records that the Lord often told his disciples to 'fear not.'"

The other angels were eager to hear the captain's answer.

"You are wise to question me, Adaam-Mir," said the captain. "Fear not does not mean, do not *feel* fear. It means do not *obey* fear. No son or daughter of Adam can make themselves not feel fear any more than they can make themselves not feel lust or anger. But they can reject the ungodly feeling and still obey God. This is what it means to walk in the spirit."

Adaam-Mir's head went back slowly as he looked upward. "I see. I see. The flesh is fallen. The carnal mind is enmity against God. Emotions and feelings come and go. A saint can't judge his walk with God by how he feels." He took a few steps and pondered more. "And he can't wait to get rid of fear to obey God." His countenance was bright as he looked at the captain, then at the others. "Otherwise, most of them will never do anything for God. They can't be ruled by their feelings."

Enrid spoke up. "So it is best, Adaam-Mir, that we leave these demons of fear alone. They can handle them."

They, the ones of whom Enrid spoke, could not have disagreed more as they headed toward *Mayhem.*

***

The cars rolled slowly past the *Mahem Courts* sign as though it read *O K Corral* and that any minute they'd be bushwacked by the bad guys in black hats. They parked on the street. It seemed a better idea than to park in either of the lots filled with vintage cars and lots of men with bad attitudes. Bad attitudes that seemed aggravated by their presence.

No one got out of the vehicles.

Jonathan rolled down his window and propped his elbow on the door. "Well, they got good eyesight." A guy sitting on a classic Camaro seemed to be looking directly into his eyes. "Lil Johnny, you know that guy staring at us?"

"Which one? They all staring at us," he answered.

"The one on the Camaro. What year do you think that is?"

"Oh, Lawd," moaned Lil Johnny. "That's Pretty Tony."

Elizabeth looked past Jonathan. "Humph," she said, and sat back and resumed praying.

"That's my girl," said Jonathan. "Is he bad news?" he asked Lil Johnny.

"Put it this way. Sonny is the fat Satan. Pretty Tony is the tall Satan," he said. He put his skinny hand up to his face and shook his head. "Oh, Lawd, have mercy."

Jonathan looked in the rearview mirror. "You're scared, Lil Johnny?"

"Scared? I wish I was just scared. I'm terrified," he said.

"Good. So am I. I'm usually scared." Jonathan chuckled. "Or terrified. But mostly just scared. Do you want to make your life count, Lil Johnny?"

He answered immediately. "Yeah."

"I know you do. If you didn't, you never would've publicly prayed for salvation. You wouldn't have been baptized, either. If you're going to make your life count for eternity, you gotta learn to fight scared." Jonathan looked at Edwin get out of his SUV. "You see that man, Lil Johnny?"

"Edwin? Yeah, I see him."

"He's not scared. He's terrified. Not just for him. He's got a wife, a daughter, a son. He's terrified for all of them. But look at him. He's the first out of the car. They're all scared. Well, maybe not Sharon. But she doesn't count. She's not human. Lil Johnny, you understand what I'm saying?" asked Jonathan.

Lil Johnny hopped out of the SUV. Apparently he did.

Everyone disembarked and gathered at Edwin's SUV.

One of Ava's wild friends, a white woman about sixty who used to work as a prison guard, said, "Gideon had a few more people than this, but we're better lookin.' Right, Ava?"

Ava was busy rebuking the devil and binding spirits of violence. She never heard the quip.

"Right!" answered Sharon.

Ava stopped rebuking the devil. "Let's hold hands and pray," she said. They didn't move quickly enough for the tiny volcano. She pulled the arm of one of the three women who had come with her and joined it with Sharon's.

Sharon beamed as she said to her, "Isn't this just too awesome?"

"Let's spank 'em, Sharon," said the woman. "Every place we put the soles of our feet is ours. Glory!"

Ava's long, braided black pony tail sailed left and right as she whipped her head back and forth. She took another friend and joined her hand with Elizabeth. She nodded approvingly at Barbara, who was holding Edwin's and Andrew's hands with the seriousness of someone on the *Titanic* trying to prevent her slide into the dark, frosty ocean.

"Satan's not going to bend over and let us spank him," Ava said. Her intensity was too much for a lot of people. But those with naturally thick skin, and those who managed to survive the first few waves of her personality usually ended up loving her so much they'd die for her. She looked at her friend who had spoken of spanking Satan. "He spanks back, you know."

The lady smiled adoringly at her drill sergeant. "I love you, too, Ava."

The circle was complete. Everyone was holding hands. Three men. Six women. One teenage girl. One teenage boy. Eleven people.

Mahem (AKA Mayhem) Courts. Seven thousand and eight hundred and eleven.

Eleven.

Seven thousand and eight hundred and eleven.

"Lil Johnny," a man yelled from one of the parking lots.

The entire prayer circle looked across the street in the direction of the voice.

A man wearing shades and a baseball style cap turned to an angle was leaning over a green Camaro with a wide black stripe that ran from front to back. He pointed his finger as though it were a gun and pulled the imaginary trigger. He blew his finger and laughed.

"Oh, Lawd," said Lil Johnny. "We don't need to be here."

"It's okay, Lil Johnny. Remember what I said about fighting scared," said Jonathan.

"No one's going to get hurt," encouraged one of Ava's friends.

Lil Johnny looked at her with eyes that understood what this woman couldn't possibly imagine. "Lady, that ain't what that finger mean. That finger mean he gone smoke my skinny, black a—"

"Oh, goodness," the lady exclaimed more for his language than the threat he had shared. Honestly, she didn't understand what it meant for someone to "smoke" another.

Ava got back on the job. "Don't let them intimidate you, Lil Johnny. Hold hands. Hold them tight. Let's pray."

Everyone's head lowered. Jonathan and Ava prayed with their eyes open, looking at the asphalt beneath their feet. Lil Johnny prayed with the nervous edginess of a man who may have to save his life by making a mad dash to and over the eight-foot wooden fence behind the bushes.

POW! POW! POW!

The prayer circle hit the ground. Jonathan must've had a Marine Corps flashback. In a flash, he had low-crawled to Elizabeth and covered her with his body. Edwin had never been in the Marine Corps, but he was a general in the Husband and Father Corp. His anxious eyes darted until he saw Barbara. He leapt on her and put his body between her and any other bullets that may come their way.

"Andrew, Sharon!" said Edwin.

"We're okay, Dad," said Andrew. He had covered his sister.

The only person not on the ground was Lil Johnny. His *Mayhem* survival skills had ignited the rockets in his feet at the sound of the first gunshot. He was ten feet away by the third gunshot and into the tall bushes and onto the fence in just a few more seconds. He was almost over the fence when he uncharacteristically looked back before jumping to the other side.

One of the parking lots looked like a comedy club. Vice Boys were holding their sides and laughing so hard they couldn't stand. Several were on one knee and cackling like black hyenas. One dude was hopping around like a rabbit, flailing a red scarf.

Something strange, though. There were two parking lots filled with Vice Boy cars. They usually only used one of them. Everyone knew that was their lot. But they were in two lots now. Also, the Vice Boys in the left lot were the ones laughing like hyenas. The Vice Boys in the right lot all looked disgusted. And their looks of disgust were toward those in the left lot. What was going on?

The sixty-year-old lady who had talked about spanking Satan had been the first to hit the ground.

Ava was the first to get back up. She was angry. Angry at the devil. She looked at her friend on the ground. "Well, Willetta, we're not going to spank the devil's butt lying on the ground like a rug. Get up from there."

Jonathan popped up next. He helped Elizabeth up. She was shaking her head and intermittently looking toward the parking lot. "And this is funny," she said with disgust as she brushed dirt off her pants.

Edwin and Barbara were still on the ground. The only two people on the ground. They were snuggled up to one another, Edwin's body conforming to her body from behind.

Barbara laughed lightly as she squeezed his hand and pressed it into her chest. "Edwin, what are we doing in a place they call *Mayhem*?"

The question didn't surprise him—*What were they doing in a place they call Mayhem? Had he gone crazy?*—but his wife's laughter did. Was she in shock? "Are you okay?"

She laughed again. This time it wasn't a short, light laugh. It was a long, light laugh. Her abdomen bounced as she laughed. "Edwin," she said through the laughter, "we're in *Mayhem*. You...me...the kids...we're in *Mayhem*. I've never been more scared in all my life."

Edwin was about to apologize.

"And I've never felt such joy, Edwin," she said. "I—am—terrified. But I've never felt as free as I do now."

Edwin propped up on one elbow and turned her face to him.

"Okay, this has just gone from bizarre to embarrassing," said Jonathan. He motioned to Sharon and Andrew. "Come here, children. You don't want to see your parents behave like this. Hopefully, they'll still make it into the kingdom."

They went to him with raised eyebrows and funny smiles.

Jonathan had both arms draped around the necks and shoulders of Andrew and Sharon. "Lil Johnny, what are you doing on that fence?"

"They shot at us," he said matter-of-factly.

"They were just trying to scare us," said Jonathan.

Lil Johnny hopped off the fence. When he landed, he said, "Maybe they were just *tryin'* to scare you, but I gotta change my drawls."

"Lil Johnny," Sharon scolded.

Andrew burst out laughing.

Drill Sergeant Ava rounded everyone up again for prayer. The little woman looked up into each person's eyes. "We're going to pray. No matter what they do, we're going to pray. You understand?"

There were some nods and yesses.

"*Whatever* they do," added Jonathan. "We've all seen those civil rights videos, right? People beating up people who refused to fight back. But they were fighting back. Their weapon was nonviolence."

Lil Johnny lowered his head and put his hand to his forehead. He shook his head. "This ain't gone work. *Mayhem* ain't no circus. We can't come up in here with some kind of tricks."

"We're not talking about tricks, Lil Johnny," said Jonathan. "We're talking about prayer. Now we have to trust in the same God, and use the same power that these people have to use. If we can't trust God to keep us for a day in *Mayhem*, what right do we have to tell someone who lives here that Jesus will take care of them? If it doesn't work for us, we need to leave these people alone."

Pretty Tony knew what Sonny's stupid crew was about to do.

"Look, they're leaving," said Sharon excitedly.

Lil Johnny interpreted the exodus differently. "Uh uh," he said, shaking his head. "This ain't right. Somethin' goin' down."

***

Jonathan looked at the last car leaving the lot on the right. He looked at the cars on the left. Actually, he looked at the guys near the cars. They were gathering around a few cars parked near the edge of the lot closest to them.

"Ladies and gentlemen, this is it," he said. "Join hands. Quickly." Sharon grabbed one of his hands. He whispered in her ear, "If this doesn't go too well, meet me by the Tree of Life."

She looked up with a smile. "Tree of Life."

"Lord, she's smiling," he muttered to himself about Sharon. "Pray everybody. Ask God to free these people. Take authority over the demons that rule this place. Take authority over the Vice Boys. Hurry."

In a moment, desperate cries and intercessions erupted from the circle of eleven saints who had dared to invade the stronghold of *Mayhem* with the gospel and love of Jesus Christ.

In a moment, Satan answered.

POW! POW! POW! POW! POW! POW! POW! POW!

On and on and on it went.

POW! POW! POW! POW! POW! POW! POW! POW! POW! POW! POW! POW! POW! POW!

Silence. Then another barrage of gunfire. One that lasted so long, it seemed that it would never end. When it did end, it was a mess. But not a fatal mess. Jonathan's SUV had been blasted with what would later be determined to be sixty-three bullets. Not counting the windows.

Sonny Christopher's crew stared wide-eyed at the *still* praying Christians. They watched in stunned, confused, and murderous silence as the eleven held hands and walked towards the open field.

The field where Prince had been shot.

The field where LaQueesha's body had been dumped.

Chapter 35

Slavery watched the blue mist for several minutes until it dissolved. He waited several more minutes before approaching. He feared that he would find his friend destroyed. He entered the darkness.

"What took you so long, baby?" Heroin's arms were wide open to Slavery. His outfit, depending on whether it was described by Slavery or Heroin, was either a ridiculous display of demonic insanity, or the fashion statement of a fashion king. This time it was pink. Cape. Feathered hat. Flowing cape. All pink.

It wasn't the color that was offensive to Slavery. For what did he care about colors, especially as they pertained to humans? It was having to suffer through a brilliant demon's deranged and shameful obsession with human fashion.

Clothes. Human clothes. A demon wearing human clothes. That was stupendously bad and inexplicable. But Heroin had to take his insanity to levels that would qualify him for shock treatment if there were such a thing for demons. The clothes were ridiculous, but taking on the exaggerated antics of humans had always worn on Slavery's last nerve.

Heroin waited with open arms for Slavery to come to him. He wanted to hug him and pat him on the back. Slavery knew how hypersensitive Heroin was, but crazy or not, he wasn't going to be hugged. He just didn't have the patience for this foolishness today.

Heroin dropped his arms. "You hurt me, baby. You hurt me bad." His saddened expression turned cheery. "But I'm okay, Daddy-O.

You remember fine, little Holly? That cat, Jared, is going to bring me another one."

It was impossible for Slavery to not feel something delightfully evil at hearing this. Slavery was his nature, was it not? But one slave could hardly take his mind off his troubles. "That's lovely, Heroin. The war is lost," he stated bluntly. "Now it's about minimizing our losses. We can still have a formidable presence here. I need your help."

Heroin looked at Slavery so long and saying nothing that Slavery moved to say something. Heroin held up his hand. "You hear that?"

Slavery listened. "What?"

Heroin took off his cape and threw it to the ground behind him. He pointed to his own feet with both hands and slowly raised his hands over his head. As he did, his clothes changed. The pink hat was gone. In its place was a black-brimmed hat. The rest of his clothes changed, too. Tight black pants that appeared too short. Black jacket with sleeves that appeared too short. White shirt. Black shoes. One glove.

"What is this?" Slavery tried hard to not let the menace he felt come out in his voice.

"Fedora, baby."

Slavery was unsuccessful at diminishing the angry glare in his eyes. "I know what kind of hat it is, Heroin. What is *this*?" He pointed at the whole get-up.

Heroin's eyes popped wide. They darted around. He started popping his one gloved hand. He let out a yelp and put his hand on his hat. He lowered his head. "I'm bad."

"You're what?"

Heroin started walking. He took short jerky steps, popping his head to the left and right. He bounced his shoulders and spun in a complete circle. He stood in a pose, one hand reaching for the sky. The other resting on his crotch.

Slavery looked at the demon bouncing his waist upward like a pathetic human in heat. "What is this?" he screamed. "What are you doing?"

Heroin didn't answer. He stood in a wide stance and squatted. Both hands were on his thighs. He rolled his neck in a circle and yelped again. He popped up and tossed his hat with a backhand and crossed one foot over the other. He was still. Perfectly still.

Slavery felt as though he were in a pot of boiling water. The fury that drove him to kill Annihilation was nothing compared to what was boiling him now. He followed the spins and hops and yelps and robot moves and crotch grabbing and crotch pumping until his rage could stand it no more. He was about to reach for his sword.

Heroin started walking backwards. No, he floated backwards, but he made it look like—

Wait a minute! thought Slavery. *Is he moonwalking? Of course, this is why he's acting like this.*

"Heroin," Slavery screamed.

Heroin looked at Slavery, bouncing his shoulders one moment, rolling his hands the next.

"Do you think you're Michael Jackson?" he asked with the patience of a cannon with a short, lit fuse.

"No." Heroin kicked up his leg and popped it to the side. "I *am* Michael Jackson. They thought I was dead. But baby," he paused, then he smiled as though it were an afterthought, "I'm too bad to die. I'm going on tour."

Slavery's hand trembled on his sword. He looked at the dancing spirit. His rage was pushing him to take Heroin's wiggling head off his neck. Yet even in his rage he knew that once it subsided, he would regret losing such a valuable ally, holding desperately to the hope that he'd recover one day.

Slavery watched Heroin prance back and forth mimicking the dead performer's dance moves. He had never seen him have an episode as long and as bizarre as this. He had never even heard of him being prone to such intense lunacy.

"Slavery," Heroin said in a whisper, looking around as though someone might hear his secret.

"What, Heroin?" answered Slavery with a grimace.

"I never liked Tito," he said.

This demon is crazy, thought Slavery. He took his hand off his sword. He suddenly felt quite alone. Everything was going so badly. What were the odds that Heroin's insanity would erupt in such a new and devastating way right when he needed him most?

Then it clicked.

"Oh, darkness." Slavery's words were slow and heavy with his oversight. He had feared when he saw the Holy Spirit's presence in the prayer mist that he would find his friend dead, and was relieved and happy that he was not. He had concluded that the mist had been just another of the enemy's diversions. But it wasn't a diversion. Somehow the enemy had pushed his friend over the edge of what little sanity the demon had left.

Prayer was dismantling the Mayhem stronghold behind the scenes.

"What else could go wrong?" he said, looking at his crazy and now totally worthless friend.

Heroin had retrieved the fedora. It was back on his head. He stood with one leg crossed over the other. He put his hand on the hat and looked at Slavery. He tossed it toward him.

Slavery watched with a tired heart as the hat sailed toward him.

He gasped when a flying knife slammed it against the dark wall. He approached it with the arrogance of a demon who had tried to kick God off His throne. He snatched the knife from the wall, letting the hat fall to the ground.

"Rashti," snarled Slavery, and tossed the knife on the floor, his contempt and fear fighting for supremacy.

***

Slavery left Heroin sitting in the darkness holding his hat, and literally crying that the hole in the hat was noticeable. "It's just me now," Slavery said, as he walked by a large tree.

"And me." The voice came from behind Slavery.

Rashti! Slavery spun with his weapons poised. He looked with surprise at the angel. He'd always thought that the legendary warrior both sides called the Sword of the Lord—although his did so secretly—would be larger up close. More intimidating.

He wasn't small, but he wasn't large, either. Actually, Slavery judged, the angel was significantly smaller than himself. "Rashti," said the unimpressed ruler demon. The word gurgled from deep in his throat and fought a mouthful of spit to get out, "I was expecting more. I thought the Sword of the Lord would be...if not as large as me, at least larger than you."

"Captain Rashti is more than your darkness will ever comprehend," said the angel.

Slavery was surprised. First, that Rashti spoke of himself in the third person. Second, that the angel spoke at all. He wasn't expecting an answer. Angels rarely spoke to demons. "An angel with a tongue. Have you come for conversation, great Rashti?"

"Obviously, I am not Captain Rashti," said the angel. "If I were, you would be dead already and confined to the Dark Prison to await your final judgment."

Slavery's face twisted. "What? Who are you?" he demanded.

"I am Adaam-Mir, servant of the Lord God Most High and of the sons and daughters of Adam."

"You are not the Sword of the Lord." The demon said this fighting back laughter. "You are an Adaam. Unbelievable. I am being challenged not by a mighty warrior, but by a glorified foot washer." This time the laughter came. "I could use a good foot washing. Would you mind filing down my claws before you wash my feet?" Slavery's laughter was heavier.

Something went through Slavery's big mouth and came out the back of his thick skull, pinning him to the tree. The demon's shocked eyes appeared to be crossed as they looked at the sword that had been rammed into his mouth.

Adaam-Mir's sword had started the death process, but left to himself, Slavery would linger in agony until he joined other vanquished demons in God's holding place for such demons. But Adaam-Mir had no intention of leaving Slavery's presence until the job was complete.

He let go of the sword that was buried into the tree via the tunnel he had made in the demon's big mouth. Its large handle covered Slavery's mouth like a children's pacifier. A pacifier of spiritual metal.

The angel stood toe to toe with the shocked, dying demon. He held both of the demon's wrists by his thighs. He would not be allowed to pull the sword out of his mouth. There'd be no second acts. His days of enslaving God's people were over.

"I am an Adaam. I am a glorified foot washer. A ministering spirit sent forth to minister for those who will inherit salvation. The great captain told me that you were a great warrior who had conquered and enslaved vast multitudes. He told me that I was new to the front lines, and that I had no experience as a warrior. He told me I had almost no chance against a spirit of your power."

The ruler spirit felt his life ebbing away. He had to free himself before the last of his energy drained out of his body. He pushed his powerful arms upward. They didn't budge against the angel's iron grip. Either the angel was strong, or Slavery was now weak.

Adaam-Mir's nose neared Slavery's face. He looked into the demon's eyes and said, "Then the captain told me to read the story of David and Goliath. I had read it thousands of times before. I love the story. But I read it again. I read it and realized that you are Goliath. Big. Proud. Boastful. Arrogant. And careless.

"I went back to the captain and told him that your pride would make up for my inexperience and lack of power." Adaam-Mir's face was hard as he said, "And the ambushment of my brothers? Don't blame Ferocious. His idea was brilliant. We just tweaked it a little. Have you never read in the blessed book, 'Their swords will pierce their own hearts'? And again, 'Keep me safe from the traps set by evildoers, from the snares they have laid for me'?"

The demon gurgled.

"Enough." The angry word came out at the same time Adaam-Mir's dagger plunged into Slavery's dark heart.

Adaam-Mir watched the demon's eyes close. In one motion, he yanked the sword from Slavery's mouth and the dagger from his chest. He walked with the weapons hanging in his hands and rejoined the angels who were watching in awe from afar.

"Where did you learn to fight like that?" asked a beaming Myla.

"You killed a ruler spirit by yourself," said Enrid.

Captain Rashti said, "But you were not alone, were you Adaam-Mir?"

The angel that Slavery had mocked as a glorified foot washer looked at the half-circle of the captain and his distinguished warriors. His unsheathed sword and dagger were dirty with demonic blood. "No, I was not alone. The God who helped David kill Goliath was with me."

Captain Rashti looked at his angels. "The God of David isn't through. Goliath is dead, but there is still work to be done. Let's go."

Chapter 36

The eleven would-be Mayhem stronghold busters walked in near silence for about fifty feet. The near silence was the fact that although no one was talking to one another, everyone was talking to God. Their words weren't loud, but they were urgent. There was something about the Vice Boys using Jonathan's SUV as target practice that put everyone in the mood to pray.

"Funny, I don't recall this street being this long," Edwin said to Jonathan.

Jonathan looked at the crowd of Vice Boys on the other side of the street who had followed them step for step, eyeballing them as though any minute there would be another round of target practice. They were brazen about letting their guns be seen. This place truly was like something off of a cowboy movie. "That could be because of our fan club across the street."

"Jonathan, remember when you were in Mexico?" asked Sharon.

"Which time?" he asked.

"The time when you were beaten up by—"

"Sharon, darling," interrupted Ava, "there's a time and a place for everything. Jonathan got his miracle. We need to get ours. It's time to pray for a new testimony not talk about an old one. Jonathan. Edwin."

Jonathan waited until Ava wasn't looking and mimed to Sharon, *She's bossy.*

"You're right, Ava" said Sharon, and glanced at Jonathan who had already gotten back to pleading for *Mayhem*. Sharon looked around at *Mayhem*. Something was different. She cocked her head on one side, then the other as she tried to figure out what was different. "Jonathan," she said.

Ava looked at her.

"Ava," said Sharon, "something's different. I mean, the air. It's not heavy any more. Do you feel it, Jonathan?"

"I think the bullet holes in my vehicle are messing with my spiritual antenna," he answered. "What do you feel?"

"I know those guys shot up your truck, Jonathan, but something's different. The power's not the same. It's like whatever was ruling this place is gone. I think the ruling spirit's power has been broken."

Lil Johnny looked across the street at the Vice Boys. "There's eight rulin' spirits right there, with those guns in they hands. There's another one. The big ruling spirit. He live right up there on the twelfth floor. Number 1201. His name is Sonny Christopher."

"Wait a minute, everybody. Listen to me," said Sharon. They stopped. The Vice Boys stopped, too. "Lil Johnny, the Bible says, 'We wrestle not against flesh and blood, but against principalities and powers, against the rulers of the darkness of this world, against spiritual wickedness in high places.' There are evil demonic powers behind strongholds like this. People like Sonny are used by them to do what they want done. Sonny's just a puppet."

"Sharon," said Lil Johnny, "I don't mean no harm—I just got saved. But you talkin' 'bout demons we can't see. If Sonny's a puppet, he a puppet with a lot of guns. And those puppets across the street, those puppets got guns, too."

A soft look of understanding came on Sharon's face. "You're right, Lil Johnny. I'm not saying Sonny and the Vice Boys aren't real. We do have to deal with them. I'm just saying that before a stronghold can be taken down in the natural, it has to be taken down in the spirit—through prayer." She looked upwards to the sky, with her arms partly extended. "I think that has happened, Lil Johnny. I think Sonny's power has been broken because the saints have broken the power of the ruling spirit that gave him his power."

Lil Johnny looked across the street. “Somebody need to tell them they ain’t got no mo’ power.”

“I think that’s why we’re here, Lil Johnny,” said Sharon.

“Sharon, are you sure you feel this?” asked Ava.

“She has strong prophetic gifts, Ava,” said Jonathan.

Sharon shook her head, but she wasn’t saying no. “I—it’s hard to explain. Something’s lifted. Something’s gone.”

Barbara spoke tentatively, not wanting to be presumptuous. “Is it a spirit of slavery?”

Sharon’s eyes bulged. “Mom!” she said excitedly.

“And death?” she offered with an equal amount of fear.

“That’s it! That’s it! Mom, Dad, that’s what it is. There was like a blanket of evil over this place. I know the Vice Boys are over there with their guns, but the spiritual battle has been won. God has given us the land. Now we have to take it.”

Lil Johnny eased his way over to Jonathan. “If God gave it to us, why we gotta take it. That don’t make no sense at all,” he whispered.

Jonathan whispered back. “That’s the way it works, Lil Johnny. God doesn’t work for us. He works with us. If you want to see God do incredible things, you gotta do your part. We live through this, I’ll explain it to you later.” He smiled and winked at him.

“Bet that,” said Lil Johnny.

Ava took off, her short legs propelling her across the street toward the Vice Boys.

Elizabeth looked at her mom not with shock—she could be unpredictable—but certainly with alarm. “Where are you going?” Her voice carried that alarm.

“Sharon said God has given us the land. I’m going to tell these Egyptians to let God’s people go.” She looked at her friend. “Willetta, are you going to spank the devil by Skype? Get over here?”

Willetta was like a sprinter waiting for the sound of the race gun. Ava was the gun. She hurried toward her, saying something about uncircumcised Philistines.

Lil Johnny looked at Ava and frowned in confusion. He looked at Jonathan. "Egyptians? What she smokin'? Them niggas ain't from Egypt. I grew up with 'em right here in *Mayhem*."

Jonathan looked at Elizabeth. "See why I love that lady? She makes me look tame." He joined the two ladies who were crossing the street.

Lil Johnny put his hand to his head and rocked it. "Oh, Lawd, why don't they leave these killers alone."

Ava, Willetta, and Jonathan approached eight Vice Boys. Ava was about to say something. Jonathan recognized three Vice Boys. He put his hand lightly on Ava's shoulder.

"Q. Last time I saw you, you were trying to get Jantell's drawls," said Jonathan. "I hope that didn't work out for you."

Q seemed to wear two expressions. One was respect of the preacher. The other was fear of his friends. Jonathan understood what was going on in Q. He wouldn't put him on the spot too much—yet.

"And, my man, Antoine. How's your back?" asked Jonathan.

Antoine didn't answer. He seemed even more conflicted than Q. Jonathan could also tell that he was putting more effort into his bad boy persona than this friend. That could be bad news. A man trying hard to impress his friends could do things in front of them that he wouldn't do if he were alone. It was dangerous to push a man like this.

Jonathan pushed. He took a step toward the man. "Antoine, most people like to think of Jesus as they think He was when He lived in the world. Always smiling. Always forgiving. Always taking people's crap. Dying on a cross. They're uncomfortable with what the rest of the Bible says about Him. Or even what He said about Himself."

Jonathan looked at the Vice Boys in front of them, and those to his left and right. The others had gotten in back of them. This wasn't going too well.

Save Antoine. Save him now.

Jonathan's eyes widened at the thoughts. He knew this was God. He looked at the man with hopeful eyes. Suddenly, he felt as though he were hooked to an IV, receiving a love transfusion from the Holy Spirit.

Antoine frowned. This dude was smilin' at him like he was a punk or something.' "What the hell you so happy 'bout, nigga? You 'bout to get shot."

"Antoine, the Lord is calling you. He's calling you now. You remember I said God wants what's His? He wants what's His, Antoine. You're His. He created you. He created you to know and serve Him." Jonathan shook his head as he motioned with his hand towards the *Mayhem* area. The moisture in his eyes had turned to hopeful tears running down his cheeks. "He didn't create you for this. He didn't create you to hurt people. He didn't create you to live in sin. He didn't create you to go to hell."

"Go to hell?" said Antoine. His response sounded more like he was insulted rather than him asking a question.

"Antoine, God sent me and Edwin to where you were so He could show you His power. Your back, how long did you have that condition before God healed you?"

Antoine had not kept his healing a secret. It was not something he could have kept a secret if he wanted to do so. It had happened in front of three Vice Boys. They had told folks. Plus, he had told people about it. But that had been under different circumstances than what this preacher was doing.

When Antoine and the other Vice Boys had talked about it, it had been just something to talk about. Like a spectacular shooting star racing across the darkness of the sky. An awesome sight that excites the senses for a moment, but not awesome enough to demand a change of lifestyle. But this preacher was putting the shooting star of Antoine's healing in a context of God personally reaching out to him. This dude was making him look bad, like he was weak. For in Antoine's mind, why else would this preacher talk to him like this?

When Jonathan stepped closer to Antoine, the young man said through clenched teeth, "You better get out my face, preacher."

The hope that had given Jonathan's eyes their energy dimmed. His lips parted slightly, but no words came out. Nothing that would shake this young man out of his drunken sleep. But there had to be something he could say to make him see the error of his ways. How could someone receive such an incredible healing and not want the God who had healed him? It was a question Jonathan had asked himself a million times. But he had to ask this time, too.

"Antoine, Jesus healed you. How can you take His healing and not want Him? God intends for His goodness to lead you to repentance. How can you escape His judgment if you neglect salvation so great and so freely offered to you? If you reject His mercy, there's nothing left but His judgment. Is that what you want, Antoine? There's only heaven and hell. There's nothing in- between. No second chances after you die."

Jonathan's watered eyes were pleading as desperately as were his words.

"That cracker's yo' God, Preacher, not mine."

"But He healed—"

"Look," said Antoine in a raised, hard voice, "I didn't ask that cracker to do nothin' fo' me." The man's eyes glared a hatred that Jonathan was still hoping wasn't real. Maybe these were the eyes of a coward instead of a man who truly despised the Christ who had so graciously healed him.

"Okay," Jonathan said sadly. "I can't make you choose heaven over hell."

Ava had heard enough. Since Antoine was the one Jonathan had been speaking to, he was the one she confronted. She took four determined little steps and planted her five-foot frame in front of Jonathan and before the man. Her chin was raised high as she looked up at the man. She pointed a finger at his chest without touching him. "The Lord God Almighty loves these people. Each and every one of them." Her sentences snapped rapidly. "He sent us here in answer to prayer. This place belongs to Jesus now. You have a choice, young man. You can go with God or against God. What is it going to be?"

The Vice Boy was stunned that this midget had fronted him like this in front of the others. And right after he frowned his face and said, "What the hell?" she was stunned too. For his left hand came across and slapped her for her mouth and Jonathan's.

The little woman hit the dirt like a cartoon character. No stumbling to an awkward fall. Instead, there was simply *SMACK!* and hard dirt.

Jonathan's love for Ava moved him before his self-control could stop him. In a flash, he closed the distance between him and the Vice Boy. His balled fist raised to take the man's head off his neck.

Antoine raised his gun to Jonathan's face before his fist arrived. "Go 'head, nigga. Be a hero," the man challenged.

Jonathan froze. Not because of Antoine's gun, nor because of the several other guns now pointed at his head. He dropped his fist because he had heard the Lord speak in his spirit. *Vengeance is mine. I will repay.*

"Least we know you pee standin' up," said Antoine. He looked at Willetta. She was just getting over the shock of what had happened. "You come down here thinkin' yo' white skin gone keep you from gettin' smoked."

Willetta turned to help Jonathan who was now kneeling over Ava. She bent down to assist, and the bottom of a Vice Boy's foot found her butt and pushed her hard into the dirt. She landed like a meteor, face first.

The Vice Boy pointed his gun at Jonathan, who was staring at him, then at the other fools starting to cross the street. They stopped in their tracks. All but one. That crazy, fine white girl that Sonny liked. He lowered his gun. She could come over if she wanted to.

"Sharon," her father called. She stopped and stood there, staring at the Vice Boys for a few moments before she turned and reluctantly went back across the street.

Antoine watched her. He remembered the picture of her that Edwin had shown them of his daughter. *That picture wasn't lying.*

"You can come back if you want to, Sharon," yelled the Vice Boy who had kicked Willetta to the ground. "My name Jamarcus."

Jonathan picked up Ava. She was draped across his arms, still knocked out.

Willetta's face was sore and dirty and her nose was bleeding. But she was on her feet, muttering something about uncircumcised Philistines.

They walked back across the street to join the others. They were thoroughly shaken up. After several minutes Ava revived and looked up at the faces looking down at her. "Where am I?" she asked.

"*Mayhem*," said one of the faces. It was Elizabeth.

"Get me up from here," said Ava.

Everyone knew it would be a losing battle to say no. They helped her up. She looked at Willetta. "We showed that devil, didn't we?"

Both ladies laughed. "We sure did," said Willetta. "I'd always pictured spanking the devil would be a bit different."

They laughed. This time Ava's other friend, Ethel, joined weakly in the laughter.

Ava looked at Jonathan, Elizabeth, and Sharon. "What's wrong with you sour pusses? You'd think they had found the body of Jesus the way you people look."

"Look," said Andrew, pointing across the street towards the Vice Boys. One of them had his shirt off, and almost all the others were staring at the man's back. The only guy not looking at the man's back was a guy holding his own leg. "What's going on with them?"

***

It happened the moment Antoine slapped Ava. He felt something sting him in the back. The sting had grown more painful as he pointed his gun at Jonathan. By the time Sharon went back across the street, he felt the sting spreading across his back.

Whatever it was, it was itching and burning like crazy. He had tried to ignore it, but he couldn't. His back felt like it used to feel before he had been healed when that preacher had prayed for him. The pain from the cloth of his shirt rubbing against his back was unbearable. He snatched his shirt off.

Q cursed and jumped back. "Aww man, that crazy"—he cursed—"is back! It's worse than it was! It's spreading all over yo' back, Dawg. Man, it's goin' up yo' neck!"

Antoine forgot that he was tough. He forgot that he was a killer. He forgot that he was a Vice Boy with a reputation to protect. He panicked. For a moment, he spun in a circle looking over his shoulder, like a dog chasing his tail. But he was chasing the worse flare-up of erythrodermic psoriasis he had ever suffered.

The Vice Boy's eyes were filled with horror as he looked at his friends. They were keeping their distance whenever he spun too close to one of them. Their fear of him touching them increased his panic. They could see what was on his back, and it was scaring everybody. It must've been as ugly as it was painful.

When Antoine felt the itchy, burning pain spread slowly to his butt and down the back of his legs, he looked across the street at the preacher who had prayed for him before.

Call him, Antoine. Ask him to help you. He will.

Antoine didn't call him.

For his pride and fear of man was greater than the panic he felt.

Off alone was Jamarcus.

The moment he had lifted his leg to use it to assault a daughter of God, and to use it to stop the gospel, an angel on assignment to help in the battle for *Mahem* conferred with God. He reminded Him how King Jeroboam had reached forth his hand against a prophet and he had withered his hand. Did not this man's actions, and the circumstances surrounding such an action, warrant a similar judgment?

The Lord agreed with the angel's assessment. However, He reminded the angel that King Jeroboam had received mercy when he cried out for relief from his judgment. The angel left the presence of the Lord with authority to execute judgment mixed with mercy.

Jamarcus had felt no pain when the angel touched his leg. What he did feel was something shrink in the leg he had used to kick that woman. Something in his hip, thigh, and calf. He tried to walk, and when he did he found that his right leg was several inches shorter than it had been. In one moment, he had become a cripple.

He stood alone, dumbfounded, hunched over and holding his right thigh with both hands. Somehow he knew that he was crippled because he had kicked that woman.

Ask that woman to forgive you and I will heal you.

Jamarcus looked across the street.

Chapter 37

The Glory Tabernacle saints made it to the field without further incident. This wasn't because the threat was gone. Rather, the threat was preoccupied. The Vice Boys had mirrored their steps on the opposite side of the street until Ava got the smack down and Willetta was face planted in *Mayhem's* hard dirt.

Now the Vice Boys were huddled around Antoine and his burning, crusty, puss dripping body, and Jamarcus's shrunken leg. Two of the eight thugs were out of commission. Six shooters of this crew were left, and one of these had inside knowledge. Knowledge that was also known by Burning Man and Shrunken Leg. That was that God was behind this.

Mike knew this because he wasn't a fool. And also because he was there in the house when Jonathan had prayed for God to show Himself to them. That was when Antoine had been healed. He didn't know what to think of the healing when it had first happened. Only that it *had* happened. This wasn't some fake dude on television running a game. It was real.

At the time of the healing, the preacher had asked him what it was going to be. He didn't know what to do with that question then; he didn't know what to do with it now. The preacher had also told him that God wanted what was His, and that he was His. He also didn't know what to do with that statement.

What he did know then, and what he knew now, was that either the God of these people was real, and that for some reason He had come to *Mayhem*. Or these people had a lot of strange coincidences.

And there was one other thing he knew. If their God was real, and if this God wanted him—that was hard to believe—it would cost him his life to serve Him. It was a dangerous thought, one that made no sense, but today he'd have to answer that preacher's question.

But there was one question his mind refused to engage in. This was because the answer was obvious, irrefutable. And that answer took all the ifs out of his reasonings. It put him at a crossroad he had never seriously considered. One that would not have even made sense until these people showed up. The crossroad was whether he would spend eternity in heaven or hell.

The question with the obvious, irrefutable answer, the one that his mind had immediately put in the basement to protect itself from the spiritual crisis that Mike was now in was, How did they all miss when they tried to shoot the church people from across the street?

This would remain a mystery to all involved until the Day of Judgment. On that great day of revelation they'd see the Lord Himself walking with the saints and holding out His palm to shield His family from Satan's bullets.

***

The eleven disciples of Jesus stood in the field. Honestly, they didn't know how they had made it this far without being shot. There were as many Scriptures promising tribulation as there were promising deliverance. But so far they had only one shot up vehicle and two beat up women. What was next?

"Where is everybody?" said Ava.

Jonathan looked around. The place was still. Every window was closed. He didn't wonder how a place this large with so many residents could suddenly look like a ghost town. He looked up in the direction of Sonny Christopher's apartment. "Little Satan. Sonny," said Jonathan. "These people are scared to death of him."

"What do we do now?" asked Edwin. "Pray some more?"

"Nope," answered Jonathan. "There's a time to pray and a time to act." He modified his statement. "This time we'll pray as we act." He slowly looked around in every direction. Vice Boys stationed at every building's entrance. Vice Boys in the little kiddie play area, or at least what used to be a little kiddie's play area. But there were people peeping out of their closed windows. Sonny could make them close their windows, but not their hearts. "We're going to preach," he said.

The saints watched him walk away about twenty feet and stop. He turned toward Sonny's building and lifted his hands halfway above his head. His eyes were closed.

Sonny's eyes looked through his high-powered binoculars. He could see the preacher's face clearly. "Big head sucka's praying," he said to himself.

Sonny's low voice masked the rage that had consumed him and turned his mind into one long train of murderous thoughts. He didn't know the moment his own rage had entered the demonic stage, or that he was even being controlled by such a demon, but this is where he was.

The demon of rage had followed the well-worn, routine path of human sin to gain control of his victim. This certainly wasn't the only path, but it was the widest. The spirit's influence within Sonny had grown to such a degree that there was little to no resistance from him. He was at the *What have I done?* stage.

The *What have I done?* stage was what demons called the moment after an otherwise rational person committed an uncharacteristically violent act, and they looked at their own action in shocked horror after the fact and said to himself, "What have I done?" Prisons were filled with people like this.

Sonny put down his binoculars. He didn't know what the preacher was praying, but that preacher was going to be shocked at the answer coming his way.

Jonathan's hands were still raised when he opened his eyes. He saw somebody from Sonny's apartment looking at him through binoculars. He turned and walked back to the others like a man who had just received orders.

"You're not going to preach, are you?" Sharon asked Jonathan.

"No," he answered. He looked at his wife. "Liz, you remember Tepotzlan?"

"I remember," she answered.

"I do, too," said Ava.

"What's Tepotzlan?" asked Sharon. She was always milking Jonathan for his stories. It was like sitting at the feet of the apostle Paul. "What happened there?"

"Got into a little tif with a family of shamans," he answered. "Mexico's got a lot of shamans. Just a fancy name for witch."

"What happened?" she asked with wide eyes.

"Had a few power encounters with them. I'd so something. They'd do something. I'd do something. They'd do something."

"Something like what?" asked Sharon excitedly.

Ava loved Jonathan—he was a true apostle—and adored Sharon—she was an angel—but this wasn't the time for one of Jonathan's long stories. "Sharon, you familiar with Moses and the Egyptians he faced when he tried to free his people?"

"Yeah," she answered, salivating for more.

"That's what happened." She turned to Jonathan. "So we're going to do proclamations?"

He looked at her with a smile and shook his head as he answered. She had cut short a very good story. "Ava, you're the loveliest scissors I know. Yes, we're going to proclaim the word."

Ava spun. "Listen up," she said. "The word of God is alive and powerful. God is watching over His word to perform it. Don't worry about those closed windows. We are going to speak God's word over this place."

"What do you mean?" asked Barbara. "We're going to quote Scriptures."

"Yep," answered Ava. "Quote Scriptures and anything else the Lord brings to mind. Speak blessings over this place. Be specific."

"Then what?" asked Andrew. His fourteen-year-old mind needed more than this.

"Then God," answered Ava. This answer brought her a number of quizzical looks. She followed up. "If there's anything else to do, we'll know what to do when it's time to do it." She looked at Jonathan. "That about it, Jonathan?"

His love showed in his grin at her. "Couldn't have said it better myself."

"Okay, get to it," Ava ordered everyone.

Barbara was the first to speak. She narrowed her eyes and pointed her delicate finger at one of the buildings. "We speak life to this place! It is no longer Mayhem Courts! It's Mahem Courts! The God of Lazarus is here! In Jesus name, all of you are free to serve the Lord!

"Goooo, Mom," said Sharon, and joined her with her own blessings.

Ava's friend, Ethel, had been in the background, saying very little until now. Apparently, she had a thing for declaring Gods word. It was also apparent that she only had one decibel level—loud. She began like a bullet out of a barrel. Loud and fast.

"Call unto Me, and I will answer you, and show you great and mighty things that you do not know!" said Ethel. "That's what You said! Well, I'm calling...."

Elizabeth wasn't loud or fast, but she had first learned the power of the spoken word of God over a stronghold when she was still in bondage in Argentina, and she had learned even more with Jonathan since then. The words came powerfully out of her mouth. "Let God arise and let His enemies be scattered! Let those who hate Him flee before Him! As smoke is driven away, so drive them away...."

Andrew pointed at various buildings as he declared over *Mayhem*. "I declare the crooked paths straight. I declare light in the darkness. I declare life where there was death!"

***

The distraction of Antoine's sudden attack of enraged erythrodermic psoriasis and of Jamarcus's sudden shrunken leg had been interrupted by a phone call from a Sonny Christopher who was talking like a man who had gone insane.

"Kill 'em! Kill 'em all! Right now!" he ordered.

He was on his way down twelve flights of stairs with four Vice Boys to join the carnage. They were going to smoke these fools and dump them and their vehicles somewhere else. No one in Mayhem would tell. They never told.

His phone rang. He put the phone to his ear as his heavy body stormed down the stairs. Whatever he heard on the other end stilled the storm. He stopped and listened. He didn't want his guys to hear this. He pushed the phone to his chest. "Go on." He waved them on. "I'll catch up with you."

The Vice Boys went on without Sonny. They didn't need him for what they were going to do to those church people.

***

The tentacled blue mist that was already in Mayhem grew hundreds of different arms when the saints began declaring the word of God. Its arms went in every direction. In each stream of blue were angels that every demon feared irrespective of rank.

The massive, large-mouth mercy angels walked in and out of the blue. Their swords were drawn—for a specific purpose. They were here to minister to every person in Mahem Courts. Every person would decide for or against Christ today, and they'd do it without interference from Satan—if the last phase of the plan occurred.

This wasn't merely unusual; it was rare. The saints had done such a great job of intercession that the stronghold of darkness had been all but destroyed. There were still pockets of resistance—there always would be—but the overwhelming gravity of evil that had pulled down the people of Mahem was spiritually gone.

The other extremely powerful and game-changing thing that the saints had done was they had showed up. They had added legs and hands and hearts to their prayers. So often saints overlooked the basic foundation of the kingdom of God, and that was that God's power followed His love, and that love could be seen in its actions. No actions, no love. No love, no power.

How often the saints had overlooked the Scriptures that said "Jesus was moved with compassion and healed their sick." Why should such an obvious and fundamental and highlighted truth, that God's power followed love, be treated like a baffling mystery?

Had they never read, "He who walks in love walks in God, and God in him"? What did this mean? Was it a mystery? No. Its meaning was obvious. Children of God who behaved like God were empowered by God.

Yet, as exceptional a job as the Glory Tabernacle saints had done in intercession and showing up, there were other spiritual considerations that went into taking down a stronghold that was in Mahem's category. There was one other thing that must occur if God's plan for Mahem were to come to pass.

Chapter 38

It was something that had not been discussed by the eleven saints who were walking in the Mayhem field and quoting Scriptures and declaring freedom to the captives. Time was running out. Something wonderful or something horrible was going to happen soon. Everyone's pace quickened.

"Let these people go, Satan!" ordered Sharon. "You can't have them!"

Barbara was close by. "You've exploited and crushed them long enough." Her voice wasn't loud as Sharon's, but her words carried the brokenness she felt in her heart for Mayhem. No one should have to live like this. She wouldn't let Satan have his way with these people. "Lord, You said, 'Ask of Me, and I will give you the heathen for your inheritance and the uttermost parts of the world for your possession.' I ask You for Mahem Courts. Give us Mahem Courts." Her attention turned. "Satan, I demand that you give us Mahem!"

Edwin kept a close eye on his family as he declared the word of God over Mayhem.

Willetta rubbed the burning scrape on her face. It stung. She reached into the bag she had draped over her shoulder and pulled out a polished shofar that she had purchased on her Holy Land tour. It was a ram's horn. In the Bible, it was often used to announce the arrival of holy days, the commencement of religious ceremonies, or the beginning of battles.

Willetta was going to battle. She put the horn to her mouth and blew. She blew as hard as she could. The low sound didn't match the energy of her soul. She blew anyway, believing that God would make up for her weakness.

Willetta was right.

For Jesus blew His horn each time she blew hers. And each time He blew His horn, a shock wave blasted through the remains of the Mayhem stronghold that crumbled buildings and sent demons hurtling.

Sharon stopped her declarations and looked with surprise at the approaching car. She took a couple of steps in its direction and said, "Dad, look."

He looked. Then he looked again as though he could focus his eyes like binoculars. "Kim?"

"That looks like her car," said Sharon in disbelief. Kim had been adamant about never setting foot in this place again. *Is that her? Couldn't be,* she thought.

"She has someone with her," said Edwin.

The car parked in front of Edwin's car. Kim got out of the car, closed her door, and walked around to the other side. The passenger door opened.

The Vice Boys who had been trailing the saints and that had opened fire on them weren't facing the street. They were looking down at Jamarcus and Antoine. Jamarcus had taken off his pants. He and his friends looked with horror at a right leg that had shrunken and dried. He sat on the nonexistent grass and cried like a man who wasn't a thug. And right now none of his thug comrades were judging him harshly for crying. A couple of them even had watery eyes.

But it was Antoine who was truly the horror movie. The Vice Boys watched as the psoriasis spread inch by inch. They could actually see it enlarging over his body. First, it was his back, then they watched as the skin on his neck progressively turned blistery red. Now the redness was encroaching from his left and right ribs to the eventual meeting place in the center of his torso. There was only about a six-inch path from his neck down to his crotch that was untouched by the growing plague. But the six-inch path had been a twelve-inch path. So it was just a matter of time. Mercifully, his face and ears had only small blotches of red, and they looked worse than they felt.

Mike had enough. He couldn't look at this any longer. He was a hardened criminal, but these were his friends. He had grown up with Antoine and Jamarcus. He turned away from his tormented friends for a moment of relief. He saw something that couldn't be. His eyes relayed to his brain what they saw. His brain rebelled. He took a couple of dazed steps towards the mesmerizing image.

In a moment, the other Vice Boys, including Antoine and Jamarcus, were staring in disbelief at that new girl, Kim, and the person who was with her.

***

The Vice Boys were shocked to see a dead man walking around. Three of the eight who had shot Jonathan's SUV were also among those who had shot Prince dead. The other two, plus Mike, Antoine, and Jamarcus, hadn't taken part in the shooting, but they knew he was good and Vice Boy dead.

The saints couldn't put it past the Vice Boys to try to kill him as he lay in a drug-induced coma. So it had been a closely guarded secret among them that Prince was still alive and in critical care at Grady Memorial Hospital. They had spent a lot of time in Prince's hospital room praying for him. Yet even though his recovery was progressing remarkably fast, they were surprised to see him up and about—and in Mayhem of all places.

One saint in particular, Kim, had spent more time at the hospital than she had at the Styles's home, where she now lived. Like everyone, she laid hands on him often and prayed. But her prayers were different. For when she laid hands on him, interesting and embarrassing thoughts went through her mind—absolutely nonsensical. Then one evening her thoughts graduated to the insane stage.

Kim had tried to discreetly get prettied up—something that required very little effort. She must not have been discreet enough because Sharon had forced her way into the restroom with Kim to help her prepare to see, as Sharon put it, "Your Prince." Sharon had joked about reversing the fairy tale. In Sharon's version, Prince Charming was the one brought out of the coma by being kissed by the beautiful damsel.

On the night Kim's thoughts went to the insane stage, it happened like this. Kim innocently placed her hand on top of Prince's hand. She looked at his face and lingered. Then her innocent eyes fell upon his wide, dark chest. She meant nothing undamselike. This, however, didn't stop her heart from quickening. She liked dark men. She knew this, but she wouldn't discover just how much she liked dark men until the insanity came upon her with a vengeance.

Prince had a tube that was inserted into his chest to help him breathe. Kim looked at the tube and realized his grim condition. A slight frown hinted her thoughts. She'd had enough of looking at that tube. Her eyes went back to his face, his dark and lovely face. She lingered. She lingered too long.

The deer and lights phenomenon hit with all its fury. Kim looked at the light of Prince's full lips and before she knew what was happening, an animal instinct drove her inexplicably to the lights. Her lips puckered for a delicate and brief smack. But at the moment of the planned smack, she was betrayed. Her lips parted and she kissed him deliciously. She did it again. When she finished molesting this beautiful man, she slowly pulled her head back with her eyes closed, savoring the moment.

"Thank you, Kim," said Prince, his voice faint, his eyes too weak to open.

Kim's eyes popped open, only inches from his face. Her sanity returned. What had she done? She would later blame Sharon for using mind control.

Things progressed quickly between Prince and Kim. So quickly that when on one of her visits Prince told her that a doctor he hadn't seen before came into his room and laid his hand on his forehead and said, "Rise, Octavius, it is time to deliver your people," he never said anything to Kim about accompanying him to Mayhem. He didn't have to. It was a foregone conclusion.

"I'm going with you," she had told him. "You died for the Lord once, all alone. The next time you die for God, we die together." Prince had opened his mouth to shut this idea down. She cut him off. "I'm never leaving your side, Prince."

So here they were. In Mayhem. Prince and Kim facing their greatest threat together.

"Prince," Sharon came running, "you're up! Oh, Jesus, you're up. You're here."

Prince leaned on his cane. He could walk without it, but his body, and especially his right lung, had been through a lot of trauma. Plus, walking with the cane helped his breathing.

The rest of the team gathered around Prince. They gushed and hugged and squeezed. Prince told them about the doctor who had laid hands on him and prophesied. They all agreed excitedly that he had to have been an angel. Their excitement was interrupted by the sight of Vice Boys approaching from several directions.

Jonathan turned to the saints. "This is it."

Sharon said, "What are we going to do?" Her question was filled with the possibilities of seeing and being involved in one of those fascinating Jonathan stories.

Jonathan looked to their left. Vice Boys. To the far center. Vice Boys. To the right. Vice Boys.

"Almost like General Custer," said Sharon. She smiled like someone who must not have known that the general was killed by Indians.

"Bad example, Sharon. Not even close," said Jonathan. "That rascal didn't have the Holy Ghost." He winked. But it still hadn't come to him what they were to do next. *If I be lifted up, I will draw all men to Myself.* Jonathan rested his finger on his lip.

"You got something, don't you?" asked Ava. "Let's hear it, Jonathan."

"That's right," said Edwin. "If you've got something, this would be a wonderful time to let us in on it."

"Prince," said Jonathan. "The angel told Prince, 'It is time for you to deliver your people.'"

Everyone looked anxiously at the man recovering from twelve gunshot wounds.

Jonathan looked over Ava toward the building directly behind her. A window on the third floor had opened. Three people were in the window. "That," said Jonathan, pointing to the people. "I assume their shock is due to seeing a dead man stand here with us. You know those people?"

Prince looked up and smiled. "I don't know the girl in white, but I know the other two."

Jonathan knew they were running out of time. "Prince, tell them to call everyone they know in Mayhem and let them know that you have been raised from the dead, and that you are here in the field. Tell them to get out here now!"

Prince did as he was asked.

The Vice Boys were nearly upon them. Less than a minute away. Not nearly enough time for Jonathan's plan to work.

Chapter 39

The moment was way beyond awkward. The saints were surrounded by Vice Boys. Vice Boys who had killed Prince. Vice Boys who had killed Lil Johnny's sister. Vice Boys who had shot Jonathan's SUV clean into the world to come. And Vice Boys who were looking at one another as though they were enemies. What in the world was going on?

There was something else awkward about the moment.

The men who had murdered Prince were intermingled among the various little groups of Vice Boys. There were at least forty or more Vice Boys here. Yet their body language and expressions didn't reflect their advantage of numbers and firepower. Questions had paralyzed their actions.

Prince took three steps forward. Kim quickly joined him at his side. She took his hand and looked at the Vice Boys with a bravery she did not feel. What she did feel was deep love for the man Prince had become. And that was enough to give her the strength to stand next to him. That and the fact that Jesus Christ was now her God.

It appeared that none of the Vice Boys had anything to say.

Prince pointed at the Vice Boys. "You killed me. I went to heaven." It was apparent that he was reliving what he was describing. "I saw God. I saw angels. I saw some of the people who wrote the Bible. I saw my aunt, Sonny's mom. I saw the things God has created for those who love Him. I wanted to stay." He pointed behind him without looking. "But they wouldn't let me stay in heaven. They wouldn't let go of my spirit. The Lord told me I had to go back because they wouldn't let me go. He said the reason they wouldn't let me go was because my work wasn't done."

Something remarkable happened. As Prince spoke, four people bravely walked across the field and joined together as they journeyed toward the crowd. The saints greeted them with hugs and tears and "Praise God."

The first of the four to reach Prince was one of the two men. He was the oldest, about sixty. He looked into Prince's eyes with tears in his own. "I gave my life to God when you preached. I felt something good happen inside me. I had never felt like that in my whole life." The man started crying in shame. "But when they killed you—" The man's shoulders bounced as he cried with a covered face. "When they killed you, I got scared. Then when these people came back and preached, I wanted to get baptized. I was scared of Sonny though and didn't do it. Then they killed that young lady."

Lil Johnny said heavily, "That was my sister they killed."

This was the first Prince had heard of LaQueesha's murder. He groaned with closed eyes. He opened them and made himself focus on the man before him. "But you here now," Prince said to the man.

"Yeah, I'm here now. And if they kill me, they kill me. But I'm not gone be scared no more." The man looked at the Vice Boys. "I'm not gone be scared no more.""

The other three said almost the same thing as the first man.

A Vice Boy spoke up. "That's what it's gone be?" he challenged the four. "Y'all know what Sonny said about messin' with these fools. You ready to die for 'em?"

"Xavier, you haven't hurt enough people?" asked Prince.

"Naw, nigga, I ain't even got started," he answered.

"Xavier, you can't win. You're fighting against God," said Prince.

"Naw, nigga, you can't win. You fightin' against the Vice Boys."

Prince saw Mike's face in the Vice Boy crowd. "Is that right?" he said, as he looked in his direction.

Mike's mind went into overdrive when Prince said they were fighting against God. Antoine burning up over there on the dirt, looking like a reptile. Jamarcus all shriveled up. Prince smoked and now right back in their faces. This was like watching *The Ten*

Commandments on television. But this time he was in the movie. *I ain't gone be one of them Egyptians.*

Prince didn't get an answer. But maybe he did. A steady trickle of people came out of the buildings as though they had conspired to appear at the most dramatic moment. "You're going to kill all of them, too?"

The Vice Boys looked around at the disobedient people. One of those who had shot Jonathan's SUV took several angry steps into the field. He screamed, "Get yo' crusty butts back in the house!"

They kept walking.

He pulled a gun and shot three times into the air. "What I say?" he demanded.

They stopped.

He pointed his gun in the directions of several people who had dared to try to go to the church people.

"Jonathan," said Elizabeth, when she saw the people intimidated by the Vice Boy.

He put his hand on her shoulder. "Let's just trust God and see what He does. It's not over yet, Liz."

Another figure came out of a building. Out of Sonny's building. It was Sonny. The phone call he had received was the last straw. He had been told that if he couldn't handle Mayhem, they'd replace him with someone who could. The phone call, coupled with the rage demon's growing control of Sonny, made him a very dangerous man.

Sonny's feet pounded hard and angrily on the field he owned as he walked toward the crowd. He wasn't thinking rationally. He was thinking desperately. He was thinking demonically. The guns he held in each hand were proof of this.

When the Vice Boys who were about to go after the people on the field saw Sonny, they stopped. Even from a distance, they could see that he had that look in his eye. He wasn't coming down here to scare people. He was going to kill somebody. They turned around and went back to the rest of the Vice Boys.

As Sonny got closer, the crowd of Vice Boys parted into two sides. He now had two rows of Vice Boys, a dirt path leading directly to the church people.

Jonathan tugged the four brave converts back. He stepped forward and stood next to Prince.

Sonny still had some distance to cover, but his eyesight was good. He came to a sudden stop, like he had hit a wall. His thick neck jutted out the hat he wore. *Can't be. That nigga dead,* he thought. He shook his head and resumed his murderous march. He stopped again. *That nigga ain't dead.*

Rage exploded inside of him.

"That nigga ain't dead!" he screamed at himself, and took off in a brisk walk toward Prince. He had thirty bullets. He was going to use every single one of them.

Edwin stepped up and stood next to Kim. This caused a quick chain reaction. Barbara, Sharon, and Andrew huddled around Edwin. Elizabeth and Ava gathered with Jonathan. Ethel stepped up next to Ava. Lil Johnny stood behind everyone and bent down, trying to make himself a smaller target. And Willetta....

Willetta snatched the big flap across her large bag that hung over her shoulder. She reached inside and yanked out the shofar. She ran down the path of Vice Boys and stood at the beginning of its opening. She pointed her finger at the big, green-suited menace coming at them with a gun in each of his hands. "In the name of Jesus!" She put the horn to her mouth and blew as hard as she could.

"What that crazy heifer doing?" Sonny snapped to himself. His rage lifted his right hand. He pointed the gun at her face. He was going to put a bullet right through that horn.

Beeeeeeeeep! Beeeeeeeeeeep! Beep! Beep! Beep!

Everyone turned.

A bus rumbled toward them, horn blaring.

Sonny lowered his gun and stared at the bus. Buses didn't come into Mayhem. What was this fool doing?

The fact that the bus driver drove up over the curb and onto the grass and headed toward them was strange enough. But even more strange was there were other buses behind this one, and cars. It sounded like every single driver was laying on the horn. The other buses jumped the high curb and joined the first bus on the field.

Sonny looked at the sudden crowd of invaders. Every bus and car and van was filled, and the caravan seemed to have no end. This development drained him of his irrational rage. In its place was left something that resembled common sense and self-preservation. “What are these crackers doing now?” He huffed and quickly stuck his guns in his waist.

People started getting off the buses and getting out of cars and vans. He watched what must’ve been a hundred people take to his field. His field. And still there were buses that hadn’t been emptied yet, as well as a long line of buses backed up as far as he could see.

Sonny’s bewilderment left when he looked at Prince and his church friends, and how they were looking at the invaders. They knew these folks. The invaders were church people, too. He cursed. *What the hell am I going to do with five hundred church people?*

He’d figure this out later. Right now he had to get out of here. Sonny started walking back toward his building. The Vice Boys looked at one another and did likewise.

Something told Sonny that there was an element to this church invasion that was even freakier than it looked. His criminal instinct would prove this accurate.

Three empty church buses drove toward Prince and his people, then took a left and drove alongside the Vice Boys. One church bus went up ahead and circled to the right. The next thing that happened explained that freaky feeling Sonny had.

In a few seconds, the Vice Boys were staring at sixty members of the FBI’s Enhanced Special Weapons And Training (SWAT) team. The armed bullies of Mayhem offered no resistance. They were on their knees in a flash and instantly obeying every command.

An FBI agent walked over to where Sonny was handcuffed and on his belly. He got on one knee beside him. “How you doing, Sonny?”

This was awkward. Sonny didn’t know what to say. “I’m alright.”

The agent shook his head with a smile. His eyes twinkled as he said, "You don't look okay. Did they read you your rights?"

"Yeah," said Sonny.

"Ohhh, that's good. That's real good, Sonny. 'Cause you're in a lot of trouble. You ever heard of RICO?"

"Naw." Sonny was defiant.

The agent was genuinely surprised. "You kidding me. A man in your line of work, and you don't know RICO?" He wiped his brow. "Whew. This is hard to believe. I always thought you'd be smarter than this. Well, let me begin your advanced education in federal law by saying that RICO is some kind of a bad mutha. RICO. Racketeer Influenced and Corrupt Organizations.

"This is the catch-all law we use for criminal enterprises. Like, say, the Vice Boys. All we have to do is establish a pattern of naughty behavior." The agent snapped his finger. "Just like that, even before we go to trial, we seize your goodies. That means your lovely little loft in Atlanta—"he paused for effect—"your place in the burbs, cars, bank accounts—gone. All gone. And RICO penalties," the agent looked around as though he were about to share a secret, "draconian. Could've been written by Fidel Castro. Up to twenty years for each offense of your *criminal* enterprise. Look at me, Sonny."

Sonny turned and looked at the special agent.

"It's not just the big stuff like your multiple murders or the drugs or the rapes. It's stuff like, uhhh, extortion. You'd call them taxes. Remember I said the law was draconian? Oh, and that means severe. You can get twenty years for every time one of the residents here paid their monthly tax to you and your Vice Boys. I'm not the best at math, Sonny, but even I know that alone is worth thousands of years in prison."

The special agent seemed to have no end of conversation for Sonny.

"You tryin' to talk me to death?" Sonny asked angrily.

"No, Sonny, I just talk a lot. Always have." The agent helped up his prisoner. "Pretty Tony, he talks a lot, too. What happened? You had a good thing going here. You want my opinion?"

Sonny didn't answer.

"We know an awful lot about you and your chump friends. We know a lot about who you work for. But I'm getting off track," said the agent. "I think it all started going down hill when you tried to kill Octavius AKA Prince Monroe. That's what I think. What you think, Sonny?"

Sonny blurted a curse word in three quick successions.

The FBI agent offered some helpful advice. "You may want to slow down with that. The toilet paper's rationed where you're going."

"I'll be outta jail in two days," said Sonny.

"Really?" The agent smiled. "I'm pretty sure you're not going to be given bail. And even if the judge did go crazy and grant you bail, you're broke. Uncle Sam's got your money."

"Two days," said Sonny.

***

The saints were as shocked to see Sonny and the Vice Boys arrested and hauled off as they were at being hauled off. But the busloads of Christians, that was equally amazing. What was going on?

"Dad, is that Reverend Winston?" asked Sharon.

Edwin looked at the large figure trying to make his way over the rough field without twisting an ankle in a gopher hole. "I—do—not—believe my eyes," he said.

"Believe it, Dad. It's him."

The large man came to a stop before Edwin and the team of saints. He bent over and shook his head in an exaggerated rest, leaning on his flabby thighs. "Edwin, you got to do something about that ground. I like to broke my neck." He looked sideways from his doubled over position. "Hello, Sharon."

"Hi, Reverend Winston." Sharon looked around with wide eyes and a face filled with wonder. "What is this?"

He stood up straight and looked at Edwin's whole crew. "This, my darling, is the Holy Ghost cavalry—come to rescue you." He looked around at the hundreds of milling people. "Well, most of us got the Holy Ghost." He said in a whisper, "There are a surprising number of Baptists and Methodists represented in this formidable army. Who would've thought?"

"Maybe they've got more of the Spirit than you give them credit for," said Sharon.

He smiled largely and bobbed his head as he spoke. "Yep, yep, yep. I stand corrected. Some of the meanest people I know speak in tongues and prophesy." He lowered his head and put his hand over his heart. "God rest her soul." He looked up. "Oh, somebody close to me came to mind when I said that." He chuckled. "Anyway, Sharon, I was just testing you." He smiled at her. "You passed."

Edwin looked at Reverend Winston with a look that said he was trying to sort out this abrupt turn of events.

Reverend Winston looked at Edwin with a serious expression. "Reverend Styles, people look at me and get lost by my good looks. They hear me speak and are mesmerized by my charm. I'm more than that. I'm an incredible man of God." He changed expressions and moods in a flash. "Okay, enough of that," he said quickly. "There are two other reasons I'm here. First, my lovely daughter, Jennifer. My Lord, my Lord, she can torment you worse than the antichrist if you don't do the right thing. I don't know why we ever let that girl learn to read. Second, the Holy Ghost. He's got my number, man. He can put a torment on you like all get out." He pushed his face forward to Edwin. "See any bags under my eyes?"

"Actually, yes," said Edwin.

"Holy Ghost. Won't let me sleep. Rocks me all night long," said Reverend Winston.

"But where'd all of these people come from?" asked Edwin.

Reverend Winston lowered his head and looked up at him and the others with his eyes rolled up. Edwin knew the man was about to give a comedic answer. This was the sort of thing in the man that used to irritate him to no end. But now he found himself liking the guy and actually awaiting his answer.

"Edwin, you know I'm full of the Holy Ghost and speak in tongues and prophesy. But, Edwin, some of you charismatics are STR strange. I mean *strange.* On one of those nights I was being tormented by the blessed Comforter, a lady calls my house. Now did I mention it was two o'clock in the morning? This lady tells me that God told her two things. Number one, God told her to cook me a pot of ox tail stew."

Prince looked at the man intently. "Ox tail stew?"

"Yep. I was about to hang the phone up on this nut. But then," he stretched his words, "she reminds me of the conversation I had with my wife the day before about my mother's ox tail stew." The preacher squinted his eyes. "Now how'd she know about that conversation? Number two, God told her to remind me that He has commanded the church to go into all the world to preach the gospel. He also said that He expected *me* to help *you*."

Edwin's eyes and face lightened. He appeared ready to say something.

Reverend Winston looked at him with his mean look. "Edwin, I'm a godly man, but if you say it, I'm going to stuff you into one of those gopher holes you tried to kill me with."

"This lady who called you," said Jonathan, "how's her stew?"

The reverend shook his head several times with an expression that said it all. "Lordy, lordy, had I known you were going to be here, I would've brought you some. Let you taste what kind of food they eat in heaven."

"Maybe we'll have to go by your house after this and get some," said Jonathan, with a sly grin.

"All gone. Ate it all. Every piece of meat. Every carrot. Every ounce of liquid. Every grain of rice. They've all gone on to meet the good Lord," said Reverend Winston. He looked at Sharon. "What are you crying for, Darling?"

"God's tender love," she answered with light tears. "How He speaks to us. The fact that He speaks to us. It's beautiful. I want to hear His voice more. I want to grow as a prophetess of the Lord. I want to be like the lady who called you."

Reverend Winston chuckled. "Oh, so you want to be a holy nuisance, do you? Well, young lady, I'm going to have to hook you up with Prophetess Ebony Monroe. Make sure you say Prophetess *Ebony* Monroe. Made the mistake of calling her Prophetess

Monroe. Tightened me up right quick and in a hurry. She said God saved and anointed all of her. *Prophetess Ebony Monroe.* She and her church are here somewhere."

Prince broke out laughing. "I knew it. I knew it. Moms and that ox tail stew."

"Oh, my God!" said Sharon. "That's your mom."

That's why that name sounded so familiar. The saints shared a good laugh. After all they had been through, they needed a good laugh. They needed something else, too. Jonathan brought it up.

"God has begun this work, and only He can finish it," he said. "Let's pray together."

"Jonathan, you mind if I pray first?" asked Prince.

Jonathan looked at him like a proud father. "No, not at all. I think we'd all like that."

Everyone agreed and encouraged him.

"And can I pray after Prince?" asked Lil Johnny.

"Of course," said Edwin.

Prince let his cane drop in front of him. "Let's hold hands." They did and he looked around nodding. He bowed his head.

> *Lord Jesus, I was in darkness, and You brought me to the light. I was stuck in quicksand, going under fast, and You reached down and pulled me out. You set my feet on a solid foundation. There was no hope for me...until I met your servants, until they had mercy on me, until they saw beyond who I was to what I could become. Lord, I don't know where I'd be if I had never met Edwin and Jonathan—if they had never come down here. I didn't know those kind of Christians existed.*
>
> *Lord, thank you for Sharon and Andrew and Barbara and Elizabeth.* Prince shook his head. *Lord, thank you for Kim, for this beautiful woman you have given me. Help me to be the kind of man she deserves. Help us to work together for the rest of our lives to bring You glory.*

Lord, I don't know how many people have seen the things you've let me see. I don't know how many people have been raised from the dead. I don't ever want to take this for granted. I'm Yours forever.

Lord, there's still a lot I don't know, but I know that nobody could've taken down Sonny. Nobody could've stopped the killing and raping and all the other stuff. I know Sonny would've killed all of us today had You not stopped him. And God You stopped him through my mama. You stopped him through Reverend Winston. You stopped him through all the saints who showed up here today.

Lord, I honestly thought I was about to die again. Prince smiled. *I guess when the church believes God, and when it works together like it's doing today, all things are possible. Amen.*

Chapter 40

Captain Rashti looked at the faithful angel and budding warrior. "What do you see, Adaam-Mir? Tell me of the Creator's wisdom here." He spoke of the crowds of Christians who had gotten off buses and out of vans and cars.

The excited angel could hardly contain himself. He pumped his alternating fists and did likewise with his feet as he jerked a short march of triumph. "Look at them! What a mighty army they are! See how they go into every home. Look at all of the people they've brought to the field. The people are crying out to the Creator for forgiveness."

Rashti pushed the angel into understanding more. "This is the *work* of the Lord. Now tell me of His *ways.* Explain what has happened."

Adaam-Mir's giant smile didn't altogether leave, at least not all at once, and not entirely. The moment was too grand to completely remove it. He looked at the captain with a radiant glow. His growing thoughtfulness furrowed his brow. "God used intercession to break the power of Annihilation and Slavery. Once this was done, they joined forces and came here to save Mayhem and the Bluffs from the wrath to come."

Captain Rashti looked at the angel with a tenderness the angel felt. Yet the captain's expression also told him there was more. He was right. "Adaam-Mir, Sharon and the others were right when they discerned that the dark powers had been broken over *Mayhem* and *The Bluff*. But what she and the others, and Satan himself, don't yet fully realize is that Mayhem and the Bluff were secondary targets of the Lord. The primary target was the church."

"The church? I do not understand," he answered.

"In the blessed book—"Adaam-Mir's face lit up at the sound of the blessed book—"it says that where sin abounded, grace did much more abound. In another place it says 'For, behold, the darkness shall cover the earth, and gross darkness the people: but the Lord shall arise upon thee, and his glory shall be seen upon thee.'

"Adaam-Mir, this has happened. You have seen a way the Creator often works. It is not the magnitude of sin or the intensity of the darkness that gives it such power. It is the absence of grace and light that gives sin and darkness their power. Do you understand?"

"I think so." Adaam-Mir's answer wasn't confident.

"Do you remember when the Lord said of the church, 'You are the salt of the earth. If the salt has lost its flavor, how shall it get it back? It is therefore good for nothing, but to be thrown out and trampled on by people.'

"Yes," said Adaam-Mir.

"In many ways the church has lost its flavor, but God is committed to presenting to Himself a church without spot or wrinkle. So He did something Satan did not anticipate. The evil one thought the target was *Mayhem* and T*he Bluff*. It was, but only as they related to the main target—the church."

Adaam-Mir put both hands to the sides of his head and rocked his whole body side to side as the revelation dawned on him. "This is too much. Too much, Captain." He dropped his arms to his sides and lifted his face to the heavens. His eyes were closed. He spoke with them closed. "The Lord is not using the church to save Mayhem as much as He is using Mayhem to save the church."

"Yes!" the captain exulted. "Do you understand what this could mean to the church if they ever come to its full truth?"

Adaam-Mir let his mind soar until his chest was filled with euphoria. He thought of Moses and Pharoah. *Pharoah brought out the best in Moses.* He thought of Samson and the lion. *The lion brought out the best in Samson.* He thought of David and Goliath. *The giant brought out the best in David.* He thought of Jesus and the cross. *The cross brought out the best in Jesus.* He opened his eyes and looked at his captain. "They would look at darkness and trials and impossibilities differently."

"How would they see them?" asked Captain Rashti.

"They'd see them the way God sees *Mayhem*—something that could bring out the best in His people," Adaam-Mir answered. "He knew that it would take something dramatic, something so horrible that it could not be ignored, to awaken the church from its slumber. The Creator used Sonny to awaken the Atlanta church, and to gather it to this great battle.

"The presence of much sin and intense darkness should not repel or intimidate the church. Instead, this should incite it to action—like when Sonny killed Laqueesha and left her body out for all to see."

Captain Rashti took a few steps to where the angel was. He put his large hand on his shoulder and squeezed. He didn't speak. The squeeze was enough.

"What will happen to the two who were disciplined of the Lord, and of their friend, Mike?" asked Adaam-Mir.

"The one who kicked God's daughter to the ground has repented in his heart of the evil. God has mercifully put an open door before him. He will be restored little by little as he learns the fear of the Lord. Mike also has repented. The Lord will be with him in prison."

Prison? Adaam-Mir frowned.

"Forgiveness does not always mean one escapes being paid the natural wages for one's sins. But God will have mercy on him at his sentencing and during his confinement," said Rashti.

"Captain, what of the other?" Adaam-Mir asked thinking he may not like the answer.

The captain took a deep breath. "Do you remember when Esau sold his birthright for a bowl of food?"

"Yes. I wept bitterly when I read the story," said Adaam-Mir.

"I wept bitterly when he did it. I was in the area with Michael, the great prince who fights for Abraham." Rashti looked hard at the angel. "Adaam-Mir, after Esau had filled his belly, he realized what he had done and wept bitterly, seeking to undo his sin." Captain Rashti's head lowered. He raised it with moist eyes. "As it is written in the blessed book, he did not find repentance. The deed was forever done."

The finality of God's justice hit Adaam-Mir hard. He staggered back a step, with a hand over his chest. He thought of Adam and Eve. He thought of the people who died during the great flood of Noah's day, whose moment of mercy passed when God shut the door of the ark. Then his mind went back to Lucifer's rebellion, and how he could have suffered the same fate as that deceiver. *Eternal damnation!*

"Adaam-Mir," called Rashti.

"Oh, I..." he had to recover from such a fearful thought, "I was just thinking of something. What were we talking about?"

Captain Rashti noted the angel's demeanor. "You chose correctly. I chose correctly."

The angel's eyes were thoughtful and wide. "What if we hadn't?"

"Then," he paused, "we'd have no hope. The one who is burning, Antoine. God has not dealt with him as He dealt with Esau. But the son of Adam did say no to the Holy Spirit when the opportunity for full and immediate healing was before him."

"So he will never be healed?" asked Adaam-Mir, hurt at this possibility.

"I cannot say *never*, for the Lord's mercy is from everlasting to everlasting to those who fear Him. However, I have been shown that even if there is true repentance, and he cries out to God for healing, it will only happen after a considerably long time. He must learn the preciousness of the body of Christ. In this case, a quick healing would do more damage than good. God knows what is in man. The Creator is perfect in all His ways."

Adaam-Mir had now fully recovered from his recollections of the Great Rebellion. "Yes. He is perfect in all His ways." He looked out at the ruins of the former *Mayhem* stronghold. "What and where is the next assignment?"

***

Diane was on the sofa. Rosa was in her wheelchair. They both sat before the television and watched the news in shock. Rosa wouldn't be so presumptuous to think she alone had been the cause of what was going on in Mayhem. But she no longer wondered whether her prayers had been having any affect.

Terry Night of CNN had been talking about *Mayhem* and *The Bluff* all night. He was asking a lot of hard questions, a lot of them quite accusatory. One that he constantly asked was, "How could something like this go on for so long without there being very powerful local people involved?" He had apparently already developed contacts who were supplying him with shocking information.

He even produced a disturbing and incredible video of a young girl with a hood over her head and tied to a chair. That was the disturbing part. The incredible part was that the video caught her sailing through the air from a raised porch and landing on one of her kidnappers. A member of a ruthless gang that called itself the Vice Boys.

That evening Rosa went to bed feeling not good, but better. She'd forever be a prisoner of her own limp body. Her paralysis a cruel warden. But she could at least participate in the world through her prayers. This redemptive thought lasted but a little while until despondency got the best of her and she finally and mercifully fell asleep with tears in her eyes.

That night she dreamt that an angel entered her room and put his hand under her back and touched her spine. Once the dream was over, a hungry and loud female horse-fly flew in erratic paths all around the room. It flew around Rosa's face several times before landing just to the side of her nose to grab a bite to eat. She bit the sleeping woman and barely escaped with her life when a hand slapped the spot it had just vacated.

The next morning Diane was not awakened by her alarm clock. She was awakened by screams coming from Rosa.

***

Barbara was beaming. Her kitchen and living room was filled with happy and hungry people. Including her and her family, which now included Kim, there were sixteen people. Jonathan, Elizabeth, Lil Johnny, Prince, Prophetess Ebony Monroe, Dante, Aisha, Ray-Ray, Ava, Willetta, and Ethel.

The only thing that could've made this evening better would've been had she prepared the meal. But then again, maybe not. So much of what had happened centered around Prophetess Ebony Monroe's ox tail stew that it made sense for it to be served at their celebration meal.

Jonathan spooned the last of his stew into his mouth and chewed with closed eyes. He opened them and rubbed his belly as he said, "Forgive me, Father, for I have grievously sinned."

Elizabeth looked at him as though he were a five-year-old who had tracked mud onto the floor. She shook her head. "Three bowls qualify as more than one sin, Jonathan."

"I only sinned with bowl three, Liz. And, technically, it was really only half a sin because it was only half a bowl. And since Scripture says nothing of a half sin, I may not have sinned at all." He grinned at her and slowly nodded his head a couple of times and ended his defense by clicking his tongue twice.

Elizabeth just shook her head.

"Prophetess Ebony Monroe," said Jonathan, giving Prince a sly grin for his mother's preference of being addressed this way, "*now* we are ready for the ox tail chronicles. You promised us a story. Let's hear it."

Everyone appeared eager to hear the story of how God used her ox tails to take down the Vice Boys.

"Yeah, let's hear it, Prophetess Ebony Monroe," said Sharon. Sharon hoped she'd one day have prophetic gifts as strong as this lady—and Jonathan. But Jonathan's level seemed light years away. For now, she'd settle for less.

Prophetess Ebony Monroe stood behind her son and placed both hands on his shoulders. She squeezed them. Her happy attitude changed. Her face looked troubled. "I should have acted sooner," she began. "For years I knew my nephew, Sonny, was terrorizing everybody."

"You talked to 'em, Mama. You talked to me, too," said Prince.

"Yeah, I talked. I talked and talked and talked. And I prayed and prayed and prayed. And I tried to help as many people as I could. But I was so scared of my own nephew that I was content to just doing first-aid on people he ripped apart. I should've done something."

"Something like what, Mama? You did what you could? Until Jonathan and Edwin went down there, I didn't see nobody else tryin' to do somethin'. You got a church full of people you kept from that madness."

Prophetess Ebony Monroe thought about what her son said. "Something like what I did."

"What you do, Mama?" Prince turned around.

"The day they shot you—before they shot you, I had just driven up to see Tessa. You know she lives across the street from Sonny's building. I was about to get out of my car when her little boy, Troy—he's only seven—came running around the corner like he was being chased by the devil. He was crying and hugging a rifle to chest. A rifle."

"A rifle? How'd that little peanut head nigga get a rifle?" asked Lil Johnny.

Prophetess Ebony Monroe cut a hard, unChristian stare into Lil Johnny's one eye. "If that's what you want to call yourself, you go right ahead. But da—"the prophetess caught herself—"don't you call nobody in my church family a nigga. There's not one nigga in *Worldwide Apostolic Church of International Deliverance and Glory*. I'm a prophetess. Sanctified and full of the Holy Ghost. I got a church mother. We got two deacons. We got two deaconesses. We got seven ministers-in-training. We got a choir director. We got a Sunday school teacher. We got somebody over the children. Did you notice what I didn't say, Lil Johnny?"

The stunned man looked at her glaring eyes, wishing his other eye was patched. "No."

"I didn't say anything about any *niggas*, now did I?" She didn't sound angry, just intense.

The room was quiet.

"No, ma'am," Lil Johnny answered nervously, thoroughly chastened.

"Mama," said Prince. "Lighten up. He got a patch over his eye, not a hood on his head. He ain't KKK."

She shook her head with a new lightness. "Now when did I become *ma'am*?"

Lil Johnny gave his head a Ray Charles wiggle and said, "When you started goin' gangsta on a—"

Prince gave him a warning look.

Lil Johnny smiled. "On a *child of God,*" he finished.

"There you go. There you go," said the prophetess. "Got to renew yo' mind. Only say what God says about you."

Prince winked at him.

Sharon looked at her parents and shook her head in slow motion. "So *that's* how it's done, huh?" She smiled. "You respond to threats and violence."

"I da—aaarn sure do," he said.

Prophetess Ebony Monroe playfully pushed the back of his head.

Everyone laughed.

"The ox tail story," said Ava.

Prophetess Ebony Monroe looked at Ava approvingly. "I like you. I like your style."

"And I like yours," said Ava.

"Ox tail story, please," said Jonathan. "Little boy. Rifle."

"So Troy runs around there carrying a rifle. He looked scared to death. I called him and he sped up. He didn't stop until I said, 'It's Prophetess Ebony Monroe.' He stopped in the middle of the street. I said, 'Boy, where'd you get that rifle?' He said that it fell from Sonny's window. That's when I jerked him into my car and took off outta there."

"He got Sonny's rifle?" asked Prince. This was hard to believe. Sonny had shot a lot of people with that rifle.

"Why'd that little boy run off with Sonny's rifle?" asked Lil Johnny.

"You know Sonny killed that boy's daddy with that rifle," she answered. "I guess it's the same one."

"Oh, yeah," said Lil Johnny.

"He said he didn't know why he took the rifle," said the prophetess. "He said he heard a voice tell him to go around the building. When he got to the corner of the building, that's when he saw the rifle fall out the window. He hid behind the corner. Then a voice said, 'Get the rifle and run, Troy.' That's what he did."

"Mama, you got Sonny's rifle?" said Prince.

"Nope. The FBI's got his rifle," she said.

"FBI?" said half the people there.

"Yep. I called the FBI office in Atlanta and told them I wanted to talk to someone about Sonny Christopher. Ooohh, glory to God, they wanted to talk about Sonny. I told them that I had the rifle he used to kill people. The man on the other end started breathing and talking so fast I had to call him down. I prayed for 'em. Led 'em to Christ over the phone. But I think he was just trying to get that rifle."

"Mama," Prince stood up, "the FBI has Sonny's rifle?"

"Yeah. Gave it to 'em the day after they shot you."

"So that's why they all showed up like on TV," said Lil Johnny.

"Prophetess Ebony Monroe is not through with her story," she said.

"There's more?" asked Sharon. Her mouth was wide as she looked around the room.

"They love my ox tail stew. Sonny. Pretty Tony. All the Vice Boys like my stew. So I went around to all the Vice Boys houses and dropped off some stew." For dramatic effect, she stopped talking. She started looking at her nails.

"What else, Mama?"

"Dropped off some other stuff, too."

"Like what?" asked Barbara.

"Like some bugs," she said.

Lil Johnny frowned. "Bugs? You put bugs in the stew?"

"I don't think Prophetess Ebony Monroe means living bugs," said Edwin, looking at her.

Andrew's mouth gaped. He looked around quickly and spoke before anyone else could. "FBI bugs? Like the Mafia?"

"I sure did. After the FBI got that rifle, and I told them that Sonny is my nephew, they asked me to bug him."

The FBI was ecstatic to get their hands on that rifle for more than one reason. It had started a chain event that allowed them to get wider authorization to use one of their most potent, and relatively recent, weapons against the Vice Boys. This weapon was called the roving bug.

The roving bug method allowed the FBI to remotely manipulate and activate a suspect's cell phone to use it as a microphone and transmitter. This could be done even if the phone was off. So a suspect didn't have to consciously use the phone for it to provide valuable information to the FBI. The suspects were in effect using the phone any time the FBI chose to use their phone as a microphone. The only defense against this was to take the battery out of the phone. But who was in the habit of removing their battery for fear of the FBI listening in? And who viewed the other guy's phone as a microphone when it was not in "use?"

The FBI's roving bug discovered interesting and quite incriminating chatter among the Vice Boys. Who was Officer Crandal and Officer Brown? Why were they so chummy with the Vice Boys?

These chatter-prompted questions were enough to get authorization to widen the electronic surveillance net. So now the FBI turned the phones of the dirty police officers into microphones. This paid off almost immediately. For these cops were as dirty as pigs in mud, and as talkative as they were dirty. Compliments to them, now the assistant police chief had the interest of the FBI. Who knew where this probe would lead?

Prophetess Ebony Monroe's revelation to the group of working for the FBI dominated the rest of the evening's conversations. But there was a life-changing side conversation that occurred among

Aisha, Ava, Willetta, and Ethel. Long before the conversation was over, Aisha was crying so hard for joy that she couldn't speak.

Ava and her friends had decided that it was their responsibility to make sure that Aisha became a doctor.

There were two doctors in Ethel's family—her husband and one of her sons. Ethel would have Aisha over for a family dinner, and the young woman would get to talk to some doctors firsthand.

Willetta didn't have any doctors in the family. All she had to offer was a bunch of love and a bunch of money. She was a loaded widow whose deceased husband had been exceptionally gifted in equities and real estate investments.

Ava, well Ava was full of faith and love for young girls. Rescuing them was her specialty. Some would say she had done a good job with Elizabeth. She'd do a good job with Aisha.

When Aisha could finally stop crying, she looked up into Ava's eyes—she was sitting on the arm of the sofa and hugging her—and asked, "Why are you doing this?"

"Because we love Jesus," Ava answered simply.

Willetta added, "I owe the devil one for kicking me in the butt down there in *Mayhem*. I can't let him get away with that, can I?"

Aisha laughed, "No. Then she burst out in joyous tears again.

This was the moment Dante gave himself to God.

***

Sonny had defiantly told the FBI agent that he'd be back on the streets within two days. That bravado had proven to be a false prophecy for a few reasons.

First, he had never heard of a Nebbia Hearing. Sonny learned that the government wasn't as stupid as he thought it was. Making bond wasn't as simple as paying ten percent and going to the house. The Feds wanted fifteen percent, not ten.

Plus, they had a problem with accused criminals paying bail with money that may have come from criminal activity. So they used the ruling from *U.S. v. Nebbia*, 357 F.2d 303 (2d Cir.1966) to place a hold on the payment of bond. The hold could be satisfied by the person posting bond proving through acceptable documentation that the money used to pay the bond was earned through legal means.

Third, bail. He had smirked at the FBI agent when the judge said she was going to allow bail. But then the FBI agent smirked back when bail was set at one million dollars. Fifteen percent of that was one-hundred and fifty thousand dollars. Bail would've been more had the Feds not done such a thorough job of showing they had frozen all of his assets. Still, where was he going to get that much money?

Nonetheless, Sonny Christopher was happier than the FBI felt he should be. But this was unavoidable. For although he had made his Muhammed Ali-like prediction, a second-round knockout of the FBI, off the cuff, rather than from inside knowledge, he was finding that he had powerful, unseen friends.

One of these friends, which he had met since his arrest, was a lawyer who promised him everything would be okay. He told him that he had bad news and good news. The bad news was that he had been unable to get the Nebbia hold lifted. The good news was that Sonny's unseen friend had a work-around to handle this situation.

Two full days had passed and Sonny wasn't out yet. But that was cool. He had the invisible man working for him. The next day he got a phone call from his lawyer. He finished the call and immediately began talking trash.

"This is day three," he yelled in his cell. They probably were listening. "I'm about to do a Jesus Christ on you crackers and rise again!"

In a couple of hours Sonny Christopher made bail and was free awaiting trial.

***

The drugged man's head bobbed in unchoreographed directions. Left. Left. Back. Front. Left. Right. That signaled one of the men in the abandoned house to snatch the hood off of Sonny.

Something about that hood being snatched off sobered him immediately. His eyes were alert; his senses heightened. The dude he felt standing behind him wore cologne that under other circumstances he would have described as tight. But the tightness of the ropes that bound him to his chair made his thought of the man's cologne ridiculous.

Sonny looked around at the three serious-looking men. Their faces weren't covered. That was bad news. He looked in all of their eyes. Not a one of these crackers looked like they had a soul. What prison had they broken out of?

Sonny looked directly across from him, about four or five feet. They had another hooded dude tied to a chair. There was something familiar about the man.

"Let me help you out," said one of the men. He snatched the hood off.

Sonny's bladder and bowels started acting up.

Another of the men spoke. He wore an expensive-looking dark suit and was clean shaven. His hair was dark, long, and combed to the side. The cat looked like an evil model. "Makes sense now?"

Sonny and Pretty Tony looked at one another with eyes that competed for the *I'm More Scared Than You* title.

"Naw," said Sonny. "What y'all want with us?"

The model looked at his *Montblanc* watch and looked at Sonny with an expression that said him being there with him and Pretty Tony was an inconvenience. "Sonny, this man made a phone call a few days back and said you were doing some dumb things. We saw you losing control of *Mayhem*. We were still in deliberations about how to handle your lapses of judgment. Then Pretty Tony makes a second phone call and says you have ambitions. He said you told him that you had some leverage that would compel us to make certain concessions to you. Those weren't his exact words, but you get the picture."

Sonny looked at Pretty Tony. "Nigga, what have you done?"

"Now, now, no need for name-calling," said the evil model.

Pretty Tony looked at the evil model. "I told y'all—this didn't happen. Me and Sonny had a fallin' out and—"

The evil model looked at his watch again and started walking away. Without looking back, he said, "If that's true, Pretty Tony, that's the worst mistake you've ever made—and the last one. Handle this," he said to the other men just before he went out of sight.

The remaining two men walked over to a table and each picked up a short, thick club. They walked toward Sonny and Pretty Tony at a deliberately slow pace.

"I think both of you are familiar with the sticks?" said one of them with an evil smile.

"Wait a minute," came the anxious plea from Pretty Tony. "Why y'all got me here? I was looking out for the business."

One of the two soulless killers looked like he belonged on a Hell's Angels' motorcycle. He stepped forward and patted the club in his hand. "The boss wants you to know he appreciates your loyalty. It hurts him that it has to end this way." He exhaled a calloused breath. "But it ends today."

Sonny's eyes bulged at the savage blows that quickly ended Pretty Tony's life.

The other man looked at Sonny's open mouth and perspiring face as though his grudge was personal. "Your treatment's going to take a bit longer."

Sonny's unseen boss was quite upset with him for letting his inexplicable vendetta against the church take down the Mayhem business. He had cost them a lot of money, and had put a lot of powerful people in jeopardy. So the men followed the boss's orders meticulously and were quite patient in their treatment of Sonny.

Finally, the last blow cut his ties with the earthly life. Sonny stood up from his bloodied chair. There was no period of confusion. He understood immediately what had happened. He was dead and on his way to hell.

"I can't die now. I ain't ready." He jumped back in the chair and tried to get back in his empty body. He sat on the body's lap and pushed, but couldn't reenter. He pushed repeatedly. Each attempt was more desperate than the previous.

Sonny was too busy to see him.

The dark spirit was not amused. "You were a fool in life, and now you make yourself an even bigger fool in death. It's over, Sonny

Christopher. It is appointed unto men once to die, and after that the judgment."

Sonny's eyes bulged at the demon's appearance. His eyes darted up and down at him. His arms shot out behind him as though he was searching for a wall to his rear. Condemnation was all over him. He felt like a cornered rat. The monster in front of Sonny made no move toward him. But he didn't have to. Something was coming for him.

The ex-king of Mayhem moved in a tight circle of confusion looking for the threat.

SNAP! SNAP!

Sonny's frightened eyes shot to his feet.

The dark spirit now moved forward. His face full of hatred; his voice full of anger. "You lived in sin and died in rebellion. It's now time to pay for those decisions." The spirit glared at the man who was staring at the chains that had suddenly taken hold of his ankles. "Hell is waiting for you."

Sonny was snatched downward. He screamed all the way until he reached the gates of hell. Then his screams began again—and never ended.

The End

A Note from the Author

May I ask you a favor?

Would you mind writing a review online at wherever you purchased the book? Many people determine from book reviews whether or not a story is worth their time. Your review (even a short one!) can help convince others to join the fun!

Let's Stay In Touch!

Visit me at ericmhillauthor.com for a **free spiritual warfare short story** or a **free book!**

Here's my contact info: ericmhill@yahoo.com or
Facebook.com/ericmhillauthor or
Twitter.com/ericmhillatl.
God bless you!

Other Books by the Author

Spiritual Warfare Fiction

Fire Series
Book 1: Bones of Fire
Book 2: Trial by Fire
Book 3: Saints on Fire

Demon Strongholds Series
The Spirit of Fear
The Spirit of Rejection
The Spirit of Ugliness (Coming)

Other Fiction

Out of Darkness Series
Book 1: The Runaway: Beginnings
Book 2: The Runaway: Endings

Three Sisters Detective Agency
Finding Angel
Saving Daddy

Non-Fiction

You Can Get Answers to Your Prayers
Deliverance from Demons and Diseases

Made in the USA
Middletown, DE
12 March 2024

51349801R00258